THE SECRET OF THE PHOENIX

THE SECRET OF THE PHOENIX

The Phoenix Series

S. R. BREAKER

Zeta Indie Publishing

Contents

2

THE FLIGHT

3
THE RISE

I

the fall

I

the vision

Was it a dream?

No, it couldn't have been. I'm sure it really happened.

I can still feel the hot wind swirl over my skin as the once majestic kingdom of Centeria burned to the ground.

I can still remember how the mountains surrounding the kingdom shook violently with every step of the enemy coming closer.

I can still hear that voice assuring me that everything would be okay, telling me that he would never let anything happen to me...

"Stop it! Stop it! I'm warning you!" I protested, laughing as I backed up.

Two blond five-year-old boys were chasing me around the yard with their plastic toy squirt guns. They were trying to hit each other but I supposed they found it more amusing to team up against the hired help.

Yes, it was Torture Tuesday.

It was a popular opinion that babysitting for my mom's friend's twin sons Timmy and Tommy Matthews qualified as torture.

But I was a pure soul with a kind heart. *A saint, a martyr, a model daughter—*

"Hey Sarah," a male voice called from next door, across the white picket fence.

I jumped and looked over.

Derek Richards, every teenage girl's dream guy, lived next door to the Matthews.

—who deserves every reward possible for her enormous sacrifices. I smiled back, waving casually at him. "Ow!" I squeaked as the twins tackled me to the ground.

Timmy or Tommy, one of them, squirted water at me as I fell back on the ground, while the other one ran circles around us, laughing and shooting water into the air like a fountain. It rained down on us.

"Oh, cripe—" I hissed under my breath before I was able to sit up. I shot Timmy—or Tommy, the squirting one, a warning look before lunging at him for the gun. Pinning him down, I squirted water back at him. "Like that, huh?" I tickled his stomach and he squealed with laughter.

A deeper laugh made me stop and turn around.

I flushed red. I almost forgot about Derek. Clearing my throat, I shot him a playful, offhand grin. "Sorry 'bout that."

The kid I'd knocked down jumped up, grabbed his gun from me, and tore off after his brother.

"Hey, Timmy—Tommy!" I called out. "Not too far, guys!" I shook my head as I straightened up, brushing off my jeans.

"Quite a handful?" Derek walked closer to the fence.

"Ohh yeah—" I looked down at myself and stopped in aghast. Way to look good for a guy. My jeans had mud and grass stains, my shirt had splotches of water, and my hair was damp and probably frizzy too.

Derek must've noticed my dismayed reaction to the sight of myself, he chuckled.

What was he laughing at? I furrowed my eyebrows back at him, trying to think of a snappy retort.

Smiling, he reached over to tuck a strand of hair behind my ear. "See you around, Sarah." Then he walked back to his house.

I bit back a wide smile, stunned, and didn't move for a second. Then I saw Timmy or Tommy dash across a yard—Mrs. Andrews' yard, the one with the prized petunias, and I snapped to attention.

"Timmy—Tommy—whichever!" I waved them back.

I could go home now. Hell, I could very well die now.

"And Pathetic Peters strikes again," my friend Ena Johnson teased the following day as we walked back to her house. We were part of the local baseball league with some of the students from school and we'd often hang out at the dug-out in the afternoons on hot summer days.

I swung my bat around as we strolled along though I didn't think Ena had been referring to my batting average.

"Why didn't you ask him out? All the bases were open," Ena suggested.

"Look at me, Ena." I gestured down at myself in ridicule, muddy jeans and all. "This was me yesterday. You know that line they use in the movies? That 'you clean up real nice' line?" I laid it out flat. "Fact: I don't."

Ena rolled her eyes. "Hello? That's the movies. Fiction? Pretend? This is the real world, Sarah. And this isn't any of your made-up stories either."

"Oh, don't start." I sighed. "You're like Annette. You never get off my back." I mimicked my obnoxious older sister with a high-pitched whiny voice. "*When are you going to stop daydreaming and grow up?' 'All of Sarah's friends are imaginary.' 'Why don't you go outside and spend more time with the three-dimensional people instead of always burying your head in your little notebook?'* "

"Think of it as...motivational," Ena phrased with a mischievous tone.

"Silent support would suffice, thanks."

Ena chuckled. "How's that all going anyway? I thought you'd given up on that hobby after your last writer's block."

Shrugging, I dragged my feet as we passed the rows of identical-looking houses in our quiet, little suburban neighborhood. "I'm waiting to get inspired, researching some things..."

"How? In those Japanese animated cartoons you've been watching lately?" Ena mocked. "Aren't they kind of immature and...sort of cheesy? I mean, my brother watches some of them. They're pretty weird."

I shrugged again. "Hey, at least it's something. I mean, my life pales in comparison. Nothing ever happens to me."

"Again, let's keep in mind, those are cartoons. They're fiction. Imaginary." Ena ticked off her fingers meaningfully. She shot me a look as we arrived at her front porch. "Besides, if you had asked Derek out when you had the faintest shadow of a chance, maybe things would start happening in your life and you can stop complaining."

I paused at her house's front walk to lament, "Blah blah blah...fear of striking out," butchering the old saying before I turned to go.

"Whatever you say, sport." Ena waved me away. "See you tomorrow!"

I waved back and started for home.

Oh yes, the story of my life. Always a dull moment rather than never.

Nothing interesting ever happened in our little suburb of Chicago. And since discovering that writing was a very effective means of escape, every night, I exchanged the boring humdrum of normal life for the always exciting, twisting, and turning fiction of thrills and adventure. I preferred it that way. Because over there, in the world I created, I could do anything.

Of course, Annette thought I took my 'writing nonsense' way too seriously. But I didn't see what could be wrong with being drawn to fictional worlds, worlds where anything was possible, worlds where the only limit was my imagination.

I paused in mid-stride when I thought I saw something move out of the corner of my eye and I glanced over to the alley.

Trees swayed in the breeze. Leaves rustled along the street as the wind blew them around. Nobody else was outside. It must've been the heat. This year's summer was a little hotter than usual and on a day like today, there wasn't a cloud in the sky.

Starting to walk again, I wiped the perspiration off my forehead with my sleeve. The sun was beating down on the ground. I shielded my eyes from the sun's rays.

All of a sudden, the sun changed colors—from bright yellow to fiery red. I stopped and looked back down. There in front of me was a wide field of fire... ruins of some sort... crumbling structures and... what looked like... *robots...?*

The heat seemed to emanate from the ground. I swallowed and squinted. *What in the—?*

There was a high-pitched cry behind me and I turned. My eyes widened as a big, fiery bird flew right past me with a loud whoosh. I tried to take a step back away from it when all of a sudden, the ground beneath me gave way and I started to fall...

I fell back on the concrete sidewalk with a thump. "Ow," I groaned, snapping back to reality. I cursed, rubbing my rear as I pushed up to stand. Down the road, a red sports car zoomed away, tires screeching. *Jerk must've knocked the wind right out of me.* I shook my head to clear it before I continued walking home.

That was the first time I felt that weird, creepy feeling.

2

another world

"Sarah, turn off the damn lights," Annette mumbled, burrowing deeper under her covers.

I rolled my eyes and didn't budge. I was finally on a roll in the middle of writing a story. Okay, well, in the middle of starting one. I'd gotten an idea to write an adventure story about a heroine who gets magically transported to another world, and I was at the part when she first meets the hero because, of course, he saves her from some bad guys and—

"Sarah, for god's sake, I'm sleeping here!" Annette whined.

"Yeah, in a minute," I said, exasperated. "This is my room too, you know?"

"Yeah? Well, it was my room first," Annette reasoned stubbornly. "Now, knock it off or I'll ask Mom to make you move into the garage."

"Yeah, right." I turned back to my notebook. "You'll miss me when I'm gone, Annette."

"Don't count on it," she grumbled before turning over in bed.

I shook my head. *Where was I?* I read my work over.

The mysterious stranger let out a breath as if fending off five sinister monsters was no more than a brisk walk in the park and he turned to face her.

Swallowing, she edged back against the wall, giving him a wary look.

Hmm... I paused in thought, my pen poised to write.

Annette was still tossing around in bed, turning over several times, and I had to roll my eyes again. When I heard a fluttering noise, I thought it was just Annette falling off the bed. I frowned in annoyance and was going to yell at her when a strange breeze whispered across my skin—a dry, hot gust of air.

Except the windows were closed.

I looked up at the mirror right above my desk. Something was glowing. Something behind me. Blinking, I got that weird, creepy feeling in the pit of my stomach again, but I just figured it must've been that reheated turkey steak I ate at dinner. So I opted for the more realistic and more enjoyable option of turning on Annette.

"Annette, for the love of god—," I started to say as I turned around. I nearly fell out of my seat, gasping in wide-eyed fright and backing up against my desk.

It was the bird I'd seen this afternoon in the street. It hovered in the middle of our bedroom, right above the aisle between the beds. The bird's wings were spouting what looked like liquid fire, and when I met its gaze, its eyes gleamed so brightly that I had to shield mine. "What the—?" I blinked hard several times to check if I was hallucinating.

I was not.

I glanced over at Annette, peacefully sleeping in her bed, oblivious to anything that was going on. "Annette," I hissed, loud enough to wake her up, but she didn't even so much as groan to shut me up.

The bird let out a screech and I looked back at it in dread. I was frozen where I stood, waves of heat and wind undulating around me. "Annette..." I breathed heavily, my breath coming out in short gasps. Darting my gaze around the room, I looked for something I might use to whack the bird away.

But it must have read my mind or caught on as it let out a short defensive squawk, tilting its head to one side. It was preparing to attack.

"Oh shit." I tried to summon a smile. "Nice birdie."

Before I could blink, the big bird thing began to fly, or more accurately whoosh, *straight at me*. I couldn't even move to scramble away. "Oh, shit—Annette!" I cried, squeezing my eyes shut to brace myself from being scorched in the fire.

When I opened my eyes again, I was falling—from the sky.

"Oh shiiiiiiiiiiiiiiiiiiiiiit!"

"Ow!" I squeaked as I landed with a hard thump on the ground. Before I could wonder how I could have survived such a fall, something ran me over. "Ow—ow!" I yelped, tumbling in the dirt.

A few feet away, someone sprawled on the ground. He had been running and tripped over me.

"What in the—?" Hissing, he cast an annoyed look back at me then up over my shoulder at something and his eyes widened.

I followed his gaze, bracing myself again, and sighted an angry mob running toward us with a big cloud of dust. "Oh my g—" I scrambled up and started running.

The guy reappeared, running a few feet ahead of me, and when he ducked into an alley, so did I.

He grabbed me, covered my mouth, and pinned me against the wall.

My gasp cutting off, I squeezed my eyes shut again. *Holy shit. What the hell was going on?*

The commotion rushed by and was a distant fog in the din before I dared to open my eyes.

The guy kept my mouth clamped. He checked around the corner, and when he saw the coast was clear, he shot me an irritated look and pushed me away. "Where the hell did you come from?"

I shot him an equally irritated look, after I regained my balance, that was. "What? Who the hell are you?" I retorted. "Where in the hell am I? How in the hell did I get here?"

The dim light made it difficult to focus. We were in some type of grungy town alley. Laundry hung on wires across windows above us. Barrels of an oozy substance leaking from them were stacked in a corner. Rats scurried alongside the back wall. *Ew gross...* I made a face in distaste.

The guy shot me a dark, suspicious look. He was wearing torn, grimy clothes and some sort of weird cape. His hair looked like a tornado had run through it, his face dirty, his jaw set.

There was only one explanation.

"Ohh okay... I get it." I nodded at my epiphany. "This is a dream! I'm having a totally vivid, totally screwed up dream." I backed up, looking around. "I was just writing about another world and then I dream about it—okay, okay, makes sense." I laughed. "Although this whole dark alley thing is sooo cliché. And you—" I pointed at him, still laughing. "Yeah, I'm ready to wake up now, Chief."

"What the hell are you talking about?" His expression didn't change.

"I'm ready to wake up," I told him pointedly, fighting the inklings of panic and dread. "Come on. I have to get out of here and wake up now. You know, snap your fingers or something."

"I don't have time for this." He turned away, but just as he did, his cape flew up a little and I saw a familiar marking.

A fiery bird.

That *goddamn* annoying bird.

My eyes widened. "Oh, no, no, no, wait." I went after him. "You have to help me, please."

He paused gruffly, giving me a scrutinizing look. "Oh, all right." He sighed. "How much do you need?"

A nerve in my neck stiffened. "*What?*" I asked in a skeptical, quick-short-burst-of-a-word, my voice shifting to a higher pitch.

He shot me a plain look. "How much do you charge?"

It was a knee-jerk reaction. My hand flew to his face. "You pig!"

His head flicked back at the force. He stopped before slowly looking over, his smoldering gaze met mine.

"Just because a girl says she needs help doesn't mean she's for sale," I informed him, heaving.

He crossed his arms over his head nonchalantly. "Well, excuse me," he drawled. "My mistake. You are dressed like that in a place like this."

I gritted my teeth. What was he expecting me to be wearing—a ball gown? I was about to go to sleep before all this! "Never mind," I dismissed crisply, turning to stalk off. "I guess I'll just have to go and find that stupid firebird on my own then, won't I?"

He was blocking my way within a split second. "What did you just say?"

I shot him a suffering look. "That weird bird thingy on your cape, which by the way, is *so* dated." I rolled my eyes as I started to walk away again.

He grabbed my arm. "How do you know about the phoenix?"

"*Ow*," I said pointedly, loudly, and he dropped his hand. I gave him a fake gracious look. "Well, your stupid 'phoenix'," I relayed, mocking quotation marks with my fingers, "appeared in my bedroom, and the next thing I knew, I was here. You do the math."

"The stupid phoenix," he echoed in offense, "is the insignia of my country."

"What country? Thailand?"

"Centeria."

"What?" I sucked at geography but I was pretty sure I'd never heard of such a grandiose-sounding name for a country. "Where in the hell is that?"

"You have to come with me." He pulled me along behind him.

"*Ow*—stop grabbing me." I shrugged him off in exasperation. "I'm not going anywhere until I get some answers here."

He had started to groan when he paused, his gaze halfway to the sky. "I have a feeling you'll be changing your mind."

I shot him a wry look. "Yeah, sure."

The sudden explosion behind me made me flinch. I turned to see a huge black and indigo robot crash through two building structures. The ground shook and I held on to the wall for support. "What the—?" My jaw dropped as I recognized the robot from the vision I'd seen this afternoon on the street, just as the thing seemed to look over and point that mechanical arm weapon in our direction—in *my* direction.

The shot it fired obliterated the top of the structure above us, making debris tumble down. I jumped aside and to the ground. "—the hell?" I gawked up at the thing.

"Change your mind yet?"

With no time to answer, I scrambled up and started running down the street again. I looked around, baffled. I'd watched enough television to figure out that robots were supposed to fight other robots. But these ones seemed to be chasing us—not anyone or anything else. *This has to be the stupidest dream in the entire world!* I noted just as another robot wove into view right up in front and this one wasn't looking any friendlier either.

I skidded to a stop. "Oh shit."

The guy stopped as well, took two furtive glances left and right, and the next thing I knew, he'd scooped me up and we were—rather, *he* was running faster than the wind.

The landscape blurred past us and I closed my eyes, my chest heaving. *Oh god, if this is a dream, wake up, Sarah. Wake up! Wake up!*

After a few moments, with a sudden rush of wind, we stopped again. Opening my eyes to take a peek, the view of the top of a cliff was before me, but the robots were nowhere to be seen. When I met the guy's gaze, he took it as a cue to drop me.

Luckily, I landed on my feet. "Ow, thanks a lot."

He shot me a disapproving look before turning his back. But he didn't leave. Instead, he took off his cape and tossed it at me.

Surprised at his gesture, I shrugged. "Thanks." I put the cloak on over my shoulders, pulling it closed in front of me. The fabric was warm around me. I hadn't even realized I was cold. I frowned at the ground. These sensations were too vivid for this to all be a screwy dream. And after almost being crushed by those idiotic robots, if I'd had any hope left that I would simply wake up soon, it was *so* gone now.

I rubbed my bruised arm at the very real pain. "So, what the hell were those?"

He was gazing out to the horizon or somewhere. "Relics. Robot spies from Malken."

"Riiiight..." I replied blankly. "And a Malken would be?"

"It's a kingdom due south."

"South of what?"

"Here."

"Here where?"

Unable to restrain his irritation, he whirled around. "Who are you? Where did you come from? What are you doing here and—how do you know about the phoenix?" He shot out one question after the other.

I winced at him. "Jeez! Does everyone in this world have no manners?"

"This world?" he repeated. "Are you telling me you come from another one?"

I threw up my hands. "I don't know! I don't know where I am!"

"How do you know about the phoenix?" he demanded again.

"I told you," I relayed, exasperated. "It appeared in my room and the next thing I knew, poof! I was here—wherever here is."

"Nobody has seen the phoenix." His tone carried a stubborn conviction. "It is a mission for the people of my kingdom to seek it out, to save Centeria from its enemies."

"Really? *Oooohh...*" I mocked sounding impressed. He scowled and I rolled my eyes. "All right, all right, I'm sorry," I said, not really sorry. "So look, if nobody's supposed to have seen this phoenix thingy then what the hell was it doing in my bedroom?"

He looked away. "I don't know."

"Great—this is just—great! This is perfect." Pacing, I mocked a laugh at myself. "This-this is all my fault. When I said I wanted adventure, I meant to *write* one!" I yelled at the sky.

He was watching me like I was crazy, which I figured wasn't a far-off diagnosis.

"So, okay..." I rubbed the bridge of my nose, trying to make sense of things as much as I could. "Why were those people chasing you?"

"I knocked over a couple of stands in the market."

"While shopping?" I asked in incredulity.

"Evading the relics."

"And why were those chasing you?"

"They know I'm from Centeria."

I huffed. "They can smell that, huh? You must be pretty popular in your kingdom."

He didn't respond.

"So, what's your name?"

"Gradd."

I feigned a shiver. "Ooh, creepy."

He shot me another dark look.

I took a deep breath, having relatively calmed down. "Well, I'm sorry I slapped you earlier, Gradd," I apologized. "My name's Sarah. Sarah Peters."

"Sarah...?"

The way he said my name sent real shivers down my spine and I made a face. "Right. Whatever." I shook my head and turned away.

"We have to go. You're coming with me," he announced.

"Am I?" I prompted in ridicule. "Where?"

3

the legend of centeria

After the cursory weighing of my options—none of which were at all promising, and most of which ludicrous and terrifying, I found myself hitching a ride on the next hay bale cart that we had come across.

I was trying to get some sleep, but the hard surface of the back of the cart was purpose-built for grass, not naps. Every bump along the mountainside trail didn't make the trip any more bearable either.

I happened to glance up by the edge of the cart where the guy from earlier was leaning against the railing, his arms crossed over his chest, his eyes darting furtively around—probably still watching out for more robots. He hadn't slept a wink, hadn't moved an inch.

His eyes darted up to glare at me.

I met his gaze somberly for a second and just pulled his cloak closer around me before looking away.

The landscape around us had noticeably changed, from the desert mountain areas to the green lowlands and valleys we were passing now. And on the path that had been deserted most of the way, appeared people walking alongside the roads of what must have been a town, first a few handfuls, then more.

Narrowing my eyes, I observed the natives.

They were strange-looking people, with subtle animal features—horns, big ears, whiskers, all walking by the side of the cart in clumps, or scurrying around, carrying sacks, and crates, going about their business. I only then realized that the cart driver himself looked like an anthropomorphized big, old wolfman.

I craned my neck around in marvel. *Well shit, I'm definitely not in Kansas anymore.* I tried to shake out my nerves. Either way, these people gave me the creeps. This whole place gave me the creeps.

After hours of possibly pretending he was a statue, Gradd finally turned. To look at something.

I had to stand to follow his gaze. Over the horizon, a great structure was materializing against the sunrise. A majestic stone castle with high walls and a quaint wood and metal drawbridge was set upon rolling green hills, dotted with quite a colorful crowd.

Then I saw it. High above the castle, waving on a pole, there was a flag with a big, red crest, standing out against the orange sky of sunrise. A Phoenix. The wind blowing through it made it seem like the image, the bird, was actually flying.

"Wow," I breathed in wonder.

Gradd heard me. The expression on his face was as much pride as he could probably muster.

He was home.

As the cart drove into the castle's stone-walled gates, clusters of people swallowed it up. I looked around at all the people, who seemed to be in celebration.

I furrowed my eyebrows in puzzlement. *Was the circus in town or something?*

Several older men were waiting in a row, right up front in the middle of a wide courtyard, clad in armor and formal-looking garb, long thick velvet capes, similar to the one I was wearing. They watched as the cart pulled closer. Grimacing in near panic, I wondered if maybe we were being arrested for something.

I glanced over at Gradd. He didn't look scared. Of course, I was assuming that he was capable of any emotion at all. He merely nodded regally at the men in armor, as if in greeting.

Boy, when he said popular, he meant it, I thought in amazement. He was probably some kind of a head soldier, or a knight, or something.

Gradd jumped off the cart and straight toward the row of distinguished-looking men, right to the one in the very center, to give him a hug—the kind men do, with resounding pats on the back, as if Gradd were his long lost—

"Oh." I blinked as I got it. "Huh." *Well, that explains the hot air.* But before I could think any more, Gradd leaned over to say something to his father and they both looked up at me.

I swallowed hard.

Uh-oh.

"This is just perfect," I muttered as I paced. "Ungracious behavior toward a member of the royal family. Uncouth, uncultured, disrespectful, damn straight insolence, and reckless endangerment to the prince. The prince—of all people!"

I'd been locked up in the 'quarters' I had been led to once we'd gotten off the cart. I mulled over what my punishment might be. "Possibly thrown in the dungeon," I guessed, shaking my head. "Maybe life imprisonment. Skinned at dawn. The guillotine. Ugh," I groaned as I fell back on the bed.

Trying to look on the bright side wasn't making me feel any better either.

Sure, I was alive, except I didn't know where I was alive at. I was pretty certain that I was most definitely no longer on my Earth. I was alone. I had no idea how I got here. I had no idea how I was going to get back. And who even knew if these people were more likely inclined to lock me up forever or outright kill me for trespassing into their realm?

"Jeez, what is going on here anyway?" I whined. It wasn't fair. I had always been led to believe that knights in shining armor saved people. So far, the arrogant "prince" I met hadn't saved me from the bad guys or anything. He, in fact, had put me in danger with all those stupid robot relics.

And now that I was thinking about it, those robots were chasing him, weren't they? *Why didn't I just get out of the damn way?* "God Sarah! You are so dense!" I let out a haggard sigh.

I shifted on the bed as something bulky was against my hip. I reached down, remembering what it was, and sat up with a frown, pulling the cape out from under me. It was a heavy thing. I wrinkled my nose, trying to hold it up to see, but it was way too wide, so I stood up and laid the cape out on the bed.

I frowned at the hand-stitched pattern.

It was that damn phoenix again.

A chill ran up my spine as I looked into its eyes and I quickly tossed the cape to fold closed.

"Lady Sarah?" A voice accompanied the tentative knock on the door and I whirled around.

Lady *what now?*

Two girls dressed in what looked to me like gypsy renaissance fair costumes were at the door carrying a pile of clothes. They both gave me curious stares.

I stared back at them.

One of them, in the pink gown, put the clothes on the side of the bed. "His highness sent these for my lady's needs," she said, curtsying a little.

I raised my eyebrows. "You're kidding, right?"

The two girls looked at each other in confusion.

"I'm sorry. You must be mistaken," I amended, shaking my head. "My name is Sarah Peters. I'm kinda new here, so I'm pretty sure you must have the wrong room."

The other one with the long green hair nodded. "Yes, Lord Gradd gave instructions to bring the new lady guest something appropriate to wear."

"Appropriate? Well, but—" I looked from one to the other then dismissed my protest. "Oh, forget it," I said. "Thanks anyways."

They both curtsied again and bade me, "M'lady," before scurrying away.

I examined the pile of clothes up close. *Lady Sarah.* I almost gagged.

I was 'sent for' a few hours later. A pair of bison guards escorted me down the hall to the main court. The large chamber was decorated with high ceilings, and tapestries, the entire room was filled with phoenix paintings and murals.

Making a face, I fidgeted in my dress as I followed the guards. The abomination they had given me to wear was a real pain, and as it was, I rarely wore dresses. Nobody seemed to care that I had put the dress on over my own clothes, then again the dress itself seemed stiff enough to stand on its own.

As I entered the room, Gradd and the 'King' were seated at the dais at the head of the room, their heads together in deep discussion. They both looked up when I was announced.

I cringed at the term 'Lady Sarah' again and considered hiding behind the ostrich herald but he'd already stepped away.

The King looked me up and down.

I forced a sheepish smile onto my face but everyone in the room was intently watching me, as though expecting me to do something.

After a few moments, Gradd must have realized I wasn't going to budge and his eyes narrowed.

"Curtsy," someone hissed at me from the sidelines.

Curtsy! Oh, of course! I flinched in realization. But I could already barely walk in the damn dress, let alone curtsy properly. I didn't want to embarrass myself in front of the royal family any more than I already had. Still, I figured I had better try, no matter how awkward, in case that was considered a hangable offense. Hoping I didn't end up sprawled face-down on the marble floor, I struggled to grab the sides of my big, floofy dress.

Except Mr. Prince decided to get impatient.

Gradd shot me a stern look. "You're supposed to curtsy in front of royalty," he declared so loud everyone startled as though he was yelling at them.

I shot him a look with daggers in it. He may have been a Prince, but he wasn't *my* Prince. Besides, who did they think I was? I wasn't one of their royal subjects. I wasn't even from this world! I huffed in indignation. "This dress weighs a ton. I'll fall over if I try to sit, much less curtsy." Audible gasps from the room made me flinch again. "...uh, your highness," I added in an attempt to recover from my aggressive auto-response.

Oh, jeez, don't antagonize the natives!

My stomach was churning in dread but instead of giving a royal rebuke, the elderly King laughed

Gradd shot his father a skeptical look.

"Lady Sarah," the King began.

I blinked, snapping to attention. "Oh, Sarah, please," I cut in on instinct, belatedly realizing I probably shouldn't interrupt the King when he was speaking.

But he didn't seem offended. "Very well. Sarah." He smiled warmly at me. "My son tells me you've had a vision of the Phoenix?"

Gasps and murmurs arose in the crowd once more, the King had to hold up his hand for attention and the crowd hushed.

I cast a wary look around the room before meeting the King's gaze again with a nod. "Uh, yeah, in my bedroom, but I don't really—"

Too eager to let me finish, the King went on, "Are you aware how important the Phoenix is to our kingdom?"

Blinking again, I surveyed the room once more. There was not a spot in the entire hall without an image of the phoenix. The paintings, the carpets, the flags all over the place, not to mention everyone's clothing. "Uh, yeah, I think I have a vague idea."

The King leaned forward. "Has my son told you of the Legend of the Phoenix?"

"Well..." I fidgeted in my stance. "He said something about a mission to look for it to save the kingdom from its enemies or something."

"Yes, but there is another part," He added with an enigmatic nod. "The legend foretells of such a time as when the kingdom is faced with grave danger that a savior will come...a person who will save Centeria."

"Oh, really? That's pretty cool." Then his full meaning struck me and my eyes popped out. "Ohh no." I shook my head, backing up. "No, no, no, no, no. You don't mean me. You *can't* mean me. I don't know anything about fighting wars, much less saving countries."

"But you are exactly as the legend says." The King gestured to me. "A strange person from another world."

I broke a frown at being called 'strange' but didn't get a chance to respond.

"I knew it!" Gradd burst out. "This is complete nonsense! You can't expect us to believe that this girl will defeat the Malkens. She couldn't even defend herself from two relic spies. How do you expect her to defeat a whole army?"

"Hey!" I piped up in annoyance. "Those robots were after you, wise guy. And if you had just left me out of it, I wouldn't even be in this mess!"

"Well, maybe if you hadn't gotten in the way, I wouldn't have had to save you from them," he countered, "which by the way, you haven't thanked me for yet."

"Thank—" A nerve ticked under my eye. "Thank you? What am I supposed to be thanking you for? For dragging me into this? For running me over? For almost getting me killed? Oh, of course, this is another world!" I threw up my hands in anger. "You're supposed to thank people who put you in danger, silly me—" I stopped short as a brilliant red light flashed from beneath me. *What the hell—?*

The people in the room began to whisper among themselves and jostled around to have a closer look.

The King stood up in alert.

Gradd looked taken aback.

I didn't understand what was going on. Despite the heavy dress, my feet lifted off the floor, and the next thing I knew, I was floating away. The crowded royal chamber before me fizzled out and I was instantly somewhere else.

"Ball one! Strike two!" Jamie Carter called from home plate. The sun beat down. A hot haze rose from the ground.

Matt Owens, the pitcher, set up.

"Come on, Peters!" Ena hollered from third base. "Bring me home!"

"Sarah, grow up. I'm sleeping here," Annette whined from out of nowhere.

"See you around, Sarah." Derek smiled.

The brightness of his smile grew in intensity until the stark whiteness overwhelmed my eyes.

In another blink, everything turned pitch black.

I swallowed from the creepy feeling in my stomach again.

With a scrape of a matchstick, a small light appeared up ahead. And then voices...

"They've found the girl," a man's voice said. "Relics spotted her with the prince."

"It doesn't matter," a deeper voice dismissed. "A little girl can't stop an army of relics."

Were they talking about me? My pulse raced. I struggled to focus my eyesight but it was like I was floating in a cave or a dungeon.

"What about the legend? What if she's the one?" the first voice prompted.

"She can't very well fulfill a legend if she's dead, can she?"

I gasped and then I was falling through a black void again. I couldn't hear myself scream.

Someone's strong arms caught me. When I opened my eyes, I was back in the main hall of that kingdom—Centeria. Looking up in a daze, I saw a prince.

He yelled out, "She's fainted, get some water."

4

❦

battle stations

The sky was red.

The fierce wind was on my face when I woke up. *What the—?*

My pulse raced again as I was hurled up into the sky and then somehow whooshed back down. Cold metal pressed against my skin, constricting me. One of the big metal robots, like the ones from the marketplace earlier, had me in its tight grip.

Chest heaving, I tried to scream but there was a lump in my throat. I pushed at the hard vise that enclosed me but my human arms were no match for a robot monster.

It was taking me away from the castle—*the castle!* I gasped as I craned my neck back to see.

The castle was on fire. People ran amok, in panic, in the courtyard, on the hills, and all over town. People were screaming in anguish. Large structures crumbled down as more giant relics tangled together in battle. A large crash perked up my ears, and when I glanced over, part of the castle collapsed from a powerful blast of some sort.

Centeria was falling!

The majestic flag bearing the golden phoenix crest on top of the castle had caught on fire.

Oh no! I panicked and tried again to free myself from the monster's claws to no avail.

The giant mech slowed down and I noticed we had arrived at the edge of the forest surrounding the kingdom. To my surprise, the metal monster extended its arm to set me down gently on the grass.

I straightened up, confused. From the ground, I studied the robot more closely. This one did look like the relics in the marketplace, except it was a different color. Olive green and brown, not indigo and black.

A whoosh saw the relic's faceplate open. I only needed to squint for a moment to recognize him.

It was the King.

"Stay hidden, Lady Sarah," the King bade, his hoarse voice urgent as he called down to me. Then his faceplate closed again and the giant robot turned to head back toward the fighting.

"Wait!" I whirled around. "Wait a minute!" But he was too far away to hear me.

I stood at the edge of the cliff, the edge of the valley, and watched helplessly as a wildfire spread across the dozens of thatched houses in the surrounding villages, the fire engulfing more structures and temples. Meanwhile, more green robots continued to fall.

I swallowed hard as I recognized the vision I'd seen from the street walking home the other day. "No." I froze in dread. This couldn't really be happening.

The ground shook and I steadied my knees to keep my balance but I couldn't stop staring at the utter destruction before me. This had to be some kind of huge coincidence.

Another loud crash caught my attention.

The King's relic was across the valley. It had fallen on his back and somehow was bursting apart as if something was tearing it to pieces. I frowned. For some reason, I couldn't see what was attacking him.

"Oh no, somebody help him." I searched the field for any other green relic but the ravaged landscape offered no glimpse of any other giants, except for the ones likewise beaten, collapsed on the ground.

A keening noise and an echo of a loud bang saw the King's relic explode and shatter.

"No." I clenched my jaw to steady my trembling chin, my heart pounding in my ears. I squeezed my eyes shut. "No!" I screamed again and collapsed on the ground.

It took a while for the pounding in my head to stop, for the fire that ravaged the Kingdom to die down to a low crackling. The wind still blew hot but it was over.

Centeria was gone.

Lying on my side, I picked at the grass in front of my face. *What the hell was I supposed to do now?*

So much for their legend. Some savior I turned out to be.

The ground trembled for a second and I sat up in alert. After another moment, it came again. The trees swayed in the wind and disturbed birds flew up as something appeared from behind the tall trees.

My gasp caught in my throat. *Another relic!* It paused when it saw me. My eyes widened in dread. *Uh-oh.* I'd scrambled up and gotten ready to bolt when the robot's faceplate opened and there was a vaguely familiar voice.

"Sarah!"

I whirled around. Looking up, I was a bit relieved to see that this robot was green. "Who's there?"

"It's me." Something landed in front of me with a hard thud.

I jumped back in surprise but then I met his sharp green gaze. *Gradd!* I was half-relieved and almost glad to see him. "Oh, you're hurt." I winced, noting his bleeding forehead.

Gradd reached up as if only realizing he was wounded but then dismissed it. "You have to come with me now." He grabbed my arm.

"Ow!" I shrugged him off. "Jeez! I'm not a goddamned piece of furniture you move around! If you want to take me somewhere, how about try asking?"

Gradd shot me an incredulous look. "Is everyone from your world like you?"

"Like what?"

"Incredibly annoying."

"Haha, that's so funny." I gave him a suffering look.

He turned away and headed for his relic. "Just come on."

"Where are you going?"

"I have to take the relic into the forest. The Malkens will easily spot one lying around in the open." Glancing back, he raised an eyebrow. "Why? You want me to leave you here?"

"No, but—"

"Then come on."

I frowned. "Do you have to be so rude?"

"Oh, hold on and let me candy-coat all this, especially for you." Sarcasm dripped from his words. "Harden up."

I feigned a retch. "Arrogant pig," I mumbled.

He must've heard me because he sighed in annoyance. "Look, my father left specific instructions about making sure you were brought along to Thorb when we regroup. Since you're obviously still here, I guess the dirty work is mine." He ran his fingers through his hair in clear frustration. "My father thinks you're the one from the legend. He thinks you're important."

"But Centeria's..." I trailed off, gesturing to the ashy ruins. "I mean, I'm not saying I'm buying into the whole thing, but even if I was the one in your legend, what exactly would be left to save?"

Gradd shot me a look. "Do not underestimate the people of my kingdom. The phoenix stands for exactly that. Centeria will rise again," he declared.

"Huh." I nodded in approval. "Okay, I suppose that's pretty cool."

"Tch," he huffed in derision. "Anyway, come on." He waved me over. "We have to go meet my father at Thorb."

I paused at the evenness of his tone. He seemed a little less in mourning than I would have expected. Then it occurred to me that maybe I had just seen wrong. Perhaps it wasn't the King's relic I had seen explode into a million pieces.

"Uh, when did your father last speak to you?" I tried to ask, all casual.

"At the castle," he replied, not breaking his gait. "Just after the Malkens attacked. I went out with the first wave of relics. He told me that if things went south, we needed to make sure you were safe."

He didn't know, I realized with a sinking sensation in my stomach. "Your father was really nice—*is* really nice," I amended quickly.

He shot me another already annoyed look. "Look, if you're going to go off on a tangent about how different my father and I are, keep in mind that I don't like this situation any better than you do. If my father didn't believe in you so much, I couldn't care less where you go. In fact, I wouldn't care if the Malken relics get you either 'cause it really doesn't matter to me, okay?"

I frowned again at his outburst. I had wanted to tell him about what I had seen happen to his father. I was planning to be sympathetic to his loss. But if he was going to be a jackass about it, I wasn't going to do him any favors.

"Oh, yeah? How about you keep in mind one very important detail here," I proposed, crossing my arms over my chest. "I actually don't have to go anywhere with you. But because of some stupid legend that your father is so dedicated to—which by the way I don't believe for one second, *you're* the one who needs me. I'm the one making the big sacrifice here and you should be grateful."

"Look, I don't need you any more than my father needs you," he countered. "And for the record, I didn't believe in that legend either. Legends don't save kingdoms. Anyone who believes differently is delusional or bewitched. By the way, that little magic trick you pulled off in the castle was a pretty convincing hoax."

"Magic trick?" I made a face.

Gradd rolled his eyes. "The big lights show you did at court where it looked like you were fading away? Oh, and pretending to faint was a nice touch."

I narrowed my eyes in deep thought. Was that when I had seen that new vision?

She can't very well fulfill a legend if she's dead, can she?

Recalling the strange voice, my heart thumped in my chest as the realization hit me. "The Malkens..." The Malkens had attacked Centeria to kill me. The attack, the fire, the relics—they had all been meant for me.

I was the reason Centeria had burned to the ground. I was the reason Gradd's father, the King, had been killed. They had all died saving *me*.

My stomach turned over. I clamped my hand over my mouth to tamp down my nausea.

Gradd shot me a wary look. "Now what? What kind of trick are you doing now?"

Dropping my hand, I shot him a dark glare. *Insensitive jerk.* He didn't even seem at all sad about his kingdom that lay in ashes behind us. He wasn't worried about his father. He wouldn't give me a chance.

He leered. "You're trying to cast a spell on me, aren't you?"

In a hot flash of anger, I slapped his face. It was the second time in two days and I had a feeling it wouldn't be the last one.

I spun on my heel and stalked off into the woods.

Gradd didn't follow. He didn't move. He stared in shock.

By nightfall, I was still in the woods. I had given up the thought of going back for him. I had given up trying to see if he was somewhere behind me. I didn't have to save anything or help anyone.

I just had to get home.

You'll miss me when I'm gone, Annette, I remembered with a shake of my head.

I frowned as I inspected my arms and legs, getting all scratched from the forest's shrubs and weeds. That dumb, heavy dress was slowing me down so I had left it behind. It would probably be some animal's nest come morning. My only relief was that I hadn't worn my usual, ratty, holey clothing to bed the other night. Not that a tank top and shorts were suitable clothes for hiking in the woods at night.

Wondering about the seasons in this world and hoping winter was far, far away, I made my way through the thick, dark forest.

I didn't have the first clue what to do if I had to stop to camp out for the night. I rubbed my hands over my arms but it wasn't so much the cold as it was dread. I didn't even know where I was going.

I cursed aloud when I snagged my arm on another branch. "Oh dammit," I muttered, examining my arm as I kept on.

There was a snap and the next thing I knew, my legs slipped out from under me, and I was hoisted up into a big tree, ensnared in a net. "Whoa—Ow!" I cried though it was more of annoyance than pain.

The rough rope scratched my skin. I was quite high off the ground. "Oh, man—" I groaned aloud and tried to struggle free from the net but it only made my position even more awkward as I dangled in mid-air.

I groaned again, squinting in the dark if there was anyone that might be able to help me, but the forest was eerily quiet. Perhaps this trap had been laid out for a bear or something. Perhaps poachers were camping in the woods. Then again, this was a whole other world. Who knew what manner of terrifying creatures lurked in the area? Perhaps one of them was getting ready to eat me or something.

I tensed up when another twig snapped in the darkness. *Are those the monsters now?*

Two shadows approached underneath my net.

"Hello? Who's down there?" I tried to make out their form.

They looked like people but they didn't reply. Several others like them came.

My stomach churned in caution. Perhaps not a good sign.

"Uh, hi guys!" I greeted them with an artificial cheer. "Could you like, help me down, or something?"

They still didn't respond.

I frowned. "Come on, guys." I eyed the strange people as they circled under me. I sincerely hoped it wasn't a prelude to some gruesome ritual sacrifice, wherein I was the sacrifice. I swallowed hard as one of them raised a sharp, pointy thing. "Hey—uh—let's not be too hast-eeee!" I cried as, with one swoosh, the net holding me up fell to the ground with a loud thump.

"Ow, I think I broke my back." I moaned, even as I managed to sit up, still tangled in the net. Upon closer inspection, the strange people looked like a lost jungle tribe, their clothing made of animal skins and bones, their faces painted.

One of them poked me with a sharp stick.

"Ow," I said again, still trying to wrestle my way out of the net. "Look, there's obviously been—ow—some mistake here. I am not—ow—food, and if you could just let me go—ow—then maybe we could—" I struggled to try to stand.

"Hey!" A familiar voice from behind made me turn to look.

It was Gradd, his sword drawn.

The tribal people sensing danger sprung to action, several of them letting out battle howls as they jumped toward Gradd—and left me alone.

I stared at them. "Uh, hello?"

Although Gradd was doing well, fighting off half a dozen armed locals, I wasn't watching because nobody had thought to help me out of the stupid net first. *Damn!* Every girl for herself!

When I finally managed to crawl free of the rope, I blew out an exasperated sigh.

Gradd was facing only two of the tribal people left standing. The rest of them were lying on the ground but I could tell they were still alive, merely subdued.

Gradd lunged at the two guys with his sword as if taking on two at a time made no difference to him.

He was probably fine on his own, but his haggard expression seemed near his limit, so I moved forward to help. But just as I'd bent down to pick up a fallen tree branch with which to defend myself, another loud snap saw Gradd fly up into the air—right into another net trap.

"Oh sh—" I straightened up and jumped at the blunt end of a wooden stick weapon against my back. "Oh great," I muttered as I dropped the branch and raised my hands in surrender.

5

aella

"Oh, don't give me that look like it's my fault," I snapped. "I got out of my net."

Gradd continued to glare at me.

Ignoring him, I turned back to peer through the wooden bars of the cage on makeshift wheels we were being carted in to head to what I assumed would be the tribal people's camp.

A big bonfire lit up a clearing in the dense forest. Thundering drums and howls of songs echoed up the trail. Eerie shadows flickered against the woods we went past before our wooden cage was dropped, settled right by the edge of the clearing.

I only hoped whatever tribe this was, they didn't eat or sacrifice people.

Groaning, I rattled the bars in restlessness. I glanced over at Gradd again who hadn't moved and was still glaring at me. "You know, I'd always been led to believe royalty have good breeding," I relayed. "I mean, as a writer, I wouldn't even write a prince character like you. Princes are supposed to be gallant, charming." I ticked off my fingers. "And most of the time, they're like freaking knights in shining armor who save people." I pointed at him. "You, on the other hand, haven't done anything so far except put me in danger," I prattled on. "I probably would have been better off if you hadn't butted in. Or maybe if you'd thought to look where you stepped in the forest earlier, we wouldn't be in this mess—"

His gaze was smoldering as though he was trying his damnedest not to explode at me. "If you had come with me instead of overreacting, maybe I wouldn't have had to come after you, and then *maybe* we wouldn't be in this damned cage."

"Hey! If you had one shred of compassion and stopped being an arrogant jerk for two minutes, I wouldn't have had to get mad. Jeez!" I threw up my hands before slumping against the cage bars. "What did I ever do to deserve this?" I whinged in desperation. "I'm too young to die."

"For god's sake, shut up," Gradd barked. "No one's going to die here today."

"Why?" I prompted wryly. "They only sacrifice people at dawn?"

He scoffed in ridicule. "This is a Kiffad camp. They're peaceful people. If we don't hurt them, they don't hurt us."

"Oh, is that so? Then what are we doing locked in this fricking cage, huh?" I demanded, shaking the bars with a hollow rattle.

"Would you calm down?" Gradd snapped. "Nothing's going to happen. Now sit down and shut up."

A wave of commotion outside made me look over. Several of the tribespeople were starting to crowd at the entrance to the clearing.

"What's going on?" I craned my neck but the crowd was too thick to see.

Gradd's face didn't betray any emotion.

Squinting, I blinked in surprise when the two gypsy girls from Centeria stepped out of the crowd. They were followed by several other people who, judging from their features, I was pretty sure also came from Centeria.

My eyebrows furrowed in confusion. "Hey, aren't those—?"

Gradd merely stood up as if he was expecting this.

Even more Centerians appeared mixed in with the masses of tribal people. Then a particularly big group of people moved surrounding a person of whom all I could see was a tall feathered headpiece.

Curious, I tilted my head. "Who's that? Their leader or something?"

"Chief Onnahawk." Gradd approached the bars beside me.

I was already creeped out. "Is he nice? Do you know him? Tell me you've got some kind of peace treaty or something with them. I mean, he's gonna let us go, right?"

The group around the Chief moved toward us. I swallowed in anxiety. If the Centerian people were here, they were either refugees or prisoners. I wished Gradd would show some sort of expression instead of that poker face of his, so I could decide whether to be panicked or relieved.

Then again, even if the Chief and the Centerians were friends, there was still no guarantee he'd be happy with someone weirdo like me hanging around.

I tensed in nervous anticipation as the milling crowd began to part like colorful fans to present their leader.

"Lord Gradd, what a pleasant surprise."

I blinked, taken aback at the sweet melodious voice of the Kiffad Chief.

She was tall, wearing a majestic tunic of animal skins adorned with feathers and a fur collar underneath spiky armor. Her long hair was twisted around a rough rope and hung down her back. She had black warrior stripes under her eyes and a garland around her neck. Not quite elegant, but still regal, strong, and very beautiful.

She walked up to the cage as someone opened the door and faced Gradd with a warm, almost personal smile.

"Aella." Gradd gave her a curt nod.

The Chief raised her eyebrows at Gradd as though in an amused warning before she turned to me.

A chill went up my spine as I met her gaze. I tried to smile. "Uh...hi."

Chief Onnahawk shot me a puzzled look before meeting Gradd's gaze again.

He was already shaking his head. "You'll have to excuse Sarah

Peters." He dismissed with a wave. "She comes from a place with no procedure."

"Hm." The Chief regarded me with another look before merely turning away.

Gradd fell into step beside her.

I peeked out of the wide-open door to the cage for a wary moment then dashed off to follow the two of them before I figured anyone else could object.

Walked a few paces behind them, I overheard talk of certain evacuation procedures, and I guessed that Centeria did indeed have some sort of agreement with the Kiffads for assistance in the event of adversities.

My stomach churned again as I remembered that it was entirely my fault that Centeria was a burning pile of rubble. I couldn't help a heavy sigh.

Gradd glanced over his shoulder at me but he didn't break off communication with Chief Onnahawk.

When Onnahawk and Gradd arrived at the edge of the clearing, what looked like the tribe Chief's honored post before the big bonfire, Gradd stood beside her.

Shifting uncomfortably on my feet, I stopped short of the dais as I certainly didn't want to distinguish myself and stand with them. Looking around, I recognized the two gypsy girls near the back and decided to walk over to them instead.

Gradd caught my arm. "Where are you going?"

I pulled away. "Just over there—jeez!" I shot him a weird look, but he let me go, narrowing his eyes to watch me leave.

As I walked, Onnahawk's voice thundered over the crowd.

"Let us welcome our friends from Centeria," Onnahawk began. "Tonight, a lot was lost." She paused as a shadow passed over her face. "But my father always said it is the challenges in life that make us strong and that we should look at every tragedy as a new beginning. A chance to start over—"

Her expression softened at the mention of her father. Beneath the rough and regal Chief act, there was probably still a real person under there.

The people cheered as Onnahawk's speech finished. The music re-started, and as people went back to business, the Chief and Gradd walked off together again.

Arriving where the gypsy girls were, I approached them with a smile. "Hi."

The two of them jumped in surprise and stared at me in a fluster.

"What's wrong?" I asked.

But both girls curtsied and scooted away, leaving me gawking at their retreating backs.

"Was it something I said?" I mumbled in puzzlement.

"Cursed," a voice rasped behind me.

I whirled around. In the dark, I could just make out a cloaked person holding a staff, sitting by the sidelines. "Pardon?" I prompted.

"Cursed," he-she-it repeated with more conviction. "Stranger from another world...bring downfall to Centeria."

I froze. *No.*

"Yes," its voice countered as though it read my mind. "Stranger burns down kingdom. Brings fear. Brings curse to Centeria. Brings curse to us all."

"No." I set my jaw and stepped closer to see.

The old woman had long, silver hair, wrinkled skin, and beady black eyes. The amulets around her neck jangled with every move-ment over her worn brown cloak. She raised her hand to point a shaky index finger at me and as she muttered something, her eyes gleamed red.

"Witch."

I wrinkled my nose in distaste, clenching my fists. "Hey, speak for yourself."

A heavy hand landed on my shoulder and I gasped, whirling around.

Gradd withdrew his hand quickly. "What are you doing?"

A bit annoyed, I gestured to the old woman. "What does it look like I'm doing?"

Gradd glanced over at the bushes, his eyebrows lifting in expectation.

The old woman was gone.

My jaw dropped. "What the—?" I looked up at Gradd again. "I swear there was an old... I know there was a—"

"Let's go," Gradd beckoned.

"But there was an old woman there," I insisted. "I talked to her. You believe me, right?"

Gradd glanced behind me into the forest again but he just shrugged. "The forest is a strange place. Sometimes the fog can play tricks on your eyes. Now come on. Chief Onnahawk requests our presence for dinner."

"Are you sure she meant me too?"

"Don't start," Gradd warned.

Shivering in fright, I took one last look into the forest to make sure before following him.

6

flipside

"Sarah Peters." Chief Onnahawk nodded graciously as Gradd and I arrived at what I could only describe as a 'royal picnic mat.'

"Oh please, call me Sarah." I gave her a tentative smile.

With her feathered headpiece beside her on the ground, Chief Onnahawk didn't seem as intimidating as she was before and I certainly didn't want to keep the formality.

She gestured downward. "Please have a seat. I do apologize for how you arrived at camp. We are on high alert these days. My people were only doing their jobs. You understand?"

Gradd sat down first. I followed.

A variety of fruits and weird half-burnt animal parts I'd never seen before in my life were spread on several bowls and plates before us. The steaming food made my mouth water. Then again, maybe I was just starving.

The Chief watched me eat. "So, Gradd tells me you're the one talked about in this legend."

I glanced over at Gradd who didn't seem willing to participate in the conversation in any way. He was looking off somewhere, oblivious to the world. "Uh...okay." I shrugged passively.

"That would mean of course that you are…from another world?" she prompted, curious.

"Uh, yeah, but honestly, I don't know how I got here or where my world is." I met her gaze, hopeful. "It's called Earth. Maybe you know it?"

Onnahawk shook her head. "I am sorry. I've never heard of it before. Maybe you could ask Agarpa, the seer of our tribe," she suggested. "She often speaks of spirits and other worlds."

"Oh." I deflated in my seat. "Maybe."

She leaned forward. "If you don't mind my asking, what were you doing in the middle of the woods at such a late hour? Unaccompanied, I might add. I would have thought the legend of the Centerian kingdom would have been heavily guarded."

That question I could answer. I sneered at Gradd. "Well, you see—"

Gradd cut me off. "She wandered off."

"I stormed off," I corrected and gave the Chief a sweet smile before gesturing to Gradd. "Because *he* is an asshole."

Onnahawk almost spit out her drink. She turned an amused look toward Gradd. "Well, that's something I haven't heard before."

But Gradd was scowling at me. "Why don't you tell her about how I've already saved your neck about ten times?"

"Haha, saved me from trouble you get me into," I clarified.

"Oh, don't start that again," Gradd huffed, folding his arms. "If you hadn't appeared out of nowhere yesterday, you wouldn't have gotten in my way. Just like if you had listened to me earlier instead of walking out on me, you would have saved the trouble of being caged."

I groaned in disbelief. "Are you kidding me with this? If you had left me out of it, I wouldn't have had to run from the marketplace at all. And if you had been a little more compassionate about your stupid kingdom like I was trying to do, instead of acting all know-it-all, maybe we wouldn't have been captured." I leaned forward, my lips curled. "Or maybe if your kingdom could fend for itself without relying on some stupid legend—"

Gradd gritted his teeth.

"—without relying on me for that matter, I wouldn't even be here. Did you even think—"

Without warning, Gradd grabbed my chin. "One more word out of you and I shut you up myself."

Gasping in instant alarm, I jumped away and out of his reach.

Eyes wide with amusement and surprise, Onnahawk simply looked at each of us in turn.

Still glaring at him, I brushed myself off. Sticking my chin up, I huffed away without another word.

Conceited, arrogant, moronic, sadistic— Scowling, I wandered around the clearing. It wasn't like I had anywhere else to go. And everyone I passed by was making sure to keep their distance, their watchful eyes on me wary, if not terrified. *That damn legend. This is all its fault.*

Gradd and Onnahawk hadn't moved from the mat. They were now talking and laughing (or at least she was laughing.) Even from across the bonfire, I could tell they were already familiar with each other. Maybe they were friends. Maybe even lovers. Maybe that was why he called her 'Aella.'

A hissing from behind me made me turn. There was that old woman again from earlier, just then disappearing around the bushes.

That old hag. A bit annoyed, I went to follow her. She needed to explain what she had meant by all that curse business. But her spooky shadow moved through the woods and kept vanishing around the trees.

I lost her in another dark clearing before I realized I'd wandered too far from the party and the cold breeze brought chills to my spine again.

"Get out here you old witch," I called.

For a minute, silence, save the wind blowing through the trees. Then when I turned again, the old woman was right behind me.

"What are you doing?" I put my hands on my hips.

She beckoned me to follow her.

I craned my neck as she disappeared into the entrance of a creepy cave almost hidden under a thick layer of vines, amidst more shrubs and trees.

Shifting on my feet, I already broke goosebumps peering into the entrance. "Okay, this is beyond creepy." But a strange glow emanating from inside the cave drew my attention and curiosity took over. Grimacing, I let out a resigned sigh. *Sure, what the hell?*

Cobwebs brush against my face as I stepped through the narrow opening. "Ew-ew-ew—" I hurried through, waving the sticky, stringy crap away with my hands, trying to feel around in the dark. I almost tripped over some rocks until I found the source of the light.

It was the sun.

The old witch was standing within a projection in a hazy puff of smoke, a floating representation of the solar system which filled the cave with an eerie glow.

But I made a face as her hologram thingy seemed to be missing quite a few planets.

She crooked her finger at me. "Come here, witch."

I shot her a look. "Seriously? You look like that and I'm the witch? I mean, between the two of us—"

"Quiet!"

I winced at her booming voice. "Fine!" I blew out a breath as she skulked around the smoky haze. "So what is all this?"

She pointed to the planet Earth within the 'hologram.' "Anthuria."

I shot her a weird look. "No," I disagreed. "That's Earth."

She shook her head. "Listen, witch!" she hissed and pointed to Earth again. "Anthuria." When she waved her two hands to cross each other and back, a strange gust of wind rose to spin the hologram all around us in the cavern.

I tucked my hair behind my ear and squinted up at the new formation of planets before me.

There were now two sets of planets orbiting the sun, one seemingly a mirror image of the other set which wasn't there before.

The new set looked exactly like the solar system I knew.

The witch pointed to the third planet in that image. "Earth."

Eyes widening, I shivered again.

Anthuria and Earth were on completely opposite sides of the sun, following the same orbit, as though Anthuria was the flipside of Earth.

I gawked then shot her a wary look. "Is this some sort of joke?"

Growling as she took offense, the witch turned to leave.

Panicked, I went after her. "No, wait!" She might have been the creepiest thing I'd ever met so far but I was desperate for information. "H-how do I get back?"

Mumbling something incoherent, she gave me a dismissive wave.

I supposed I could have been more polite. She did seem like she was trying to help me. I pursed my lips. "Please," I called out.

The witch stopped in mid-stride. But she turned to slowly walk back over to me.

When she held her wrinkled hand out for mine, I hesitated for a second before putting my hand in hers.

Her hand was cold. Like she was dead.

But before I could freak out about that, a surge of energy shot through me.

A vision overtook my mind. The burning form of the phoenix was rising up from the ground, soaring high before landing again as tumultuous waves of fire. It swallowed up entire forests, mountains, and grand structures. I was in a field of fire and the intense heat emanating from the ground hurt my eyes. When the ground shook, my gaze snapped up in alert. A strange-looking relic was weaving across the way, one I'd never seen before. I didn't know why or how I knew but somehow, I knew it was Gradd's. His new relic was in mid-battle with another unfamiliar large dark red relic and Gradd looked like he was in trouble.

My heart pounded in my chest. *What is this? How does this help me get back home?*

Gradd's relic seemed to turn to me, in the strange, indeterminate haze where I was, and there was a shout. "Watch out!"

Furrowing my eyebrows, I glanced over my shoulder for any cause for alarm.

I found it.

An extending mechanical claw appeared out of nowhere from the trees behind me and whooshed right in my direction. I held my breath, frozen in place, and could only widen my eyes as the relic claw crashed into me and the ground around me.

I screamed as the impact tossed me aside like a pebble. Rocks and dirt flew up and I shielded my face as I fell. My whole body ached from the direct hit of the monster's heavy metal claw as if I'd broken every bone in my body. My head whirled and hurt like hell. Blood oozed out of my eyes, my nose, and my mouth...

Then everything went black.

7

the curse

Gradd shook me awake.

Groggy, I came to, still aching all over. I took a few seconds to remember what had happened. I was in Gradd's arms. He was carrying me again. I tried to push off to come down but for some reason, I had no strength.

"What did you do to her, you witch?" Gradd demanded of the old woman.

The three of us were still in the dark cave.

I guessed Gradd had gone to look for me *again* and I must've fainted *again*. I groaned in annoyance. I was sick and tired of being the damsel in distress in this story.

"She came to me." The old woman's response was hollow, throaty. "I merely answered her question."

Swallowing, I turned my head. "No, you didn't." I narrowed my eyes but my forceful demand was feeble in my raspy voice. "What did all that mean? How do I get home?"

The old woman leered at me and her beady eyes glowed again. When she spoke again, her ominous words sent chills down my spine.

"You don't."

My heart stopped.

I don't get back home... I die...

"Alright, that's enough!" Gradd barked at the witch.

She cackled before disappearing into the dark shadows. But her laughter echoed in the cave, echoed in my head...

Squeezing my eyes shut, I trembled in dismay.

She was wrong. She had to be wrong. I do *so* too get back home. *Somehow.*

When I opened my eyes, Gradd was looking down at me with that disapproving frown.

I returned his frown. He was going to lecture me again on wandering off and how I was an annoyingly huge burden that he had to look after every second.

But he didn't say anything. He just took a deep breath and walked us back to the camp.

Onnahawk was waiting for us. Relief was clear on her face when she spotted us coming out of the forest. "Where was she?"

"She was with Agarpa." Gradd set me down to my feet on the grass.

I stopped at the name in dejection. That was Agarpa? I struggled to regain my balance as I made a face. Some help *she* was.

Onnahawk led me to a nearby tent to sit down.

"I need to prepare my men," Gradd told her then he glanced over at me before he shot Onnahawk a meaningful look.

She nodded and he walked away.

It was impressive how they easily understood each other.

Gesturing for me to settle down on the mat, Onnahawk disappeared inside the tent for a second and came out with a wooden bowl. "Drink this."

"Thanks." I sipped the warm drink, whatever it was.

"You're welcome." She sat down beside me.

It was curious. Onnahawk seemed like she had two personalities. When she had her big headpiece on, she was 'Chief Onnahawk of the Kiffad tribe.' Powerful. Intimidating. Scary. And you wouldn't expect her to sit down with a weirdo like me and be all Florence

Nightingale. But when her headpiece was off, it was like she was a normal person.

"Was Agarpa able to help in any way?" Her prompt was gentle.

I almost choked on the drink, my eyes watering from coughing, and I had to blink several times.

"Oh, I'm sorry." Chuckling under her breath, she thumped on my back. "Usually Agarpa's very wise. I'm sure she didn't intend to scare you or be too blunt."

"Yeah? I'm pretty sure that's exactly what she intended." I cleared my throat as I put the drink down.

"What did she tell you?"

"Well." I feigned a cheerful expression. "She said that uh...I would die in Anthuria."

Onnahawk curled her lips. "Oh, I suppose that is pretty bad." But she waved her hand. "But you shouldn't take everything Agarpa says to heart. Often, she only glimpses one possibility among thousands. What you saw may have many interpretations. And..." she paused, a catch in her voice, "she has been wrong before."

The vision was still fresh in my mind, the warm, clammy blood, the broken bones, the searing pain... I wasn't sure it was a memory that would leave me soon. I cleared my head with a brisk shake. "She just seemed so sure. She even knew where I came from."

"Was it called...Earth, did you say?" Onnahawk's eyebrows rose in a prompt.

"Yeah. And apparently, it's on the other side of the sun from this world. Or so Agarpa said." I heaved a huge sigh as I looked around. "It's very...different from this place. For starters, we don't have huge fighting robots like you have here. Well, except, of course, in cartoons," I added offhand.

She cocked her head in question. "What are...cartoons?"

"Uh..." I opened my mouth to explain but then dismissed it. "It's complicated." I went on with a wave. "Anyway, where I come from, kings and queens and kingdoms are more like tourist destinations, and we've got democracy and stuff."

Onnahawk absorbed this information with narrowed eyes. "I see. This is why you aren't familiar with our traditions. I have to say I've never seen Gradd make allowances for anyone before."

I couldn't help a frown. "Gradd—is an arrogant jerk."

Onnahawk shook her head in silent laughter. "Oh, he might surprise you," she assured with a tone of authority in her voice.

I pursed my lips. But of course, she would say that. It was obvious the two of them knew each other pretty well. I hesitated before asking what I had wanted to ask since earlier. "Um, may I ask why he called you Aella?"

She stiffened a little, but in surprise, not offense. "Onnahawk was my father's name," she explained. "It's the name I used ever since he passed away and I became the head of my people. Gradd knew me before I got the title."

Wincing a little bit, I gave her a small consoling smile. "Your father must've been a great man."

"He was." Onnahawk's nod was full of pride. "We believe he still lives among us, within the people. In spirit."

"Oh yeah, it sounded like it." I jerked my thumb back toward the dais when she made her 'my father' speech.

Her pretty face colored slightly. "I try to make big speeches like my father used to. Speeches that encourage people. Lift their spirits. I try to make my people believe I know what I'm talking about. To inspire confidence. But sometimes, I'm not so sure I have it myself." Her countenance dimming, her revelation allowed a peek underneath her all-calm, fearless leader façade.

I studied her expression. "Must be hard, huh?"

She blew out a breath as though to indicate I had no idea.

I happened to spot Gradd at the far end of the camp with a group of Centerians. I couldn't help a small sigh as I remembered his father. Pretty soon, Gradd would have to handle pretty much the same stuff that Onnahawk was having to and he didn't even know about it yet.

"Have you told him?" Onnahawk's voice was quiet but firm.

Wary, I turned my gaze toward her. "Told him what?"

She merely met my gaze. She already knew. And she knew that I knew as well.

I shook my head. "No. I...couldn't. How did you find out?"

Onnahawk's mouth simply curved up. She had her sources.

I looked over at Gradd again. "Are you going to tell him?"

"He'll find out when he's ready." She regarded me with an inquisitive look before following my gaze. "Are you worried about him?"

Gradd, as though sensing we were talking about him, glanced over at us. But not seeming to care, he just went back to briefing his men.

I pursed my lips in consideration.

Gradd was tough. His expression was always calculatedly neutral. Impenetrable. He didn't seem the type to falter or weaken at all. I was sure he would handle it just fine.

In any case, my response was the same. "It's not really my business."

8

the invisible enemy

When Onnahawk left me to attend to tribe business, I lay back on the mat with my arms crossed under my head as I stared at the sky.

I supposed the sky looked the same as Earth's. Except Anthuria had two beautiful moons, one almost overlapping the other in the sky.

I made out several familiar-looking constellations and took a deep cleansing breath. Being under a somewhat familiar sky made me feel a little bit better. It was almost as though any time soon, my mom would poke her head out the kitchen door and call me inside for dinner.

With the sky being clearer, the kind of view you'd see if you drove up to the mountains, outside the city, I glimpsed a tiny, un-twinkling red spot in the sky. I thought perhaps it was a planet since I remembered a documentary saying on really clear nights on Earth, you should be able to see Mars.

I was wondering whether Anthuria had such a neighboring planet when suddenly, Mars began to glow brighter—unusually brighter.

Pushing myself up on my elbows, I furrowed my eyebrows.

Mars glowed even more in that strange manner and I groaned when it struck me what was now about to happen. "Oh, not again," I muttered as the red planet 'fell' from the sky.

It sped down like a glowing fireball before subsequently turning into the form of a phoenix.

When I floated off the ground, I gasped, "Whoa." I tried to turn around and found myself staring into the dark forest. Into nothingness. Right before a shadow materialized from the black, a silhouette of a robot with a mechanical arm. The giant robot appeared to solidify from clear liquid metal, solid and very visible when just a moment ago it was invisible... As if it was cloaked...

Its arm shot out again at me and I screamed.

I sat up with a gasp.

I had fallen asleep.

Trying to normalize my breathing, I regained my bearings, forcing a shiver to clear the dread.

I was still in the Kiffad camp except everything was quieter now. The fire burned low and dimly and only a handful of people were walking around, probably scouts or guards, standing watch at the perimeters of the clearing.

"Something wrong?" a voice to my left asked and I whirled in alert. But it was just Gradd. He was sitting beside Onnahawk's tent as he examined the dents on his sword. He raised his eyebrows at me in a calm prompt.

I shook my head. "No. I just...uh...nightmare."

"What did you see?"

His question surprised me because he seemed genuinely interested.

I flustered and tried to grasp the fragments of my dream before they slipped away. "I saw the phoenix...and..."

He nodded for me to go on.

"And some robots—relics that appeared out of nowhere."

He sat up straighter. "What do you mean out of nowhere?"

I furrowed my eyebrows and shrugged. "I don't know. They seemed to be cloaked or something."

His eyes lit up. "Cloak?"

"Yeah, you know, have some sort of way to hide. Like a...camouflage so they can't be seen," I explained, matter-of-factly since the concept was quite obvious to me, being in many movies and TV shows on Earth.

It didn't seem obvious to Gradd.

"That's right." He nodded as if figuring something out. "The invisible enemy. The Malkens have developed some kind of new technology. Their relics are camouflaged and that's why we couldn't see them." He looked over at me to prompt again, "What else?"

I shot him a weird look. "It was just a dream."

He shook his head. "I think it was more than that." He paused for a second before relaying his theory. "I think perhaps you have the ability to see things that may occur in the future through these visions, these flashes. Perhaps because you're...different, you can somehow see things that haven't happened yet."

My blood ran cold. The future...? I saw myself die. Was that my future?

Shivering again, I hugged my knees close to me. This was not at all amusing. In the beginning, being in another world, and being chosen as a supposed 'savior of legend' of a kingdom seemed to have its merits. It all seemed so surreal. But the thought of dying here in a far-off world, all alone, was certainly not one I wanted to even entertain.

"Did you see anything else?" he pressed. "Think hard. It could be important."

I bit my lip, shaking my head. I didn't want to see any more. I was already a witch and a curse. I didn't want to know what else these people expected me to do.

Sensing my retreat, Gradd stood up and came over to kneel beside me.

Eyeing him warily, I stiffened. "What?"

"Aella told me what Agarpa showed you." His face was solemn as he peered at mine. "And I want you to know, that's impossible."

I shot him the driest look ever. "You just said I could see the future. Well, I *saw* myself die. And if that's the future, how is it not possible?"

"Because." Gradd's gaze on me was steady, his tone firm. "I would never let anything happen to you."

I opened my mouth to voice my skepticism but then I met his sharp green gaze. There was no hint of doubt or uncertainty in them. He meant what he said. And right then, I knew it was true. Nothing save hell could get past Gradd. Somewhat reassured, I nodded.

"Good," he noted my acknowledgment and stepped back. "Now if the relics are hidden, there has to be some kind of trigger for them to be revealed. And once they are visible, defeating them should be easy."

He paced, seeming to be forming some kind of plan in his mind. He sure was driven. He'd make a great king, no problem. Of course, technically, he already *was* King, but there was no way I'd tell him that.

Onnahawk arrived. "You're awake."

She was wearing her official Chief headpiece so I just gave her a nonchalant shrug. "Uh, yeah, nightmare. No biggie."

She turned to Gradd with an air of authority. "I've briefed my people on tomorrow's mission. The Centerians will be convoyed to Eleria by noon. They'll be safe there."

I almost sagged in relief. I didn't think I could handle any more fighting. And too, if I was safe and sound in this 'Eleria' place, there was no way I'd be dying soon. Maybe I wouldn't even need Gradd's protection.

"If the Malkens attack Thorb," Onnahawk went on. "You should fall back to Eleria immediately. Do not—"

"Got it." Gradd whirled to leave.

Onnahawk grabbed his arm. "Do *not*—" She gave him a pointed, knowing look. "Attempt to take your stand at Thorb."

"I got it." Gradd shrugged her off, his voice rough.

"Gradd, your army, as it is, doesn't stand a chance against the Malkens," Onnahawk said. "You need to regroup and rest. You all do. And it won't do Centeria or anybody any good if you die fighting a lost cause."

His face darkened. "The restoration of Centeria is not a lost cause."

Onnahawk held up a finger. "Just—don't do anything rash, okay?"

Gradd? Anything rash? Hell no! I almost laughed. Even I knew that would be a difficult one to swing.

"And Sarah can join the head of the convoy," Onnahawk concluded.

"No." Gradd shook his head. "She's coming with me."

My face fell in indignation. "Am *not.*"

"No offense, Aella," Gradd started. "But I don't trust anyone else for the protection of the legend."

"What?" I scrambled to straighten up in protest. "The other day you couldn't wait to get rid of me!"

"You could be helpful to me," Gradd stated. "You know things."

"Oh, but you said you don't believe the legend," I reminded him but he turned away, effectively closing the subject. I made a face in protest. "There's no way I'm going with you."

Turning back to make his point to my face, he declared, "You are coming with me. Even if I have to drag you and that's final."

My jaw dropped as he walked off. "Jerk," I scoffed.

9

trust me

At sunrise, I made a decision. I was going to tell Gradd about his father. He had said that if his father hadn't wanted to see me at Thorb, he wouldn't care where I went. And if his father wouldn't be there at all, it stood to reason that there sure wasn't any reason for me to be either.

The Kiffads were preparing the convoy, loading up the carts and supplies. On land, it was a long travel to Eleria, as to Thorb, but if I flew on Gradd's relic, we'd probably be at Thorb in no time.

I passed Onnahawk on my way to Gradd who was by his relic. "I'm going to tell him," I announced loudly, not stopping.

"He'll kill you." She didn't look the least bit surprised.

"I'll die anyway."

As soon as I was in his sight, Gradd was already in disagreement. "You are coming with me," he repeated as he prepared his relic. "I don't need to explain my reasons to you and you're not changing my mind."

"Your father is dead." I didn't bother softening the blow.

That, at least, made him stop for a moment before he went back to fixing his relic.

"It's true," I assured. "He died in the battle at Centeria. I saw his relic blow up under attack from an invisible relic just before you found me."

Gradd kept working on his relic.

I frowned at his non-response. "Hey, doesn't that mean I don't need to be at Thorb anymore? You said he was the only one who wanted to see me there—hey!" I snapped to get his attention.

He paused again with his back still to me. Then, shaking his head, Gradd turned to meet my gaze. "Now, you're really coming with me," he concluded before he brushed past me to keep working.

"What?" I followed behind him, groaning in frustrated complaint. "This is so not fair. You said you didn't need—oh come on!"

Gradd jumped up into the relic's pilot seat without a word.

"Hey! Did you even hear what I said?" I called up to him.

The relic moved and one of its giant metal hands scooped me up. "Whoa!" I yelped and held on as the relic lifted me off the ground.

"Stay there," Gradd bid before jumping back down to finish setting up.

"What?" I sputtered in annoyance. "Oh, for god's sake." I folded my arms over my chest.

It only took a few more minutes before Gradd jumped back into the pilot's seat. "We're going," was all he said before the relic thundered and shook.

"Yipes!" I squeaked in panic.

Way down on the ground, Onnahawk mocked a salute at me as the relic lifted off the ground.

I cast Gradd an incredulous look across his seat.

He wasn't really going to keep me out here in the robot hand the entire way, was he?

The relic took off and I grabbed onto the mechanical hand even as it clamped a little tighter around me. We flew higher and higher and higher. Eyes wide, I watched the camp shrink smaller from my view and the ground speed past us.

My mouth turned dry. "Ohh my god oh my god oh my god..."

The relic's faceplate cranked open and I caught Gradd's gaze as I looked over.

"Having fun?" Gradd prompted nonchalantly.

"No!" I cried out in indignation. "Put me the hell down!" The wind was whipping at my hair, flying in my face. "You're such a jerk. I order you to put me down right now!"

"Why didn't you tell me sooner?" he called out his question. "About my father."

At about the same time, the relic swooped. "Aaahh!" I screamed. "I wasn't sure." I squeezed my eyes shut so I wouldn't see exactly how high we were. I wouldn't say I was afraid of heights. I was afraid of falling to my death and crashing into the sharp rocks in the canyon that was zooming past below.

"But you're sure now?"

"Onnahawk confirmed it. We didn't want to worry you. You had enough problems."

"Why did you finally tell me then?"

"Because you said you'd leave me if your father wasn't whoa—," I yelped as the relic swooped again. A hint of nausea was beginning in my stomach, I was glad I hadn't eaten much at the Kiffad camp. This was exactly the sort of carnival ride I never usually got on.

But Gradd had more questions. "Why didn't you want to go with me?"

"Oh, god—put me down. Please!"

"Why?" he insisted.

"Because you're a walking target and I don't want to die!" I screamed again.

Gradd didn't reply. The turbulent wind whipped past my ears but Gradd had gone quiet.

All of a sudden, the relic's hand opened and let me go.

Gasping, my eyes flew wide open.

I was falling. He let me fall. The jerky asshole *let me fall.* He wanted me to die. *That arrogant son of a—* I clenched my teeth in anger and disbelief as I torpedoed straight down to my certain death.

My heart pounded in my chest as I kept blinking, still trying to see through the wind. But I was way past panicking. I was flailing through thin air. There was nothing to grab onto. My body tilted one way and the sun was in my eyes. The relic was nowhere in sight.

I let out a resigned breath. So this was it.

I stopped fighting and allowed my body to go limp. I supposed it made little difference whether a Malken relic killed me or I fell a hundred feet from the sky. I was still going to die here anyway.

But at the last moment, something large swooped down and caught me.

When the relic landed on a high cliff, its metal hand set me down on the grass to release me, and I crumpled to a trembling heap on the grass.

Gradd landed with a thud in front of me. "Now what do you have to say for yourself?"

Glaring up at him, I was sure my face was red as it felt hot. Maybe he thought this little legend was indestructible. Maybe because he was a cold, unfeeling soldier, death was just a joke to him. I was so ready to blow up in anger. But when he peered into my face, my eyes welled up with tears, and instead, I burst out crying.

Gradd shot me a weird look like he couldn't figure out why. "What..." He nudged me with his toe. "Hey, get up."

I was so weak and dispirited, I couldn't stand. I couldn't talk. I just kept crying, from fear, from relief, whatever. Or maybe the entire gravity of my situation was only just dawning on me and I was suddenly and completely overwhelmed by absolute and sheer hopelessness.

"Oh shit," he mumbled, almost inaudibly.

Strong arms curled under my knees and around my back. Sitting back on the grass, Gradd cradled me in his lap with a heavy sigh of resignation. "I'm—sorry," he said like he meant it.

But it only made me cry harder.

He groaned again, stroking my back. "Oh come on, I wouldn't really let you fall. I just wanted to show you that you could trust me. You should know that by now."

I tried to get a hold of my breathing. For god's sake, if that was his reason, then that had to be the dumbest 'trust fall' ever in the history of the entire universe.

"I'm sorry," he said again.

Sucking my breath in as I regained a short burst of energy, I pushed away and gave him a murderous look. My terror had turned into hot molten anger.

Gradd didn't resist.

I stumbled away, managing to straighten up before breaking into a run—which was ridiculous because I had nowhere to go. What the hell was I supposed to do now? Wiping my eyes with the back of my hand, I groaned out a loud curse as I ran past some trees in the dense forest beneath the cliff.

Straining to think, I gritted my teeth. Maybe if I concentrated hard enough, I could just will myself to go home. Maybe I could summon that phoenix creature and beg for it to send me back. Maybe it could even be reasoned with. There had to be a way. There *had* to be.

As soon as I figured I was far enough away, I ducked behind a tree and slumped down. Sitting cross-legged on the grass, I squeezed my eyes shut in concentration and tried to summon the phoenix.

But it didn't take long for the ground crunching underneath his boots to announce Gradd's arrival.

"What are you doing?"

At the incredulous tone in his deep voice, I could already imagine his glare of ridiculous mocking and that arrogant, insensitive, cold sneer on his face.

"Going home," I snapped in pent-up fury, my eyes still shut. "Leave me alone."

"Sarah..."

I waved carelessly. "Look, I don't know what you were expecting but I'm really not supposed to be here. And there is absolutely no reason for me to do any of this," I rationalized. "I don't have any responsibility for your stupid kingdom whatsoever. You can go find some other strange person to be your stupid legend. Your father was stupid for believing in me. You're stupid for bringing me along. I'm stupid for believing any of it and I've had just about enough of you." I paused, opening my eyes to level a glare at him. "Now if you'll excuse me, I'm trying to apparate back home." I shut my eyes again, trying to focus.

"Sarah," Gradd started with a tired sigh, the air shifting when he crouched in front of me. "Please don't kill my kingdom because you hate me."

I didn't move.

He touched my knee. "I should have explained. I should have been more clear," he conceded. "The reason I wanted you to come with me is because my kingdom needs you. And if something happens to you, it's my neck—more so now that my father is gone." His voice shook a little bit. "But I have to do what's best for my kingdom. And right now, I can guarantee, the safest place in this world for you is with me."

I was trying not to hear him, trying not to consider his words, trying to ignore the sincerity in the timbre of his voice. It was highly irritating that what he'd said made sense. He had just lost his father. There was no way I could imagine what he was going through. He probably wasn't thinking clearly either.

I heaved an annoyed sigh of resignation at the wave of pity that washed over me. But when I opened my eyes again, Gradd had already trekked back up to his relic.

Dropping my gaze, I stared at a blade of grass on the ground. I had to face the fact that I had less than zero options. And whether either of us liked it or not, this train had already left and I was so on it.

Pushing up to stand on shaky legs, I wiped my face dry some more. I so loathed crying. I didn't see why I had to cry in front of His Royal Jerkiness. But I dusted off my hands and made my way up to the edge of the cliff where Gradd landed his relic.

I was rubbing my sniffling nose when Gradd glanced up at my arrival.

I could tell he already knew I'd given in. It aggravated me even more how much of a stuck-up, self-assured, know-it-all he was. He merely waved his hand to gesture me toward the relic.

"You're a real asshole, do you know that?" It was more a point of fact than a prompt.

But that only made the corner of his mouth turn up in amusement.

I narrowed my eyes up at him. "Are you going to try to kill me again?"

"I promise I will only protect you from now on." His steady gaze met mine but I wasn't ready for his words, I almost flinched.

Refocusing, I stuck my chin up. "And if you think I'm riding on that damn hand again, you've got another thing coming."

Gradd tilted his head to give me a pointed look. "Stand back," he instructed as he jumped into the relic's pilot seat.

I stepped back and sure enough, just like in those cheesy cartoons, Gradd's relic transformed into a great winged mechanical beast, a hovering aircraft with boosters underneath and a couple of seats along the open ridge across the spine. One of the wings was tilted down to the ground like a ramp for getting on or off.

Slightly impressed, I blinked. *Huh.*

Gradd held out his hand to me. "My lady?"

Still wary, I eyed his hand and wrinkled my nose at the relic's new form. "Is that even safe?"

"It is with me," was all I got in response.

I supposed I shouldn't have expected anything else.

The wind blew against my face as I held on and I was glad to finally have a calm flight to take in the scenery.

Anthuria was such a beautiful world. We flew through the clouds, over valleys, mountains, and streams. Old-fashioned castles stood on rolling green hills dotted with grazing animals while clumps of cottages lined paths winding around village settlements.

From his seat behind me, Gradd leaned forward to point out a different type of relic tending a large garden with bright beds of colorful flowers so I could see.

With a smile, I nodded acknowledgment. I turned to one side to ask him. "How far is Thorb?"

"Not long now, why?"

I shook my head, not bothering to reply.

As we flew, Gradd pointed out a few other breathtaking landscapes —fields, towns, forests. I was pretty sure he didn't have to but it was like he was giving me a little tour. I couldn't see his face but the pride in his voice was evident.

After another turn, the view beneath us turned flat and ashen gray as we flew over a barren land with scorched ruins and scattered debris.

Gradd frowned and took a detour.

Even from behind me, I could sense his tension. "Did they do that?"

He didn't reply. I assumed yes. I could imagine there were many similar sites of ruins left behind from enemy relic attacks and battles across their entire land.

I furrowed my eyebrows. "What do these Malken people want?"

"They're looking for something."

"What?"

He paused before posing his question, "Do you remember when we first met?"

I almost scoffed. "Like I could forget."

"The relics were chasing me because I had escaped from Malken captivity"

"What? Were you abducted?"

"Taken prisoner," he corrected, his voice a bit hollow. "I sometimes visit relatives, outside of Centeria. Except for this time, the Malkens were waiting for me. They destroyed everything."

I couldn't see his face but my heart sank at the remorse in his voice.

Before a few days ago, I couldn't have imagined the guilt Gradd must have felt, having been responsible for these tragedies. Of course, now I carried guilt for the destruction of his entire kingdom. And for the first time, I felt as though I almost understood.

"I wouldn't give them what they wanted. It was…" he broke off, likely unwilling to relive the experience. "Anyway, it took me weeks to escape but I finally managed."

"What did they want from you?"

"The Phoenix." His reply was matter-of-fact. Then he must have caught my sideways confused look, he explained, "The phoenix is a very powerful creature. It would be a disaster if the wrong hands were to gain possession of it. But the Malkens believed in our legends too. They wanted me to give them the phoenix." He paused, an exasperated sigh under his breath. "But I couldn't give them what I didn't have." Leaning forward to conclude, his tone was urgent. "Do you see how important you are?"

Uneasy, I fidgeted in my seat. I didn't like the idea of people, whoever they were, thinking that I was some sort of prize in a power play, but at least his story answered a few questions.

The Malkens believed in the legend too. That was why they wanted me. I took a deep breath, my stomach churning in dread. "They know you have me. I saw it. In a vision. They wanted to kill me."

His response was firm, absolute. "You're not going to die."

Blinking to get a grip, I tried to hold on to that thought. "So what happens at Thorb?"

"A lot of rest, I hope." Gradd's demeanor had subdued, wearied.

"That sounds good." I nodded in approval before glancing back at him. "*Are* you tired?"

"Hmm," was his reply. He sounded half-asleep.

"Can I drive?" I joked.

"You can*not*." Gradd perked up in an instant and I had to laugh.

10

knight in shining armor

We passed by more and more fleets of brown and gray relics as we flew closer to Thorb. There was a handful of them guarding each entrance to the heavily fortified, forbidding gray castle. And within the castle walls, familiar-looking green robots—Centerian relics were gathered.

Gradd set us down a short distance away from the main gate.

The ground thundered as the half-dozen guard relics stepped forth to raise their weapons.

Startled, I edged back in my seat. "I thought you said this was a friendly kingdom?"

"Relax," he instructed before clearing his throat to raise his voice. "The King of Centeria demands entry to the castle."

"What do you think you're doing?" I hissed in alarm, swallowing hard.

The relic guards shifted in their stances as they assessed the threat we posed and the ground thundered again.

"Hang on, Sarah." With a push of a button and mechanical whirring, Gradd transformed the aircraft around us back into its previous robot form.

The transformation caught me off guard, I didn't have time to hang on to anything, and when the relic stood upright, my seat retracted and I slid right into the single pilot seat, right in Gradd's lap.

Before I could complain, another gray relic landed in front of Gradd's with a loud whoosh. This new relic was more intimidating and way cooler than any of the plain guard relics standing at the gate. It also even glinted silver in the sunlight. This was obviously not any ordinary relic—or person.

Gradd didn't even flinch.

"The King of Centeria has better manners than you," a deep voice replied. "Identify yourself or prepare to fight." As it said that, the silver relic drew its massive sword.

Gradd called out his firm reply. "The King of Centeria backs down from no challenge."

Wide-eyed in disbelief, I glared at him. Was he seriously trying to pick a fight with this robot while I was in here? "Gradd, what the hell are you doing? This is so not funny."

"Sshh," he shushed me.

"Draw your sword then, stranger," the other relic said.

Gradd drew his relic's sword and our relic shifted in its stance.

Trying to remedy my awkward position, I shifted in my seat as the robot rocked. "Are you freaking crazy?" I shook his shoulder in distress. "Let me the hell out of here! If you want to die today, that's your business."

"In a minute," Gradd dismissed me before he called out to the enemy again. "The King—"

I pinched his arm.

"OW!" Gradd yelped.

The other relic stood fast, puzzled, and its faceplate opened. I couldn't see but a curious query called out of it. "What happened?"

With an exasperated sigh, Gradd pushed a button to open his relic's faceplate. He met the gaze of the other pilot, still with a wince on his face.

I was still on edge from the threat of my imminent demise. "I don't know what the hell you're trying to pull but I've seen my death and this is not supposed to be it, you got that?" I declared in complete annoyance.

The other pilot stared at us.

Gradd turned dull eyes to meet his. "She pinched me."

All of a sudden, the other pilot burst out laughing.

Not bothering to disguise his groan of aggravation, Gradd scooped me up and jumped us both down off his relic. When he set me down on the ground, I brushed myself off. "Thank you."

The pilot of the other relic landed in front of us with a heavy thud. He was tall, blond, built, and also wearing armor. Tilting his head, he shot Gradd a look then put his hand out which Gradd grasped and pulled forward for a brotherly hug—another one of those 'guy hugs.'

"Nice to see you made it," the other pilot said.

"Almost didn't," Gradd replied with a smirk, thumping on his friend's back.

I blinked. Oh, for god's sake. They were friends. I shot Gradd another glare before elbowing him in the ribs. "You scared the hell out of me! You could've just told me you were playing."

Gradd stretched out his arms with a haughty shrug. "I told you to relax."

The other pilot turned to me. "And you must be the famous Centerian legend."

"Uh, yeah, hi," I replied offhand, putting my hand out to shake. "I'm Sarah—"

He bent low, took my hand, and raised it to his lips. Like a *real* prince.

"Oh." I froze. *Hel-lo—*

"Scott Darabont." Still bowed, he looked up at me with a gorgeous smile. "Pleasure."

Flushing deep red, I bit my lip. "Uhh..." It took me a moment to compose myself but I glanced over at Gradd, my hand still in Scott's. "Oh look, what a refreshing change," I noted pointedly. "Some manners."

Gradd shot me a suffering look.

Scott chuckled as he straightened up. "Always happy to oblige an enchanting lady." He smiled at me again and I gave him a sweet smile back.

My hand was still in his.

Clearing his throat out loud, Gradd strode between us to push past. "Can we get down to business please?"

Dropping his hand, Scott watched him head toward the gate first. "Of course, let's not keep the new King of Centeria waiting. My men will take care of your relic." He snapped his fingers and soldiers appeared to rise to the task. With a swish of his cape, Scott caught up with Gradd to lead the way into the castle.

With the two walking in stride, I fell back as we entered the castle.

Looking up at the archways high above me, I hushed in awed wonderment. Stone carvings and tapestries adorned the wide hallways. It struck me that the castle at Thorb was just as majestic as the one at Centeria, only the former seemed to lack warmth. I supposed that was because Thorb was primarily a population of soldiers.

"Where are my people?" Gradd asked.

"In good hands." Scott led us up a gold-embellished carpeted staircase. "What news of the Malkens?"

Gradd's face was dark. "Not good."

"The Malkens haven't exactly been an ally of my kingdom," Scott began. "But they have never instigated any offensives against us. Hopefully, they won't look for you here." He paused, his tone strained as he added, "I only just heard about your father. I am sorry for your loss. He was a great man."

Gradd dismissed with a brusque wave. "It's fine, forget it."

Scott assessed him with a look. "So, how's it feel to be King?" he prompted as we reached a room at the end of the hall.

"Sucks," Gradd muttered, plowing through the door.

Scott hung back and met my gaze. "He's...tense?"

I shot him a you-have-no-idea look before we followed suit.

The room was a bedchamber. A lady's quarters. Chiffon curtains, pink bedspreads, and flowers adorned the large cheery space.

Forehead creased in confusion, Gradd threw up his hands. "What are we doing here?"

"Nothing," Scott replied with a gesture to me. "This will be Lady Sarah's quarters."

"Oh." I gave him another appreciative smile. "Thank you so much."

Great smile, good looks, manners, a castle. Scott would quite easily knock Derek Richards out of the water. I had to stop staring.

"I thought you would be tired from your journey," Scott relayed with a warm smile.

"Great." Gradd turned on his heel and beckoned Scott. "Let's go. We've got a lot of important things to discuss." He started to head out but not before meeting my gaze to give me a stern 'Behave' look.

I ignored him.

"I'm sure I'll see you later." Scott nodded me farewell.

"Later." Gradd gave a careless wave before pulling Scott out the door with him.

I winced as the door slammed shut. A lot of important things to discuss. I rolled my eyes. Like I shouldn't be there because it was important.

I flopped back onto the bed and was surprised at how good the firm mattress felt against the flat of my back. I was a lot more tired than I thought.

I'd never had to be burdened with the responsibility of an entire legend before. I was never the bravest kid in the playground. Then again not once in my life did I ever think I would witness epic robot battles, be locked up in a cage, or fly on a relic's back before. This whole other world was wreaking havoc on my sense of normalcy, forcing me out of my comfort zone, and I'd only been here what, two—three days?

I thought back to what I might have been missing back on Earth right at this moment. All the average human chaos, bad news, mundane problems, school politics, my friends... I wondered if my parents had called the cops to report me missing yet.

Frowning, I stared at the canopy ceiling.

Anthuria was the furthest thing from any teenager's paradise. Despite their advances in robotechnology, the world still lived like it was in the medieval ages. There were no phones, television, or computers. Perhaps children learned to operate heavy machinery here first instead of learning to ride their bikes. It didn't surprise me that everyone I had met so far was so gloomy and grumpy.

Yikes. I hoped it wasn't starting to rub off on me.

I blew out a sigh, shifting to make myself comfortable in bed. But I didn't want to sleep. I didn't want to get another one of those freaky traumatic visions.

I I

the kingdom of the tiger

I was stirred awake on the brink of my nap by a firm knocking on the door. Squinting at the sunlight pouring through the windows, I sat up on my elbows to respond. "Yeah?" Except the knocking didn't stop. Not wanting to leave the bed, I groaned in displeasure as I had to stand up to open the door. "Yes—?"

I was cut off as about four maids whirlwinded in, carrying clothes and sponges, spouting off their master's direct orders to get 'the lady' cleaned up.

I didn't get to say much because I was then efficiently dunked into a tub of water, scrubbed down, dried, and dressed in minutes flat.

Then the lady who looked like she was in charge informed me that meals were to be served shortly at the main dining hall before she and the others bowed out through the doorway.

As the door closed behind them, I stood in the middle of the room, still a bit dizzy from the sudden bustle of activity. I had to hand it to these Thorb people. They sure knew how to be efficient.

I stifled a yawn. Figuring if I had to wait any longer in the room I would likely fall asleep, so I decided to take a walk outside instead and do a little exploring.

Peeking out the door, I found the hallway empty. My clunky shoes

70

clacked against the polished wooden floor as I meandered down, stopping every few minutes to inspect the strange things displayed along the way. Stone sculptures stood on pedestals, painted portraits were mounted on the walls, and ornate, gothic chandeliers hung on the ceiling.

Judging from the multitude of tiger sculptures all over the place, it was probably safe to guess that the mascot for this kingdom was the tiger. I shook my head in ridicule. This whole entire world seemed obsessed with symbols and legends.

As I passed the main stairwell, servants peered curiously at me. Uneasy, I returned the same wary looks as I hurried past them. I guessed the rumor about my terrifying curse had already reached their ears.

I cocked my head when the clashing of swords from somewhere in the castle broke the eerie silence, and with the castle so deathly quiet to begin with, it wasn't that hard to tune in to the sound to find where it was coming from.

A few soldiers exiting a room up ahead of the hallway craned their necks upon spotting me.

Passing a large baroque mirror mounted low against the wall, I stopped in mid-stride and blinked at my reflection in surprise.

I hadn't paid much attention to what the ladies had dressed me in except to note it was significantly more comfortable than the last outfit I had been given to wear. I didn't even care that it was pink. But with sleeves down to my elbows, a decent neckline, and a length to the floor, I looked just like one of those ladies-in-waiting from a Renaissance fair in the dress. The dress fit snugly, I couldn't sneak my own clothes underneath them. The maids had even fixed my usually lifeless hair in a loose bind with ribbons down my back.

Grinning in pleasure, I suddenly wished Ena could have been here too. She adored these classic dresses and we both would have had a blast trying on these types of clothes.

A door burst open behind me and I whirled around.

The tall statures of Scott and Gradd were unmistakable. Swords in their hands, in the center of the room, the two of them advanced and parried. They sparred as though each move was choreographed.

It only took a few moves for it to be apparent that Scott was easily the better swordsman. Scott was probably a few years older than Gradd so it would make sense that he was more experienced. But while Scott moved with effortless grace and reserve, Gradd's moves emanated passion and determination.

Entranced, I couldn't help moving closer to the doorframe to watch.

They both groaned and grunted as they kept going. Two other soldiers in the room turned to exit through the same doorway I was standing by just as Gradd and Scott crossed swords once more.

Gradd glanced over, spotted me, and stepped back with a start, flinching as though someone had pepper-sprayed him in the face.

Scott followed his gaze and met mine. "Ah." He straightened up and beamed a gracious greeting at me. "Sarah."

I waved a small wave, feeling sheepish at having disturbed them. "Hi. Sorry, I didn't mean to interrupt. I was just watching—"

"It's no bother at all," Scott dismissed at once. "We were just training." He slung an arm over Gradd's shoulder. "Gradd seems to be getting a little rusty."

Gradd rolled his eyes. "It's an unfair advantage. You've been training since you were five."

"Oh, come on, Gradd." Scott patted his back before correcting, "I was three."

That made me laugh.

Scott gave me an appraising look up and down before a nod of approval. "You look wonderful."

My cheeks coloring, I smiled back. "Oh, thanks." I couldn't remember ever looking 'wonderful,' at least not since junior prom.

Gradd just wiped off his forehead with his sleeve, that same ever-so-neutral expression on his face.

I turned to Scott again. "I heard meals would be served soon."

"Oh, of course!" Scott piped up. He walked up to me to hold his arm out. He didn't look or seem the least bit exhausted from the training. "Shall we?"

I accepted Scott's arm with another smile and glanced back at Gradd with my eyebrow raised. "Coming?"

connections

After the meal, Scott gave me a grand tour of the castle—the libraries, gigantic hallways, beautiful gardens, huge dining tables, carpets, tapestries, and ancient chandeliers. My jaw was sore from almost being unhinged as I'd dropped it so often to marvel at everything.

According to Scott, the castle's structure had been well-preserved since its erection centuries ago, and since Thorb had such a strong military reputation, I needn't worry about the Malkens ever attacking.

Of course, I doubted he was aware of the invisible robots and the growing power of the Malkens. But I didn't want to disagree with him.

Scott was clearly the master of his kingdom. And he had been since his parents died, his father falling in a war somewhere far away, his mother having had a breakdown.

My heart squeezed at the recognition that out of all the people I had met in Anthuria, three of them—Onnahawk, Gradd, and Scott —no longer had any family. Despite Scott mentioning that most of them had a few relatives across other lands, they were all technically orphaned.

Scott was orienting me on the political landscape of Anthuria and ranking kingdoms and countries based on the strength of their military forces when Gradd found us in the garden.

Noting his presence, I turned to Scott. "What about Centeria?"

"Centeria's a relatively young kingdom." Scott nodded a greeting at Gradd. "But their military force is good. Isn't that right, Gradd?"

Gradd inclined his head to acknowledge his statement. "Of course, you have to say that because most of our training was done here."

Standing up from beside me, Scott patted Gradd's back. "Well, it's always good to learn from the best."

"Haha." Gradd made a face. "You just wait. One of these days, I will beat you."

"Such optimism." Scott ruffled Gradd's hair and Gradd shrugged away from his reach, grimacing like a little boy, I couldn't help but laugh.

With another smile, Scott turned to me with a slight bow. "I have to go attend to some business. I'll see you later."

"Bye," I called out as he walked away then I looked over at Gradd whose face was still crumpled in displeasure, I had to tamp down the urge to laugh some more.

Gradd clicked his tongue. "That's Scott for you. Good form, big head."

"You two are close, huh?" I prompted as he sat down on the bench beside me. "You seem almost like brothers—except of course, for the staggering difference in disposition."

He shot me a deadpan look. "Oh, go on."

Shaking my head in mirth, I lifted my eyes to the sky to watch white puffs of clouds sail by. "You know what your problem is?" I ventured.

Gradd's tone was more than surprised, challenging. "My problem? Suddenly you're the expert?"

I nudged him with my elbow. "You need to lighten up. I mean, let's consider my situation. Not to be a one-upper or anything but I *am* trapped in this whole other world. Everyone thinks I'm cursed. I get these strange visions. I know I'm going to die—" I stopped before he could object. "Or not," I amended before going on. "And I'm probably fighting a losing battle but I figure I have to stay focused on the bright side."

"That's easy for you to say," Gradd countered. "You're not going to be responsible for a thousand lives, maybe more."

"I'm not?" I mocked, aghast. "But I'm the legend of Centeria! I'm supposed to save an entire kingdom from its powerful enemies who have invisible robots. I'm supposed to find a phoenix." I gave him a deadpan, exasperated look. "It's literally a mythical creature. And oh yes, let's not forget, all the people trying to kill me left and right."

He met my gaze, a corner of his mouth turning up. "This is focusing on the bright side?"

"Yes," I agreed wryly. "Your severely infectious seriousness has no doubt rubbed off on me. Thanks a lot, by the way."

Gradd leaned forward on his elbows. "The truth is the Malkens have never been a threat to us before. It's only recently that they acquired this technology as you described to 'cloak' themselves. It's almost as though they've found a new source of power. I really don't understand it." Pausing, his expression sobered as he averted his gaze. "And I have to be serious. My kingdom is all I have especially now that my family is...well..."

Tentative, I peered at his face. "But we can't lose hope, right? And whatever else is happening, I have to believe it's going to get better." I heaved a big sigh. "Because if I don't, I may as well throw in the towel and give up."

"So you don't?" There was a catch in his voice. "Give up?"

I huffed airily. "Are you kidding me? I can't give up now."

I thought I heard him chuckle. "That's good to hear."

Cracking a small smile, I looked up at the sky again and took a deep, cleansing breath.

Gradd elbowed me back. "That's really good to hear."

13

ouch

As I looked out the window from my room, the entire landscape was bathed in the stark orange sunset. I closed my eyes for a moment in its fading warmth.

I had just gone one whole day without doing battle or running for my life and there was an unusual lack of that heavy dread in my chest. It felt good. As though I was actually going to get through this.

If only every day in Anthuria were like this, I'd probably never want to leave.

The clashing of metal to metal from the courtyard beneath my room grabbed my attention.

Several dozen soldiers were in training, including Scott and Gradd near the front of the assembly.

Scott was coaching Gradd again, demonstrating some moves with his sword.

Nodding, Gradd rested his hands on his knees. He looked exhausted. I couldn't even remember if he had slept a wink in the last three days.

I pursed my lips in concern. I was no expert, but surely, he would be no good in a real battle in his current condition. Meanwhile, I had been resting on and off since we had arrived. I wasn't really of much use otherwise.

The vision came to me with a pummeling force—like being hit behind the head with a baseball bat the size of a cargo truck. My knees buckled, and I collapsed on the floor, unconscious.

When I came to, the sky outside my window was already darkened. With the blankets tucked tight around me in bed, I could barely move. I guessed one of the maids who had been knocking every thirty minutes to see if I needed anything had found me indisposed and alerted what seemed like the *entire* castle because when I looked around, my room was close to crowded.

Several maids, a few soldiers, a physician, Scott, and...there he was, standing by the window, Gradd.

As if sensing me awake, he turned around.

Just when he met my gaze, I grimaced as my head throbbed.

Gradd's eyes lit up and he hastened to my side.

Noticing Gradd walking over, Scott turned to see me awake as well. Coming to my other side, he leaned over. "Hey, you're awake. How are you feeling?"

As if on cue, the entire room fogged with the relieved or curious chattering of the rest of everyone and my headache intensified.

"Everyone leave this room at once!" Gradd barked out loud.

Nobody had to be told twice.

Save Scott and Gradd, the room was empty in an instant.

Gradd's forehead was creased as he looked me over. "Are you okay?"

"Hey, I had another vision." My voice was raspy despite my eagerness.

"Later," he cut me off. "Are you okay?"

Surprised, I blinked. "Y-yeah." Nodding, I took a deep breath. "I'm fine."

Straightening up, Gradd seemed satisfied with that.

Scott sat on the other side of my bed. "The doctor says you're alright. Of course, if this sort of thing does happen with every uh...vision? That you get?" His eyebrows rose as worry tinged his tone. "Your health could be compromised."

"Thanks. That's good to know," I scoffed in helpless bemusement since I had little to no control over the visions.

Standing up, Scott patted my arm. "We should let you get some rest. The maids will be right outside the door if you need anything." He pointed a stern finger at me. "Don't even think about getting up."

I tried to mock a salute at him but I could barely raise my arm. "Sir, yes sir."

Amused, Scott pursed his lips. "Well, gotta get back to work."

When he moved toward the door, Gradd started to follow him.

"Gradd, wait," I called and they both stopped to look back. "Hey, why don't you have a seat?" I gestured to the deep armchair right by the bed.

Gradd shot me a curious look. "If I sit down now, I'll fall asleep."

I gave him a meaningful nod. "Yeah-huh. Exactly."

Scott turned to him. "You know, she has a point, Gradd. You've been running ragged these last few days. You really need to take a breather."

Eyes wide in indignation, Gradd looked back and forth between the two of us. He seemed almost in disbelief that he was getting ganged upon.

"Tell you what." Scott gestured to the door, a catch in his tone. "I'll go ahead. You can come along. If you want." He bid me a pointed nod before exiting the room.

When Gradd promptly moved to follow him, I jerked up in bed, "Wait—" which was a terrible idea since my head turned all woozy. "Ohh..." I moaned, flopping back down.

Gradd's eyes widened in alarm and his forehead creased. He hissed out a curse and stalked toward the chair.

"That's a good boy," I coaxed. "Now sit."

His glare on me was dark the whole while that he begrudgingly slumped into the armchair.

Cracking a teasing smile, I was relieved he didn't put up any more fight about it. "I can make you do anything now, huh?"

He folded his arms across his chest. "I am just sitting down for a few minutes to rest."

Exasperated, I rolled my eyes. "Would you stop being a stubborn ass for two seconds? You need to sleep! You're not going to do anybody any good if you doze off in the middle of a sword fight. It won't do *you* any good. It won't do *me* any good. It won't do Centeria any good—"

He didn't like my tone. "What do you even know about it? Just mind your own business."

Red spots blotted my eyesight as I jerked to sit up again but I needed to make my point. "My business? Don't make me tell you what my business is. My business is I don't want to die in this world!" I threw up my hands. "But unfortunately, for me to manage that, I need you. You may not like it, I may not like it, but that's the deal. And if I think you won't be able to do that half-asleep, you can bet all your damn legends, that is absolutely my business, so don't you be telling me what to mind and what not to mind."

By the time I finished my incensed rant, my head was all woozy again. Swallowing hard, I leaned on my one hand to keep myself propped up. But when I looked over at Gradd, he had already fallen asleep in the chair.

14

the other guy

The next day, I was pleased to find that my own clothes had been returned, cleaned, and laid out by the foot of the bed, but didn't put them on just yet.

Today's dress was a gorgeous, floor-length, royal blue dress with a V-neckline and sleeves to my wrists. I almost didn't even mind the cold, impersonal, and expedient manner of the assisting maids. Surely, they had better things to do than to deal with a weirdo like me.

Scott and Gradd were discussing plans to restore Centeria during breakfast, most of it in hushed undertones.

I was eating whatever passed for bacon and eggs in this world and not paying them mind.

At some point, the two of them had begun to argue about something then Scott happened to cast a glance over at me. "It's the only way," he was telling Gradd.

"There are other ways. I won't have her do that," was Gradd's curt reply.

My ears perked up at 'her.' 'Her' being obviously me. Looking up, I raised my eyebrows in expectation. "Have me do what?"

"Nothing," Gradd barked.

Scott gave him a pointed look before turning an amiable smile at me. "I was asking Gradd if you thought you might be able to help locate the Malken army on a map," he began. "There's a theory that their base is mobile since we have never been able to pin them down. We've even sent scouts to where Gradd had been captured before only to find the place deserted." His eyes narrowed in purpose. "But since you have these...visions, it might be our only chance to try. It could be important, Sarah."

"No." Gradd's tone was firm as he turned to Scott. "You said so yourself. She could endanger herself if she kept having these visions and you want her to force one?" He shot me a terse look. "You're not doing it."

I looked at each of them in turn. "If it's important, I want to try to help."

Gradd's jaw dropped in mocking. "Wasn't that you I heard last night saying you didn't want to die in Anthuria?"

I pursed my lips to implore. "Yes, but I've been resting so much and I haven't done anything to help in days. Besides, the visions...come to me. I've never tried willing one to come before. It might not even work."

"Honestly, I don't want to do this either," Scott admitted with a shake of his head. "But we're out of options. If we could discover where the enemy is hiding, for once, we'll have the upper hand. It might be just what we need to win this whole war."

His darkened gaze pinned on me, Gradd stood up to come to my side. "Look, you're always saying I should protect you." He shook his head. "I can't help you in these visions. What if something happens?"

I met his gaze evenly. "You could win this war. End all this," I reminded him. "What if this was exactly what I was meant to do to help you? Wouldn't you let me at least try?"

I regretted those words the instant Scott unfolded the huge map of

Anthuria on a table in front of me. "Maybe I can't do this after all." I wrinkled my nose.

We were in a small part of the library, a cozy, quiet area, free of distractions.

"All you need to do is try," Scott reminded me.

Gradd merely sulked in one corner.

I turned to him to prompt, "Can you show me where they took you that time? Maybe some landmarks, things you saw, somewhere for me to start?"

"I've told you it's south." Gradd's reply was flat, in no way co-operative.

"Try down here." Scott gestured to the map. "Ignore him."

Been trying for three days, I wanted to note. Instead, I shifted to get comfortable in the chair.

This was probably going to take all day. I didn't even know how to do this. I mean, conjure a vision?

My heart pounded as I surveyed the huge map before me. Anthuria was such a big world. It looked so different from Earth, with fewer continents and different shapes of land masses. It looked so strange. So alien.

Shaking my head to concentrate, I tried to focus on the area Scott had shown me, tried to focus on the Malkens and on what I'd seen them do in my earlier visions. But nothing came to me.

Blowing out a slow breath, I ran my fingers over the map. If I could just find the enemy then maybe I could feel a little bit useful around here. Maybe I could be a hero for once.

An hour passed according to the big clock over the arched doorway of the library and still nothing.

Scott had shuffled in and out of the room a few times. Gradd shifted in his seat before pacing back and forth across the floor.

Frowning, I concentrated a little harder. I squeezed my eyes shut and tried to get a feel of the south area again. I didn't know if the room was getting warm or if I was breaking out in a sweat from the anxiety.

I leaned back against my chair to look up at the clock.

Another hour had passed.

Getting frustrated, I heaved a huge sigh.

A warm hand rested on my shoulder and I glanced up to meet Gradd's solemn gaze. I forced a smile as I didn't want to appear as utterly exhausted as I was.

"Alright," Scott spoke up from behind us. Sitting in a chair across the room, he stretched his legs out, his tone resigned. "Perhaps we've tried long enough."

As if on cue, a burst of warmth shot through my chest, and the map glimmered red before me. I shot up in my seat. "Oh."

Gradd stepped back in surprise. "What?"

The light disappeared.

What? Frowning, I blinked. "I saw...a light, but it disappeared."

Scott came closer. "What were you doing exactly? Can you do it again?"

"I-I don't know." I tilted my head to try to recall the exact moment.

"Where did you see the light?" Gradd moved to rest his hand on my shoulder once more. "On the map?"

My eyes widened when a faint red light emerged from the map again. Furrowing my eyebrows in curious puzzlement, I turned toward Gradd and put my hand over his.

The red glow around the map brightened.

Wary, Gradd was staring at my hand but he didn't pull his away. "What?"

Another surge of warmth shot through me again and the library began to fade away. The map grew out of the parchment, like 3D images rising all around me, and the next thing I knew, I was in it.

I was flying over mountains, rivers, forests, and seas. I sped faster and faster until a dark fortress loomed in front of me. It stood on a huge, weird, floating rock, surrounded by several other floating rocks, some small, some big, hidden behind huge marbled mountains.

I flew closer and closer through the arched entrance until I was inside the floating fortress itself. I rushed past a faceless crowd of people before whooshing through a long, dark hallway leading to a larger main chamber.

As I moved forward, my heart began pounding all over again. Already creeped out at what I might see this time around, I swallowed hard. I couldn't turn back. I couldn't move my body any other way. Arriving at the end of the hallway, the main chamber was dark, and a heavy feeling engulfed me. Suddenly, a light—

I squinted in the dimly lit room. Two men were up ahead. One of them was wearing a heavy black cloak. He was bald with a deep scar across his left eye. As I caught sight of the other man, my gasp caught in my throat.

The man suddenly laughed out loud and it was as though I was thrown across the chambers by his laughter. I tumbled out of the room, out the door, out of the fortress where I, of course, began to fall. Again.

The lump in my throat prevented me from screaming and as I fell, my arms flailed around, hopelessly trying to catch a grip on something.

Finally, there was something firm beneath my fingers and I opened my eyes with a startle.

Falling never seemed to fail to scare the shit out of me.

My heart was still pounding as I looked around, but to my great relief, I was back in the library at Thorb. I took a few deep breaths before withdrawing my white-knuckled hand from having grabbed Gradd's.

Gradd stepped back again and Scott walked over.

"Well?" Scott prompted.

My anxiety grew again as I tried to call back to mind what I'd seen. My mouth turning dry, I turned panicked, wide eyes up to Scott. "I s-saw—I saw—oh my god, they ha-have—"

Scott furrowed his eyebrows. "Slow down, Sarah. What are you trying to say?"

I clutched at his arm fervently. "Scott, there's a man. I-I mean, I saw rocks. It's the Malkens. They—" I swallowed again. My head was swirling with too many thoughts wanting to burst out, jumbling together, and my mouth was having a hard time keeping up. I kept seeing the darkness before my eyes, kept sinking into it...

A loud crash from outside made the three of us look up.

My heart pounded harder again and I froze in my seat. "They're here."

15

visions and battles

Scott darted an alert look at me and then at Gradd before he raced outside.

Another loud crash made me wince. The enemy was getting closer.

Alarmed, I turned to Gradd.

He met my gaze, grabbed my hand, and bolted.

I gasped as we ran down the castle hallways. "Don't you guys ever have some peace and quiet around here?" I tried to joke.

"We used to," Gradd replied. "Then you arrived."

I was going to retort but the wall to my side exploded and I screamed, jumping back and bumping into Gradd.

Catching me, Gradd glanced up at the collapsing wall. "Oh shit—" He yanked me forward and ran even faster.

When we arrived at my room, he practically threw me into the doorway before whirling to head back outside with a quick "Stay there!"

"Wait!" I called out. "Where do you think you're going?"

"I have to fight. I have to help Scott."

"Onnahawk said to fall back to Eleria." I pulled on his sleeve. "You can't—"

"Scott has to know about the invisible enemy or Thorb will fall. Do you want that?" Gradd's eyes blazed with the challenge.

"No, but—"

He didn't let me finish and hurried away.

Cursing aloud, I rushed to the bedside. "Like hell I'm staying here," I muttered as I quickly changed out of the princess dress and back into my own clothes. Tying my hair up impatiently, I ran out the door despite his instruction.

My head spun. Thorb wasn't prepared for this. There was no way they could defeat the Malkens in this state. Scott's army was strong but he needed a plan. There just had to be a way to uncloak those robots.

I skidded to a stop at the top of the staircase.

Maids, servants, and even soldiers were running around, terrified. I could imagine Thorb being the peaceful, efficient kingdom it had been for so long, despite everyone's training, this reality was crashing down hard on all of them.

I bit my lip. They had to get out of here. Looking left and right, I clattered down the steps, yelling, trying to gather everyone around and beckon them to follow me out. But none of them seemed to be listening.

I grabbed random people I passed by. "You have to get out of here!"

But fear and panic were all over their faces. There was no space for rational thought.

The head chambermaid crossed my path and I ran to her. "Excuse me," I called over the noise of the fighting outside and the panicked shrieks. "We have to get—"

She wasn't listening to me either.

I grabbed her by the shoulders roughly. "Listen to me!"

When I shouted in her face, she jumped startled, and finally met my gaze.

"We have to get everyone out of here," I told her. "You have to help me get everyone out, okay?"

She nodded, if a little flustered, but I could see she had snapped to attention.

The two of us began to herd people out of the castle.

My throat was raw from shouting but it didn't take much longer for us to gather most of the staff to lead them outside, out of the open, away from the fighting.

I ran out of the front entrance to search for cover myself.

Some distance away, Thorb's relics were trying to steer the fighting away from the castle.

There weren't any more green relics in battle but at least none of them were lying around destroyed either.

I supposed Gradd had already given the order to retreat to Eleria. I was about to feel relieved until I spotted Gradd's relic among the fray, still fighting the Malken relics.

That idiot! My jaw dropped in disbelief and annoyance. Looking around anxiously, I tried to think of what else I could do to help.

There was a loud flurry from behind me and I spun around. Dozens of birds flew up from the trees just then, their wings flapping, squawks echoing in the din.

My eyes widened as I spotted—actually *saw*—several strange-looking relics lift off from the forest.

My jaw dropped again they soared into the sky before landing across the field and then subsequently completely disappearing into thin air once more.

I narrowed my eyes. These relics looked nothing like the black Malken relics that were chasing me before. These new ones were dark gray with fairly large, sharp-looking metal spikes on their shoulder caps. They kind of reminded me of a suited-up football player, only bigger, uglier, scarier, and more deadly. These relic monsters also had retractable extending arms with pointed spikes on the end.

I could almost remember the excruciating pain I'd felt when a similar heavy relic arm had crashed into me in my vision.

Wincing, I closed my eyes before quickly shaking it off.

A terrified cry made me look back up at the castle. It took a minute to see where the cry was coming from with the fire having spread across the castle but I finally spotted her. It was one of the maids that tended to me in the morning. She was in one of the upstairs rooms, crying out the window.

Casting a glance to make sure the head maid and the others were all trailing to safety, I ran back into the castle, up the front steps, and turned onto one of the castle wings.

"Hello?" I shielded my eyes from the heat of the fire that was spreading on the floor and the dust from the crumbling ceiling. "Hello?" I was practically wading my way through the overturned furniture and the rubble. Running down the hall, I glanced into the rooms I passed and stopped when I found her near the rearmost suites.

The maid turned around from the window.

"Come on!" I waved her over.

She didn't budge. She kept crying and I figured she must be in shock.

"It's okay," I tried to reassure as I took a tentative step forward. "You'll be okay. Come on over."

She kept shaking her head and didn't budge.

Looking around, I frowned helplessly. The way to her was an obstacle course through debris and burning furniture. I made a face, having been left no choice, and I started to make my way across the room. "Listen, we have to get out of here." I tried to keep my voice calm as I stepped over an overturned bureau. "It's gonna be okay."

"We're all going to die!" she shrieked, seemingly losing it.

"No, no, please," I insisted, coming closer, trying to get her to calm down or at least stop crying.

She shook her head again and stepped back against the window.

I was like six feet away. I held out my hand. "It's okay," I assured again. "Come on. Take my hand."

She cried again, tears streaming down her face, mixed with soot, her voice quivering. "Stay away."

"Look, it's dangerous for us to be here," I tried to reason as I edged closer. "Please listen to me—"

"This is your fault!" she rambled, all hysterical, shaking her head. "This is all your fault!"

I froze in my tracks, taken aback—in time too as just then, an invisible force crashed right into the window and the maid disappeared with a loud shriek as she fell out, along with the rubble and debris.

Stumbling back, I gasped in fright. I tried to stand but for some reason, my arms lacked the strength to push me off the floor. My left shoulder was bleeding like hell. "Oh shit," I whispered as I crawled backward.

There was another explosion and winced. A cloaked relic materialized in the hole in the wall before it tipped over and crashed to the ground. Then a shiny silver relic appeared in the gap in the wall.

I recognized Scott's relic even before the faceplate opened.

He shot me a stunned look. "What are you still doing in there?" His relic's arm extended to scoop me up to carry me out of the castle.

"Scott!" I yelled out. "We have to get out of here!"

"I know!" Scott replied. "I've ordered a retreat. Have you seen Gradd?"

Shaking my head, I clung tighter to the mechanical hand.

"There he is."

I followed Scott's gaze.

Gradd's relic was badly broken up but he was running over to the castle to look for more enemies.

Scott called out to him as we got closer.

Gradd saw him and his relic face plate opened. Looking at each of us in turn, he nodded. "There are still some relics on the other side."

"No, Gradd, we're leaving." Scott's tone was firm. "We're no match for them."

"We can still win this," Gradd insisted, turning to beckon us over. "We can't give up. We can't let them walk away this time."

Scott shot him a look. "Gradd, don't be stupid."

"Yeah, leave me alone!" Gradd snapped. "What do you care anyway?"

Scott's jaw clenched. "Fine!" He extended his relic arm over and dropped me into Gradd's open relic, right into his lap before he could object. "I will," Scott bid before his relic launched off like a rocket.

I met Gradd's furious gaze.

His eyebrows furrowed and he lifted his relic hand. "Get on." He gestured to the hand. "I have to go back and fight."

Aghast, I frowned at him. "You most certainly will not."

"Get off my relic, Sarah!" he yelled out, trying to maneuver his relic hand to pick me up.

I looped my arms around his neck to hold on to him. "I'm not getting out. You're not going to fight."

He groaned in aggravation. "Sarah, you have to get out of here. It isn't safe for you. You have to go to Eleria without me. I have to stay and fight."

"You're crazy!" I insisted. "I'm not leaving you here."

"Look, I'm not going to say it again," Gradd bit out. "Leave. My kingdom needs its savior."

"Your kingdom needs their king too," I argued, trying to look him right in the eyes even as he kept trying to move away. "If you die here, it's over. I may be their savior but I can't do it by myself. Look at me!" I barked and he finally met my determined gaze.

I was heaving as I spoke, "I need you."

Gradd studied my face, his expression changing.

"Don't be stupid," I pleaded with a soft shake of my head.

His deliberation felt like hours but it was only a moment. With a deep sigh, Gradd clenched his jaw at the same time that he pushed a button and the relic took off.

I had to blow out a breath of relief. "Thank you," I whispered hoarsely. I was absolutely drained. Leaning my head onto his shoulder, I gave his chest a small poke in jest. "I can make you do anything, huh?"

Getting a bit groggy, I didn't check to see if he responded.

I also didn't have to check to know that Thorb was burnt charcoal either.

The heaviness was back on my chest. I really was a curse. Wherever

I went, everything shattered. At that devastating thought, I sighed again.

The faint sunset filtered through the small window of Gradd's relic as we sped off and headed for another kingdom. Eleria.

***

2

the flight

16

i can't hear it

"You're in big trouble, young lady." Mom shook her finger at me as she stood at the kitchen counter.

"Me? Why? What did I do?"

"Like you have to ask." Her face was dark with disapproval. "You've burned down two whole countries. You ought to be ashamed of yourself."

"But I—I didn't!" I protested. "It was the Malkens. They've got invisible robots and—and—"

"Like anybody would believe you." Ena's voice came from behind me. She was in our kitchen too. "You can't even ask Derek out on a date. That is so pathetic."

"Ena?" What? Why was she betraying me like this? And what did Derek have to do with anything?

"So pathetic," Annette mocked as she materialized beside Mom. "Just like those stupid stories you keep writing."

"But they're real," I insisted. "They really are. I saw them. The robots. They burned down the castle! They tried to kill me—"

"Save your excuses, Sarah," Ena cut in.

"It doesn't matter though." Gradd came up to me from nowhere and gave me the same dark look before glancing at the others. "She's gonna die,

anyway. I mean, she says so. She saw it in a 'vision'," he ridiculed before he
burst out laughing.

"That's truly some bizarre imagination." Annette laughed with him.

"Why can't you be normal, Sarah?" Mom asked before she started
laughing too.

Pretty soon, everyone was laughing at me.

"Witch." Agarpa's face popped up in mid-air.

*"It's all your fault." The maid from Thorb who fell to her death also
appeared.*

"Curse," Agarpa taunted with a cackle.

*Stepping back, I swallowed past the lump in my throat. "No. Please don't
do this to me."*

"Don't do what?" Gradd asked.

Gasping, I sat up. I'd been dreaming.

Blinking a few times, I looked around to get my bearings.

Night time. Burning fire. Forest trees. Gradd.

"Vision?" His eyebrows rose in a prompt even as he inspected
his sword.

"Nightmare." I rubbed my face with my hands. "Just your garden
variety kind." Shivering, I pulled my knees up to put my arms around
them. I looked around again. "Are we in Eleria?"

"No," Gradd answered. "Had to camp out for the night. Eleria's not
far away. We'll go again at daybreak."

"Oh." I guessed I'd been out cold because I didn't even remember
landing at all after having left the charred battlegrounds at Thorb.

"How's your arm?"

My gaze automatically went to my shoulder. It seemed Gradd had
already bandaged up my wound. I'd almost completely forgotten that
I'd been injured while escaping the castle. And now that I remembered it, it began to sting like the dickens. But at least I wasn't losing
any more blood.

I dismissed it. "Fine. Thanks."

"Go back to sleep," he instructed.

I nodded and started to lie back down when a rustling in the forest caught my attention. Darting a suspicious look behind us, my eyebrows furrowed. "Someone's—I think someone's in the forest."

Gradd stopped. "What did you—?" He cut off, looking sharply to the left before his posture relaxed.

I blinked at him. "What?"

He gave me an odd look. "You didn't hear that?"

"Hear what?"

Gradd called out. "Hey, Scott! Would you stop lurking back there already?"

My eyebrows rose when Scott emerged from the shadows behind the trees. "Hey," I greeted in surprise. "What are you doing here?"

"Looking for you," Scott replied with a smile. He nudged Gradd's shoulder as he walked past him across the fire toward me. "I knew she'd talk some sense into you." Evidently, Scott knew his plan of leaving me with Gradd was a guarantee of his retreat.

"Didn't expect you this early," Gradd noted.

"You always underestimate me, Gradd." Scott sat down on the ground before turning to me. "Hey, how are you feeling?"

Smiling back, I rubbed my arms. "A little cold."

"Oh!" Scott quickly took off his cloak and threw it around my shoulders before shooting Gradd a pointed look. "Of course she is. Gradd, didn't it occur to you that she needed a blanket or something?"

Gradd looked irritated. "Oh, I'm sorry. I'll remember to make a note for the next time I babysit."

Scott rolled his eyes.

I merely shook my head before peering curiously at the object in Scott's hand. "What have you got there?"

"Ah...this." He held out what looked like a wooden flute. "My father made it. You didn't hear me playing it just now?"

"No." I glanced up at Gradd again. It must have been what he'd heard before. Turning back to Scott, I inspected the flute more closely. No bigger than Scott's finger, the small wooden flute had a beautiful intricate design carved on it.

Meeting Scott's gaze, I indicated a silent prompt for permission to try it out.

"Yeah, sure, go ahead." Scott handed me the flute.

I put the flute to my mouth and blew once softly, then again harder. I heard nothing. I blew on the flute as hard as I could, and for some reason, Scott and Gradd winced. But I heard nothing. "I don't hear anything." I blinked, confused.

"What?" Scott took the flute back from me to test it himself, and nodding satisfied after a moment, he shot me another look. "You didn't hear that?"

"Hmm." I pursed my lips. "Maybe there's something different about how I hear sounds because I'm not from this world," I guessed. "On Earth, there are also instruments that play frequencies so high only ears as sensitive as dogs' can hear them."

Scott exchanged a glance with Gradd. "Did she just call us dogs?" He met my gaze again and I laughed.

But Gradd just sneered, not seeming entertained.

I gave him a teasing look. "Aw, poor Gradd, so uptight because he couldn't keep playing with the big, bad robots."

Scott grinned before handing me back the flute. "Here, you can keep this."

"What?" I blinked and shook my head. "No way. Your father made that for you."

"I'd be happy for you to have it," he conceded. "Who knows? It might be of use to you someday."

"What? Oh, wow." I beamed at him. "Thanks, Scott. This is such a nice gesture."

Gradd cleared his throat. "I hate to break this little moment you guys are having but there is a war going on."

Exasperated, I rolled my eyes. "Can't you stop being a complete stick in the mud for two seconds?"

Gradd gave me a deadpan look. "You know, I would absolutely love to." He threw up his hands. "Hey, maybe if I didn't have to save your life every other day, I could put my feet up and relax. Or maybe if you weren't a total magnet for all kinds of trouble, I could just throw caution to the wind. But no, I have to go around cleaning up your mess. Sarah Peters, the whiny little legend who never does anything except destroy countries wherever she goes."

My stomach dived. My eyebrows snapped together in offense but I couldn't exactly refute his statement. "Yeah? Well...you're a jerk!" I slumped back down to curl up into a ball on the ground, facing away from them.

"Let her sleep," Gradd told Scott. "We have things to discuss about tomorrow."

Important things, I supposed with a grumble to myself. Pulling Scott's cloak closer over me, I figured I might as well try to go back to sleep.

I sulked for a while before drifting off. I still overheard them discuss the Elerian kingdom, a King Cornelius, and several princesses' names. I was relieved to know that there would be other girls in the next kingdom. I only hoped these princesses weren't arrogant, spoiled little brats too.

I hoped they would like me.

And I hoped I wouldn't burn down their kingdom.

17

two kings

I woke up as the first rays of the morning hit my face. Stretching as I yawned, my blanket seemed heavier than it was last night. Opening my eyes, I glanced down. Through the night, Scott must have found another blanket to put over me to make sure I stayed warm.

So nice, I thought to myself as I looked across the clearing.

Scott and Gradd were both readying their relics.

On some levels, they were so similar. They were both soldiers, brave, courageous, and skilled, but that was the extent of it. Scott was by far more personable, friendlier, and so much more considerate. On the other hand, Gradd was very much like his relic. Big, with a hollow head.

I stood up with a groan. The coarse ground was definitely not the most comfortable surface to sleep on. My hair was inexplicable. I shook it out, struggling to run my fingers through it since I didn't have any kind of hairbrush handy before gathering it back up into a ponytail. When I turned around, I found both Scott and Gradd watching me.

I raised my eyebrows at them in a prompt. "What?"

Gradd simply averted his gaze.

Scott smiled. "Good morning!"

Smiling back at him, I picked up his cloak and walked over.

The camp had been packed up, the fire already doused. Everything was ready to go.

I realized they had just been waiting for me to wake up. Embarrassed, I made a face. "Oh, gosh, sorry, did I take too long to wake up?"

"Don't worry about it," Scott dismissed. "We weren't ready yet anyway."

"Now we are," Gradd interjected.

Scott glanced over at him. "Great." He cast me a glance. "Are you all set?"

Ignoring Gradd, I gave Scott a nod. "Yup."

Scott paused for a moment when nobody moved to go. He looked at Gradd and me in turn before his gaze settled back on me. "Well, would you like to ride with me this time?" he offered.

I perked up. "I'd love to!"

"Yeah, whatever," Gradd muttered as he hopped into his relic.

Scott's relic was bigger than Gradd's so thankfully, there was more space on the pilot seat. And while Gradd's was just a Class 3 training relic, Scott's robot, I learned, was a more advanced type of relic.

According to Scott, there were many different kinds of relics, each with its own special features. The first ones I had seen in the marketplace were classed as 'spy relics.' Then there were the ordinary battle relics. Scott's relic was a Class 5 dubbed 'The Silver Saber.' The only other kind of special relics that he didn't mention were the ones that the Malkens had, the ones that could camouflage, which I guessed were probably relics in a whole other class of their own.

As we flew to Eleria, Scott also told me more about the kingdom. Eleria was a very peaceful place and the way he described it made it seem significantly more appealing than the previous countries I'd come across. King Cornelius had three daughters: Leanna, Lessandra, and Leila.

"I hope they'll like me."

"I'm sure they will," Scott replied gaily. "Especially Leila. She's a cute kid. A bit feisty, but she's a lot of fun."

"How old is Princess Leanna?"

Clearing his throat, Scott's face darkened. "Princess Leanna died a few years ago."

My eyes widened in alarm. *Oops.* "The Malkens?"

"No." He shook his head. "The Malkens have only become a threat for a few seasons. Leanna was...lost in an earlier war." He paused for a moment, torment on his face as if he was reliving the event in his head.

I could already guess that he and the Princess must have been close.

"But Lessandra's around your age," Scott began again. "You two should get along famously."

"I sure hope so."

After another tentative pause, Scott started, "Hey, listen. I'm sorry about last night."

My smile faded as I remembered my highly unflattering characterization from last night as described by Gradd.

It was like it wasn't enough that I was alone and stranded in this foreign world. I also had to deal with the fact that I drew death and destruction everywhere I went. But it wasn't like any of it was in my control.

"I'm sure Gradd is sorry too," Scott noted.

I scowled at the mention of his name. "Why don't you let that jerk speak for himself?"

"Perhaps." Scott chuckled. "If he was capable of speaking for himself. Gradd's not exactly the forthcoming type."

"I'll say," I scoffed.

"He's a soldier. He has rarely the need for words or emotions," Scott tried to explain. "But he was upset and tired. I'm sure he didn't mean what he said about you."

"You don't have to make excuses for him. It's not like it matters anyway. I'm just a stupid legend. I'm like a myth, right? I probably don't even exist right now."

"Of course, it matters," Scott argued with a frown. "That is not how a person, much more, a future king, behaves before a lady. He should have known better."

I couldn't help studying his face in wonder. "How come you're so nice?"

Looking pleased, Scott broke a grin. He leaned over and kissed my cheek.

I blinked, flushing completely scarlet.

Fortunately, he didn't let the awkward note settle.

Scott gestured to the relic's controls. "Do you want to try this?"

"Do I?" I burst out in excitement, making him laugh.

Scott pointed out several important buttons and levers before letting me fly the relic. He coached out instructions and guidelines before bidding me with a, "Just take it easy."

When I grabbed the controller, the weight of the relic was heavy in my hands. "Whoa." Feeling challenged, I steered the relic, carefully swooping down. I had never in my entire life controlled anything with this much power before and a gratified sense of self-confidence filled my chest. When the ground got closer and closer, my heart pounded as I could almost make out the texture of the jagged rocks. Then I pulled up hard. The Saber was like a manual-controlled roller coaster, only quicker and more agile.

"Whoo!" I whooped, turning an easy spiral in the air and Scott chuckled in amusement. His smile was easy, his shoulders slack. He didn't appear nervous at all.

"Whoa, what's going on over there?" Gradd called from outside. "Are you okay, Scott?"

Scott called out his reply. "It's fine, man. I'm just letting Sarah try out the Saber."

"You're what?" Gradd's disbelief was not disguised.

"Calm down. She's a natural."

Grateful, I beamed at Scott.

"If you have a death wish, that's your business," Gradd drawled.

Scoffing under my breath, my mood soured. "Do you have rockets or something, Scott? I'd really like to blow him out of the sky right now." I wished I could say I was only half-kidding.

Scott just laughed again.

18

competition

Much to the surprise of everyone, we did not crash. Upon arriving in Eleria, Scott assisted me to put the relic down on the ground across a wide field that led to a huge walled-in kingdom. It wasn't the smoothest landing ever but I was so proud of myself. I was still beaming when Scott and I dismounted the Saber.

Having already gotten off his relic, Gradd was rolling his eyes.

I had decided to ignore him for the rest of his life, which given the odds I was betting wouldn't be so long in any case. *So there*, I thought haughtily.

The neighing of horses made me turn.

Whoa.

Several white horses stood in formation to meet us. Soldiers holding staffs bearing the logo of a crab sat stiffly upon each steed. Another horse stood apart from the line, front and center, its rider making a graceful dismount.

She was no doubt one of the princesses of this kingdom. With her long, curly blond hair and pale skin, she wore an elegant pink riding habit and carried herself with a very poised, royal air.

Scott and Gradd bowed down.

Gradd knocked my knee in as he bowed beside me. Sinking into a very awkward curtsy, I hissed out a curse word disguised as a cough.

The girl stepped closer, and stopping in front of Scott, she held her hand out. "Lord Darabont."

Scott bowed deeper before he kissed her hand. "Princess Lessandra. It's good to see you again."

"You haven't visited in a while," the Princess said with a catch in her voice. "We've missed you."

I stole a glance up at her in amusement. She was so very obviously coming on to Scott.

Scott straightened up and proceeded to introduce us. "If you recall, Lord Gradd, King of Centeria," he announced and Gradd bowed lower. "And Lady Sarah Peters." Scott gestured to me. "The maiden of the legend of Centeria."

I attempted a more proper curtsy, bowing my head so she couldn't see the grimace from my effort but when I straightened up, she was giving me a critical look.

However, a dismissive "Hm," was all she said before she tipped her chin up. "Welcome to Eleria." With an impersonal smile, she turned back to her horse. "Come. My father expects us back at the castle for breakfast."

I was a little bit disappointed as that didn't exactly go as I thought it would. The Princess didn't seem to like me at all.

The soldiers gave us each a horse to ride back to the castle. Scott had to help me to get on mine— something which Lessandra was keenly watching.

She spoke her request as though an afterthought. "The soldiers will take care of your relics. Scott, would you ride with me, please?"

Scott led his horse to ride beside the Princess up front.

I groaned because that meant I had to ride with Gradd. That meant putting up with his cold silence.

"Jealous?" Gradd's prompt was wry as he watched me.

Not meeting his gaze, I made a face.

Lessandra obviously liked Scott. Though my main concern was that it seemed my being friends with him was going to be in the way of the Princess liking me. I didn't need a member of the royal family hating me before I'd even done my inevitable damage.

Besides, how could I possibly be jealous of a Princess? Obviously, Scott would like Lessandra in return. She was beautiful, graceful, classy, poised... It was seriously no contest.

So, yeah, sure, I wasn't jealous at all.

We arrived at the castle and were each led to our quarters to freshen up. My room was a giant, fully-furnished loft at the end of one hall, with pale yellow walls, yellow curtains, big windows, flowers, bedspreads, old wooden bureaus, and cabinets. There was a big mirror beside the cabinets. As usual, the suite was first class and much grander than the one I had at Thorb. All I needed now was my own bathroom, I thought. And possibly a TV and a phone.

I had barely finished exploring every corner of the room when someone knocked on my door.

It was one of the maids informing me that breakfast would be served shortly and I thanked her before she left.

Sighing, I walked over to the window to check out the view. On one side, the Kingdom of Eleria was green as far as the eyes could see, with fields, and rolling hills of grass and flowers. People worked on the land and in the huge sculpted gardens. A few small houses were scattered on the hills and I could see animals and children running around. Looking to the other side, the ocean sparkled crystal blue in the sun.

Eleria was very beautiful and very peaceful indeed.

The landscape before me set on fire as burning rubble and crumbling to the ground while the hot winds blew flashed in my mind. Squeezing my eyes shut, I forced the images out of my head. My chest constricted at the possibility of another entire kingdom being destroyed by me.

There was another presence at the doorway but when I turned to look, all I glimpsed was the tail end of a dark cloak with red stitching.

I heaved another sigh, turning back to the window. I had given up trying to understand what was going on inside Gradd's head. *Talk about blowing hot and cold.*

It wasn't like he wasn't capable of feelings or anything as I'd initially thought. There were even times when he was perfectly sane, perfectly nice.

I promise I will only protect you from now on...

A different rustling came from behind me and I whirled around. *Now what?*

I narrowed my eyes around the empty room but the sound came again. My focus darted to the closet. Okay, was I now hallucinating? I almost dismissed the thought just as something sprang out from behind the bedside table.

"Boo!" she yelled.

"Aaaghh!" I jumped back.

A little girl with sparkling eyes, gold pigtails, red ribbons, and a frilly red dress giggled as she began to circle me like a bird of prey, studying me with a curious look on her upturned nose.

"Hey—what—" I turned around to keep an eye on her.

Peering at my weird clothes, she poked me in the side with her finger.

"Hey!" I yelped and made a grab at her. "What do you think you're—" But she slipped away, tugging at my hair. "Hey!" I exclaimed and she dashed to the bed. She stuck out her tongue at me, jeering.

I almost had to rub my eyes in disorientation. *Was it Tuesday again?* I took a step toward her. "Look, kid," I started but she ducked away, tugging on my shirt as she passed me. "What the—?" I kept trying to grab her but she was too fast. "Quit it!" I cried out, and the next minute, I was chasing the little girl around the room, around the bed. "Get back here, you!"

She seemed to be enjoying the chase which frustrated me even more. She kept laughing.

Man, this kid was agile!

She dashed toward the door but this time, someone managed to scoop her up.

"There you are," Scott announced, trying to handle the struggling kid in his arms.

I sighed in relief. "Scott."

Scott shot me an amused look. "I see you've met the Princess."

"Princess?"

"Leila." Scott's tone turned firm as he spoke to the girl and she stopped wriggling for a moment to look up at Scott. "Say hi to Sarah."

Princess Leila gave me an almost toothless grin with her bright greeting. "Hi, Tharah!"

I had to laugh. She seemed at the age that had trouble with S's.

Scott shrugged his apology. "Sorry about this. She gets quite hyper-active in the mornings."

I waved it away. "Don't worry about it. I needed the exercise anyway."

Leila let out another squeal, wriggled down from Scott, then scrambled away before he could grab her. "Oh, man." He shrugged. "Well, there she goes."

"Aren't you gonna go after her?" I craned my neck to watch the little upstart skid across the hallway.

Smiling, he offered his arm to me. "I think I'd rather walk you to breakfast. Are you ready?"

My cheeks warmed. "If you insist, but uh...wouldn't there be a certain Princess to object to your, shall I say, familiarity with me?" I asked with a catch in my voice.

Scott suddenly looked uncomfortable and I knew he knew exactly who I meant. "Lessandra and I...are just friends. She's like a sister to me, that's all."

I pursed my lips in full knowledge. "Whatever you say."

19

my home

King Cornelius and his entourage were waiting for us on the patio in the garden. Gradd and Lessandra were already there. Leila was running around the rose bushes, her father beckoning her to come along. His tone was reprimanding, but his expression was warm. He was very proud of his energetic daughter.

The King looked up when Scott and I arrived. "Ah, Scott."

Scott bowed. "Your majesty."

Oops! I jumped, remembering to do my awkward curtsy.

"You must be the maiden of the legend," the King noted.

Scott gestured to me. "Your majesty, Lady Sarah Peters."

"Uhh..." I flustered and bowed again. "Nice to meet you, your majesty."

The King's laughter boomed out. "This must all seem strange to you."

"Pardon?"

"I have heard stories of this world of yours," the King continued. "I hear you do not have any of this formality."

I began to nod.

"I'd like to hear more about it," he proposed, musing as we walked along toward his place at the head of the table. "This world that has done away with royalty, traditions, and customs? It sounds very controversial."

I met Scott's gaze. Word sure traveled fast around here. "Uh, I'd be happy to tell you more about it, your majesty."

I didn't know who arranged the seats at breakfast but I found myself seated between Gradd and Scott. Scott was on the left side of the King with Lessandra across from him. Other members of the court filled the table, several older men and women.

"It's an honor to have the King of Centeria in our midst today," General Tunney spoke up amidst the light and carefree conversation during the meal. "I have heard stories of your bravery in the battle of Durenberg."

Gradd cleared his throat. "Uh...no, that was my father."

"Oh, forgive me. I can be so forgetful." General Tunney let out a chuckle. "So, how is the old chap? Last I heard—"

Gradd's jaw tensed. "He's dead."

Wincing, General Tunney flustered his apology as the entire table hushed. "Oh, heavens, my sincerest apologies and condolences. I hadn't heard."

I couldn't blame the General for being rattled. Gradd's expression was hard as stone. He hadn't once wanted to talk about his father at all.

The King cleared his throat out loud and regarded me with a look. "So, tell us, Lady Sarah," he began to change the topic. "I've heard a great many rumors from the people who arrived with the Kiffad a few days ago, but I must admit many things still confuse me, especially this notion I've heard that you have no kingdoms in your world." His eyebrows rose in curiosity. "Where do people live then? Who makes the laws? Who takes care of the land?"

I shot Gradd a tentative look over but he was staring coldly into nothingness. "Well," I started. "I live in this city called Chicago..."

"City?" one of the court members to my left echoed.

I stopped short. *Oh boy.*

And so throughout the meal, I tried my best to describe in the simplest terms—Chicago, the government, baseball... Everyone had questions about everything. I struggled to compare Earth stuff to Anthuria stuff.

Lessandra wanted to hear about talking pictures. Leila wanted to hear about theme parks. General Tunney made me practically recite the Declaration of Independence. Scott asked about the fast horseless carriages. Gradd, however, ate nonchalantly as if he'd heard all this before.

I must have talked for hours, and while everyone was courteous, wholesome, and seemed genuinely interested, I barely managed to eat one bite.

It did feel good to be able to talk about Earth though. It made me feel like I was closer to home somehow. And I was glad even Lessandra seemed engaged in the conversation for a change. Not to mention, it was a refreshing change of pace after hearing nothing but 'the plan' for the war or what evil deeds the Malkens had committed.

The King was very nice and warm. He struck me a lot like Gradd's father. Noticing that I was getting tired, the King stood up to announce the end of the meal, suggesting that we all retire to our quarters to rest.

But having been wound up by all my talk of Earth, I couldn't possibly rest now!

I let Leila pull me along after the meal. She said she wanted to show me something. I merely laughed at her enthusiasm.

Across the garden, Lessandra was gracefully promenading up to Scott.

Remembering his earlier hesitation about the subject, I had to shake my head. *Good luck, Scott.*

Then I happened to glimpse Gradd by the pillars. When he met my gaze, my smile vanished. Then my view of him was obstructed by the tall green plants as Leila pulled me into the greenhouse.

The greenhouse at Eleria was full of exotic plants and flowers. I marveled at all the strange plants I passed. I had to admit the gardens at Thorb were nice, but like everything else over there, they were very formal, even cold. These Elerian plants, on the other hand, seemed to benefit from extraordinary care and maintenance. The blooms all seemed so alive. The greens were so crisp and fresh. It was a garden tended to with love. Someone from the family obviously had a green thumb.

"Where are we going, Leila?" I asked as she pulled me deeper into the garden.

"Here." Arriving at a rack of plants, she pointed to one flowering pot with a light blue orchid-like flower with a strong scent, almost like jasmine.

"Wow," I praised. "Is this your plant?"

Leila's nod was proud. "Yup, and I take care of it all by myself, too."

A raspy chuckle behind us made me turn.

Walking up to us, the old man adjusted his white hat, his weathered skin seeming to denote a certain wisdom, and his kind eyes crinkled when he smiled.

"Starso!" Leila exclaimed. Of course, it sounded more like *Thtartho*.

"Hello, child." He looked up at me. "And who is this young lady?"

"This is my friend, Sarah," Leila supplied. "She's from another world!"

Starso raised an eyebrow at me. "I see." He put his hand out to shake mine. "You must be the much-talked-about legend of Centeria then."

"Uh...I don't know about legend but 'Sarah' it is. It's nice to meet you." I gestured around us. "Are you the caretaker of this garden? It's quite beautiful."

Starso's smile widened. "This is Princess Leanna's garden. I merely watch the plants for her."

A bit confused, I furrowed my eyebrows. *Leanna, the dead princess?*

Starso easily read my mind. "Her spirit takes care of the garden," he amended with a slow shake of his head. "When she was alive, she loved this garden and these plants show the character of their owner. That's why they're so beautiful."

My eyes widened. "Wow."

Starso watched me for a while. "You must have a unique spirit yourself."

"Huh?"

"The plants." He nodded in the direction of the flowers behind me. "They bloom their best around people with good hearts."

"Oh! Thank you." Blinking, I couldn't help another grateful smile.

Starso turned to Leila, his voice warm. "Now, shall we go and check on your pet fish, child? Did you remember to feed them yesterday?"

"Oh, you're right!" Leila dashed off without another word.

Starso chuckled before bidding me farewell and he turned to follow Leila.

Still smiling to myself, I moved to leave as well, admiring more plants as I went along, humming to myself.

Rounding a corner, I almost ran into Gradd and jumped in fright, and for a moment, I forgot that I was supposed to be ignoring him. "Whoa! Where'd you come from?"

He didn't respond. His forehead was creased as though there was a dark cloud over him.

I guessed breakfast hadn't been as therapeutic for him as it had been for me. I peered up at him in sympathy. "What are you uh...doing here?"

Gradd gestured to me. "You shouldn't wear that anymore while we're here."

"What?" I was taken aback by his abrupt tone.

"People are staring at you," he relayed nonchalantly. "You should wear something more decent."

My jaw almost dropped in disbelief. And here I thought he'd come to call a truce for what he'd said about me last night in the forest. But no, he just wanted to insult me some more.

My eyebrows snapped together in aggravation. "You—are unbeliev-able. First, you drag me around like I have to be everywhere, then you criticize me because I don't do anything but cause trouble. When

I try to have some fun for a change, you have to butt in and drag everyone down. And now I can't even wear what I want?"

Regretting that he'd flipped that switch, he groaned. "Look, I didn't come here to argue with you."

I scoffed in ridicule. "Well, this is an odd way to show it."

"I came to apologize."

I stopped short again, now incredulous. "What?"

"About last night." His gaze was on the floor. "What I said about you not doing anything but get into trouble. I know I shouldn't be blaming you for what happened to...to my kingdom or anything else. It's just...easier to..." He broke off and cleared his throat. "Either way, I'm sorry. I was out of line."

Still giving him a wary look, I had to sigh in concession. "Well...thanks. I do understand that you're under a lot of pressure right now. You've got a lot going on. I'll really try to stay out of your way as much as I can." I nodded in assurance before shrugging offhand. "And anyway, Scott already apologized for you this morning so—"

His narrowed gaze snapped up to me and the sneer was back on his face. "Well, that was awfully perfect of him."

I rolled my eyes sky-high. "Oh my god, why can't I say anything without you biting my head off? And what the hell is your problem with Scott anyway?"

"I don't have a problem with Scott," Gradd told me.

"Don't give me that. You're clenching your jaw," I pointed out. "You said you two were like brothers. Scott's never done anything to you. I don't understand why—"

"Forget Scott!" He threw up his hands in exasperation. "Why are you always talking about Scott?"

I winced. "Is that what this is all about? You're jealous because you think I like Scott? And even if I did, I don't see how that's any of your business."

"Don't be absurd," he mocked. "Every time you are within the vicinity of Scott, you turn into a giggling heap of mush. But whether

I like it or not, you're supposed to be the one who's going to save my kingdom. And if I think you won't be able to do that when he is around, then that is absolutely my business," he declared using the exact same tone I had used with him back at Thorb.

At a loss for words, I stared back at him, my jaw having dropped again. I wanted to tear my hair out in helpless frustration. I didn't know what to make of the situation so I whirled to leave, but Gradd caught my arm.

"What?" I tried to pull away, seriously ticked off now, but when I met his gaze again, his eyes darkened even as he held me firm. I furrowed my eyebrows in exasperation as I studied his face. "What?" I asked again.

When he tugged on my arm, I spun into him, his other hand catching my hip to hold me still. Gasping at how close he was, I met his gaze again but even he looked surprised.

Gradd gave a small shake of his head, the struggle clear in his eyes. It was as if he wanted to tell me something but he didn't know how, as if he wanted to do something but couldn't figure out how to begin.

My heart pounded in my chest but I didn't move. Scott had said that Gradd was a soldier who rarely had the need for words or feelings. Maybe for the first time in a long time, with the continuous onslaught of disasters surrounding him, Gradd was having to expand his emotional vocabulary, and he was coping really badly. No wonder his reactions were all over the place.

He slowly raised his hand—to touch my cheek, I realized. But instead of pulling away, I instinctively turned my face into his touch.

His eyes narrowed in question at my gesture, but then instead of asking, he leaned his head down.

Wide-eyed, I gasped again and drew back an inch in bewilderment.

Just then, a squealing kid tore off from the bushes across the path and came barreling toward me.

When I jumped in surprise, Gradd dropped his hands and stepped back a few feet.

"Sarah! Sarah! Save me!" Leila wrapped herself around my leg. "The monster is after me!" She pointed excitedly toward the bushes where Scott emerged, hunched down, his fingers curled up like claws as if he was Leila's monster.

I burst out laughing.

Spotting us, Scott's eyes lit up and he straightened up. "Hey, what's up, guys?"

"Aaaahhhh!" Leila screeched and started running again, round and round the fountain.

20

lessandra

It was only my second day this week of an entire day with no enemy relic attacks. I was glad to retire to my room after a full evening meal. Looking out the window at the water, I admired the way the moons reflected on its calm surface. The night had gone quiet with only a handful of people wandering about town. It was so peaceful, I had to sigh.

I was feeling pretty good. I was feeling that maybe I wouldn't burn down the kingdom this time.

There was a knock on my door and it was one of the maids informing me that Princess Lessandra had requested an audience with me.

I wasn't about to say no to the Princess so I let the maid lead me wherever she wanted.

It was a bit of a walk right across the castle. I wouldn't have been surprised if the Princess had an entire wing of the castle to herself. When we arrived at the pale pink door, the maid gestured me in.

The Princess's room looked like an indoor courtyard in its own right. Most of the décor was pink like it was a giant cupcake. And in the middle of the cupcake was Princess Lessandra. She was sitting in what, to me, looked like a salon chair, while half a dozen maids tended to her hair and her nails. It was some form of medieval mani-pedi.

"Hello," the Princess greeted me while two maids brushed her long blond hair. "Would you like to have a seat and someone can tend to you?"

Her prompt didn't sound like I could say no to it either, so in no time at all, the maids had my hands soaking in a beeswax bath. I propped my arm up to make sure not to get my bandage wet.

Lessandra nodded toward my arm. "Battle wound?"

"Oh, not exactly. Back at Thorb, when the Malkens attacked, I...guess rocks from an explosion scratched me or something. It doesn't hurt that much anymore though."

"I've never had a real wound before." Lessandra's tone was regretful for some reason. "My father doesn't allow me to do anything dangerous."

In full understanding, I had to concede, "Hey, if my father knew what I'd been doing lately, I'm pretty sure he wouldn't approve either."

"That's easy for you to say since your father isn't a king," Lessandra drawled with a haughty tinge in her tone. "My father has spies everywhere. I couldn't do anything he wouldn't find out about."

"I'm sure he just wants you to be safe. Fathers are strange like that," I remarked a bit sarcastically.

"Safe," she mocked. "Who wants to be safe when there's a big exciting world out there? And yours sounds even more wonderful and exciting." Eyes gleaming, she turned to me. "Tell me, what do you do for fun back in your world?"

I furrowed my eyebrows, not understanding her interest. "Um, not much really. My life's pretty boring."

"Boring?" Lessandra echoed in ridicule. "Are you locked up in some castle, forbidden to do anything? I'm sure you can do anything you want in your world. How might it be boring? Do you simply do nothing?"

"No, of course not," I replied in my defense. "I do stuff. I mean, I play sports with my friends, we hang out a lot, and watch movies."

"That's...all?" She looked at me with an expression of distaste.

I wrinkled my nose in slight offense. "What do you mean by 'all' exactly?"

"Oh, I don't mean to sound patronizing. It's just..." She waved her hand. "You could do so much more, like travel the world. It's something I've always wanted to do but alas, I admit I've never gone very far from this kingdom." Her eyes shone. "This must be really exciting for you. Being here. In a different world altogether."

I made a face again. "I don't know if 'exciting' is the word I'd use to describe it. Though I would definitely have to say it's not boring here. Your world is pretty scary, with this war, and battling monster relics. It's exhausting. It's dangerous—"

"I wish my life was as dangerous as yours," Lessandra cut in. "I think I would have loved to live in your world. Where I could simply be someone else, to go anywhere I wanted, to be able to do *anything*." Her gaze turned far away, dreamy.

In my world? I had to blink at the reversal. "Hey, my world is scary too." I felt I had to enlighten her. "And I'm not just talking 'you could die' scary. Take high school for example," I relayed. "Maneuvering certain social school politics gets tricky. You have to be really careful what you do and what you say. You don't want people talking about you behind your back. Some mistakes can haunt you for the rest of your life."

Disappointed, she frowned. "I don't understand this. You have all the freedom in the world and yet you take it for granted. If I lived in your world, I would make all the mistakes I could ever make and I wouldn't regret anything." She shook her head at me. "Why should you regret who you are? Who cares what people say behind your back?"

I cast her a pointed look. "That's easy for you to say."

Lessandra shot me a look of incredulity. "What is this? The great legend of Centeria isn't afraid to battle monster relics but is afraid of a few silly rumors?"

I chuckled. "Trust me, from my point of view, both are equally as life-threatening."

"Well, regardless." She waved again. "I don't believe my father would ever let me do anything even remotely exciting or dangerous."

I had a feeling Lessandra probably didn't understand the scope of what she was asking for, as by having parents myself, the King's restrictions for Lessandra made total sense to me. Although I had to wonder how much of his protectiveness was influenced by the untimely death of his eldest daughter. Either way, it was an interesting insight into Lessandra's affairs.

"I'm sure your father is just doing what he thinks is best for you," I proposed.

"Oh, yes. He's an expert on what I want." Lessandra rolled her eyes.

"Why don't you just talk to him about it?" I ventured. "He might understand. I'm sure he just wants you to be happy."

She narrowed her eyes at me. "How do you sound so sure about all this?"

"Hey, if I was a Princess and I was as pretty as you, my dad would have a righteous headache keeping me out of trouble."

Lessandra smiled at my compliment even though she didn't look surprised. "You're very kind." Then she mused aloud almost to herself, "How come men never say things like that?"

I hid a smirk. "Are you talking about Scott?"

Lessandra's gaze snapped to mine as though she hadn't expected me to guess so accurately and she blushed big-time.

"Lucky guess," I dismissed offhand.

"Oh, that. It's—it's nothing. Nothing," she flustered. "Never mind. We're just—"

I pursed my lips, trying not to give her a knowing look. Who was she trying to fool? *Moi?*

"Anyway," Lessandra waved the topic away. "I should say you are very lucky to be in Eleria right now. Did you know that my father has arranged to have Lord Gradd's formal coronation ceremony here? That means there is going to be a glorious banquet and a big celebration. We are known for holding the best ones."

Nobody, and I meant *nobody*, could usually get past me with the change-the-subject routine but the mention of Gradd scrambled my circuits. "Really? When?"

"Four nights from today," Lessandra answered. "I heard them discussing it after dinner."

"A formal coronation, huh?"

So Gradd was officially accepting the baton in front of an entire Kingdom or three for that matter.

"Even the Kiffad chief is coming. We're expecting a really big turn-out."

"Oh, is that Aella?" I paused to correct, "I mean, Chief Onnahawk?"

"You've met Aella?" She tilted her head, curious. "How do you know her real name? Have you already been told about Gradd and Aella?"

Not responding, I narrowed my eyes at the tone in Lessandra's voice as it indicated that I had guessed correctly. Then again it was already obvious from the assembly at the camp. There *was* something between Gradd and the Chief.

But Lessandra went on, eager to share. "They courted for a while, but when the late Chief Onnahawk died, Aella chose the tribe over Gradd. Of course, there are always stories that the tribe's seer foretold of a great loss in the future if the two were to unite so it never was."

I involuntarily retched in my head. "Agarpa."

Lessandra's eyes lit up. "I see you get around." Then she moved to cover her yawn. "Oh my, it's getting late."

I agreed with a silent nod and let one of the maids dry my hands but the wheels in my head were already spinning.

I didn't sleep well that night. I kept thinking about curses, great losses, crowns, and...beeswax. If only everyone else's didn't keep getting in the way of me minding my own.

21

the plan

"Good morning," I greeted with a small smile as I arrived at the breakfast hall the next day. Gradd and Scott were already at the table. The maid had informed everyone earlier that the King and his court would not be joining us since they had to attend to some business.

"Looks like you're happy today." Scott turned in his chair to see me approach.

I gave him a big, cheesy grin. It was Day Two in Eleria and I still hadn't burned down the Kingdom yet. I hadn't even had a vision since we'd arrived either which was even better news.

Looking up, Gradd met my gaze, and the slight smile he gave me stirred butterflies in my stomach.

Swallowing hard, I averted my gaze. Between whatever it was that happened with us in the greenhouse yesterday and last night's eye-openers from Lessandra, I decided that I had better not open that particular can of worms.

Taking the seat farthest from him at the table, I was about to ask after Lessandra when the Princess's voice floated out from the hallway.

"I know, I know. Tell my father not to worry about it." Lessandra strolled out to the patio, followed by her handmaid whom she immediately dismissed before calling out her bright greeting, "Good morning!"

"Good morning, Princess." Scott gave her a charming smile. "I trust you've had a lovely morning so far?"

Lessandra's eyes darted over to meet mine as though wary of what she knew I knew. I didn't even say anything but she blushed anyway. "Yes, thank you." She cleared her throat before sitting down at the head of the table. "Uh, Sarah." She seemed eager to focus the conversation on something else. "After breakfast, would you perhaps like to go riding outside the castle? My father has some very handsome horses and it would be a great way for you to see the rest of my beautiful kingdom."

Pleased at her kind offer, my eyes lit up. "That sounds great." But then I grimaced. "I'm not that good at horse riding though."

She dismissed my concern. "You'll do fine. Perhaps we might find some adventure for ourselves after all," she added with a self-satisfied grin.

"That sounds like an excellent plan, Princess," Scott piped up. "Provided you have suitable escorts?"

I gave Scott a pretend haughty look. "Um, excuse me. We're trying to do a girl bonding activity. You can't go."

Lessandra pursed her lips. "Actually, Scott may have raised a fair point. My father will likely have concerns if we were to ride out on our own." She gestured to Scott and Gradd. "This way, my father would be more at ease and not insist that we bring along a fleet of royal guards."

"You know him too well." Scott's tone changed to mischievous. "Besides, this might be Gradd's last opportunity to have some fun for a while."

Curious at his tone, I looked at Gradd for a second. "Oh, really? Why?"

Gradd, of course, sat stone-faced, not volunteering any information.

Scott answered for him. "He has to complete his training before 'the' day." He reached out to thump on Gradd's shoulder. "Isn't that right?"

Lessandra turned to me to explain. "All royalty must complete their training before they are crowned. It's tradition. And one Gradd certainly cannot escape," she added with a light-as-air giggle.

"Oh. Right." I happened to meet Gradd's eyes again. He raised a prompting eyebrow at me but I turned away again, clearing my throat before he could make me have to talk to him.

Something about what Lessandra had said about Aella and Gradd was nagging at me. Like maybe I was more right than I thought. Even Aella had mentioned that Agarpa wasn't always a hundred percent accurate in her foretelling.

What if, somehow, Agarpa had simply misread their fortune? What if when Agarpa had seen destruction, she had merely been referring to my arrival? I was the one who had caused total and complete destruction to Centeria. And if that were the case, her visions of Gradd and Aella might have been misread altogether.

It meant Gradd and Aella still had a chance to be together. The King of Centeria with the Chief of the Kiffad—which totally made sense. Certainly way more sense than anyone getting involved with someone like me, the weirdo from a whole other world.

Notwithstanding all that, I was pretty certain I couldn't afford for things to get any more complicated than it already was anyway.

Lessandra noticed my thoughtful silence. "Is something wrong?"

"Huh?" Snapping to attention, I beamed a quick smile. "No, of course not."

Nothing was wrong, nothing was right. *Po-tay-to, po-tah-to.*

Lessandra let me borrow one of her riding habits. It was a very elegant dark green ensemble, except that I was pretty sure her being taller and more filled out than I was didn't help me with how elegant it should have looked. In any case, my other outfit of choice, which would be my Earth clothes, was inappropriate in more ways than one.

Scott and Gradd were already waiting outside with four horses and two grooms, both of whom Lessandra dismissed right away as soon as we arrived.

The two grooms looked at each other but merely shrugged in obedience to her direct order before ambling back to the castle.

"Like I was seven," Lessandra muttered in displeasure.

Scott was looking up at the sky. "Looks like the weather's turning out fine."

"That's good." I nodded at him then got distracted by Lessandra's sudden incapacity to mount her horse. My eyebrows furrowed, and I watched her strangely until Scott, taking notice as well, gallantly jumped to the Princess's aid.

I had to shake my head in disbelief. The Princess sure was subtle.

"Oh, thank you," she told Scott in a breathy voice. "I don't know what happened. I must have hurt my foot somewhere."

I was going to laugh but then I felt Gradd's presence behind me and I froze.

"Give you a boost?" he offered in a disorienting gentlemanly tone.

"Sure. Thanks." Hell, if I knew how to get on a horse by myself.

The four of us started at a gentle gallop toward the hills within sight of the castle then farther out closer to town before heading toward the forest treeline. We rode steadily, switching places, except I always fell behind the group. The three of them were properly trained for horseback riding. Scott and Gradd were equally competent but I should have expected the same from Lessandra. She was as graceful on a horse as she was on her feet. I, on the other hand, had only taken a few cursory lessons when I was eight.

I couldn't help but cringe as I observed Lessandra's manner toward Scott. She had pretty much talked to and about not much else but Scott all morning. And even as I was sorely aware that I was no expert on the subject, I already knew there were better methods for what she was trying to achieve.

We slowed to a canter, heading for a spot near the waterfront with Lessandra leading the way and the rare occasion of Gradd riding beside her.

With the two of them discussing something that I didn't care to eavesdrop on, Scott fell into pace beside me with a grin. "How're you holding up?"

Breathing heavily, I shot him a wide-eyed meaningful look. "I think I'm...I'm not going to have—" I paused for breath. "Any trouble...getting to sleep...tonight."

Scott laughed. "Hang in there. We'll be taking a break soon." He patted his horse's mane. "We gave these guys quite a workout."

"No kidding." We must have gone for miles and miles but it wasn't even midday yet. I also had a feeling I was going to be very hungry later on.

Lessandra glanced back at Scott and me again. I almost rolled my eyes but made sure she wasn't seeing anything she would take any offense to.

The views were breathtaking and every vista was as stunning as the next. The trail we were taking was lined with unusual trees with purple-red leaves. I tried to reach out every so often to pluck a leaf off to show Scott, and when an especially low branch passed by, I leaned sideways to grasp a leaf while trying to maintain my balance on the horse. But I was pulled back quickly—by Gradd.

"Whoa—" Surprised to see that Gradd was beside me, I glanced up to see that Scott had switched forward to be beside the Princess again.

"What are you doing?" Gradd's tone was a little impatient.

I gave him an even look. "I was just trying to grab a leaf from these trees."

"Oh." He blinked. He must have thought I was falling off my horse.

I didn't want to sound defensive but I wanted to make my point. "You don't always have to rescue me, you know. Sometimes I can take care of myself."

But Gradd's response was wry. "Sorry. Can't seem to break the habit."

Stifling back a chuckle, I stuck my tongue out at him.

Gradd popped out of his seat. The movement was so fast, I hardly caught it. But when Gradd came back, he was holding a stem of the tree with a leaf and a bloom. He held it out to me. "There."

"Oh." Delighted, I examined the brilliant colors in my hand before looking back up to the trees surrounding us as their branches swayed in the wind.

Everything in Eleria seemed so tranquil. I couldn't help the hollowness in my stomach at the dreadful thought of the Malkens destroying everything here too. The thought that the entire kingdom would simply wash away with the tide.

Fortunately, Lessandra's voice broke into my thoughts. "Here we are."

Looking up, my jaw dropped. We were near a cliff's peak, above the shoreline where the big waves slammed into big rocks below, and from up here, a full panoramic view of Eleria was spread before us— the quaint seaside houses, the harbor, fishing boats, and horse-drawn carts moving along toward the colorful marketplace.

Everyone dismounted except for me since I was still awestruck. The people of Eleria lived in such harmony. Despite the less-than-advanced technology in certain aspects of their lives, they were all perfectly in synch with nature and each other. It was breathtaking.

Gradd stepped up beside my horse. He'd mistaken my lingering for inability to dismount. He held up his hands to assist me.

"I'm fine, I'm fine." Trying to wave him away, I swung my leg up and around the back of the horse. Gradd caught my waist anyway. "Whoops—" I held on to his neck as he set me down in front of him. Dropping my arms, I stopped for a second to regain my balance before I looked up, straight into his eyes. His arms were still around me.

"Um..." Biting my lip, I stepped back quickly. My pulse racing, I hurried over to Scott and Lessandra, all the while feeling Gradd's questioning gaze on the back of my head.

girls and guys

"Your kingdom is so beautiful," I remarked to Lessandra.

"Thank you." I could hear the pride in her voice.

Scott walked over to his horse. "Say, where can these guys get a drink?" He patted his horse's head.

"There's a reservoir over that way." Lessandra pointed down a path and started to head over to him. "I could show you—"

I pulled her back. "Why don't we let the guys do that? I'm sure the two of them are more than capable," I told her loudly so Scott could hear.

Scott shot me a strange look but then looked down the path. "This way?"

Lessandra just nodded but not before giving me a strange look as well.

"All right," Scott complied and waved Gradd over. "Come on, Gradd."

Gradd gave me yet another strange look, which made three, and shook his head before he led two of the horses to follow Scott with the first two.

Lessandra whirled around to me as soon as they had gone. "What was that all about?" she demanded, her royal air coming up in my face.

I winced. "Sorry, your highness. But I thought we needed to talk alone."

She prompted cautiously. "About what?"

I wrinkled my nose. "Well, I was just thinking that perhaps..." I tried to phrase my suggestion in the right way. "You might like to tone it down, you know, with Scott."

Lessandra shot me an annoyed look, probably because she knew I was right. "What are you talking about?"

I gave her a wry smile. "Look, I know I just got here and I don't know any of you all that well but I'm getting the sense that Scott is just not the kind of guy that—how shall I say this?" I paused for thought. "You know the usual stuff?" I supplied before shaking my head. "It's not going to work on him."

Lessandra didn't say anything but she was still watching me, except attentively now, instead of annoyedly.

"Like, for starters," I went on. "You know, try not mentioning his name every two seconds."

She scoffed in ridicule. "I don't do that."

I put up my hands. "Look, Princess, I'm trying to help you here. But I'm guessing you're so beautiful, you've probably never had to flirt too hard to get a guy's attention."

It was the first time I saw Lessandra look uncomfortable after having been given a compliment.

"I'm just saying," I relayed, hoping I sounded logical. "The school of thought is that if what you're doing isn't necessarily working, you might perhaps want to try something else."

That earned me another strange look. "You learn this in school?"

I had to keep myself from laughing. "I suppose. In one way or another."

She studied my expression. "So these methods of yours, they work on Lord Gradd?"

I almost choked. "What—no! I mean, I'm not doing that. I'm not trying to—in fact, it's the total opposite. Total, total opposite," I repeated with conviction.

"Why not?" She sounded in disbelief. "I thought the two of you were close. And he's really not bad looking."

I had to purse my lips at her understatement but I had to explain. "Well, because..." I waved it away. "We're just friends. And he's a—I'm a—" I broke off, distracted upon seeing the guys on their way back. "Oh, look, they're back," I announced, almost in relief.

"Scott!" Lessandra practically flew to him to ask him to accompany her for a walk down to the shore because she wanted to show him something.

I clicked my tongue, watching them leave with a shake of my head. *Whatever. I tried to help her.*

"Sarah," Gradd spoke from behind me and I turned. "What's this all about?"

I shifted on my feet. "Uh, what do you mean?"

"Don't pretend you don't know." His expression was serious. "You're avoiding me and I want to know why."

"Whaaat?" I tried to weasel out of the question and tried to think of a logical response without giving away my grand conspiracy theory. "Avoiding you? How could I possibly avoid you? I'm basically stuck with you."

His forehead creased. Yep, he wasn't buying it.

I pursed my lips. "Look, I said I'd stay out of your way, remember? I'm just...trying not to complicate things," I added as that was wholly true.

He met my gaze. "What's complicated about it?"

My heart pounded in my chest. Bad sign. Backing up, I walked toward the edge of the cliff to sit on a big, flat rock, facing out to the water.

Without a word, Gradd walked over and sat beside me, facing backward toward the meadow. He leaned forward to prop his elbows on his knees.

"Hey, I heard about your coronation ceremony," I spoke up, mostly to change the subject, mostly because I already knew how he would react, which guaranteed the change of subject. And as I expected, his body tensed.

"Don't." His voice was rough.

"I thought you would have been looking forward to it," I started. "When I first met you, you sounded really proud of your kingdom. This must be the biggest honor. Don't you think so?"

He didn't reply. He didn't even move. He sat stiff as a board.

"Gradd?"

"I said I don't want to talk about it!"

My eyebrows furrowed as I watched him stare at the ground. I could sense a shattering degree of anguish and helplessness in him despite the expression on his face not having changed as it was still as stoic as ever.

I almost regretted bringing it up. I already knew he was struggling under tremendous pressure. Gradd had lost everything. He practically had to fight an entire war and rebuild his whole kingdom. All by himself.

I wanted to help give him some perspective but I felt nothing in my own life even came close to comparing to what he was probably going through. All I could think to say was what I had been repeating to myself, the only platitude that was keeping me from the brink of insanity since I had arrived in Anthuria.

"You know, I was always told everything happens for a reason," I spoke softly. "Even bad things. They make us stronger. They shape us. Maybe...we just need to remember that nothing would ever come our way that we couldn't possibly handle." I realized I was also saying it to myself, as well as to him.

Gradd didn't say anything for a while and I let my words sink in. I took a deep breath and looked out at the surf where Scott and Lessandra were strolling along the beach. The waves crashed against the rocks below the cliff. Birds dotted the sky. Such a pretty picture.

Smiling to myself, I reveled in the serenity of the place. "We should've brought—"

In one fluid motion, Gradd turned to put his arms around me.

"Leila," I finished with a gasp, blinking in surprise as his warmth enveloped me.

"Do me a favor." Gradd's voice was a low rumble. "Don't ever stay out of my way."

23

scruples

The ride back was tense for some reason. Lessandra insisted on talking to Gradd while Scott rode next to me. Saying nothing, he stared into space.

We'd arrived late for the meal and the King took Lessandra to one side for a lecture about getting him all worried about dismissing the other grooms. She reasoned that we were perfectly safe with Gradd and Scott, sounding disproportionately irritable, which the King must have sensed because he didn't pursue his line of questioning.

Scott excused himself and kind of stalked away.

I watched him leave with a puzzled frown on my face.

Lessandra shot Scott's back a haughty look before whirling around to leave herself.

I wasn't about to eat alone with Gradd so I asked if the food could be sent up to my room instead.

But Gradd didn't want to eat.

The King waved the maids away before he beckoned Gradd over for a serious discussion.

Left standing in the courtyard, I simply shrugged in helpless exasperation before retreating to my room.

I woke up with a start and blinked several times. My sleep was almost always interrupted by the dread of that recurring nightmare or a brand-new vision. Even when there was nothing, I almost half-expected the pain and panic already. But getting my bearings back, I stared at the canopy ceiling above my bed.

Right, still in Eleria.

Yawning, I sat up. I had fallen asleep after the late meal. Not to mention I was exhausted from all that morning exercise.

The sun was setting now, sending orange and red rays of light into the room. The food service to my room had already been put away. There was also a fresh change of clothes at the foot of the bed—another princess dress, in lavender.

Hopping off the bed to get changed, I absently noticed that my own clothes were hanging on an armchair across the room. I couldn't help but think of the random circumstances from that evening, now seeming so long ago, when I had haphazardly chosen to wear those particular clothes to sleep, I never once in my wildest imaginations thought that I would get transported to a different world and get stuck with the same clothes for weeks.

My mom was always nagging me to throw out my old, ratty clothes. She would always say I looked like a hobo and better live outside the house. I couldn't help a grin to myself. I should have listened to my mom.

If I ever got back home, I was going to start wearing tidy clothes. If I ever got back home, I was going to be so nice to Annette. No matter how annoying she got. I would never pass up a chance at bat again whenever we played baseball. I'd totally take Ena up on that offer to double date. Maybe I would even finally ask Derek out. And maybe I would no longer let fear control my life and live for a change. If I ever got back home...

Home... Sighing, my arms fell slack to my sides.

Someone cleared his throat from the doorway.

"Yipes!" I whirled around as the back of my dress gaped open.

It was Gradd. The corner of his mouth turned up in amusement.

I flushed scarlet. "I'm getting changed, do you mind?" I wanted to frown at him in annoyance but I was too stunned, too caught off-guard. "H-how long have you been standing there?" I narrowed my eyes at him.

"I just got here," Gradd replied before walking over. He tilted his head in scrutiny of the dress that I was having trouble putting on by myself. "Can I help you with that?"

"I'm fine." I turned away from him, clumsily but hastily doing up the back of the dress. It was one of the downsides of medieval dresses. Buttons. Laces. No zips. One time, it took me nearly an hour to get into one. I knew Lessandra had maids to help her get dressed but I had dismissed mine. Seriously, it was just a dress.

"It's not like I haven't seen you wear less," Gradd reasoned.

I blushed again. "It's not like I do it on purpose. That's how people normally dress for bed where I come from."

"Boy, I'd love to see your world," he couldn't help his remark.

"You would," I quipped before my smile faded again. "I know I would."

Pausing, Gradd regarded me with a look. "You will." At least, *he* sounded sure of himself.

I wanted to believe him but in my current mood, my pessimistic side was overriding any fragment of hope.

When I didn't answer, he prompted, "I thought you said you weren't going to give up?"

Eager to focus on something else, I glanced out the window and thought I saw Scott down in the gardens. "Is that Scott?"

Gradd craned his neck to check. "Seems so."

Curious, I tapped my chin. "What do you suppose happened between him and the Princess out there this morning?"

Gradd leaned against the window. "I know the Princess has always liked Scott."

"That much is obvious," I had to say.

"Although back then, I remember Scott being rather close to the eldest," he recalled offhand. "But then, Leanna died and I guess Scott's still trying to get over her death."

I nodded. "Right. Scott told me about that. No wonder he sounded so sad."

"He must have felt guilty," Gradd relayed as the two of us watched Scott walk aimlessly around the garden. "I know he blames himself for her death though I don't know any more details than that."

My heart squeezed. It was like one tragedy after another with these people. "Poor Scott. I suppose poor Lessandra too."

Gradd shot me a probing look. "Why does it matter to you?"

"They're my friends." I shrugged. "I thought they were your friends too."

"I know they're my friends," he pointed out. "Do you make friends so fast?"

I shot him a deadpan look. "Thanks."

Gradd studied my face for a minute as though he'd found something new.

"What?" I raised my eyebrows at him.

A hint of a smirk was on his lips. "I've never...met anyone like you before."

"Well, obviously," I said, matter-of-factly. "I doubt many people from Earth drop by around here."

"That's not what I mean." He gave me another look that was a cross between disbelief and amazement. "You care so much for people you hardly know. You go out of your way to help strangers. I guess..." He shrugged. "I guess actually...Centeria's pretty lucky to have you as the legend."

I was almost taken aback by his statement. After a moment, I shot him a bewildered look. "Is that a *positive* comment from the King of Centeria? Are you feeling okay?"

Gradd simply shook his head in mirth.

24

royal airs

"Give me another one." Scott knocked on the wooden table in the garden where we were playing Poker with my crude handmade playing cards.

"No, no." I shook my head. "If you want another card, you say 'Hit me!'"

"Very well then." Scott grinned and called out "Hit me!" with dramatic emphasis.

I laughed before I dealt him another card. Then I frowned at my own hand. "This hand is terrible."

"Maybe it is who's playing it," he teased.

I had stopped counting the days that the Malkens didn't attack. I was beginning to get comfortable with the day-to-day in the peaceful, beautiful kingdom of Eleria. Everyone I had met so far was very friendly. The King and his staff never ran out of questions at mealtimes and I never ran out of stories.

Also since Gradd was always in training for the last few days, I'd spent most of my time hanging out with Scott, Lessandra, and Leila.

We had gone to town a few times. I'd managed to catch a few busking shows, taken walks along the seashore, and had picnics on the hillside just outside the castle. I'd even bought a seedling at the marketplace which with Starso's help had been potted and was sitting next to Leila's on the rack in the greenhouse. It was meant to bloom yellow flowers. Leila was much like the kids I usually babysat. I always had fun with her. Scott was even helping me improve my riding skills. And while I could feel that the tension between Scott and Lessandra hadn't completely subsided, I think they had agreed on a happy impasse and were at least always polite to each other.

In as short as a few days, I'd also gotten to know several of the castle's staff, mostly because, in an attempt to feel useful, I had offered to help babysit one of the cooks' kids. It wasn't like my diary was full anyway.

With the war still relatively unfelt in this part of the world, everything was surreal and extraordinarily ordinary, and I couldn't help but hope that it would always stay like this.

"Okay, pair queens, pair aces." I lay down my hand in triumph.

Scott stopped for a second, shot the cards a suspicious look then looked at me before dropping his cards onto the table with an exasperated sigh. "Why do I have the sneaky suspicion that you're cheating somehow?"

I merely beamed at him as I gathered the cards again to shuffle. "It's just not your lucky day, Scott."

"Whatever. I know you're cheating," Scott accused good-naturedly before he stood up and walked over to Leila who was playing with the water fountain.

I was honestly relieved that Scott had gotten out of the deep blue funk he'd been in for the past couple of days. Leila had been highly instrumental in cheering him up. I noticed that she was especially capable of making Scott smile. It was likely because of the very close resemblance that Leila had to Princess Leanna, something I had noted from looking at the portraits displayed around the castle.

I did a fancy card shuffle in deep thought. The last time I'd spoken to Gradd was in my room, that day before his training started. Since then, I'd hardly seen him, except when we would walk by the courtyards and he happened to be training there, or when he and King

Cornelius had official talks in the drawing room and we'd be in the library across the hall.

But Gradd never looked up. He seemed really focused on his training. I supposed he had to concentrate because obviously being King was a really big deal. Not that I knew anything at all about it but I could imagine it probably was.

On those occasions, he no longer seemed resentful about fulfilling his duty and I guessed he'd finally made his peace with it.

Ironically, things were quieter without his constant brooding and scolding. Not that I was complaining. There was plenty to do without being on tenterhooks, dreading another argument with Gradd. Still, it was kind of strange not having him around all the time.

"Hello, hello!" Lessandra's voice broke in on my thoughts as she practically floated into the garden.

Scott and Leila looked up as well.

"Look who came early," Lessandra announced as another woman stepped up from behind her—a woman wearing her majestic, feathery headpiece.

My eyes lit up in recognition. "Chief Onnahawk."

She gave me a warm smile. Reaching up to take her headpiece off, she noted, "Call me Aella."

Scott walked over for formalities. Leila simply gave Aella a sunny wave from across the garden.

"Hello, Leila," Aella called out her greeting with an amused tilt to her smile as the little princess returned to making waves in the fountain water.

By their looks, Lessandra and Aella were as night and day. Aside from the obvious difference in couture, Aella was darker and more built, while Lessandra was fairer, curvier, and more delicate. Regardless, they were both incredibly strikingly beautiful.

"Sarah, it's so nice to see you again." Aella took my hand in hers. "Truth be told, I'd have thought one of you and Gradd would have killed the other by now. But since you're still alive and well, I suppose Gradd is dead?"

Her joke made everyone laugh.

"So where is his royal ego?" Aella craned her neck to look around.

"Still in training." Lessandra waved her hand. "He's been ignoring us for a while now. Of course, we can't really blame him."

"Mm." Aella nodded in understanding. "I remember my ascension day. I was a wreck the entire week prior."

"A wreck?" Scott echoed with disbelief. "You needed the strongest herbs to calm down."

"Look who's talking," Lessandra said to Scott. "Might I remind you where you were half an hour before your turnover ceremony?"

Scott gave her a grimace.

"I'll tell you where," Lessandra whispered to me. "Throwing up on the tapestries," she quipped before laughing.

And Aella laughed.

And Scott laughed.

Swallowing hard, I forced a laugh. I had almost forgotten that for the last few weeks, I had been spending my time with esteemed royals. And while I was certainly grateful for the advantages coming with such unprecedented access, I couldn't help but feel insecure and a little bit apprehensive. These were arguably some of the most powerful people in Anthuria. Heaven help anyone who ever crossed them.

Just then, Leila skipped over to me, took my hand, and pulled me toward the fountain to show me some flowers she had picked and let float on the water like lilies.

Later that evening, I leaned out the window of my room with a huge sigh.

Dinner had been almost unbearable. Aella, Scott, and Lessandra had all talked and laughed as they reminisced old times, or for the lack of a better term, engaged in a royal pissing contest.

I was well aware that they were all simply telling it like it was. They were all titled, and entitled, and no doubt very deserving of whatever honor they claim to have received. Surely, none of their accomplishments had come easily, with even a few having come with a terrible cost.

War. Famine. Revolts.

They were all incredible, amazing people.

I was very fortunate that they were all nice enough to befriend me.

I was nobody. I hadn't done anything. I was nothing in comparison. In fact, I was incredibly out of place and I so didn't belong here. Despite being considered whatever legendary entity, I was still not from this world. I was and always would be an outsider.

Frowning, I slumped onto my elbows against the windowsill.

I happened to glance down at the small courtyard beneath my room, and among the dozens of dark suits of armor in training, there was one face looking up.

I met Gradd's gaze and my heart skipped a beat. His face was pale under the light of the moons but he didn't look away. It seemed he had been watching me too.

Holding his gaze for a long moment, I took a deep breath as if I could draw strength from his eyes.

Gradd... I sighed again.

"Tharah!" Leila rocketed into the room and wrapped herself around my leg.

Jumping in surprise, I stepped back from the window. "What do you want, squirt?"

"Tell me another story!" Leila's little face was eager as she pleaded.

I scooped her up and set her down on my bed. "All right, all right," I conceded with a smile. "I've already told you about Cinderella, right?"

"Yup," she chirped, sitting cross-legged on my bed. "And of the girl who slept all the time too."

"Right." Chuckling, I sat down next to her on the bed. "Hm." I paused for thought and looked at the night sky outside my window. "Okay. Have you heard about the princess who lived in a tower and her prince charming who always watched her from below?"

25

gradd

It was like game day at Wrigley Field. There wasn't an empty spot on the main courtyard floor. The huge space was packed with people from Eleria, Thorb, Kiffad, and of course, Centeria. Everyone had come to see the formal coronation of the new King of Centeria.

It was a party, a huge celebration. The sky was clear, loud festive music played, colorful streamers hung from the castle archways, kingdom banners flew, the crowds cheered without ceasing, and the event hadn't even begun yet.

"This is incredible!" I exclaimed, leaning out the window to immerse myself in the spectacle.

Since the main courtyard was on the other side of the castle, nowhere near my room, I'd persuaded one of my dressing maids to help me locate a room closer to the festivities.

Friendly and pleasant, Genesa was one of the people that I had gotten to know during my time here, one of the maids whom I finally let help me get into the fancy princess dresses every day. I'd almost even got her out of the habit of curtsying to me all the time. As far as I was concerned, I was no better off than her in rank. In many ways, I was also just here as hired help.

"This is the most people in the castle I have seen at any one time."

Genesa leaned beside me. The empty chambers she had found for us were right above the celebration. "I cannot believe how many people are here!"

"Yeah." I agreed though I had to shake off the uneasy feeling about the fact that part of the reason for the size of the crowd was due to half of these people's countries having burned down. Ahem, care of yours truly.

Glancing down at the main dais where King Cornelius was sitting on an elegant throne, it was easy to spot Lessandra and Leila standing by him. Scott and Aella were also standing just behind the King. Everyone was dressed at their best.

Lessandra had even persuaded Aella to wear a long formal beige satin dress. And with Aella's hair done up, care of Lessandra's hand-maidens, Aella was the most beautiful woman in the kingdom today.

But even from way up here, I could spot the hint of a scowl on her face. She had mentioned she wasn't used to wearing dresses either. Smirking, I made a mental note to make fun of her later.

"How come you aren't down there with the rest of the royal party?" Genesa turned to ask me.

I made a face. They *had* asked. I had to make sure I had an excuse to refuse. I knew I didn't belong down there, to be bowed and curtsied to, and I needed to stop trying to assume their position. I wasn't royalty. Their life wasn't my life. I was just an Earth girl and I wasn't going to be ashamed of it.

"Eh." I shrugged to reply. "With this view? Those are the cheap seats." Genesa laughed.

The loud, steady beating of drums, calling for attention, made us look down, and the hush coming over the crowd was like an undulating wave of dissipating chatter.

"I think it's starting." I elbowed Genesa.

Halfway from the front, the crowds parted forming a wide aisle flanked by soldiers carrying Eleria kingdom banners.

Eyes roving to the end of the assembly, I glimpsed Gradd's cloak with the big, red phoenix stitching.

The King of Eleria and his court all stood as royal trumpet music sounded and Gradd began his walk up the aisle at a certain pace, followed by two Centerian soldiers holding banners with the phoenix on them.

"There he is," Genesa whispered in reverence.

Nodding, I couldn't look away.

"He is really good-looking, isn't he?" Genesa murmured.

"What?" I shot her an incredulous look.

Coloring, she gestured to him. "Lord Gradd."

"Oh, well—" I flustered, glancing back out there. "I...uh...we're too far away to tell." I dismissed with a wave.

"Oh, come on." Genesa nudged me. "You're the Centerian legend. You know him."

Making a face again, I shook my head, but couldn't figure out exactly how to respond to that.

"I've heard he's kind of scary," Genesa asked. "Is that true?"

Nodding again, I had to agree with that. "Ohh yeah, that is definitely true."

As the proceedings wore on, my enthusiasm died down. It was no doubt a delightful tradition, but to me, it was just as boring as any other ceremony I'd ever watched in my life. Too much of that pomp and circumstance. I was relieved when the officiator handed Gradd a cloth-covered sword, the sword of Centeria which he accepted with a bow, down on one knee, signaling the conclusion of the rite.

The crowd erupted into loud cheers, confetti fell from above, and festive music began to play again.

Pulling myself up onto the windowsill, I clapped and cupped my hands to howl cheers into the loud din. Once all the cheers had died, I hopped off the window to dust off my dress.

Checking the time, Genesa perked up in alarm. "Oh, my! We'd better start getting you ready for the ball later."

I shot her a surprised look as she ushered me out of the room. "Ball? What ball?"

Waltz.

Genesa hummed along to the loud music coming from the main ballroom as it filtered through the halls all the way to my chambers.

I frowned at myself in the mirror. "I hate waltz. I hate dancing."

Genesa paused from fixing my hair and shot my reflection a weird look. "I don't understand this world of yours. You don't wear dresses, you don't have royalty, you can barely ride a horse," she listed wearily, "and now you don't dance either?"

"Well, I skipped dance class. It's just not my thing."

"Hm," she mumbled before she stepped back to survey her work.

All my hair was up except for a couple of tendrils around my face. It was very on-theme medieval. I just couldn't help but wonder how she'd done it without the help of hairspray.

"Hey, you're really good at that." I turned my head to each side to see. "You've got real talent here."

"It's just a hobby," Genesa relayed. "I never need to fix my hair anyway."

I turned to raise an eyebrow at her. "Never?" I stood up and gestured to the chair. "Here, let's do yours right now."

"What? Whatever for?" Genesa looked bewildered.

"Just 'cause." I pulled her down to sit, facing the mirror. "Come on, you have great hair." I ran a brush through her long brown hair.

She gave me a weird smile. "But I don't need to fix my hair. I'm not going anywhere."

"Oh, come on," I coaxed. "You did mine. Let me do yours. I hear it's always good to look your best no matter the occasion. Besides, I haven't French braided anyone in years, ever since my sister became such a big B."

Aella's voice came from the doorway. "Knock, knock!"

I turned around and smiled as Aella came into my room. Lessandra and Leila were right behind her. "Hey, guys!"

Leila ran up to me. "Tharah!"

Genesa jumped up and quickly curtsied backward.

"Hey, I wasn't done!" I exclaimed but Genesa had already disappeared through the door.

"So, are you ready?" Lessandra gave me a prompting look.

"Yeah, sure." Straightening up, I took one last look in the mirror. "Here we go."

"Let's go eat!" Leila pulled me out the door before running ahead.

"That kid never runs out of energy, does she?" Aella asked as the three of us walked abreast using the entire width of the hallway to wield the big, fancy dresses. She gave me a grin. "I suppose she relates better to you as being of the same age."

Knowing she was kidding, I shot her a suffering look. "By the way, nice dress."

Aella scowled at me and Lessandra and I laughed.

When we arrived at the end of the long corridor to the main ballroom, the music got louder. I hadn't been to this part of the castle yet and I couldn't help but marvel, almost intimidated by all the luxury and splendor.

Waiting by the door, Scott beamed at us as we approached him. "Well, if it isn't the most beautiful women in Anthuria."

"Oh, go on, Scott. You know that's a gross understatement," Lessandra replied with an exaggerated haughty tone.

"Yes, we understand your pain," Aella quipped.

Scott looked at me expecting another comeback.

I patted his back. "I think they've quite covered it."

Mirthful, Scott rolled his eyes at us and merely bent down to pick Leila up. "Come on, kid. Looks like it's just you and me."

Laughing again, we entered the ballroom.

Rather, I entered the ballroom by walking normally.

Lessandra and Aella both seemed to almost glide. They were both so graceful.

I had previously thought (maybe hoped) that, like me, Aella might be a bit rusty with gatherings such as these given that she lived in the forest, but no. It looked like Jungle Jane had gone to finishing school before becoming the Chief of their tribe.

Stopping short as I stepped onto the marble floor, I stared in awe at how big the ballroom was. Gold and crystal glittered from every corner of the room, the ceilings, the chandeliers, and the candlesticks. At least two long tables of food were decked out with shiny silverware, glittery trays, and sparkling drinks. Crisp, white linen tablecloth-covered tables with matching cushioned chairs bordered the sides of the room to make space for a huge dance floor.

Even the people glittered as they floated about like swans in a big lake, dancing in perfect synch to the music, or talking, laughing, drinking, and milling around. Music was being performed by the orchestra situated on the balcony over one big arched doorway. Big banners of Eleria hung from the ceiling. In front, two other banners hung on each side of the Elerian one—a tiger one and a phoenix one.

I had been warped into an old movie and that King Arthur was about to appear to wield his magic sword at any moment. Completely overwhelmed, I shivered.

"Something wrong?" Lessandra noticed my silence. When I didn't answer, she just pulled me along to lead us right up to the front table. "Come on."

But as soon as we sat down, my eyes caught the buffet table and I moved to leave again. "Hey, I'm just going to...go grab a bite to eat." I walked over to the food like a beacon. *Ohh bacon...*

26

earth girl

As I walked over, I waved hello to Madame Louisa, one of the head cooks manning the buffet. She was the one I usually babysat for.

"Miss, how are you this evening?" she greeted with a smile.

"Good." I nodded, a bit put to ease by the familiar face. "Where are Olly and Ravi tonight?" I glanced around for her two children who were usually getting into scrapes around her.

She cocked an eyebrow at me. "Oh, you'll see them. They'd be running around here somewhere." She sounded displeased though not bothered about the fact. "If you do see them, make sure they aren't setting fire to something."

That made me laugh.

"Here." She handed me a plate of something. "Try some of this. It's an Elerian delicacy. It come in by boat this morning."

"Oh, thank you." I inspected the item on my plate. *Meatball?* I shrugged as I popped one into my mouth.

"Hey, Sarah." Scott appeared beside me.

Mouth still full, I whirled around.

Scott set Leila down beside me even as his eyes were glued to the back of the room where the receiving line was being assembled. "Could you do me a favor and watch Leila? I have to go do a thing."

He nodded casually toward the stage. He made it sound as though receiving the royal family was a mundane little task.

I swallowed my mouthful. "Sure, Scott. Not that it seems I've been given a choice in the matter."

"Oh, haha." He made a face at me. Raising his eyebrows in a prompt, he turned to each side to give me a profile, several profiles. "So, how do I look? Do I look okay?"

I pursed my lips, almost mocking. *Seriously?* Scott Darabont was easily the best-looking guy in the room. No, in Eleria. No, in *Anthuria*. It seemed unfathomable to me that he would be insecure about his looks. I pretended to wrinkle my nose. "Weeell…" I tilted my hand from side to side. "Just don't look anybody straight in the eye."

"Sarah," Scott groaned.

I laughed again. "You look fine. Very, very King-worthy," I assured crisply, proceeding to pop another meatball into my mouth.

He gave me a slow smile. "Great." Then he promptly added, "Will you marry me?"

I almost choked on the meatball.

Scott's smile widened and he patted my back. "Answer later," he bid before heading off toward the assembly line.

Watching him leave, I blinked back tears stinging my eyes from almost choking on the darn meatball.

"Come on, kid." I held my arms out to carry Leila with a wary look around. *Did anybody hear that?* I furrowed my eyebrows. Come to think of it, I was pretty sure I didn't hear that. He had to have been joking. Scott was always joking. Or he must have been out of his mind.

I shook it off as best as I could and headed toward the seafood platters where Leila was pointing.

I stifled my yawn while another official proceeding went on. The royal assembly had entered the room looking very solemn and serious. Banners, flags, marching, trumpets, and speeches. Of course, the

King of Eleria had to practically individually welcome and acknowledge every single titled person in the room. Aella and Lessandra were in their seats, beaming regally at the crowd. On the other hand, Leila seemed content to raid the fruit section of the buffet, not even paying attention.

"Pst." A short hissing came from behind me.

"Hey, Genesa." I glanced back with a smile. I had to whisper so as not to disturb the King's speech. "I thought you would be working in the kitchen tonight?"

"I think my mistress has become a bit intoxicated." Her grin had a tinge of mischief in it. "She has been in a good mood all night and shooed everyone away to attend the party instead of our regular duties."

"Is that right?"

"And also the presence of her excellency, the Chief of the Kiffad, Chief Onnahawk," the King was saying, but because I was talking to Genesa, I wasn't paying attention. When he announced the King of Centeria and the maiden of Centeria's famous legend, the metaphorical limelight turned to me.

I froze. "Whoa—what?"

Everyone was looking at me in expectation.

Oh boy. "Uhh..."

"Curtsy," Genesa hissed again.

"Oh!" I exclaimed before sinking into a now-effortless curtsy.

The audience applauded then and I almost rolled my eyes as Genesa merely muffled her laughter.

Once the speeches were over, I took Leila back to our table with her plate-load of fruit.

Except we hadn't even gotten far from the buffet when several people from the crowd intercepted me to ask what seemed like a million questions—about Earth, what it was like, what we did there, what I thought about this world, how I got here. And it wasn't like I could just brush them all off.

Ten minutes later, Leila got bored with the discourse and walked away. I wasn't so pleased myself as even more people gathered around me to ask even more incessant questions left and right, at the same time, on top of each other.

It was heartening that they all seemed interested in me, and at least none of them seemed afraid, but soon, the mass of people thickened so much I could no longer see past the crowd. I was cornered back to the buffet table and getting really hot in the middle of the throng. It was like being hounded by paparazzi.

Genesa was standing behind the table but she could only give me a helpless look.

"So, do you think the Malkens will attack tonight? Tomorrow?"

"I want to see the strange clothes I'd heard about. What are they made of?"

"Do you really have no kings in your world? What is 'car'?"

"Is there a Centerian curse?"

"Do you have special powers? I want you to show us your powers."

"And just what is going on here?" Lessandra's commanding voice boomed over the din and the crowd stopped chattering in an instant.

Apparently, Leila had called on the cavalry to help me out.

The crowd backed away, muttering pardons, and I gave Lessandra and Aella a grateful smile. "You guys."

"You look kind of pale," Aella noted in concern. "Are you okay now?"

"I'm sorry my father had to call attention to you," Lessandra apologized.

I let out a nervous laugh. "Yeah, well, thank goodness for Leila." I watched the pigtailed princess stand up on tiptoes to reach over the table for some crackers. *Thank goodness, indeed.*

27

odd one out

The sky was a dark shade of navy outside the massive skylight windows when the ball began to wind down. I had eaten so much, I was sure I would burst. Leila had dozed off and was stretched out across a couple of chairs at the royal table, and I found myself talking girl stuff with Lessandra and Aella who were also seated at the table. The two of them were taking a little break from dancing.

Aella nudged me. "So Sarah, how's Eleria been treating you?"

Lessandra turned to me with a raised eyebrow as though to see that I answered correctly, in other words, favorably.

Not that she needed to. Eleria was as close to paradise as any place I'd ever been. "Honestly, this is the most beautiful place I'd ever seen," I replied and Lessandra tipped her chin up in approval. I smirked and glanced at Aella. "Lessandra has her own salon. You ought to try it."

Aella shrugged. "Oh, no, I really should be getting back to the tribe soon."

"Oh, come on," I coaxed. "Surely, you can stay longer."

"Come on, Sarah." Lessandra's tone was teasing. "Aella probably can't wait to go back to all those half-naked guys in her tribe."

"Oh, of course." I put my hand to my mouth. "Hey, maybe we should actually just come with you."

And we laughed.

"Besides," Lessandra began with a pointed meaningful look at Aella. "I know at least one person who'll be glad if you stayed here longer." She jerked her chin in the direction of the stage.

Knowing she was referring to Gradd, Aella flushed and shot Lessandra a quick look. "What are you talking about? That's ancient history," she flustered. "That's ancient history," she repeated to me with more conviction.

Somewhat puzzled at her emphasis, I gave her a faint smile. "Sure, okay."

"Hey, maybe you could clear up some things for us," Lessandra's eyes were bright with the potential scandal. "Why did the two of you break up? What happened there?"

Fidgeting in her seat, Aella looked uncomfortable but then her eyes lit up and she shot Lessandra a look. "Oh, I don't know. Wouldn't it be more interesting to talk about you and—" She cleared her throat instead of completing her sentence, nodding her head in the direction of the other side of the platform. She was referring to Scott this time and Lessandra turned scarlet.

Shaking my head in mirth, I looked from Aella to Lessandra on either side of me. "Guys," I cut in, trying to be neutral. "Maybe we can switch to some other topic of conversation?"

Aella and Lessandra met each other's gaze and their expressions turning conspiratorial before they both turned to me.

"Say, what about you, Sarah?" Lessandra prompted. "Have anyone special back home?"

"Yeah." Aella cocked her head. "Or maybe you have a thing for one of the guys you danced with earlier." She looked at Lessandra. "I think she danced twice with Baron Ellingwood, didn't she? He's pretty cute, huh?"

It was my turn to blush. "Uh..."

Good thing the royal trumpets sounded off and King Cornelius stood up.

Saved by the bell!

The King's staff came up to him and accompanied him down the aisle as the people curtsied and bowed again.

"What's going on?" I turned to look.

"Father's retiring for the night," Lessandra breathed, her eyes wide. Then she smiled, almost to herself, and looked up at the balcony to meet the gaze of the conductor, who in turn nodded.

The playing music transitioned back to a waltz and Aella shot Lessandra an exasperated look. "Oh, Lessandra. Not again."

"Again?" I echoed warily. "What's going on now?"

"She does this every time." Aella was shaking her head "I hope you like listening to the waltz, Sarah. Lessandra will now dance with every male in the room. It's like her debutante ball all over again, and over and over and over and over…" she droned on.

"What?" Lessandra asked with a feigned innocent smile.

"Seriously, guys?" I had to ask in ridicule but then I caught Genesa's gaze from the sidelines.

Genesa raised her eyebrows at me and mouthed, *Look out!*

Frowning, my gaze instantly snapped up toward the windows in dread, already watching out for Malken relics. But the night was calm. There was nothing outside the windows. *What?* I wondered and cast a glance around.

Then I spotted what manner of chaos Genesa was possibly referring to.

Gradd was walking over from across the room while Scott walked over from the other side of the room with their paths on a direct collision course to this table. Lessandra and Aella hadn't noticed yet.

I supposed it wasn't a surprising turn of events. It seemed natural that the handsome Princes would ask the beautiful Princesses to dance. It was like prom night all over again, except this time, I was going to be the awkward fifth wheel instead of the fly on the wall.

With a sigh, I glanced over at Leila who was still dozing. I wouldn't even have anyone to talk to.

But I looked up just as the guys arrived at the same time—stopping in front of me and I blinked up at them.

Scott and Gradd looked at each other, down at me, then at each other again, before they each turned to one side.

And Scott held his hand out to Lessandra.

And Gradd held his hand out to Aella.

And the four of them glided toward the dance floor.

I swallowed hard, not entirely aware of the potential trouble we had all dodged, and then settled back to watch the two couples dancing. Genesa waved me over to the buffet table again. I glanced over at Leila, still napping before walking over.

"Close call, my lady?" was her teasing greeting.

"Close what?" I echoed blankly even as I swiped a fruit stick off one of the remaining trays on the table.

"You know what I think?" Genesa went on. "Lord Gradd is just as handsome as Lord Scott. But the latter seems friendlier."

"Scott is friendlier," I agreed, turning to lean against the table to watch them all again. "They all look so good together, don't they?"

Genesa shot me a flat look. "Oh come on, they both like you. Can't you tell at all?"

I hissed. "Don't say that. Lightning might strike us."

"You like Lord Gradd better though, don't you?" Genesa prompted. "I can tell."

I made a face. "No, I don't." But after a pause, my frown deepened. "And even if I did, you so cannot tell."

"Here he comes."

"What?" I turned pale.

Genesa laughed. She was just kidding.

I scowled at her before stating my playful warning. "Do you dare risk the wrath of the Centerian curse?"

She feigned a shiver. "Oh no, will you make me eat your terrible cooking?"

And I had to laugh before I could respond to defend myself.

28

responsibilities

Genesa stopped again, looking past my shoulder. "Oh, here comes Lord Gradd."

"Very funny. You can't fool me twice," I sneered, starting to turn. "Yipes!" I yelped as I really came face to face with Gradd, who likewise jumped in surprise at my surprise, and I stepped back.

"Your majesty." Genesa curtsied away but not before shooting me a mischievous look.

I glared back at her before glancing over sideways at Gradd. "Hey." I nodded my nonchalant greeting.

I hadn't spoken to him in days. It felt like we were back to when I had only just met him.

Awkward.

Except he looked really good tonight. Really, *really* good. In his crisp, navy blue tailored suit with intricate yellow stitching around the cuffs and lapels, he looked a hundred times elegant and genuinely royal.

I had to check myself to slow down my pulse.

"Hey." He cleared his throat. "What was that all about?" He turned to get a drink from the table.

I dismissed it. "Oh, Genesa's just being weird."

"Who?"

"My dressing maid," I relayed. "She's really nice though."

"Oh." Nodding, he finished his drink and then set the glass back down on the table.

"So—" I shrugged.

"So..." Gradd repeated.

I shifted on my feet and wondered what he was doing back here instead of dancing with Aella. I searched the dance floor. Aella was now dancing with Scott while Lessandra was taking a turn with Baron Ellingwood. I supposed Aella had not been exaggerating before about Lessandra's plan to dance the night away.

Gradd and I watched the dance floor for a minute then he turned to me, hesitating about four times before he finally began. "Hey, uh..."

I looked up at him.

"You wouldn't—want to..." He gestured to the dance floor, his forehead creasing. "Would you...?"

"Me?" I wrinkled my nose. "Ah...well...I'm—I'm kinda..." I started to shake my head.

"Tired?" he supplied.

"Yeah, but you know." I waved it away, flustered. "It's fine. I don't...uh..."

Gradd was still nodding. Then after another second's pause, he turned to me again. "So, you want to—?"

"Yeah."

Gradd took my arm and led me out to the dance floor.

The next movement he made seemed to be an instruction on where to put my hands and how to position my arms for the dance. I realized he'd assumed I didn't know how to. I'd mentioned I wasn't an expert but it wasn't like this was my first dance ever.

I wasn't going to bother to correct him but then he started to lead very slowly as if we were in a class.

"Gradd, Gradd," I spoke up and he met my gaze. "I do know how to dance."

He blinked at me. "Oh, sorry."

That made me chuckle as it somehow broke the ice. "They put the crown on your head and everything else goes?"

Gradd shot me a suffering look but his tone was light. "It's been three days. Haven't you picked up any manners yet?"

"Nah, been too busy."

"Oh yeah? Doing what?" His eyebrows rose. "Getting into more trouble?"

I shot him a self-satisfied look. "As a matter of fact, there wasn't any when you weren't around."

Gradd gave me an oh-really look. He looked like he wanted to laugh too.

Grinning, I relaxed, looking past his shoulder.

"So, what did you do while I was toiling away?" His fingers toyed with the tendrils of my hair just by my ear.

I had to stop the shivers running up my spine to respond. "Oh, you know," I relayed almost dismissively as I ran down my list. "Sightseeing, meeting people, exploring the countryside, going to the market, going to picnics, and practicing horse riding. Leila and Starso even helped me plant something in the greenhouse, you should see it."

He looked somewhat surprised. "You've been keeping quite busy."

"Oh," I piped up to add. "And I've been teaching everyone this card game. I could teach you too. It's really fun, I promise. And don't believe whatever Scott tells you about who cheats at cards."

"Sounds like I missed a lot the last three days," Gradd noted with a catch in his voice.

"See, this is what happens when you put your important responsibilities first before having fun." I gave him another teasing look.

A corner of his mouth turned up but his smile didn't quite reach his eyes. "So, you've been doing fine without me. That's...great."

The tone of his voice caught my attention but he looked away so as not to meet my gaze.

Then he said something which I didn't quite hear.

"What?"

"I'm leaving tomorrow."

"You mean, we're leaving tomorrow?" I corrected.

Gradd shook his head. "No. Just me. You're staying here."

I furrowed my eyebrows. "Where are you going?"

"I have to continue on the mission to find the phoenix. I have to do it. I'm the only one left."

"And I can't go because...?" I prompted with my eyebrows raised.

"Because it's dangerous and you'll be safer here," he stated as though it was an obvious fact.

I cocked my head to disagree. "No."

"What?" He finally looked at me but only to give me an odd look since I hadn't seemed to understand that what he'd said wasn't up for discussion.

"No." I shook my head. "I'm coming with you."

"Sarah," he groaned, already sounding tired. "It isn't your place to argue. This is my decision. It's too dangerous for you to come along and it will be safer if you stay here. Besides, it's my kingdom. It's my mission."

"Yeah, but—" I tried to cut in but he stopped me.

"You're staying here and that's final," Gradd declared.

I winced, somewhat taken aback. Apparently, I wasn't allowed to make decisions that would directly impact me. Frowning, I tamped down the urge to get mad. It should have been clear to me right from the start. I was just a lowly peasant and he was the king.

"Sarah?" he prompted after a few moments of silence.

I shrugged, not meeting his gaze. "As you wish, your majesty."

Gradd sighed. "Sarah..."

"Hey, mind if I cut in?" Scott appeared beside us, his cheerful smile contrasting with our dark cloud.

I welcomed his timely interruption. "Of course not." I pulled away from Gradd but he held me fast. I shot him a dark, pointed look and his arms went slack to let me go. Then I turned back to Scott with a soft smile and let him waltz me away.

29

scott

"Gradd's being a real stick in the mud again, isn't he?" Scott couldn't help but prompt as he whirled us around the ballroom.

"Ohh yeah." I rolled my eyes.

"The crown goes on, so does the attitude."

I smirked. "Look who's talking."

Not offended at all, Scott just grinned. His energy was infectious and within a few minutes, I was laughing again.

After our dance, we stepped out onto the balcony, walking past the handful of other people who were making their way back indoors. Being late in the evening, Eleria was a black void. The only thing visible from the balcony was the glittering sea in the distance.

"Leila's already in bed," Scott relayed with a shake of his head. "She wouldn't settle down without a bedtime story. What stories have you been telling her? Princesses who sleep for years and men who climb towers using women's hair?"

"Oh." I had to laugh. "They're just made-up stories from where I come from. They're not real."

He blew out a breath. "Well, I guess that's a relief. I was worried you might turn into a pumpkin at some point during the evening."

I laughed again.

Turning serious, Scott paused for a moment. "Have you thought about what I asked before?"

I'd honestly forgotten. I tilted my head to ask, "What was that?" But as soon as the words left me, the bombshell he had dropped earlier flashed in my brain and my stomach dropped to my toes.

Oh right, of course. Scott was referring to the casual proposal of marriage he had thrown my way.

"I know it's sudden," he admitted soberly. "But we can be betrothed, and when the time is right, you can be my queen."

"I uh..." I was absolutely flustered. This had got to be the most bizarre thing that had ever happened to me. Sure, being transported to a magical planet was one. But now a king was proposing to me? "Scott," I fidgeted evasively. "I didn't think you were serious. Are you?"

His forehead creasing slightly, Scott met my gaze but he didn't look like he wanted to take anything back.

I had to ask the obvious question first. "What about Lessandra?"

A dark cloud crossed Scott's features. "Lessandra's a good kid..."

I read the grief on his face easily enough. "But she reminds you of Princess Leanna, doesn't she?"

Scott had already told me their story. They were in love. There was a war. He had to go. She asked him to stay. He didn't. By the time he came back, it was too late. Leanna had had a weak heart. There was nothing he could have done.

"I'm sorry." I hadn't meant to make him recall all that sadness.

He waved his hand. "It's in the past now." Resolved, he turned to face me. "That's why I need you. You've made me want to live in the now again. I know you're the only one who can make me happy."

Flushing beet red, I bit my lip. I felt like I should kick myself for hesitating for even a split second. Scott was brave, good-looking, distinguished, charming—hell, literally every girl's dream. But then, of course, there was that other obvious matter. "Scott, I'm not from around here, remember? Nobody knows what will happen to me or how long I'll be around."

"But I know you'll be happy here with me. I don't care how long you'll stay. Say yes." His smile crinkled the corners of his urgent, pleading eyes.

My stomach wouldn't stop churning in uneasiness. "Scott...you know I love it here and you're a really great friend. I mean, I don't even know what I would have done without you. I think it's really sweet of you to ask, but given my circumstances, it wouldn't be fair." Rueful, I shook my head. "*I* can't—and possibly nobody else I know will believe I'm the one having to say this but I think...it'll be for the best if we stayed friends."

Scott's smile had faded.

My chest constricted at the deeply disheartened look on him. I felt terrible but I was a hundred percent sure I was right.

After a long moment, Scott let out a sigh. I supposed he also found the reason in my logic. "Alright." But with solemn eyes, he looked at me again. "But if you're still here a couple of months from now, I'm going to try again."

I caught the slight teasing in his tone and let out a chuckle of relief. "Deal."

30

after party

"Da-da-da-dum-dum, dum-dum..." Genesa hummed as she danced with her stack of dishes.

"Hey, weirdo, the party's o-ver." Sitting on the edge of the platform in the ballroom, dangling my legs off one side, I chuckled as I watched her.

Genesa merely hummed louder before disappearing behind the doors leading to the kitchen.

Madame Louisa waved me away as she continued to clear tables. "Go on off to bed, child. It's late."

The guests had all gone home. There was no more music. The ballroom was empty, except for the dozens of staff, bustling around to clean and clear. Lessandra and everyone else had retired for the night but I didn't feel like returning to my chambers. I didn't want to be alone yet.

Especially since decisions had been made regarding where I was supposed to go, or not go as the case may have been. Because I was safe here and it wasn't my place to argue.

I frowned recalling what Gradd had said, mostly because I did understand his point. But if any search party was going to go looking for that damn phoenix, it most definitely was going to have to include me.

Genesa came back out to get another batch of plates to clear away.

Hopping off the platform, I went for the buffet table to swipe a leftover canapé.

"Goodness, are you still hungry?" Genesa asked in disbelief.

"Seeing food makes me hungry," I replied.

"Don't spill anything on your dress," she bid with a shake of her head before she disappeared through the kitchen again.

I made a face down at my outfit and kicked up the bottom frill of the dress. "This is the frumpiest dress I've ever had to wear in my life," I called out so she could hear from the kitchen. "I hate tulle."

"You said you hated dancing too but you seemed to have done a lot of it tonight," Genesa's voice sailed back out.

"Well, it seemed I didn't have much choice." Besides, Lessandra and Aella probably broke every record in the world for most dances tonight.

"Okay, you have got to show me one of your world's dances." Genesa hurried over to take my hand and pulled me away.

"Genesa!" Louisa squawked at her rush. "You are not done."

"I'll be right back!" Genesa waved at her before she led us out to the balcony again.

I shot Genesa an expectant look. "What?"

"Come on then, show me a dance," she coaxed with a prompting wave. "Surely, you have some form of dancing in your world." She hopped up to sit on the balcony railing.

I pursed my lips. "Well. Okay. But don't freak out, okay?"

"I won't."

"Here's my favorite dance. It's called moshpit." I jumped around with the repeated banging of my head as I did a very bad vocal rendition of the opening to one Nirvana song.

"Oh, good heavens!" Genesa cried in alarm, coming forward. "Lady Sarah, your hair!"

Laughing, I stopped and pushed my fallen up-do hair back behind my ear. "Oops! Sorry, I told you you'd freak out."

"That was a dance?" Her eyes were wide in aghast.

"Sure! We have all kinds of dances in my world."

Genesa shook her head. "What a strange world you come from indeed."

I put up my hands in resignation. "Hey, we have slow dances too. It's just hard to demonstrate without a partner."

"May I?" a voice from the door made us both whirl around.

Gradd was standing in the doorway, his tall figure silhouetted by the light coming from inside the ballroom.

"Your majesty." Genesa curtsied away and disappeared in seconds.

"Wait—oh." I frowned and gave Gradd a flat look as he stepped out. "I hope you know you scared her away again."

"Can we talk?" He walked up toward me.

My response dripped with sarcasm. "Why certainly, your majesty. You can do anything you please."

Gradd gave me a disapproving glare. "Don't do this."

"Do what?" I burst out then cut off with a sigh. "You know what, I'm too tired to argue right now."

"I'm not here to argue."

"You always say that and then I always end up shouting." A nerve ticked in my neck in aggravation. "Look, I think you've already said everything that needs to be said here, and obviously, I don't get any input as the decision's already been made, so if that's all then I request to be dismissed."

"Stop that."

"Stop what?" I asked in exasperation.

Gradd flinched. "Stop treating me like I'm...your superior." He cracked his neck, not meeting my gaze. "You've never had to."

"Yeah well, I didn't realize I needed to until tonight. You seem to be the only one in charge." I folded my arms across my chest. "Please. By all means."

Groaning out loud, he began to pace. "Oh my god—I just don't know what to do with you. You're the one who's always saying how you don't want to die and how I'm always putting you in danger. And now, when I'm trying to keep you out of it, you want to dive right in!" He threw up his hands. "I'm sick of being blamed for everything that goes wrong. You're staying right here, where it's safe. I don't want to be responsible for what happens to you anymore."

My eyebrows snapping together, I waved away his reasons. "Don't give me that. You're just trying to get rid of me again. You've been trying to get rid of me since day one and now that you've found your opening, you're taking it. Admit it," I sneered in his face. "You just don't want a nuisance like me hanging around while you do your all-important robot fighting—"

He cut me off by grabbing my arm.

"Ow!" I crumpled.

Gradd had grabbed a little too close to my bandaged wound.

His eyes softened and he loosened his hold immediately. "It hurts, right? It hurts because you damn near lost your arm in the attack at Thorb. It hurts because I wasn't able to protect you." He dropped his hand. "It could have been worse. So much worse, do you understand?"

Almost overwhelmed, I frowned as I understood what he was trying to say.

"If you come with me..." He met my gaze, his eyes intense. "I don't want you to get hurt. I don't know what I..." He lifted his hand as if to touch my face but dropped it right away once more.

Swallowing hard, my pulse started to race again at the confusing rollercoaster of emotions I always seemed to have around Gradd. I had to shut my eyes to focus on the matter at hand before I met his gaze again.

Taking a deep breath, I gave him a steady look. "Gradd, you asked me to trust you. You said you couldn't trust anyone else for my protection. You said the safest place in this world for me is with you. I know you never wanted this responsibility. That's tough because it's yours."

I shook my head in resolve. "But I have a mission too. And you are not just going to leave me here. Is *that* clear?" I stated with the firmest tone I could muster as I stared him down.

Gradd held my even gaze for a long moment before sighing in resignation.

Satisfied by his concession, I nodded. "Good."

He shook his head as though already regretting having caved before turning to leave. "Go get some shut-eye. We leave first thing in the morning. And if you sleep in, I'm not waiting for you either."

I mocked a salute at him. "I'll be there, with bells on."

Pausing in mid-stride, he blinked. "Bells?"

I waved it away. "Never mind."

31

calm before

"Hey." Aella knocked on my door early the next morning.

Still getting ready, I looked over. "Hi." Noting what she was wearing as she'd changed back to her own clothes, the animal skins, and feathers, I grinned. "Couldn't stand satin huh?"

She gave me the same pointed look back. "Speak for yourself."

I was also wearing my own clothes now. I didn't imagine I could go hunting for imaginary fantastical creatures wearing my big, fluffy tulle dress.

I tied my hair into its usual ponytail. "Are you leaving today too then?"

"Yes, but not until later." She sat on my bed. "Lessandra should be here in a few minutes to say farewell."

I beamed a sincerely grateful look. "I really hope we get to spend more time together, you know, when we all come back here."

"Did Gradd say how long you all will be gone for?" Aella asked.

"He never tells me anything." I rolled my eyes. "But the way I figure, at some point, we'll need to take a break, right? We can't possibly just go on an endless search." Sighing, I made a face. "I don't think he even knows where to start."

"Gradd will find a way," Aella commented. "He always does."

With that fond expression on her face, Aella obviously still cared a lot for Gradd, and the two of them made such a perfect match. They deserved each other. A bit of guilt gnawed at me for going on this mission with him as having more alone time with Gradd was not at all what I had planned or even wanted.

If I had a choice in the matter, I would rather relax at Eleria.

But since it was my life on the line, there was no way I was going to skip out on what might finally discover the reason I'd been sent to this world in the first place. I was prepared to go to the ends of this world and beyond if it meant I would find my way back home.

Aella curled her lips in caution. "This mission is pretty dangerous."

I smirked. "Don't worry. I'll be there to protect him."

She burst out laughing.

When Lessandra arrived, she merely sent Leila's regrets since the little princess had been too zonked out from last night, was still sleeping, and couldn't see me off.

"Give Leila a hug for me please," I bid.

I also asked Lessandra to thank her father on my behalf, since given last night's festivities, he too, much like the rest of the kingdom, was still deep in slumber.

Everyone had been so nice to me. Eleria had become my home away from home. It felt a bit sad to be leaving.

"Come back soon," Lessandra bade with a wave.

"Count on it." I mocked a salute. Then taking a deep breath, I started for the door. "I guess I'll see you guys later."

"Hey!" Aella called out and when I glanced back, she shot me a meaningful look. "Stay alive."

I gave her a wink. "No problem."

Gradd was preparing his relic in one of the smaller courtyards. It was too early in the morning, the area was deserted. But I supposed that had been Gradd's intention so as not to attract too much attention nor make a big production out of our departure.

I announced myself as I walked over. "Here I am, the Great Burden of Centeria."

Gradd only looked up for a split second, his tone nonchalant. "Last chance to change your mind, Sarah Peters."

Stopping short, I frowned at the ground, pretending to reconsider.

Gradd shot me a look of disbelief. "You're kidding." He wasn't even in the mood to give me the benefit of the doubt.

I stifled my chuckle behind my hand. "You need to lighten up so bad."

Rolling his eyes in annoyance, Gradd jumped onto his relic in its aircraft form before holding out a hand to help me up.

"Leaving without saying goodbye?"

My eyes lit up as I turned. "Scott," I greeted with a smile. I had assumed that like everyone else, Scott was sleeping in this morning, and it wasn't like I could just go and wake him up.

Walking over, Scott shook his head at me. "I hope you know what you're doing, Sarah." His tone struck me as very big brother-ish.

I hugged him. I was grateful for everything he'd done for me, for being a great friend, and for being a really understanding guy. I knew I'd miss his steady, good-natured humor, but it wasn't like I wouldn't ever be back.

His arms around me, Scott patted my back. "Take care of yourself."

"You too."

"A-hem." Gradd's throat clearing was as irritated as anything.

Glancing up at Gradd, Scott let me go and stepped back. He gave Gradd a regal nod in farewell. "Later Gradd. Don't talk to any relic you don't know."

I stifled another chuckle as I mounted the relic and took my seat.

"Be seeing you, Scott," Gradd bade as the relic promptly took off.

I was waving back at Scott as we flew farther and farther away from Eleria, then the relic suddenly jerked forward to accelerate. "Whoops!" I grabbed the braces on either side of me to hang on.

Out of the corner of my eye, Gradd's scowl was still darkening his face, and I had a sneaky suspicion that he'd sped up on purpose to make me stop waving.

I made a face in helpless exasperation. This was going to be a long trip.

32

the search

"Is this really necessary?" I wiped the perspiration off my forehead.

The hot sun was high in the sky. We'd reached a thick forest and Gradd had transformed the relic back into a robot again, as with the trees in this area about the same height as the relic, it could walk through the woods incognito.

We'd been walking for a while. I had no idea where we were going. I had no idea what we were even looking for.

"Come on, can't I just get down?" I moaned in complaint. "Are you worried that I might run off or that you might step on me?"

For some reason, Gradd had decided that I should sit in the hand of the relic as it walked. In its upright form, we agreed the pilot seat would be too cramped for both of us. The only other option was for me to walk along on the ground but no doubt that would have made it more difficult for Gradd to keep an eye on me.

Gradd didn't answer my question. He'd barely spoken a word since we'd left Eleria.

"Fine." I adjusted my position on the giant mechanical relic hand. "Don't talk to me."

Genesa thought I was insane for insisting on coming along on the mission. Why, instead of staying in Eleria where there were decent beds, and decent food, and she'd said "practically zero possibility of being blown to pieces by scary relics"?

But I was filled with a vague sense of anticipation. If we somehow managed to finally find the phoenix, I might be able to simply ask it to send me back home. Although that certainly begged the question, what the hell was the phoenix anyway? How would we even know if we've found it? Was it like an actual burning bird? A burning bush?

In his pilot seat, Gradd's eyebrows were drawn in determination. He didn't seem to have any doubts or questions. I knew there was no convincing him from undertaking this mission. He only had one thing on his mind and that was finding the phoenix.

Yawning, I leaned against the relic with my forehead against my arm. Having stayed up so late last night with all kinds of anxiety, I was already fatigued. But with the relic making a rocking motion as it walked, I thought if I tried hard enough, I might almost be able to imagine that I was simply lounging on the hammock my dad had put in our backyard.

Except for every time I almost fell asleep, a bump on the ground, a bird chirping, or the crunching of whatever the relic was stepping on, jolted me back awake.

The sun was beginning to dip down in the sky and we were still in the forest.

Blowing out an exasperated breath, I thought I'd ask again. "Gradd, where are we going?" Anxious and antsy combined, I almost felt like I was ready for a Malken relic to drop in our path just so there would be something to do.

"Hey, how do you know we're not lost? Are we going in circles?" I sat up eagerly. "Oh my god—look! That's the same tree we passed an hour ago!" I chattered on mostly to entertain myself. "Why don't we just fly to where we're going again? Don't you think that would be so much faster? Or are we hiding from someone? Are we on Malken territory? Are they watching out for foreign relics?"

After a few minutes of still no response, I frowned, crossing my arms across my chest. "This would be so much less stressful if you talked to me."

"No, we are not lost." Gradd's rapid-fire response was curt. "No, we are not going in circles. No, we are not in Malken territory. And no, we cannot fly, because honestly, I don't know where we're going. And if you don't keep quiet, I can't tell which way to go."

My jaw nearly dropped. "You don't know where we're going? *You* don't know...where we're going," I repeated incredulously. "You don't know where *we're* going—great!" I threw up my hands. "H-How is that even possible?"

"Shh!" he shushed. "What did I just say about keeping quiet?"

Making a face at him, I begrudgingly slumped back in my seat.

When I had insisted on coming along to this mission, I also thought perhaps some of my legendary powers might activate and then maybe I could be of some help. But I was just what I always was—baggage.

Sighing as I lay back on the robot's palm, I watched the tops of the trees whiz by against the sky turning violet with the sunset.

Something moved out of the corner of my eye—it was there, in the trees.

I furrowed my eyebrows. *Was someone watching us?* I thought about calling out to Gradd but then immediately reconsidered. It was probably just my imagination.

But then I saw it again. A big, dark, shadow monkey, jumped from tree to tree, and it was coming closer.

I wondered if there were any scary predator animals in the forest but before I could ask my question, the thing shot out from the trees right above, snatched me from the relic's hand, and took off.

"Hey—!" was all I was able to get out before the creature bolted away with me.

Quiet as the wind and quick, whatever it was, it took a few seconds of a confused daze before it occurred to me that I should yell out for help.

"Gradd!"

Except we were probably already too far away for him to hear.

"Dammit!" I tried to struggle away from the 'monkey' who had thrown me over its shoulder like a sack of potatoes. I kicked and screamed to no avail. "Hey, where are you taking me? Hey! Ow! Who are you? Where are we going? Come on! Ow!"

When we finally stopped in a clearing on the grass, it put me down.

Pushing away hard, I stepped back. "What is this? Where are we?" I squinted to see in the dark. The 'monkey' turned out to be a man, his clothes dirty, and torn, a black bandanna tied around his head.

The scratching of a match light nearly echoed in the darkness of the dense forest. When I looked around, about a dozen or so more of these men emerged from the shadows all around me.

They didn't look like Kiffads. They looked like bandits.

I swallowed hard.

Uh-oh.

33

❧

damsel in distress

"Gradd, come ooon. Get me the hell out of here," I bellowed out. "I know you're out there. Stop messing around, for god's sake! The time to help is nooow!" I continued to struggle against the ropes the bandits had tied my hands and feet with. "Gradd, if you're trying to make a point, it is sooo not funny." I gritted my teeth.

One of the bandits smacked the arm of the bandit who had captured me. "That's one chatty lass you got, buddy."

'Buddy' guffawed as he rubbed his cheek. "She's been at it all night. Scratched my face too."

Seated around the fire, the group of bandits was having what scraps of food they had to eat.

"Say, who's this Gradd fella she keeps callin'?" another one of them asked.

Buddy shrugged as he slurped his bowl of goo. "Prob'ly her boyfriend."

Indignant, I made a face. "Whoa, he is not my boyfriend."

Buddy ignored me and went on. "He was operatin' one of 'em Malken relics."

I blinked hard. "Uh, hello? That wasn't a Malken relic—"

181

"See a lot of 'em flyin' around these parts lately," Buddy went on. "Somethin's up."

"Hey—hello?" I interjected again. "Are you even listening to me? He is not my boyfriend, and anyone who knows anything should be able to tell, that relic was not from Malken."

The man beside Buddy laughed. "Hey look, the little girly's acting tough. That's good. Feisty ones usually fetch a good price."

Blood rushed up to my face.

Ohhh...this is so not happening right now.

"'Ey look, she finally shut up," the first man said.

I glared at him, wishing I could shoot laser beams out of my eyes.

The man pushed up from his crouch on the ground and walked up to me with an arrogant sneer. "Are you scared, little girl?"

"Of you? You're kidding," I tried to scoff in ridicule, tried to distract from the fact that my knees were shaking. I was hoping that I could keep it together and act tough until Gradd came to get me—which he'd better. And soon.

"Aw, you're not afraid?" He feigned a sympathetic look.

"No. Look, it's really getting cold and I'd appreciate it if—"

He drew a knife and held it up to my face.

Freezing still, I gasped, my eyes widening.

"Now are you afraid?" he prompted with a slimy grin.

I swallowed hard once more. "No..." I managed to say without my lip trembling. "Look, you really don't know who you're dealing with here. I'm a powerful being," I claimed with a regal nod.

His eyes darkened and he stepped back.

"I am," I assured, my nose high in the air. "I'm not even from this world. I come from another world on the other side of the sun. It's called Earth. And believe you me, nothing in this world is scarier than what we have back there."

"Oh really?" Already smirking in disbelief, he glanced back at the others. "What's that?"

The rest of them were watching with interest, but Buddy stood up and walked up to us. "What kind of shit you babblin' now?"

"We-we-we have...uh..." Nervous, I racked my brain for the scariest things I could think of. "Traffic congestion, and pollution, like, you can't even step out of your house and breathe clean air anymore. A- and global warming! The ice caps are melting, animals going extinct —it's a whole thing. And...and high school! That's the scariest thing on Earth!" I shook my head in caution. "Like, you have no idea."

The first man backed away another step. The odds were he probably didn't understand a word I said, but I was coming off crazy enough, he wanted to distance himself.

"That's right." I nodded again, trying to hide my relief as they seemed to at least be distracted by my lies. "And you better let me go now. Or else I'll have to—to—demonstrate my incredibly scary special powers."

Buddy wasn't fazed. "Oh yeah?" He propped his hand on the tree beside my head as he moved closer. His foul breath was on my face, I turned away with a wince.

"I bet you're all kinds of special," he breathed with that sly smirk.

"Eewww! Come on!" I yelled out in protest, trying my best to edge away from him despite the ropes that bound me. "Just leave me alone, for the love of—"

There was a loud "Oof!" of one of the other men groaning aloud.

Buddy's attention snapped over and I followed his bewildered gaze.

Tall, dark, and menacing as he stalked forward, Gradd had tossed one of the bandit men away like he was a mere sack of grains.

Alerted, the rest of the bandits stood up.

Buddy's eyes widened. "Who the hell—?"

"Gradd!" My pulse raced as the giant wave of utter and complete relief washed over me.

Gradd went to work beating up the bandits and turning the camp-site into a royal mess. Things got kicked around. People got thrown around.

"Gradd?" Buddy repeated in disbelief.

"Yes," I replied haughtily.

"Your boyfriend?"

In my fuming rage, I managed to struggle one foot free from my bindings. "He's not my boyfriend!" I kicked Buddy in the groin and he doubled over in pain. "Hah! How do you like me now?"

Several of the bandits had run off while some of them lay unconscious on the ground. Gradd still had three more on him. He hit one. He kicked one. The one left was the man with the knife.

He swung the knife at Gradd.

Gradd wove away.

The man lunged but Gradd caught his arm and there was a loud crack as he twisted.

I winced. "Ooh! That must have hurt. That's right, ladies and gentlemen, that was a broken arm," I feigned the cadence of a sports commentator.

Gradd looked over at me in ridicule.

But the one he kicked stood up again. The last thug standing.

"Watch out!" I called out in warning.

Gradd turned in time and sucker-punched him right in the face.

The man flopped over, almost right onto another pile of other fallen bandits.

"Ooh!" I wrinkled my nose. "And that's a ten from the judges." I almost wished I could applaud him. "All in all, ladies and gentlemen, a good fight. Good night and safe travels."

Gradd let out a breath before he came over to cut me free from my ropes.

With an amused smirk, I met his gaze. "Well, what do you know? You saved me."

"Let's get—" Gradd grabbed my hand.

"Not so fast."

I almost gasped.

Buddy was back on his feet.

So were three of his friends.

Buddy tossed his knife up in the air and caught it with a sly smile. "Now kid," he spoke to Gradd. "Why don't you just leave your little girlfriend there and we won't hurt you—much."

Dark with displeasure, Gradd turned to face him.

"Gradd," I warned under my breath from behind him.

Gradd held out his arm to keep me back.

Buddy chuckled in his throat. "Are you up to fighting us, junior?"

"We can just run away, Gradd—" I was saying when someone came up to grab me from behind and I gasped as he dragged me backward, his sharp knife pointy at my throat. "Okay, not now."

Gradd whirled around and his jaw clenched.

Buddy sneered. "Give it up, kid."

"Gradd," I called out.

Looking around as if measuring up his opponents, Gradd held both hands out to his sides.

"Gradd," I insisted.

"I know, I know!" he snapped. "Would you just shut up? I'm handling this."

"Handling?" I echoed in annoyance. "I have a knife in my neck!"

"Be quiet!" Gradd barked. "This is all your fault."

"*My* fault?" My jaw dropped in disbelief. "You were supposed to be watching out for me, you egomaniac."

"Well, as I'm sure you know, you sure don't make that job a walk in the park," Gradd retorted.

"Oh, I'm sorry." I made a face in offense. "Mr. Big Deal can't handle a simple babysitting task."

"For the love of god, shut up!" Gradd threw up his hands. "Why do you always have to be such a goddamned irritating—" Gradd stopped short and lunged at Buddy, who totally didn't see it coming, and he almost catapulted back with another "Oof!"

At the same time, I elbowed the man behind me and he doubled over. I kicked him in the shins and he dropped his knife. We both scrambled to snatch it up, but this particular man was scrawnier than the rest and with a scream, I pushed him away so I could grab the knife.

I held it to his face. "Hah!"

Scrawny glared at me but probably figured he couldn't take me on without his weapon. He backed up and ran away.

Gradd knocked the other three bandits down but not without taking a few hits himself.

I winced as he took each hit.

Then Buddy, knife in hand, emerged from the shadows to sneak up behind Gradd.

My eyes widened in alarm. "Gradd, behind you!" I yelled out my warning but just as Gradd turned, Buddy jabbed his knife, getting Gradd in the shoulder.

Gradd groaned out loud, at the same time as he clocked Buddy in the face again, making him launch backward and to the ground.

I ran toward Gradd. "Let's go, let's go!" I pulled on his other arm so we could escape before the other bandits could recover.

34

⤬

first aid

We ran through the woods. I assumed Gradd was leading us to where he'd parked the relic. It took a while before I was sure there wasn't anyone following us and we slowed down.

Gradd was deathly pale.

"Oh my god, oh my god," I mumbled, trying not to fall apart myself. "Where's the relic, Gradd?"

He gave a little nod in that direction before his knees buckled.

"Oh man, you better not die, okay? Do you hear me?" I draped his good arm over my shoulder so I could help him to walk.

A glint of metal in the distance hinted at the relic's location set beneath some tall trees and we hurried over. I settled Gradd down against the relic's feet. Straightening back up, I wrung my hands out, pacing back and forth in a panic. "Shit, shit, shit."

The knife was still buried in Gradd's shoulder.

I didn't know what to do. Was I a doctor? I wasn't even a girl scout!

He groaned.

"Gradd." I knelt beside him. "Gradd? Are you okay?" I asked and stopped short to shake my head. "Of course, you're not okay," I scolded myself. "You just got friggin' stabbed. Focus, Sarah!"

"Sarah—" Gradd coughed.

"Yes, yes, what?"

"The knife." He leaned forward so I could have a look. "How bad is it?"

Making a face, I peered closer at his shoulder. There was only a little bit of blood, but to me, the knife was wedged way in there. "I don't know. There's not much blood. I guess they didn't hit any—"

"You'll have to pull it out."

My jaw dropped. "What?" Aghast, I shook my head. "I can't! I don't know how to—no, no, no, I can't do that."

He grabbed my hand. "You have to. I won't be able to do it myself. Now, come on, you can do this." He coughed again. "Just pull it straight out, the way it came in."

Wrinkling my nose, my heart pounded in my chest. "Oh, god, seriously...?" Tentative, I put one hand on the knife but then I couldn't move. Breathing heavily, the rest of me felt frozen in horror. "Gradd...I can't do this," I whispered. "I can't. I can't. I can't. Oh god. What if I make it worse? What if—"

"Sarah, look at me!" Gradd barked.

I jumped at the startle but I met his gaze.

He held my gaze. "You can do this. I know you can. You are so much braver and more capable than you give yourself credit for." His eyes flickered as if he was trying very hard not to pass out.

I furrowed my eyebrows in another self-reprimand. I wasn't the one with the knife in my back and I was the one needing the comforting?

Focus, Sarah!

Blowing out a slow breath, I steeled myself, turning my attention back to the huge-ass knife embedded in his back.

"It's just a knife," I muttered to myself as if to dissolve its power over me. "It's just a knife. I've chopped carrots and celery hundreds of times. No problem." I grasped the knife firmly in both hands. My heart was still pounding in my ears. "Oh god. Oh god. Here I go—" With another deep breath, I pulled.

Gradd grunted out loud.

I opened my eyes, not realizing I had closed them, to see that the knife was in my hands and out of his shoulder. Tossing the dagger aside in relief, I blew out another huge deep breath. "Shit, I did it."

My eyes widened at all the blood and my stomach nearly turned in nausea.

Gradd gave me a weak smile. "Bandages," he mumbled before passing out.

I jumped to catch him. "Holy crap, Gradd!"

Genesa had sent a care package along with us and I was able to clean and bandage up Gradd's shoulder.

Short of including a step-by-step visual guide, Genesa had efficiently labeled the several items in the first aid kit. She must have figured we'd definitely need it.

It felt like days but pretty soon the work was done. The bandage wasn't perfect but I was hoping it would at least slow or stop the bleeding. Once I'd laid him back against the relic, Gradd was sleeping like a rock.

I collapsed on the grass, my throat raw from trying not to cry. He had been right. I shouldn't have come along. If I hadn't insisted on coming along, this wouldn't even have happened.

Turning to check on him again, I frowned at the cuts and bruises on his face. I didn't even have time to tend to them yet. I watched his breathing. He was breathing—that was good, at least. He was fine for now but he wasn't going anywhere for a while. Neither of us was.

Oh, good job, Sarah. I sighed again. I was so going to be nice to him tomorrow.

I lay back flat on the ground and watched the trees above us sway in the breeze. The sky was getting light. I closed my eyes for a second.

35

starting a fire

I woke up with a start to a low, steady beating. I sat up and looked around.

The light of a new day filtered through the branches of the tall trees surrounding our little clearing.

His eyes still closed, Gradd hadn't moved.

A bit groggy, I stood up to look for breakfast in Genesa's care package. I wondered if somehow she had packed a steaming hot cup of cocoa in there.

"You're awake." His raspy voice drew my attention.

My eyes widened as I hurried over. "*You're* awake. How're you feeling?" I put my hand on his forehead to make sure he wasn't running a fever. "You feel warm."

Gradd reached his hand up to feel my forehead. "No, you must be freezing."

"I'll be fine." Waving it away, I rummaged for the flask of water and helped Gradd take a sip. "Here."

He motioned for me to sit beside him. "Come here, sit down."

I hesitated for a moment but then sat down.

With Gradd's good arm, he pulled his cloak over my shoulders. "You've been out all night. You're going to catch a cold."

With a shiver at his warmth, I realized how cold I actually was.

He gave me a small smile. "See?"

"I have to get breakfast." I started to get up again but he stopped me.

"You can get it later. I'm not hungry yet."

"Well, I am," I pointed out and tried to get up again.

Gradd pursed his lips. "Would you please sit still for a second? Do you want to upset my wound?"

With a guilt-ridden frown, I sat back down without another word. I didn't know what else to say.

"Sarah." Gradd's tone changed. "Look at me."

I wasn't going to but he tipped my chin toward him.

"This wasn't your fault." He peered at my face and shook his head. "It wasn't, okay?"

"Yes, it was!" I insisted in helpless exasperation. "It's always my fault. Nothing good has ever happened since I got here and you can't argue with that. You've seen every horrible thing so far. And now, look! Look what I've done to you." I gestured to him. "You can't tell me it's going to stop. As long as I'm here, it'll never be safe. Not for you. Not for anyone."

"Hey, hey, take it easy." For some reason, Gradd started to chuckle.

I narrowed my eyes at him. "Oh great, do you think this is funny? I feel horrible and you're laughing at me."

"I'm not laughing at you," Gradd corrected with another shake of his head. "It's just...I can't believe what I'm hearing. You actually sound concerned about me."

I frowned again. "Well, I am, dammit. Why is that so hard to believe?"

"Sarah, given our very, very short history..." Gradd trailed off and met my gaze. "Well, I guess a lot's happened since we first met."

I huffed. Boy, was that ever an understatement.

"Look, you don't have to worry about me," Gradd assured. "I'll always be here to protect you. I mean, who else is self-loathing enough that they can put up with your nagging?"

I resisted the urge to roll my eyes but he caught me. He looked like he was going to laugh again but then he stopped short, lurching forward with a groan.

"Oh my god, what is it?" I squeaked.

Closing his eyes, he clenched his jaw to mask his pain.

Eyes widening in worry, I started to get up again. "I should get—" But he caught me around the waist.

"Don't leave. I just—" He took a deep breath. "I just need to rest."

I hesitated again but then resigned. Sitting back down, Gradd propped himself against my shoulder.

His eyes closed, even rest couldn't soften his face more than a slight. His jaw was still set, his forehead still creased in worry or perhaps pain.

I lifted my hand intending to brush his hair back from his forehead, but I stopped short, self-conscious. Sitting back with another sigh, I turned away to gaze off into the shady forest.

Staring at the pile of wood, dry weeds, and leaves in front of me, I dropped the two sticks I was holding in annoyance. "Okay, this—this is beyond me." I stepped back from the pile, exhausted and defeated.

Gradd was already being very patient as he tried to instruct me how to make a fire but it wasn't going very well.

It was so much more work than I'd thought. It seemed I had to gather about half of the trees in the forest before I was even able to pick out the suitable dry ones. I tried rubbing rocks together. I tried stones. Nada. Zilch. Zip. Still no fire.

"Oh Sarah," Gradd groaned with a shake of his head as he stood up. "There's no hope for you if you give up."

"Hey!" I jumped to his side in alarm. "What are you doing?"

"Starting a fire."

He disguised a groan by clearing his throat. I made him lean on me for support. "You're such a stubborn ass," I chided even as I helped him reach down. "You're going to tear your wound."

"We'll freeze to death if I don't make a fire," Gradd rationalized.

Eight seconds. It took him about eight seconds to start the fire I'd been attempting for what felt like eight hours.

"There," he announced.

"Show off." I scoffed before I led him back to his seat. "Alright." I blew out a breath. "Now can you stop fidgeting so I can finish this?"

Aside from the freezing cold of the forest, my tending to the cuts on his face had necessitated the fire. It had been very difficult to do so without much light before.

"Ow," Gradd moaned when I applied a cold cloth to the bruises on his face.

"Quit being such a baby," I scolded.

"Oh, now I'm a baby?" He sounded amused. "You were all concerned about me this morning."

I rolled my eyes before drawling, "Oh, the knife in your back you don't mind, but this tiny cut on your eyebrow is the end of the world?"

He made a face but said nothing more.

"I thought so." I huffed, self-satisfied. "Now, hold still."

Except now, he was just watching me. And the way he was watching me was completely unnerving.

I moved the cloth to his bruised jaw and he winced.

It made me wince too. "Sorry," I mumbled. "You know, I'm really not good at this, obviously."

He was still watching me. "I think you're doing great."

His eyes seemed so clear and earnest—and amazed. I had trouble looking away.

"Right," I mocked, dropping my gaze back down to his bruised jaw.

It occurred to me that if Aella had been here, with all their suitable training, she'd probably have known exactly what to do with Gradd's wounds. She'd have known how to make a fire. Heck, she could probably have been able to build an entire condo from the trees in the forest. And they'd be safe.

I couldn't help a frown.

"What's the matter?" Gradd had noticed my thoughts wandering.

I blinked. "Huh? Nothing."

He narrowed his eyes at me in concern. "Those men last night, they didn't hurt you, did they?"

"Oh." My eyes lit up. "Nah, I was too tough for them." I dismissed it with a grimace, trying to make light of it. I was relieved Gradd had arrived when he did. "Besides, I probably kept whining for hours straight. They couldn't stand me."

Gradd smirked. "Glad I missed that."

"Oh, you've had plenty of it," I reminded him. "I just wish I could have defended myself more, you know? I can barely even throw a decent punch. I should make a note to study self-defense when I get back home," I added casually before I realized what I was saying and my expression dimmed.

I guessed it was too optimistic to be making plans for what I would be doing 'when' I got back home. I didn't know when that would be or even if it was at all possible.

Gradd gave me a long look. "Do you miss your home?"

I met his somber gaze. It was the first time he asked me that.

"I mean, it must've sucked," he went on. "One moment, you are safe at home and the next thing you knew, you were in a totally different world."

Pursing my lips, I had to admit, "Well, it did suck at first. And I do miss home a lot. I miss my family and my friends. But, I figure given how much worse off it could have been for me—" I shrugged, rationalizing while trying to concentrate on what I was doing. "It hasn't been so bad, I guess."

Gradd nodded. "So then, it wouldn't be so bad if...you stayed here?"

A bit distracted by refreshing the cold cloth, I looked up at him. "What do you mean?"

"Well, say for example..." He looked away in deep thought. "If someone were to ask that you stay here..."

I blinked, taken aback. Never go home? Stay in Anthuria forever? No more electricity? No more TV? No more family? Obviously, my first order of business, since arriving here and until now, was first and foremost, finding a way to get back home. It had honestly never occurred to me to stay. It was unthinkable.

I must've frowned again because Gradd read my mind. "You couldn't, could you?" he said rather than asked.

"Oh, don't get me wrong." I waved to amend. "It's not like I regret coming here. Anthuria's a beautiful world with good people." I shrugged again. "But I don't belong here. I have to go home. I need to." I paused with a brisk shake of my head. "In any case, I don't think that's up to me."

He kept nodding. "I see," was all he said.

36

fates

The fire burned steady all through dinner and all I had to do was feed it a couple of dry branches every so often. After dinner, I set Gradd up to get some rest and he slept. Sitting back against the relic myself, I let out a huge breath. Getting a déjà vu of last night, I had worked all day again. I certainly barely got this much exercise at home so I was pretty drained. It didn't take much for me to pass out.

I dreamt I was kissing Gradd.

Waking up with a start, I sucked a breath in, my heart pounding in my chest. I had fallen asleep on the ground with Gradd's cloak bundled under my head like a pillow.

Still lying down, I blinked hard, trying to get my bearings.

It was still dark but the fire had dimmed.

I blew out a slow, steadying breath. *What the hell kind of dream was that?*

When I looked across the fire, I met Gradd's gaze and winced in shock.

He was awake.

My pulse raced. *Oh jeez, please tell me I wasn't sleeptalking this time.*

Panicked for a second, I forced a smile. "H-hey, what are you doing up?" Keeping my tone casual, I rolled to one side to face him.

Gradd shrugged. "Watching you sleep."

"What?" I ridiculed. "Why?"

"It's the only time I can get a word in edgewise." He teased me with a smile.

I was too fresh out of my dream to be immune to his gorgeous smile. Swallowing hard, I willed my heartbeat to slow down and let out a nervous laugh. "Yeah, right."

Pushing up on my elbows, I tilted my head to one side. "What *is* that?"

"What's what?"

Some manner of vibration was coming from beneath me. It was also what I had woken up to this morning, that slow and steady beating that seemed to come from within the ground. "The...vibrations in the ground? Do you feel that?"

"You can feel them?" Gradd's eyes lit up in surprise.

"What are they?" I wanted to know.

Gradd's gaze narrowed in the recall. "My father used to tell me stories about the legend when I was young," he relayed. "He said that the reason why the phoenix was a very powerful creature, more powerful than practically anything in Anthuria, was exactly because it was alive." He cocked his head. "He said that if I listened closely, I would hear its heart beating throughout our land. Of course, I always thought he was exaggerating because I never heard anything—"

"Until now," I finished in wonder. "Oh." I stopped again in realization. "So, that's what you were following yesterday? Well, why didn't you just say so? I would have shut up."

Gradd had to stifle his sudden chuckle. "Oh, I highly doubt that."

His knowing statement made me laugh too.

Okay, fine, so he was probably right.

With that gorgeous smile widening, Gradd gave me a look that seemed to say 'You make me laugh like nobody else can.'

My heart skipped another beat and I cleared my throat, averting my gaze. "S-so, how much longer do you think we need to be going on?" I was trying to switch to a neutral topic of conversation.

"We're getting closer, I think. Although I have to admit, I'm not that enthusiastic," Gradd added with a slight shake of his head.

Curious, I furrowed my eyebrows. "You're not? Why?"

"Why?" he echoed with another exasperated laugh. "Well, because..." His shoulders lifted in helpless defeat and he looked to one side. "If we find the phoenix, there's a good chance that you'd probably..."

My eyes lit up in hope as I eagerly finished his sentence again. "Get home? Do you really think so?" But I was puzzled by his tone. "Um, why is that a bad thing?"

"Oh, it's not bad exactly." He shrugged again. "It's just that I—well..." The brief wistful look he gave me made my stomach somersault, and somehow, I knew before he even said it. "I don't think I want you to go...just yet."

With an incredulous look, I tried to laugh it off. "Sure, of course. You're being ironic, right?"

Closing his eyes for a moment, he seemed annoyed with himself. He instantly corrected, "Sorry, what I meant to say was I *don't* want you to go." Then he took a deep breath. "I want you to stay...Sarah. I'm—asking."

My eyes widened. "What?"

His voice was solemn. "Look, I know it's probably bad timing. Or maybe it isn't since none of this would do any good if you'd already gone. But I wanted you to know how...unbelievably lucky I feel that you've come into my life." A shadow crossed his face. "Every morning, I wake up afraid you'd have disappeared. And every time, I'm always so relieved to find that you're still here. With me." His lopsided smile widened again. "Sarah, you've made me so—"

I held up my hand. "Stop." I frowned in worry. "Stop saying that. You're-you're injured." I started to pace. "You're delirious. You don't know what you're saying."

Gradd was watching me with a bemused look. "Yes, I do."

"Gradd, this is crazy." My chest constricted. This was exactly what

I had been trying to avoid. I wasn't supposed to get involved with these people. I didn't even belong in this world. "I mean, come on. It's not—we can't—it's just... It's not meant to be." I threw up my hands in conclusion.

"Wait." His eyebrows furrowed. "Are you talking to me about fate? I'll tell you about fate." His eager tone resolved. "One day, I was trying to escape some relics in a marketplace when I tripped over something. That something turned out to be a person, who turned out to be the savior from my kingdom's legends. It was you. Now tell me, how could you have happened to be exactly where I was that night? Why would the phoenix appear in your bedroom of all the bedrooms in your world? How much more meant to be does it have to be?"

I stopped pacing and let out a huge sigh. "You don't understand."

He shot me a questioning look. "What don't I understand?"

I gave him a pointed look. "I know about Aella."

Gradd looked surprised. "Aella?"

"Yes." I nodded in exasperation. "Aella. Chief Onnahawk. You two were in love. And I know you two were supposed to get married or something, except Agarpa had a bad prophecy about it. But she was wrong, wasn't she?" I prompted with a knowing look. "All that stuff about everything falling apart, she was just referring to me, wasn't she?"

Gradd looked at me but he didn't deny anything.

I made a show of throwing up my hands again. I was right.

"I don't see what difference that makes." Gradd's forehead was creased in determination. "Whatever I felt for Aella, it's in the past. She's not the one I want." He moved to get up from his seat.

"Whoa! Easy." I jumped in alarm to help him straighten up.

Those brilliant green eyes were gazing down at me. "I want you, Sarah."

The timbre in his voice saying those words made me shiver. Having to support his weight, my arms were already around him.

When he raised his hand to touch my face, my pulse raced faster.

He brushed my hair back, those strong fingers sliding into my hair from the nape of my neck. He studied my eyes intently before he spoke again. "I've never met anyone else who could make me feel this way."

"I—" I almost lost all rational thought. But then sanity kicked back in and I shook my head. "No, no, no, no, this is—this is impossible. I could be going home in a week, three days, maybe even less!" I wrinkled my nose in frustration. "I told Scott the same thing—"

Gradd dropped his hand. "You told Scott what?"

Flustered, I blinked to dismiss it. "Nothing. It's not important—I mean, what I mean is—the important thing is," I began again, my tone resolved. "This is so not the time for any kind of—" I stopped with a frown, unable or perhaps unwilling to label it. "And even if I wanted to—I just—I just don't see how this is going to work out, Gradd."

"You're just afraid—"

"Of course I'm afraid!" I cried out. "We don't know what's going to happen to us. And this isn't the sort of thing people should enter into on a whim. There's consequences and feelings. You can't just choose to forget. At least *I* can't."

"You're afraid you'll get hurt when you have to leave?" Gradd restated and his smile seemed haunted. "What about me? I don't even want to think that far ahead about how I'll feel when you're gone. I just want now. Today. You're here. I'm here. That's enough. I know I can make you happy." Lifting his hand again, he turned my chin up to him as if he couldn't get enough of looking at my face.

"Gradd, you have a kingdom to rebuild." Staring up into those deep green eyes, I struggled to stay on point. "We have a mission and this kind of distraction is not going to help. There are people waiting for both of us to get back. This just isn't the time." Averting my gaze, I heaved a big sigh. "There's probably about a million reasons I can think of why we shouldn't do this."

Gradd's gaze had dropped to my mouth. "Then stop thinking." With his husky words, he bent his head and the next thing I knew, his lips covered mine.

I had expected to be shocked, stunned, uncomfortable—except Gradd's kiss was so tender. I felt light and warm and alive. It was like a million fireworks set off within me. I could feel his heartbeat. I felt mine. I felt the phoenix too. He pulled me closer to him, deepening the kiss, waiting for me.

I wanted to. I really, really wanted to. But that fact just made alarm bells ring in my head. We shouldn't be doing this. What if everything fell apart? I couldn't deal with having this much to lose. I wouldn't be able to handle it. My chest constricted again, and already shaking my head, I pulled away.

Gradd looked pained as he dropped his hands again.

"We can't." Distressed, I backed up. "We just can't."

He was looking at me, and his expression which started confused, dejected, turned to anger and annoyance.

"I'm so-I'm so sorry—"

"Please," Gradd cut in, his expression hardening. "I don't need to hear about what we should and shouldn't do anymore. I know being the Centerian legend comes with its set of mystical instincts but maybe I've given you too much credit. You barely have the courage to trust yourself. You don't even trust what you feel."

His scorned gaze met mine. "All you want to do is live in a world with all these rules you've made up, where you think no one can hurt you. But you'll never be happy there because you know what you are?" He shook his head. "You're a coward, Sarah. You don't deserve to be the legend of Centeria."

My jaw had already dropped. Tears stung my eyelids. Gradd stepped away, settling against the foot of his relic again. He rested his head back and closed his eyes.

I could only stare at him.

Coward, echoed in my head.

My chest constricting again, I wanted to say something to my defense. But my heart had dropped to my toes. I was afraid of what else he might say. Perhaps other stark truths he had locked up inside of him. I really was a coward.

"I suggest you go to sleep now." Gradd didn't open his eyes with his brusque instruction. "So we can get an early start tomorrow and get this over with as soon as possible."

My vision blurred as I lay back down. *I'm a completely horrible, terrible person.*

I squeezed my eyes shut as another rush of tears threatened to spill. Swallowing past the lump in my throat, I reached up and tossed Gradd's cloak away from under my head before curling back on the ground.

I never should've come with him. I should never have come here.

The ground responded with the beating getting stronger, so strong the ground must be trembling. It was as if the ground shared my pain.

Somebody help, I thought in fervent hope. *Somebody help me get back home. Please.*

37

found

The sunlight warmed my skin. Squinting when I opened my eyes, I held my hand up to shield my eyes from the bright light.

Muffled sounds of people laughing made me sit up. I was at the dusty dugout in our neighborhood and the game was on. Everything seemed so bright but as I stood, I made out several of my friends on the field.

"Batter up!" Jamie Carter was always the catcher.

Someone walked up from the bleachers and I recognized Ena's carefree strides. She swung her bat around as she walked to the plate.

"Ena," I whispered.

As if she heard me, Ena turned to look and waved me over with a big smile. "Hey, Sarah! Hurry up! The game's already started without you."

My spirits lifting, I smiled. I was...home...? Finally! I'd gotten back home. I ran toward the field. "Wait for me!" I waved back at her.

"Come on, Sarah!" Ena called again. "We don't have all day!"

Nodding in acknowledgment, I ran faster. But instead of getting closer, the dugout seemed to get farther and farther away. I tried to run even faster. Sweat poured off me as the heat emanating from the ground made everything hazy and in slow motion.

"Ena, I'm coming!" I called out again.

I happened to look up just as a Malken relic appeared on the horizon from out of nowhere and my eyes nearly popped out of my head in alarm. Malken relics always looked so much scarier than the Centerian ones.

The relic took a step forward and the ground trembled.

Breathing heavily, I skidded to a stop.

The relic took another step, and this time, the ground beneath me opened up as it literally swallowed me.

"Ena!" I cried as I fell through the darkness.

But the fall was short.

I landed with a hard thump on the floor of a dark chamber that seemed eerily familiar.

My pulse raced. I don't know how I knew, but I knew. I was in that room in the Malkens' flying fortress. The room from before.

Two men were walking toward the door, on their way out, but they both turned to look over at me.

The bald guy raised his eyebrows in surprise.

But the other one...

I swallowed hard in dread.

His grin at me was sly. "There you are." His eyes narrowed as he looked at me...through me...

I woke up with another gasp. But sitting up with a jerk filled my eyes red and I crumpled back to the ground in intense, searing pain. I tried to hug myself to make the pain go away but it was little use.

My breathing labored, I opened my eyes to look across the embers of the fire where Gradd was still asleep. With all the energy I could muster, I dragged myself over to him.

We had to get out of there. They were coming. I knew it.

They were coming for us.

For me.

Reaching my hand out to poke Gradd's arm, I nudged him twice. But I must have been weak as hell and he was so deeply asleep that he didn't even notice.

Another sharp surge of pain shot through my body and I curled up again with a loud groan.

That's when I felt them.

The ground trembled. Except for this time, I knew it wasn't the phoenix.

The Malken relics were here.

I had to wake Gradd up.

I pulled myself up enough in an attempt to use my entire weight to nudge Gradd before collapsing back to the ground.

Gradd stirred. "What the—?" he muttered before he saw me on the ground. "Sarah, what—" Eyes widening, he stopped in alert upon noting that my face was twisted in pain. "What's happened?"

I was a vegetable. I took a deep breath. "They're...here..." was all I was able to get out.

"Oh shit," Gradd cursed. He scooped me up off the ground and, leaving everything else at the camp, climbed us up to the pilot seat of his relic as fast as he could. The relic mechanism came alive with a rumble and we took off, even if I pretty much couldn't move.

I saw nothing but the sky. The deep blue sky with white puffs of clouds. The sun was rising from one end of the horizon.

There was a crash and Gradd turned sharply to the right. He grunted and groaned as he began to fight it—them.

I could tell he was having trouble moving around because I was cramping up the pilot's seat. The only good thing was that, at least, I was still conscious.

I have to help him.

Recalling that day the Malkens had attacked Thorb when I was outside the castle, I narrowed my eyes. There had been birds in the trees, and when I'd whirled around, there was something...

"Gradd," I tried to speak but my voice was likely no louder than a whisper.

Gradd's face was contorted in anger, his face red, his eyebrows furrowed.

I tried to tug at his sleeve.

"Stay still, Sarah," Gradd ordered, keeping his focus on battling the enemy. "We'll be fine."

We took a hit and Gradd groaned in frustration.

I winced. I had to tell him. "Gradd..." I pulled his head down, his ear close to my mouth so he could hear me. "Fly."

Gradd shot me a look, and almost as instantaneously, the relic transformed around us. Suddenly, we were flying in the open-air relic beast.

As the Malken relics flew to catch up with us high above the trees, they materialized out of thin air. Three battle relics were now clearly visible. It was just as I thought. Their cloak technology didn't work when their relic was in flight.

Gradd shot me a staggered but amazed look.

I tried to smile at him and hold on at the same time, but as it turned out, I could only do one thing at a time. I began to slide off the relic.

"Sarah!" Gradd grabbed me as we swooped down low.

Quickly landing the relic, Gradd set me down near the base of a large tree so he could go back to fighting unconstrained. He touched my face. "I'll be right back," he bid before taking off again to fight the relics.

But the relics didn't want to fight Gradd. All three monstrous relics flew straight in my direction. I started to heave again as they came closer.

I could barely move. They were going to crash right on top of me.

Gradd's relic skidded to a stop in front of me. "Hey, your fight is with me!"

He fought them, clawed at them, and succeeded in downing one, but there were two more.

Back on solid ground, the Malken relics had turned back into nothingness and Gradd was taking fatal hits.

Groaning out loud with my last ounce of energy, I crawled away from the tree. I figured if I could lure the relics toward me, Gradd might be able to track them and then possibly disable their cloaking system.

It worked.

Gradd smacked the closest one out of thin air, making the still-invisible relic catapult back at the force, knocking down trees in its path until it crashed to the ground miles away.

Bracing my hands on my knees, I tried to breathe. I was on the edge of a cliff. Peeking over the side, the river waters raged below—way, way below the very, very high cliff.

There was still one more relic to fight and this one wouldn't take the bait and fly off. Its mission was to get me.

Gasping, I very unsuccessfully tried to run away.

"Leave her alone!" Gradd jetted in, sunk his weapon into the invisible relic, and the Malken relic materialized. With its cloaking ability disabled, Gradd could finally see what he was fighting.

The Malken relic tore off one of Gradd's relic arms. Gradd snapped off both its claws. They fought for a few more minutes, and despite his relic looking badly beaten up, it seemed as though Gradd was gaining the upper hand.

My relief gave me a little bit more energy. Swallowing hard, I stood up. I thought I was almost feeling better when a fresh new surge of pain shot through my body again. I jerked in my stance, losing my balance, and I fell...down the cliff...

"Aah—" was all I was able to get out and I screamed the rest in my mind. I had no energy left to scream aloud.

"Sarah!" Gradd cried just as he kicked the last disabled Malken relic off the same cliff.

Gradd's relic dove off the cliff in robot form. It was probably damaged so much from the fight that it was no longer able to transform.

The wind rushed past my body but it wasn't long before the icy cold water engulfed me too and then... I didn't feel anything at all.

38

crash course

It was like an underwater ballet. Bubbles rose to the surface as I, and at least two other relics, sank into the water. There was a humming in my ears, the kind that was always underwater, along with muted violent splashes from the surface. Everything was in slow motion. I would've sighed if I could.

I guess I do die here. Agarpa was right.

I was running out of breath. I wasn't normally too bad at holding my breath but the searing visions had weakened me. *It's so cold*, was my last thought before I closed my eyes.

I was humming to myself. The sun was out. It was such a nice day. I felt like going on a picnic. I smiled to myself. Yup, a picnic sounded nice.

"It's okay, it's okay. It'll be okay."

A voice was disturbing my calm reverie. Looking down, I recognized Gradd as he set down a big, blue fish on the grass.

"Hang in there, Sarah," he was saying. "I've got you."

I furrowed my eyebrows and squinted to look closer. The big blue fish was actually a very pale, very blue, very dead-looking me. I made a face in distaste. *Yikes, someone call the makeup and hair department.*

The two of us were on the tree-lined shore of some river. The river still raged but fainter, as if it was now from farther away. I figured Gradd must've dragged me out of the water. Nonchalant, I was going to shrug and walk away Gradd spoke, "No, Sarah, no. You've got to stay with me." He sounded pretty distraught and kind of worried.

I took pity on him. So I stayed to watch.

I couldn't see very well since Gradd was blocking the view from above but soon the big blue fish started to cough and sputter. Gradd started to take off wet clothes in a hurry, wrapping his arms around the big blue fish, to get warm.

Up until this point, I hovered over us. Then there were flashes as if I closed my eyes and opened them in slow intervals.

Gradd was leaning over me. "Just hang in there." His words were whispered against my mouth as he rubbed my back. He was really warm. Much warmer than me.

"Stay with me, Sarah." He tightened his arms around me and I shivered. His heart was hammering hard. I guessed he was exhausted too.

"Shh... I'm sorry too. Don't talk right now."

I was talking?

"Shh, just rest," Gradd murmured, cradling my face against his chest. "Get warm." Then for some reason, he froze, as if stunned. Then hugging me even tighter, he whispered something.

"I love you too..."

I couldn't move.

When I wrenched my eyes open, I almost had a heart attack when I realized I was pressed against Gradd's bare chest, his cloak blanketed around us.

He was asleep. He looked exhausted. But he was holding on to me like a vise.

I tried to remember what had happened. Everything seemed hazy and in pieces, like the fragments of a dream you have a hard time grasping to put together.

I remembered the relic fight. Gradd won. I fell.

I fell...into the water. And Gradd saved me? I mean, he must've. How else could this have happened?

Gradd saved my life. Again.

Despite what he'd said about how useless I was, he still almost died saving me—again. He saved me from the relics. He saved me from the water. He'd saved me countless times before.

And what had I done?

I've never met anyone else who could make me feel this way... I wanted you to know how unbelievably lucky I feel that you've come into my life ...

My aching heart pounded in my chest. Furrowing my eyebrows, I looked back up at him with a new resolve.

I was still afraid of what might happen in the future but I was no longer going to let that stop me.

Today. Now. That was all that mattered.

I reached up to touch his face and lifted my chin to kiss him. *Thank you.*

I hadn't pulled away an inch when Gradd caught my hand fast, and pressing it firmly against his cheek, he bent his head and caught my lips with his again.

"Mm." I blinked, surprised.

His eyes were still closed but his kiss was long and slow and soft.

A rush of warmth shot through me and the whole world melted away.

Relaxed, relieved, elated, I closed my eyes as his arms shifted around me.

Moving to pin me beneath him, Gradd deepened the kiss, his groan rumbling in his chest when I kissed him back.

Opening my eyes for a second, the clear blue sky and the peaceful mountains were a comforting sight. But when I closed my eyes again, the image of the mountain branded itself in my mind.

My eyes flew wide open. "The mountain!" I broke off from Gradd.

"What?" Confused, Gradd pushed himself up.

I pointed over his shoulder. "It's the mountain! We're here. The center of Anthuria. The Phoenix. We're finally here!"

"What? How do you know that?" He cocked his head to listen for the ground beating.

I stopped to listen too but we couldn't hear it anymore.

He shot me a concerned look as if he wasn't sure my head was in the right place after having sustained my injuries.

Rolling my eyes, I pushed him off of me so I could sit up. "This is where the phoenix is. I know it!" I relayed with full conviction. "Remember at Thorb? When I fainted? I saw a vision then of this exact place. And that mountain. That's where the phoenix is. I'm sure of it. We're here, Gradd! We've finally made it!"

I stopped short at the sight of him, crouched in front of me, before I looked down at myself. "Uh, where's my shirt?"

39

the center of anthuria

As soon as we were both dressed again, we prepared to set off for the mountain.

Gradd had finished explaining something about natural body warmth and hypothermia but I had barely paid attention because the boy wouldn't stop blushing. I could tell he wanted to ask about modern Earth underwear, which fortunately totally boggled his mind, as he had left mine alone. But clearly, there were more important matters at hand.

"How could you forget something as important as this?" Gradd prompted. "We've been breaking our necks all this time and you knew? All this time and you never said anything?"

I had to explain about the visions that had helped uncloak the Malken relics and how I'd known where to find the phoenix.

"Why didn't you tell me as soon as you had the visions?"

"You didn't let me," I reminded him. "Remember? I tried to but you shushed me."

He frowned. "Well, you didn't say it was important." He looked more annoyed at himself than anyone, really.

I stifled my laughter. "Well, you didn't say I should have to tell you it's important."

With a sigh, he shook his head in silent laughter. "Are you ready?" He held his hand out to me.

"Yup."

We had to continue on foot since Gradd's relic was at the bottom of the river. He estimated that we could reach the mountain before sundown. It was surely an underestimation being that I was still a bit weak from my awfully busy morning. It was a good bet Gradd was still exhausted himself, even if he wouldn't admit it.

"So, are there any more surprises you might like to share with me, you know, in case they may actually be important or dare I say, useful?" Gradd's tone was wry as we walked.

"Well..." I started to think back. "There was that one back in the library at Thorb."

He nodded for me to go on.

"I saw like a flying castle of some sort, made of..." I narrowed my eyes, straining to remember. "It's just—it was dark inside and there were a lot of guards and a lot of robots and two...men..." Suddenly creeped out, I shivered involuntarily.

"Hey." Gradd put his arm around my shoulder and squeezed. "It's okay. I'm here."

Giving him a grateful smile, I let out a breath and went on. "Um, so, one of them was this bald guy with a..." I bit my lip, tilting my head. "A scar on one eye...?"

"Yes, that's Tagbart," he supplied with a knowing frown. "He's the head of the kingdom of Malken. He's a sadistic dictator. But I can't believe he has the brainpower to think up something as large as to plan to conquer Anthuria."

"No wonder." Cold dread prickled my skin all over again. "He's got someone else. Someone to do the thinking for him." Frowning again, I struggled to describe him to Gradd.

The other man seemed much younger than Tagbart, but he was of average height, average build, and average everything, except perhaps his eyes. They were especially dark, sinister, and void.

Gradd shook his head. "I'm not familiar with anyone of rank from Malken with that description."

I was afraid of that. There was something really strange about that other guy. I just knew it.

"So, you saw where this fortress was?" Gradd wanted to know.

"Yes. It was surrounded by..." I bit my lip again and looked at him in questioning. "Big, flying rocks?"

"A rock canyon." His eyes lit up in recognition. "But there are several rock canyons in Anthuria. Do you happen to know which one they're in?"

I tried to think back to the vision again but the creepy guy's face was overwhelming my memories, not to mention the tone of his voice when he said 'There you are.'

I winced. 'There you are' seemed to indicate that he was looking for me. That he *had* been looking for me.

There you are...

I swallowed in dread. They didn't want to kill me. The Malken relics hadn't been sent to kill me but to obtain me. But for what?

It also seemed like the two men were able to see me when I saw them in the room. Come to think of it, the Malken relics almost always seemed to attack immediately every time I'd have a vision. Perhaps it meant that we had some kind of connection. Almost as though it was the only way they could locate me...

I suddenly realized how they must have found me at Thorb—that was, that time that I had even forced a vision. Biting my lip again, waves of guilt washed over me. *Shit.*

"Sarah?" Gradd peered down at me as I hadn't responded to his question. "Are you okay?"

I met his gentle, inquisitive gaze, and managed a small dismissive smile. "I'm—fine, I'm fine." I shook my head again to clear it. "I just can't get that creepy guy's face out of my head. I mean, doesn't it seem strange to you that when you were fighting them earlier, they didn't seem the least bit interested in you? And they could have easily killed me if they wanted to. It's almost like they needed me alive..."

Gradd's forehead creased in worry but he pulled me closer as we walked. Kissing the top of my head, he teased, "Now, how come you're thinking about some other guy? I'm still right here."

I laughed, immediately feeling better.

40

the phoenix

We crossed at least two rivers, waded through a whole bunch of marshes and trees, and climbed several hills before we arrived near the foot of the big, limestone mountain.

I was way past tired but I refused to be a drag and request a rest every ten minutes. I worried about Gradd. He wasn't saying anything but I knew his wound was acting up. All that cold and exertion this morning couldn't have been good for it.

We hadn't been talking for a while because talking made breathing harder and we were both out of breath. I shielded my eyes as I looked up. The sun was starting its descent directly behind the mountain. We were almost there.

Gradd had slowed down our pace. I guessed he was finally tired. I guessed wrong.

He stopped walking so suddenly, I almost ran into him. I thought he'd stopped for breath but before I knew what was happening, he turned to reach for me, pulled me closer, and kissed me. This kiss had a note of urgency and wistfulness and I realized he was thinking about my leaving.

Gradd cupped my face in his hands, his intense gaze searing into my eyes. "Tell me you'll stay with me," he asked fervently.

My expression turned somber. It was crazy to pretend that my time here was not limited. But since there was no way to know one way or the other, I nodded. "I'll stay with you."

Gradd took a deep breath, nodding as though he was satisfied with that.

I pulled away, trying to lift the mood. "Oh come on," I spoke up with an attempt at a bright smile. "I'm not leaving yet. I bet you I'm gonna be here for a long, long, long time. I mean, who else is self-loathing enough to put up with a cold, insensitive ogre like you?"

Gradd managed a half-smirk back, but when he replied, his tone was serious. "No one else but you."

As soon as we found the hidden passageway behind the brushes along the foot of the mountain and took a step inside, I wanted to step right back out. It was near-freezing cold and pitch black. Gradd held my hand as we felt our way through the dark.

Gradd had said he saw some light up ahead so we headed that way. I knew I shouldn't be scared but my heart thundered in my chest, perhaps simply in anticipation. I wondered what we would find. I mean, this was it. The finding of the phoenix. This was the end of the journey.

Coming closer to the source of light, I looked up. Sunlight was seeping through several small cracks in the mountain, striking random sections of the massive cavern around us.

My eyes began to adjust to the dark. The cave walls were growing mold. The limestone was damp and trickling water echoed from somewhere. I didn't imagine anyone had ever been here before or definitely not recently. Trying to be careful where to step, I ran my fingers along the wall to guide me as we crossed over to the other side of the cavern.

"Oops!" I almost slipped.

Gradd caught me in his arms. "Careful." His eyes glistened in the dark and I met his gaze. "Sarah," he spoke softly.

All of a sudden, the cave walls trembled, except this time in a rhythm, like a succession of beats.

My eyes widened as I held on to Gradd. "What's that?"

The mountain rumbled and sections of the cave across from us were collapsing, letting in wider streaks of sunlight that glistened across the walls.

"The heartbeat." Gradd held on to the wall for support.

I listened. Yes, it was the heartbeat, but much, much louder this time. It bounced off the walls, creating a sound wave so immense the mountain seemed to fall apart around us.

Looking up, the sunlight struck a strange spot against the rock ceiling above us and as the cave walls continued to crumble, the light beam became bigger and bigger, revealing more of the strange thing that was concealed behind the wall.

I squinted to see but there was a big, bulky thing hidden against the side of the mountain.

Then I realized I was staring straight at the Phoenix.

Gradd followed my gaze and his jaw dropped.

The Phoenix, as it turned out, was a very special relic in red and silver metal. Except unlike the other relics, it seemed to have two dark places for its eyes upon the head and a strange semi-transparent chest. It glinted in the dark. The relic must have been sitting here, undisturbed for all these years, and no one thought to look.

I gazed up at it in awe. It was the most beautiful relic I had ever seen.

Standing to my side, Gradd's intent gaze was pinned on me instead.

I guessed he was waiting for me to disappear into thin air all of a sudden or something.

I held my breath in anticipation.

After about five seconds, I let out my breath. *Yeah, I didn't think so.*

I was expecting I'd be totally crushed if it turned out that finding the Phoenix didn't mean a way home for me, but I felt strangely relieved, if not only mildly disappointed.

I nudged Gradd. "I told you I wasn't going anywhere."

Gradd's smile widened, he didn't bother to disguise his relief, his elation. He leaned over and kissed my forehead before jumping to climb up the new relic.

I had to laugh at his enthusiasm.

Gradd looked like a little boy with a new toy. "This is honestly, and by far, the second most beautiful thing I have ever seen in my life," he marveled as he ascended the robot.

"The second most?" I gave him a curious prompt.

Glancing down at me, he confirmed with a smile. "Yes."

My face warmed. I was for sure in need of at least a hairbrush, a shower, and clothes that did not resemble dirty rags—far, far from beautiful, but I had never been happier in my entire life than I was right now.

We'd found the Phoenix. Gradd could save his kingdom. There was honestly, and by far, no other place I'd rather be.

"This is really amazing," Gradd continued, sounding animated. "I've never seen a relic of this kind before. I wonder how you operate it. I wonder if it's the same with regular relics. I wonder how you get in—" He stopped short when he tried to touch the translucent chest plate, as his hand went through it like it was made of some type of gel. "Whoa."

"Wow." I breathed in amazement as the entirety of Gradd's body passed through the chest plate substance and he disappeared. "Gradd? Are you okay?"

"Yeah," his reply came after a second. He peered down at me through the window. "I think this is the pilot seat. I'm just trying to figure out how to operate this thing."

Nodding, I stepped back so I could see him up there. "So, what's the deal with this relic being 'alive' then?" I mused aloud.

The heartbeat had already stopped and the walls had stopped caving in but slivers of light shone into the cave and onto the relic, giving everything an eerie but magical look.

"I don't know," Gradd called out, sounding frustrated. "I can't get it to work."

I winced when I heard him curse. "Maybe it's broken from disuse." Frowning, I felt a bit bad for Gradd. I couldn't imagine what he would do if it turned out that, after everything we'd been through, this whole thing still didn't work out.

I studied the giant Phoenix relic. Most relics on Anthuria looked like disfigured blobs of metal, except for Scott's, which of course had been crafted to look like a tiger. But this one... It almost looked like a person, with a head, a torso, limbs, eyes... I looked up at its eyes.

The eyes were dark, seeming to have depth.

Very creepy, I thought as I stared into them—couldn't look away actually for some reason. I was frozen in place. Without warning, my heart began to pound, just as the Phoenix's restarted too, and the entire mountain began to tremble all over again.

The Phoenix's eyes glowed bright red and the sleeping relic seemed to straighten up from its seated slumber.

"Whoa, what did I press?" Gradd held up his hands in puzzled alarm.

The Phoenix began to emit a glowing red light.

I narrowed my eyes as the walls were caving in faster this time.

Debris was falling around and near me on the ground but strangely enough, not hitting me. It was as though I was surrounded by an invisible barrier.

"What's going on?" Gradd called out in confusion as he glanced down at me.

I was finally able to avert my gaze from the robot only to meet Gradd's gaze but I still wasn't able to move anything else.

What the hell was happening?

My heart pounded faster, as did the Phoenix's, as if we were one and the same...

The familiar bright red light appeared from under me and, looking down, my eyes widened.

No. I swallowed, starting to heave. Panicked, I looked up at Gradd again. I tried calling out his name but no sound came out of my mouth.

Gradd's eyes widened when he saw the light and he jumped out of the Phoenix. "Sarah!" he cried as he ran toward me, the cave debris falling in his path, behind him, around him. "Sarah!"

I could only watch, helpless.

Gradd couldn't seem to get any closer.

I struggled with the effort to lift my hand to reach out to him. But he wasn't able to get close enough before I pummeled backward into a spiral of red light.

"Sarah!"

Gradd's voice became fainter and fainter.

The cave got farther and farther away until it was reduced to a tiny black dot, and then nothing at all.

***

3

the rise

41

returned

"—mere sound of my voice strikes terror to the hearts of my enemies. See, I have a cross mark on my arm to prove it."

"Hey, how come you don't have that on your arm, Kenshin?"

"It's on my face."

Click.

"And we're gonna play this next music video request for you. Kat from Indonesia. Here's N'Sync with 'Bye Bye'—"

Click.

Static.

Click.

"In other world news, organizations bring aid to the victims of a 7.1 magnitude earthquake in Mexico —"

Click.

"There's never anything good on TV. I wish my folks would sign us up for that special cable deal that's supposed to have like a hundred channels. Like, what am I supposed to do all summer? This is such a bummer."

Annette?

"Oh jeez, hang on Andrea. I forgot all about the roast in the oven. I was supposed to reheat something for lunch since it's just my sister and me at home today. Yeah, no, I know. That lazy bum is still asleep. I know, right?"

Annette! I woke up with a start, jumping up so suddenly that I fell off my chair, tumbling back to the floor of my bedroom with a thump. "Ow, shit," I cursed under my breath, rubbing my elbow as I pushed myself to sit up.

Squinting in the bright light, I cast my fuzzy gaze around. *Oh look, this place looks just like my bedroom.* Still groggy, I yawned, trying to remember what had happened.

The mountain where Gradd and I had found the Phoenix relic had caved in.

I guessed Gradd must've grabbed me and flown us out of there like he usually did. I figured I must've fainted again. I pushed one hand down on my chair for balance as I stood.

Rubbing the sleep out of my eyes, I looked straight into my own face and almost jumped again until I realized it was just my mirror. *Oh jeez.* Shaking my head in disbelief, I leaned against my desk.

My desk...my chair...my mirror...my notebook...

Furrowing my eyebrows, I stopped short in confusion before I dropped my gaze to read the last line on the page where my notebook was open.

She swallowed and edged back against the wall, giving him a wary look.

"Whoa." Gawking, I blinked several more times to check if this was some sort of dream, a vision, or actually real. Then I pinched myself to make sure.

"Ow." I rubbed my arm.

Not a dream. Not a vision. I was...home. I was really home!

Holy crap, it was just a dream. I knew it! I couldn't stop looking around in complete amazement. *It was a dream. I had dreamt all of it.*

I was back in my room. I was back in my room, in our house. In Chicago. On Earth.

Rushing to the window to look outside, my jaw dropped.

Identical rows of houses. Kids playing on their lawns. My sister Annette was yapping on the phone while watching the very loud TV all the way downstairs.

I was home!

"Oh, my god." Laughing out loud to myself, I rushed back to my mirror to turn to each side.

No bruises. No cuts. I was still wearing my sleep clothes. But they were only wrinkled. Not soiled or tattered from weeks of adventure in some imaginary fantasy land. I checked my injury-free arm. I felt well rested. No fatigue whatsoever. In fact, I felt great!

"Are you finally awake up there, Sarah?" Annette called from downstairs.

"Ye-es!" I called out my melodious reply.

"Ena on the phone for you!"

My eyes lit up as I snapped my notebook shut and skipped all the way downstairs.

I was home!

I floated to the living room where Annette was sitting on the couch as she held the phone out to me. "Good morning!" I greeted her with a bright smile.

"Morning?" Annette echoed in ridicule. "It is one o'clock in the afternoon. You didn't even turn off your desk lamp. I had to turn it off when I woke up this morning." She was scolding me while not even looking up at me, her eyes still glued to the TV.

"Thank you, Annette," I chirped.

"I have to do everything for you," Annette complained. "I can't believe you fell asleep on your desk. Maybe you should ask Mom to throw away your bed and you can live on your desk instead."

"Why, of course, Annette. What a wonderful idea!"

Annette finally looked up to shoot me a suspicious look but I just beamed at her. She rolled her eyes and turned back to the TV. "Hurry up on the phone," she said. "Andrea's on the other line."

"Hello?" I sang into the receiver.

"Well, it's about time you woke up, Ms. Thing," Ena spoke from the other end. "I've been calling you all morning."

"Well, I'm fine Ena, how nice of you to ask," I kidded. "How are you?"

"Are you feeling okay?" Ena's tone was already suspicious. "You sound weird. And I heard you be nice to Annette just now. What's up with you today?"

"Me? Nothing." I flopped down onto the other couch with a refreshed sigh. "I'm just—happy to be home. So, how've you been?"

"I've been...fine. Since you saw me last," Ena replied wryly. "Which was yesterday."

I stifled my laughter. "Oh, right." I felt like I'd been gone for months when really, the whole thing—going to Anthuria, meeting Gradd, fighting robots, the war, the castles, and like, almost dying several times—had only been a dream. A very strange, very long, very vivid dream.

Entirely too vivid. I had to shake my head again in disbelief and wonderment.

"Well, we've already missed the game today," Ena told me. "Because you're such a sleepyhead. You up for the game on Saturday?"

"Sure," I responded. "I'm up for anything."

"Anything?" Ena echoed in skepticism.

"Sure. Anything," I repeated.

"Oh really now?" She didn't disguise her disbelief. "And what, may I ask, has brought about this sudden transformation? Aren't you 'Always-a-dull-moment' Sarah Peters?"

"Well, let's just say I did a whole lot of thinking while I was asleep," I quipped. "In fact, why don't we meet up tomorrow," I suggested gaily, shifting in my seat on the couch. "And I'll tell you all about—" I paused, reaching down as I was sitting on something. Something in my pocket. I pulled it out.

It was a small, wooden flute.

I blinked.

"Tell me all about what?" Ena prompted.

"What?" I snapped back to attention. "Oh, right... Uh, about this really weird dream I had..." I trailed off, still staring at the object in my hand.

42

home sweet home

I sat on the steps of our front porch later in the afternoon to get myself reacquainted with my neighborhood.

In the past five hours, Mr. Murphy from across the street had gone in and out of his house several times to run some errands for a very pregnant Mrs. Murphy. Mrs. Kincaid from next door had gone to and come back from the market. The Spinelli boys had cruised past our block on their bikes twice. Mary Anne Whiteman had walked past and said hello. Several cars with blaring radios had passed by, like Tony Richards' station wagon as he drove by from another 'session' with his pals. Matt Owens and company had all walked by, coming back from having finished the baseball game. And Annette had called me several derogatory names every time she looked out the window since she was lounging around the parent-free house.

The sun was dipping low in the sky.

I was still gawking at Scott's wooden flute which had somehow ended up in my pocket when I'd woke up this afternoon.

It was definitely not mine. I didn't own anything even remotely like a musical instrument. Annette had sworn she'd never seen it before. And I doubted one of my parents had snuck it in my pocket last night while I was sleeping.

*Sssoo…*how the hell did Scott-from-the-other-world's flute get into my pocket?

It wasn't even any ordinary flute either, of course. It was a dog whistle. And each time I blew on it, every dog on our block went berserk.

There had to be a logical explanation for this. Furrowing my eyebrows, I peered more closely at the flute again.

It was made of wood, had intricate carving on it, and tiny holes like a recorder or a harmonica. It was exactly like I remembered. Scott's father had made it for him. And he'd given it to me. Scott had. Scott from my dream. I could even still remember it. It was that time in the woods on the way to Eleria.

"You can keep this," Scott had said. *"Who knows? It might be of use to you someday."*

That was also right after I'd burned down Thorb.

I groaned in the recall. Some things were still so clear in my mind. *Did I dream it all or didn't I?*

I blew the whistle again and dogs barked up and down the street in response. I hung my head between my knees in exasperation with the whistle still in my mouth.

After a few minutes, something sniffed the top of my head and when I snapped my head up with a start, I met the huge eyes of a gray terrier staring right back at me.

Cocking my head to one side, I ruffled its hair as it panted, its tongue hanging out. "Hey, there. Whose are you?" I checked around its neck for a collar.

Gray, I read and rolled my eyes. *Someone's super creative.* I scooped the dog up in my arms as I stood up, looking around for a prospective leash-missing dog.

When Derek Richards strolled down the sidewalk, I blinked in surprise, almost squeaking, "Oh, Derek!"

Derek turned to look and his eyes lit up. "Hey." He walked over with a smile.

I was surprised at his expression but I smiled back as I met him halfway.

"You found my dog," Derek spoke up.

I blinked in realization. "Oh! Is this yours? She just walked up to me."

"Yeah, uh, *he* broke loose from me." Derek held up the leash. "Thanks for catching him."

"Oh, no problem." Giving the dog a little cuddle, I patted his head before handing him back to Derek. "See you around, Gray."

Derek watched me with another half smile. "Hey, how come I didn't get that type of greeting?"

I glanced up at him, surprised again. But I couldn't stop a slight chuckle, mostly in knowing disbelief.

Derek sure knew how to handle girls. At any other time in the past and I would probably have simply melted into a puddle at his feet with that comment. For some reason, his charm wasn't working on me today.

He gave me a casual wave. "See you around, Sarah."

I mocked a salute at him as he walked away with the dog. Then I sank back down to sit on my porch with a deep sigh.

There was a loud crash from somewhere to my right and my heart jumped to my throat.

I was going to think *Malkens!* and scurry back into the house for cover when I heard Mr. Murphy's cat meow and bound off the Kincaids' garbage cans.

Shaking my head swiftly to clear it, I evened out my breathing as I tucked the flute away in my pants pocket. This was ridiculous. There was no way I was going through the rest of my life like this. I had to figure out whether that whole thing was or wasn't simply a dumb dream.

It sure had felt real.

All of it. The relics. The kingdoms. The people I'd come to be friends with. Gradd.

I had left Gradd alone. I frowned as my heart constricted.

I set my jaw in determination. I had to figure out if all of it was real. Then I had to figure out how to go back.

"Go back! Go back!" I told Annette.

Annette shot me a haughty look as she switched over the channels.

"Channel 12, Annette!" I moaned in complaint.

Annette settled back on the couch to watch Gossip Girl, the TV remote control held protectively on top of her stomach while her other hand dug into a bag of potato chips.

I rolled my eyes at the TV where some girl called Blair was talking to some guy. "I can't believe they're still airing that. Gossip Girl is so five years ago." Slumping in my seat, I stared at the darkening sky out the window.

Earlier, when my parents had arrived home from work, I'd hugged them both so enthusiastically that my mom had to check if I had a temperature.

I'd just laughed. I was glad they were home. I was even glad to have been arguing with Annette today. I still remembered how homesick I had been in Eleria. I remembered wishing to go home that very first day.

I looked around the living room again.

Home...sweet home...

Still uneasy, I shifted in my seat. I had been fiddling with Scott's flute in my hands all day in deep thought.

It seriously had to have just been a dream after all. It being anything other than that was nothing short of crazy. But I couldn't help feeling like I'd been left hanging. As though I still hadn't finished what I had gone there to do, despite having found the Phoenix.

I would have been glad to be home—unbelievably glad, that was if that entire mind-boggling experience was genuinely a mere product of my overworked imagination.

"Tell me you'll stay with me."

I heard Gradd's voice in my head so clearly that I sat up and whirled around. Dousing my hopeful eagerness, I blew out a weary breath as I came to my senses.

Annette stared at me like I was mental. "Waiting for something?"

"What? Oh. No." I shook my head again to clear it and stood up. "I think I'll...just go upstairs."

Annette watched me as I headed up the stairs. "Hey Sarah, this isn't about that chicken roast I burned at lunch, is it?"

Smirking, I didn't respond as I headed to our room. I started to get ready for bed but my mind was still full of thoughts. There was no way I was going to be able to fall asleep right away.

I sat at my desk for a half-hour. I stood by the window for another half-hour. I stared up at the starry night sky and the solitary moon. I was half-expecting one of the stars to fall again and turn into a giant phoenix fireball. I was expecting some sort of vision to come and knock me out of my senses.

Then stepping back from the window with another sigh, I slumped back in my bed, checking back with reality. *It's just too quiet here, that's all*, I thought with a new resolve.

I wasn't going to go back there. None of it really happened. I never went to another planet. I never became the legend of Centeria. I never met Gradd. *He's totally not real.* It was all a dream.

With a groan of dismay, I curled up in bed.

I knew this would happen. I just knew it. Didn't I tell him this would happen? But of course, Gradd hadn't cared. He'd wanted 'today'. He'd wanted 'now'. Well, *now* what?

I frowned, getting annoyed all over again.

Don't be ridiculous, Sarah.

Holding Scott's flute up to my face, I stared intently at it. *Please, please, be a dream.*

"I wanted you to know how unbelievably lucky I feel that you've come into my life..."

Swallowing, I squeezed my eyes shut. *Oh, Gradd... Did I?*

43

✎

distractions

"So, these uh…'relics'? They fight these other kinds of relics because this guy Taggart from Maltese wants to rule the world on this other planet on the other side of the sun, or so this witch person says it is. And they want to kill you too because you…can see the future?" Ena summarized flatly before she sat back into their plush couch seat.

It was the next day and we were hanging out at Ena's house.

I nodded. "Yeah, but it's Tagbart and the kingdom was Malken, not Maltese." I watched her face carefully for a reaction.

"And…you're saying this really happened?"

"Well, I don't know exactly—" I shrugged.

"Wow." Ena laughed. "Well, congratulations. You win the award for Most Hyperactive Imagination in the whole city of Chicago. I give you points for detail though." She turned her attention back to the TV.

"It was a dream, Ena." I rolled my eyes and sat back, still fiddling with Scott's flute which I had strung on a loose leather cord necklace and now wore around my neck.

"Oh, don't look so depressed," Ena chided. "Even *if* you weren't cuckoo pants crazy and it was anything close to being anything remotely real, it's finished now. You're not going back there. So just forget about it."

Nodding slowly, I absorbed her point. She was right. I should just forget about it. It was over. Done.

But it was easy for her to say.

There was no way Ena would understand. She hadn't been there. She'd never felt the wind in her hair while riding on the back of a relic. She'd never been in the middle of a relic fight with debris crashing all around her, the explosions all sounding like a constant roar. She hadn't met any of those wonderful people. Not Scott, Gradd, Leila, or Genesa. She hadn't spent all night worrying if Gradd would be okay after getting stabbed by that bandit. She hadn't almost drowned, been on the brink of death, and then saved...

Then again, if Ena was right, neither had I.

I blew out a breath in frustration.

"Hey, didn't you say Derek passed by your house yesterday?" Ena's eyes lit up.

"Oh, yeah. His dog ran loose and wandered straight into our front yard."

Ena's grin was giddy. "It's fate. I'm telling you."

Wait, are you talking to me about fate? I'll tell you about fate—

I had to blink to clear my head again.

Ena shot me another strange look. "Sarah, seriously, you have to stop dwelling on this weird dream. Why don't you look at it this way? Consider it as a source of inspiration. I hear some writers get story ideas from their dreams and then they write about them. Hey, maybe you could even inject some of Derek in there." She wiggled her eyebrows. "He could be like your leading man."

I made a face. "Ahh, I don't like Derek anymore."

Stunned, Ena blinked. "—don't like Derek anymore?" she echoed in disbelief. "Well, hey." She put her hands up in defeat. "I'm not the one who's been sacrificing weekdays to babysit rowdy kids just to be near the guy."

Laughing, I gave her a suffering look.

I put Anthuria in the back of my mind and tried to hang out with Ena like a normal person, like I often did. We watched TV, ate popcorn, threw around popcorn, and made a mess in their living room. Something we did often enough that I'd always assumed Ena's parents had already taken out insurance for our little get-togethers.

"Come on, Ena," Ena's little brother whined a little later. "You've been hogging the TV the whole day."

"So, watch TV in Mom's room." Ena waved him away.

"It doesn't have cable." Andrew grabbed the remote and switched channels.

"Hey!" Ena cried in protest.

The sound of a crash made me jump again but it was just the TV.

"To the right!"

"You're missing him! What's the matter with you?"

"It's almost as if he can see us."

I stared at the tube, entranced. Cloaked cartoon robots. Fighting.

"Give that back!" Ena wrestled with Andrew for the remote control and she changed the channels.

"No!" Andrew and I exclaimed at the same time.

Ena flinched and shot us both strange looks. "Oh, my god. I am surrounded by weirdoes."

Andrew snatched the remote back and put it back into the cartoon.

The one robot in the middle was fighting with the five others around it. He was having a hard time. I winced, my pulse starting to race. I could almost feel Gradd's relic shudder at taking a hit. Just then, another robot arrived to help that first robot.

Scott! I sat up in alert before stopping short to drag myself back down to reality.

Holy crap, what the hell was happening to me?

I slumped back down in my seat but couldn't stop fiddling fiddle with the flute again.

How could a dream do this to me if it *was* just a dream? On the other hand, how could it have possibly been anything other than a dream?

I shook my head to clear it yet again. This was ridiculous. I obviously had too much time on my hands. Sitting up again, I formed a plan in my head. I needed to do something to occupy myself enough that I wouldn't even think about Anthuria.

When we'd finally given up the TV to Andrew, Ena and I sought refuge in the kitchen to look for more snacks.

"Hey, let's go do something tonight," I started, already eager.

"Like what?" Ena rummaged in the top shelf cabinets for hidden treasure.

I shrugged. "I don't know. Something we don't usually do. Something fun."

Ena stopped rummaging. "What is it with you and this mission of being transformed all of a sudden? Why can't we just stay home as usual and watch more movies?"

You can do anything in your world. Do you do nothing?

I made a face as I remembered what Lessandra had said. "Come on. Can't you think of anything fun to do that we've never done before?"

Ena's tone turned mischievous. "Well, when you put it that way..."

44

bottom line

"I'm not sure this counts as something that we've never done before."
I turned to Ena in the passenger seat as we drove around our quiet
neighborhood later that night. "And I can't believe my parents actually let me take the car out."

"Oh come on, the last time was a fluke," Ena dismissed with a wave
as she recalled, just as I did, that time I had been grounded for just
such an occasion. "You and I both know that dumpster totally came
out of nowhere. Besides, you have your license now which you didn't
even have two years ago."

She leaned back in her seat. "Relax, I just wanted to do some
cruising. It's not like we're joining a rally." She rolled her window
down and cranked up the radio. "Whoo!" she shouted as the wind
blew into the car.

Laughing, I sped up a little, spurred on by her enthusiasm. I gripped
the steering wheel from the adrenaline rush.

It was a warm night and the streets were quiet, with only a few
cars passing by, the houses illuminated with soft lights. As we drove
down the tree-lined streets, Ena yelled along to the music on the
radio that was blaring out a Creed song as we drove further away
from the residential area.

The exit to the highway was almost up ahead but there was something else by the side of the road. I slowed down to point. "Hey, look. What's that?"

Cars were parked in an empty lot. Bonfires that lit several barrels were surrounded by a bunch of people. As we drove closer, rap music boomed louder and Ena turned down our car radio.

"Hey cool, an Edge Party!" Ena exclaimed as we pulled to a stop at the curb. "I've heard they have these around here. This is where Tony and his buddies hang out. This is so cool! I wonder if it's a private party."

I frowned in distaste at the raucous laughter coming from the party. "I think people are drinking in there," I mumbled warily. "Let's get out of here. I'm sure it's a private party. Besides, this isn't my kind of fun."

I was starting to pull away when someone rapped on Ena's side of the car and we both jumped in fright.

"Holy cow!" Ena cried out.

Two guys, one of whom was Derek Richards were standing on the sidewalk. The other guy was slumped against Derek and looked way drunk.

Derek peered into the car. "Oh, hey, great, it's you guys." He sounded relieved. "Would you mind giving us a lift back to the burbs? This one's had a little too much sauce if you know what I mean."

Ena was making a face at the strong smell of liquor but I glanced back up at Derek. "Sure, hop in."

When I unlocked the car, Ena shot me a look of disbelief. "Sarah, they're drunk. Are you insane?"

"It'll be alright," I reassured. "Have some faith, Ena."

"Oh boy, I always knew this would happen sooner or later." She rolled her eyes. "You've finally snapped."

As soon as the guys were settled in the backseat, I drove off, headed back toward the residential area again.

"Hey, how come you guys don't have a ride?" I met Derek's gaze in the rearview mirror.

"The other guys wouldn't leave early." Derek's smile was charming. "Say, what are you girls doing out at this time of the night anyway?" He sounded slightly skeptical as if he thought Ena and I were somehow afraid of the dark and never went out.

"We were just cruising," I replied nonchalantly.

Ena nudged me and I glanced over at her long enough to see her mouth the word 'fate.'

Narrowing my eyes as though triggered, I spoke up again. "Hey Derek, do you guys know about the baseball games at the dugout? Ena and I are playing tomorrow. Should be a fun game to come along and watch, in case you were interested."

Ena's eyes were wide in shock.

Honestly, I didn't care if Derek came to the game or not, but the mere thrill of asking pumped adrenaline through my veins. It almost felt as though I had to prove myself—except I wasn't exactly sure to whom I was trying to prove myself.

"Oh wow, really?" Derek took on a vaguely interested look. "That does sound like fun, but I think I've already got plans. Sorry."

"Yeah, sure you do." I couldn't help a slightly amused shake of my head at his clearly insincere response. How I had liked this guy for so long, I seriously didn't know. Suddenly, he seemed pretentious and fake. Or possibly I was now starting to compare him to someone else.

I narrowed my eyes again as I checked the side mirror. "Uh, are you guys expecting anyone?"

The car following us was gaining speed. It honked its horn several times.

Derek glanced back. "Oh man," he groaned as the car drove alongside us, its occupants howling and jeering. "It's them, those morons." He called out the window to them. "Go home!"

Goofing around, the other car weaved to side-wind us and I jerked the steering wheel to move us away. "Whoa," I breathed, my pulse starting to race.

"Oh my god, they're wasted." Ena bit her lip.

"I'm so sorry about this." Derek shook his head. "Maybe you should just pull over or else they'll be on your tail until town."

"Mm." I stopped to think. *Was I a coward? Was I afraid? This was nothing.* After a beat, I floored the gas.

"Sarah, what do you think you're doing?" Ena looked seriously alarmed.

"Ena, did you know that you don't learn anything by playing it safe all the time?" I prompted her with a small smirk.

The other car began to race us and I shifted gears. We had the same kind of car as them, the same kind of engine, and they had two more people to boot, I was sure I could win easily.

This one's for you, Lessandra.

"Sarah, slow down," Ena hissed.

I checked the side mirrors again. We were ahead. The other car revved to go even faster and began to fishtail and weave across the road.

"Sarah!" Ena warned, almost panicked.

"Relax," I told her with the same tone of voice that Gradd had used when we had first met Scott.

The drunk guy in the backseat stirred and slurred. "Hey man, whas' goin' on?"

I was leaving the other car in the dust. I was *winning.* Loud rock was blaring out from the radio. An exhilarating buzz zinged across my skin. I wouldn't have slowed down. I wouldn't have slowed down ever, until I heard, "Ugh, high speeds make me sick," from the drunk guy.

I released the gas so fast, Ena jerked forward.

"Whoa." Derek looked stunned.

"My dad will kill me if I get puke in this car," I explained, wide-eyed.

Laughing, Ena shook her head. "Oh man, Sarah. I almost thought I'd lost you to the dark side."

I broke a grin. "Looks like they're gone anyway." I checked the mirrors again before driving a nice and safe thirty miles per hour the rest of the way into town. "Where can I drop you guys off?" I glanced up at Derek again in the rearview.

"Two blocks around the corner would be great." Derek gave me meaningful look. "Again, I'm so sorry 'bout those jerks."

"Don't worry about it." I waved away. "It's not like we can't handle a little danger every now and then."

"Hey, speak for your damn self." Ena jabbed my side.

Once the boys had gotten out of the car, Derek peered at us through the window with a somewhat impressed smile as he stood by the sidewalk. "That was some ride. Thanks again."

"Forget it." I pulled away from the curb.

"Hey," Derek called out. "I'll try to make it to that game."

"Sure whatever," I called with a quick wave, not stopping, before I turned to Ena. "Wow, that guy is such a flirt."

Ena shot me a gobsmacked look. "What on this living Earth has gotten into you? You're racing drunken guys and you're dissing Derek —after managing to finally ask him out."

"What?" I wrinkled my nose. "It wasn't like I was serious or anything."

Ena stared at me like I'd grown another head or maybe three. "Okay. Who the hell are you and where have you put my best friend?"

"Come on, what's wrong with a little excitement?" I rolled my shoulders to reason. "Ena, we have all the freedom in the world. We shouldn't waste our lives just being on the safe side all the time. Besides, if you don't make mistakes, how else do you learn?"

Ena leveled her gaze at me. "Sure, but I'd like to stay alive to do both."

I met her gaze for a second before I turned back to the road without another word.

"Sarah, turn off the damn lights. Don't make me tell you again." Annette groaned out as she rolled over in bed later that night.

Wordless, I glanced over at her. I would've turned the lights off but

I was still busy thinking. Still staring out the window of our bedroom again, forever fiddling with Scott's flute.

What's wrong with a little excitement?

You shouldn't regret who you are.

It's fate. I'm telling you.

You barely have the courage to trust yourself. You don't even trust what you feel.

I just want now. Today.

Sighing, I shook my head as I stepped back from the window.

Tonight was stupid. Reckless. It wasn't me. I wasn't a car racer. I wasn't a social butterfly or a princess. I wasn't a great savior or a hero of legends.

I walked over to my desk and sat down.

I was just me.

Opening my notebook to a clean new page, I smoothed it out with my hand and took a deep breath. Closing my eyes, I let the very vivid sensations and memories flash back in my mind.

From the beginning, when I'd first arrived in Anthuria. To the end...

Tonight, everything was as clear to me as it had been when I was there.

Pen in hand, I started to write.

Was it a dream? No, it couldn't have been.

I'm sure it really happened. I can still feel the hot wind swirl over my skin as the once majestic kingdom of Centeria burned to the ground. I can still remember how the mountains surrounding the kingdom shook violently with every step of the enemy coming closer.

I paused for a second as I remembered something else that Ena had said today. "*Hey, maybe you could even inject some of Derek in there. He could be like your leading man.*"

Now, how come you're thinking about some other guy? I'm still right here...

A smile came to my face. There could only be one leading man.

45

the game

"Sarah!"

I stirred in my sleep.

"Sarah, are you seriously still asleep again up there?"

Feeling exhausted, I opened my eyes. Where was I? I lifted my head from on top of my notebook and groaned. I had slept on my desk again.

My gaze darted to the clock on my desk. It was nearly one o'clock.

I sat up in alert. *Ena. The game. Oh shit.*

Still yawning, I stumbled on my way to the bathroom.

I had spent all night writing down the story of how I had gone to and come back from Anthuria. Writing about my trip to "Wonderland" made me feel like I had somehow lived the whole experience all over again. Not to mention, writing it all down made it seem more like fiction now, which was partly my goal.

And while I had to admit to myself that I still sort of missed it—them, being there, everything, I was also hoping to get some kind of closure upon finishing writing the story. Except it hadn't come.

I couldn't finish the story, simply because I didn't know the ending yet. It wasn't like there was any 'living happily ever after'. It was just that...hanging. An open ending.

Or maybe it's meant to be this way, I thought in resignation as I brushed my teeth. Maybe it's like Ena had said. It was an adventure. And it was finished.

"Finished," I said out loud to myself in the mirror with a firm nod.

"Everybody's looking this way," I mumbled to Ena as the two of us walked past the old, creaky gate of the dugout for the game later on.

"What's their problem?" Ena wondered, furrowing her eyebrows.

There were about a dozen guys on the field, most of whom had looked up and were watching on as soon as we'd walked in.

"Are we late?" I checked my watch but we were fifteen minutes early for the game.

"Oh, dude." Ena nudged me. "I think this might be about last night's uh…"

"Hey guys," Jamie Carter greeted as he jogged over from first base and fell into step beside us as we walked over to the bleachers where there were also a handful of people watching us.

"Hey Jamie, what's going on?"

He tugged on his backward cap and shifted on his feet before asking. "Is it true you guys like joined a drag race last night, beat Eli Thompson, and he got all drunk and pissed off at you?"

I wrinkled my nose. Well, that was one hell of a version. "He was already drunk," I corrected as I took off my Chicago Cubs cap and re-fixed my ponytail.

"Dude, it was a major car chase," Ena cut in dramatically. "Thompson lost big time. Sarah's the man!"

I shot her a weird look but just laughed.

Matt Owens and Zack Brady ran over from the field as well.

"So, is it true?" Zack spoke up. "I heard you guys got all drunk at the Edge last night and got busted by the cops."

"I heard you lost the cops in a car chase and they busted Eli Thompson for reckless driving," Matt put in breathlessly.

Ena and I looked at each other in ridicule. "No," we responded at the same time.

"Jeez, who the hell makes up these rumors?" Ena asked.

Three more guys came over to ask more questions, each of them telling a slightly different version of last night, none of which was what had really happened.

"It doesn't matter what you say. Everyone knows you're both junkies." Prissy Judy Pressman's nose was in the air. Her long strawberry curls were in a neat ponytail as she "posed" with her bat near the water station.

"Hey, wait a minute—," Ena started defensively.

I put my hand on Ena's arm to cut her off. "Don't listen to her." Then I raised my voice to holler. "Are we gonna play ball or what?"

Our team was on the field first.

Ena, at the center field, looked up at the overcast sky. "Hope the weather holds," she called out to me at second base.

Nodding in acknowledgment, I tugged on my cap before turning toward home plate as the first pitch was thrown.

With the cloudy sky, the humidity was high too, and soon, we were all as sweaty and tired as we'd have been if the sun was beating down. The heavy air hung tense as the dark clouds loomed above. It was a clear warning of rain but we often never stopped playing until it was a total downpour.

I didn't mind at all. I was having more fun than usual, running faster, catching harder, and sliding into the ground. Ena and I often worked together. She covered my back while I caught ground balls.

We struck the other team out easily and then our team went down for our turn at bat.

While Ena got us some water, I waited at the team bench.

I high-fived our catcher as he came over to sit beside me. "Hey, Jamie."

Grinning, he took off his cap to wipe his buzz-cut head. "So, what is up with you today? Did you get lucky last night or something?"

I elbowed him in ridicule. "Aw, Big Jim, are you seriously going to believe those rumors?"

"Well, honestly, I never thought I'd hear any rumor about you until today." Jamie wiggled his eyebrows and I couldn't help a laugh.

Ena came back. "Yo Jimbo, looks like you're up at bat."

Jamie glanced up and put his cap back on.

Our pitcher, Matt, was on second base. He was waving Jamie over to bat.

"Hit a home," I called as Jamie started away.

Jamie looked over at us and winked. "Watch me," he called as he jogged toward the plate.

Ena slapped me five. "I can't wait to win today and shove it up Prissy Pressman's nose."

We weren't losers or anything but on a day like today, it was looking like it was anybody's game.

I gulped down my bottled water. "Who'd have thought she was a pretty good pitcher, huh?" I noted with a shake of my head.

"You coming up to bat later?" Ena asked me.

"Hell yeah." I stood up to clap as Jamie hit a homer.

"Judy knows you can't hit fastballs," Ena informed me. "And for some reason, she hates us today."

"She's just mad because people have better things to talk about than her new mani-pedi."

"I didn't see Derek." Ena gave the game spectators a once-over look.

"I'd be surprised if he did come."

"Well, it is still early."

After two runs, Haley Morrows, our first baseman had struck out and we went to the field again. Judy's team made two runs before George Drew came to bat. Everyone knew he always hit high center field balls. Out of the corner of my eye, Ena got ready in her stance. Their team already had two outs. One more and we would be up at bat again.

Matt set up and threw the pitch. George hit a fly as expected. I watched it soar up. If it came up short of Ena, I would have to catch it. I readied my glove, watching the ball.

The sky lit up and thundered and I jumped, gasping, as a flash of a gigantic dark gray relic appeared behind the makeshift stadium bleachers in the distance.

Snapping to attention when the crowd cheered, I whirled around. Ena had caught the ball.

"Out!" the umpire called.

"Whoo!" Ena skipped forward in celebration, slinging an arm around my shoulder to lead us both back to walk down to the team bench.

Preoccupied, I looked back up at the sky, blinking several times.

Nothing.

I shook my head to clear it. That had to have been my imagination. It had to be. No doubt I was too fresh out of my overnight writing and getting too wrapped up in my fictional worlds as usual. That was all.

"Hey, Sarah," Matt called out. "You're up."

Nodding in response, I walked out to the field with my bat.

Ena thumped on my back. "Good luck!"

Shaking off the residual creepy feeling, I stepped up to the plate. Judy was sneering at me from the mound. Furrowing my eyebrows in determination, I snapped back to reality and positioned myself at home plate. Time to play ball.

"Go, Sarah!" Jamie hollered.

Judy wound up and threw. Fastball.

"Strike!" the umpire called.

I bit my lip and gripped the bat tighter.

Judy wound up again and threw. Another fastball.

"Strike two!"

Admittedly, I was a better catcher than I was a batter. Even when I did hit any fastballs, I wasn't always fast enough to make time to first base before someone managed to tag me. I was kind of hoping to ball and walk but then Judy made a big show of yawning from the mound and I made a face in annoyance.

"Come on, Sarah!" Ena's clap echoed across the field.

I set my jaw in determination. I was not going to let Ms. Priss strike me out. Not today.

Judy wound up and threw it again. I watched the ball closely and swung the bat. There was a crack and the ball flew. I shot off and ran to first.

"Safe!" the umpire called.

Breathless, I glanced behind me. Judy was only about to throw to first. Face crumpled, she put her hand to her hips in disappointment.

"All right, Sarah!" Ena and Matt called together.

Grinning, I gave them a thumbs-up sign.

Leftfield struck out. By the time Ena came to bat, I'd managed to get to third base. Our third baseman, Chuck Meeks was at first base. I clapped from third. "Bring us home, Ena!"

Judy was shooting me a dirty look as though she wouldn't let me home if she had anything to do with it.

A drizzle had started to fall. Nobody seemed concerned.

Judy pitched. Ena swung.

"Strike!"

Set up on third base, I got ready to run.

Judy wound up and pitched again.

The crack as the ball made contact with Ena's bat was accompanied by a bolt of lightning and a clap of thunder louder than before as rain suddenly came down by the buckets.

I dashed to home.

Judy's team fumbled Ena's ground ball.

I smiled as I ran. I was getting home for sure. I kept my eye on Judy's team's catcher Zack. The rain poured harder, making a gray veil of water all around us and I could only make out Zack's form.

Lightning and thunder crashed again, and suddenly, everything was in slow motion. Looking up ahead, I gasped. Instead of Zack and home plate, I thought I could see Gradd standing at home plate. Of course, with all the rain, it was hard to be sure.

I blinked in the rain. *I'm imagining things again*, I dismissed and ran faster. I had to get to home before Judy got the ball then I'd be dead for sure. *Home*, I thought fervently. *I had to get to home.*

Just then, the figure that looked like Gradd turned to run, and instinctively, I called out his name.

He stopped as though he'd heard me. My eyes widened in disbelief. *Was it real?* Gradd whirled around and my chest began to heave. It was Gradd. *He was here. Oh my god.* My spirits soared.

Elated, I ran to him. "Gradd!"

He stood still, his forehead creased as he looked. He seemed to be looking for the source of the sound of my voice but was unable to find it.

I was taking forever to get to him then just as there was another flash of lightning, a jolt of pain shot clear through me, accompanied by a deep, gravelly voice.

"It is done."

I hurtled right onto Gradd, my arms flailing as I crashed into him. Heaving, I held on for dear life.

Gradd caught me as my knees buckled. *Hello again, familiar weak sensation.* He held me up by my arms and stared at my face in shock.

Rain was still pouring in sheets and water dripping from his face.

I was soaked to the bone but I was trying to smile up at him. I missed his face. I missed his voice. If I could only hear his voice again...

"Sarah?" Gradd asked uncertainly, softly, as if in reverence.

My smile widened in relief and contentment before I passed out.

46

dark skies

"Mm." I shifted in bed as I woke. The rain was still pouring outside. Blinking to clear the darkness from my vision, I stared at the ceiling.

This isn't my room. I thought puzzled then remembered. "Gradd!" I sat up with a start.

"Take it easy, Lady Sarah," a gentle voice beside the bed said.

I squinted to recognize her. "Genesa!" Pausing to look around, I furrowed my eyebrows. "Where's—where's Gradd?"

Genesa stood up and took a seat on the edge of my bed. "I believe everyone is resting right now." She nudged me to lie back again. "You should get some rest too or your condition might get worse."

"What happened? H-how did I get here?"

The room was lit by a single candle on one side of the bed. My old bedroom in the castle at Eleria seemed eerily unfamiliar with all the shadows and shapes that the candlelight cast.

"I only caught a few fragments of what they were saying in all the commotion," Genesa started. "But I believe you showed up in the middle of a Malken attack at one of the outposts of Eleria. His Majesty and his men had to retreat and they brought you back here." Her face darkened with a frown. "I'm afraid everything has worsened since you've been gone. The war has been getting closer and closer to the castle."

Taken aback, I winced. "Since I've been—? What? How long was I gone?"

"Almost four months now," Genesa supplied.

"What?" I squeaked. "How can that be? I was just...just..." I trailed off, getting tired all of a sudden.

"Shhh." Genesa soothingly touched my forehead. "Just rest now. I'm sure everyone will be glad to see you tomorrow."

Nodding in concession, I settled back in bed.

"I have to get back to the kitchen. Your clothes are over there." She pointed to a chair in the corner where my baseball game clothes already looked freshly washed and neatly folded.

"Thank you, Genesa." I gave her a grateful smile.

"M'lady." She curtsied before heading out.

I blew out a breath—big time. Then I cast a glance at all the gray outside the window of the huge chamber.

So I was here again.

There must have been some kind of strange time difference since it appeared that I had already been gone four whole months when I was just back on Earth no more than three days.

Disheartened, I rolled over to one side. Gradd wasn't here. Didn't he miss me at all? It was four entire months.

I shook my head. I had to stop being so selfish. Gradd had a life too. Surely, he had other things to attend to—other *more important* things. I understood that now. Gradd was now King.

Taking a deep breath, I still couldn't help a small smile.

I couldn't wait to see Scott, Leila, Lessandra, and everyone else. I wondered if my plant was still alive. Hopefully, Starso had been watching it for me. I couldn't wait to see Louisa and her kids too and mess around in the kitchen with Genesa again.

I chuckled at my enthusiasm. It was almost like I'd much rather have been here than at home. Then again, I supposed Eleria had somehow also become home to me.

I frowned as I recalled Genesa's update. The war had gotten worse, closer. Was my mission now to save Eleria as well? I didn't see a crab when I arrived this time. Or a phoenix. I just...

It is done...

A chill went up my spine. Burrowing deeper into the covers, I pulled them up to my chin as I stared out the window to watch the rain still falling. The gloomy weather didn't make me feel optimistic about my visit to this world this time.

47

⸎

the morning after

The sky was overcast all morning. King Cornelius and most of his staff had left abruptly in the middle of breakfast since they were busy with war business. I'd overheard mentions of certain battle outcomes, relic shortages, and the multitude of casualties.

Even after the King and his company had left, the table was still very tense. Lessandra was eating quietly, gracefully as usual, but she seemed not to be inviting any conversation her way. Gradd was staring off into space. Scott seemed mildly preoccupied with other things. Only Leila seemed happy to see me.

I cautiously dug through my breakfast. Not exactly the welcome back I was expecting. Then again, I rationalized, I shouldn't be under any illusion that I was someone important. I hadn't come back having deviously escaped enemy capture or victorious from some faraway battle. I was just...back.

Gradd puzzled me most of all. He wouldn't even meet my gaze.

And to think I almost took him seriously and pined away for him back on Earth. But then I also supposed, as far as everyone at the table was concerned, I had deserted them for four whole months. What else could I expect?

"Hey, Tharah." With a cheerful face, Leila tugged on the sleeve of my dress for the day. "Are you staying here now?"

I gave her an uncertain smile. "Well, actually, I'm not sure yet. But while I'm here, I can tell you some more stories. Would you like that?"

"Yes!" Leila beamed.

I chuckled at her enthusiasm. "I'm sorry I wasn't able to say good-bye last time."

Leila wrinkled her nose. "Aw, it's okay. I knew you'd come back."

"Did you?" I ruffled her hair.

"Of course," Leila replied gaily. "Starso got me a new fish. I'm going to take extra special care of it. Do you want to see?"

"I'd love to," I agreed with another smile. "This table's no fun any-way," I muttered as Leila pulled me away from the royal ice cubes.

Starso seemed happy to see me. After showing me Leila's new fish, he led me to the plant I had gotten the last time I was here. It had grown so well. Somehow, the entire greenhouse was larger than I remembered with even more new plants and trees growing. It was sort of heartening, that at least in here, it was as though there was no war going on.

Leila thrust a pink bloom to my face. "Hey, Sarah, smell this."

"Mmmm...that smells good."

Her grin brightened.

"Hey, your teeth are almost back."

"Yup," she chirped proudly before dashing off to pick out some other flower to show me.

Rueful, I shook my head. "At least I know Leila missed me."

Starso's eyes disappeared when he smiled. "The war and the weather seem to be getting everyone down. It's been overcast for weeks. But don't worry. At some point, it will all turn around."

I gave him an appreciative smile.

"Tharah!" The yell came from outside the greenhouse.

"That's unmistakably Leila," I guessed with a laugh. Turning to leave, I bid Starso a wave. "I better go see what she wants."

"It's hide-and-seek," Starso told me with a knowing grin. "I can sense hide-and-seek from far away."

Still chuckling, I arrived near the fountain area. "Leila? Where are you?"

I spotted the movement behind the bushes but pretended not to see it. Instead, I walked over to sit beside the fountain. "Come out, Leila. Where did you go?" I reached up unconsciously to fiddle with Scott's flute still around my neck. "Lei—la," I sang out before distractedly putting the flute to my mouth and blowing into it.

I still heard nothing.

Frowning down at the instrument, I tried to play it like a recorder or a harmonica—slowly, clumsily.

When the bushes rustled behind me, I whirled around, thinking it was Leila. "Got you, Lei—" I broke off in surprise as I met his gaze. "Scott, hey!"

Leila dashed to me from her hiding place behind the well. "You didn't find me," she jeered, dancing around the courtyard. "You didn't find me!"

"Leila, go hide again." Scott waved her away and Leila jumped to it.

"She just never runs out of energy, does she?" I mused with a shake of my head.

Sitting down beside me, Scott's eyes caught the flute in my hands. "I thought I heard something familiar. Are you able to hear it now?"

"Nah." Holding it up for him to see, I gestured to the holes on the flute. "Are these for notes?"

"Yes." Scott reached over to point. "See, this is one, two, three, four, five, and six."

"Hmm, scales." I tried to play the notes one after the other. "Was that right?"

Already wrinkling his nose, Scott suppressed his mirth. "Sure. Close enough."

I curled my lips in disappointment. "Oh, then I guess it's no use. I wish I could hear it."

"I wish you could too." Scott tilted his head in sympathy but there was a heaviness to his expression. "Listen, I wanted to apologize about breakfast today. Everyone's been quite tense lately and we weren't able to welcome you back properly."

I was going to reply that it was totally fine but he went on, his tone exasperated.

"It's just a lot's gone on. It's been hectic. Crazy at best. The war's...well, it's not good news."

"What is the news?" I wanted to know.

"The enemy is getting stronger with every battle." Scott's face darkened. "They've attacked a lot of other countries. It's starting to look desperate. Our armies are nothing compared to their invisible ones."

"But didn't Gradd tell you about the cloaks and how they wouldn't work in flight?" My eyebrows furrowed in puzzlement and concern.

"Yes." Scott nodded. "And it helped a lot—at first. Especially since Gradd obtained the Phoenix relic. But the Malkens just keep being one step ahead. They've created new flight relics with a cloaking ability. They're easily over a Class 5 relic. It doesn't look good right now." He shook his head. "That's why everyone's in such a bad mood."

I pursed my lips in understanding. "I'm glad you told me. I was beginning to think maybe I'd done something wrong."

"No, of course not," Scott dismissed with an earnest smile. "We all missed you—terribly."

Grateful, I returned his smile. "Thanks, Scott. You're the best."

Scott brushed my hair back. "I have to go check in with King Cornelius now but I'll see you later."

I started to nod. "Sure—"

Cutting me off, Scott bent his head to kiss me once on the lips before he stood up to leave.

"Oh." I blinked in surprise but he was already walking away. "Uh, bye," I called out, flustered.

Stopping for a moment, I recalled what Scott had said about trying again with me in case I was still here after a few months. But I shook my head to clear it. I was here on business—and only business.

This time, I should know better than to get mixed up with these people any more than I already was. If it wasn't clear before, it definitely was now. I so did not belong here.

I frowned as my chest tightened. The last time with Gradd was just a fluke too. An accident. It was probably even better that Gradd was already ignoring me. That way, I didn't have to worry about any more distractions.

I had a mission. I had to do it. Then I had to go home. End of story.

Satisfied, I nodded to myself.

"You can't find me, you can't find me!" Leila's jeering broke into my reverie as she jumped from behind the tall ferns, squealing before running off.

Laughing as the pain in my chest eased, I stood up. "Okay, Leila. I'm going to find you this time."

48

counterpoint

Lessandra invited me to have tea later in the day and I was so relieved. It sure would have been difficult to hang around the kingdom if your only friend was the five-year-old.

The Princess had had tea service set up in the brightly lit parlor toward the back of the castle, where despite the cloudy sky, it was like summer inside. The room was cozy, sunny yellow, with padded wrought iron tables and chairs set out among more beautiful plants.

However, after the initial formalities, asking after Aella, who was back in the tribe to oversee their war efforts, talking about the weather, and other casual conversation topics, Lessandra slipped far away into her own world and went quiet.

"Something the matter?" I asked even as my gaze distracted briefly toward Leila who was seated next to me and playing with her food.

Lessandra blinked absently. "What?"

"Uh..." I gave her an uncertain smile. "Are...you okay?"

She blinked at me again. It seemed to take a while before my question registered in her mind and she waved her hand. "Oh, of course, of course. I'm fine."

I narrowed my eyes. "Are you sure? Is-is the war getting you down too?"

Her eyebrows snapped together. "Oh, I don't care a fig about the war."

I winced at her brusque tone. "Then what's wrong?" I bit my lip in worry. "Are you...mad at me or something?"

Lessandra looked at me and shook her head. "Oh, no, of course not, it's just..." She frowned again in deep frustration before giving me a meaningful look. "You already know."

And I got it. "Ahh, of course."

She gave me an imploring look. "Has he said anything to you? I mean, you two talk a lot, don't you?"

"Um, yeah, sure." Shifting uncomfortably in my seat, I belatedly realized that it was highly likely that Scott had not told anyone about the fact that he had proposed to me at Gradd's coronation ball. Since if he had, no doubt it would not have gone down very well with Lessandra. Or Gradd. But I shook my head to clear it so I could focus on answering her question first. "I think," I began carefully, "what I have heard Scott say is that...he sees you as more of a sister, because of—"

"Oh, Leanna, Leanna, my poor sister," Lessandra cut in. "He can't still be in love with my sister. She's been dead for years! Scott still sees me as a child even though I've been trying to do everything to show him that I'm all grown up."

"Maybe you shouldn't try so hard." Making a face, I made my suggestion as gently as I could. "I'm sure he'll come to his senses eventually. I mean, I honestly can't see how he can do any better than you. You just have to be yourself."

That made her smile. "I can see why people find it so easy to talk to you. You have a way of making light of the gravest things and your candor makes people feel at ease. Including Scott. It almost makes me feel jealous of how close you two are."

"Oh, there's nothing going on between us," I interjected right away. "Scott and I are just friends."

"Oh, I know that." She waved it away again before giving me a self-assured smile. "I know you wouldn't do that to me. And besides, one look at Gradd and there was no doubt in my mind."

I shot her a curious look. "What do you mean?"

"You should have seen it," Lessandra relayed with a rueful shake of her head. "When Gradd came back and said you were gone, it was like the lights went off. Nobody could talk to him for days and he mostly just sat in that new relic of his or training in it, day after day for months."

My cheeks flushed red but I didn't say anything.

"Even Scott was always distracted in the middle of meetings, making wisecracks to himself. But now that you're here, everything can go back to normal." Lessandra's smile brightened.

I laughed a nervous laugh. "Sure, sure."

"Boom!" Leila's exclamation stole my and Lessandra's attention. The little princess was making a mess. Her food was scattered all around her plate, all over her face.

"Oh, Leila." I leaned over to clean her up. "Give me that." I was trying to grab the spoon from her but it slipped from her hands and flew up in the air—splattering sauce right onto Lessandra.

Lessandra jumped up from her seat with a shriek.

"Oops." Looking over at her, I made a face.

Lessandra's dress was spotted with sauce. She did not look happy.

"I'm so sorry—" Meeting her gaze, I tried to stifle my laughter.

She shot me a seriously annoyed look.

But the next thing I knew, Leila called out "Bam!" and cold gel oozed down my arm.

"Ah!" I glanced over aghast and both Leila and Lessandra burst out in giggles.

I gave them both a suffering look before an idea struck me. Cracking a mischievous smile, I spooned some mashed potatoes and without warning, catapulted it toward Lessandra.

Her eyes widened in horror before—SPLATT! She shrieked again and shot me a dark look. "You—" Eyes wide with indignation, Lessandra reached for her own spoon.

Pretty soon, the three of us were making a royal mess of the room and ourselves.

Leila was rolling on the floor. Giggling uncontrollably in her chair, Lessandra clutched at her stomach. Wrinkling my nose, I examined my sticky hair in distaste. But when I met Lessandra's gaze again, we both just laughed some more.

Madame Louisa was going to kill me.

After getting all cleaned up, Genesa scolding me all the while through getting dressed, I ran out to the hallways. Leila was hiding from me again. Dashing across the main staircase, I slid across the floor to the other wing. Leila could have been anywhere in the huge castle.

As I hurried past a doorway, strong arms grabbed me around the waist. "Whoops—" Turning around, I laughed, recognizing him. "Scott!"

Looking amused, he put me down. "What are you doing? I almost thought you were Leila running around."

I gave him an impish grin. "We're playing hide-and-seek. Have you seen Leila anywhere?" I craned my neck to look over his shoulder.

"No."

Narrowing my eyes at him, I echoed in suspicion, "No?" There was rustling in the room and I called out, "There you are, Leila!"

The little princess zipped out the door past the two of us. "You have to catch me first!" she yelled and disappeared down the hall.

I shot Scott a feigned disapproving look. "And here I thought you would be on my side."

Scott chuckled. "I heard you made a mess of the sunroom."

Blinking, I put my hands up in my defense. "Hey, it wasn't just me. Leila started it. And Lessandra was there too."

He was shaking his head in disbelief. "I *cannot* believe you made Lessandra mess up her dress."

I beamed my boast. "What can I say? I bring out the best in everyone." I elbowed him to tease, "Hey, she was talking about you again today."

The frown on his face was instantaneous. "Oh, come on."

I threw up my hands in incredulity. "Oh, why not? She's sweet. She's smart. She's beautiful. I mean, come on, she's drop-dead gorgeous!"

"Stop that," Scott insisted. "You know how I feel about Lessandra."

"Yeah. Sure." I shrugged. "I just don't get it."

Scott turned to face me. "Sarah, you know how I feel." He reached over to brush my hair back from my face.

Freezing, I swallowed hard.

I was probably going to have to come clean and let Scott know he was barking up the wrong tree. But the last thing I wanted to do was hurt him. And if Lessandra was any indication, these royal types sure didn't deal with rejection very well.

Movement caught my eye just above Scott's right shoulder. Glancing up, I sucked in my breath.

Gradd was standing at the top of the staircase. He was watching us with the usual unreadable look on his face. But before I could decide what to do about the situation, Gradd turned with a huff to stalk in the opposite direction.

49

bliss

I crossed my arms behind my head as I lay back on the ledge bordering the fountain in the garden. The weather had miraculously cleared up. The stars glistened and twinkled in the dark velvet sky and the two moons, one of them half visible, the other full, again shone clear in the night. A light breeze swirled around the rustling leaves on the ground.

Today had ended relatively well. Everyone had seemed more cheerful at dinner. Scott had relayed several amusing stories and told the King about the mess 'the girls' had made in the sunroom which fortunately the King thought was hilarious. Leila and Lessandra both seemed happier. Although, Gradd was his same neutral self. Everyone ignored him.

I told myself today was like a warm-up. Tomorrow, I had to get up off my butt and start thinking about my new mission and how I would complete it this time around.

That's right. No more slacking off.

With a determined sigh, I closed my eyes and let my fingers run over the cool water beside me. Surely, the sky clearing up was a good omen.

I enjoyed a few minutes of peace and quiet before someone arrive beside me at the same time that he leaned down and kissed me on the mouth.

Needing to maintain my balance on the ledge, I couldn't move, except to tip my chin up.

When he pulled away, I opened my eyes and blinked up at Gradd in surprise. "Oh, it's you."

Gradd had knelt beside the fountain to lean over me. His eyebrows snapped together, his eyes flashing a brilliant green straightening up. "Who else are you expecting to greet you like that?" he demanded, his tone a mix of anger, dismay, jealousy, and confusion.

"Uh, nobody." I bit my lip as I quickly sat up. "You just surprised me. I mean, I thought you weren't speaking to me."

Gradd was standing with his back to me.

I shrugged again. "I just assumed you were mad at me."

"I was," he started under his breath. "I thought...you were never coming back."

"I'm sorry." I tried to explain, my nose wrinkled sheepishly. "But as you know, that wasn't up to me."

His sigh was heavy, deep. "I thought I never wanted to see you again." Turning his head, he gave me a sideways glance. "I already convinced myself that what had happened was absolutely crazy and that I didn't need this kind of complication." Frustration lacing his tone, he went on. "But then you did come back. And now everything is mixed up again."

I couldn't even express how fully I understood his statement. My chest constricted as I assured him, "It doesn't have to be. I think, now that we know this really isn't going to work out, we should just, you know, be friends." I shrugged yet again. "You said it yourself and you're absolutely right. We don't need this kind of complication."

That made Gradd finally turn around and meet my gaze. "What?"

"Come on," I chided. "You know as well as I do, that makes much more sense. What happened with us last time was just—" Shaking my head, I was hesitant to use the label but said it anyway. "An accident. I had come here for a reason and once the mission was completed, I had to go back. I helped you find the Phoenix and when it was done, I went home."

Gradd's expression darkened.

Dispirited, I furrowed my eyebrows. I intended for my explanation to make sense. To be rational. To make him feel better. Except it seemed to have had the opposite effect.

"I mean, I think I understand it now," I reasoned with an earnest nod. "The Phoenix could have summoned anyone. It would always have been a temporary situation. I was never supposed to have fallen in love with you."

His eyes lit up.

I shot him a look. "What?"

"Say it again."

I blinked, puzzled. "Say what?"

And before I knew what was happening, Gradd had pulled me toward him. His eyes closed as he pressed his forehead against mine. When he spoke after a pause, there was relief in his tone, a release. "You did fall in love with me..."

I sighed in exasperation. My heart pounded in my chest at his closeness and I lost all willpower to struggle away. "Are you kidding me?" His arms were around me, hugging me tight, and I couldn't stop myself from hugging him back. I missed him so much. I may only have been gone for three days but it might as well have been four months.

"I still can't believe you're here," he breathed against my hair before meeting my gaze intently. "I tried to stay away but I..." Sighing again, he shook his head. "I missed you like hell." His confession was more like a soft groan. "Did you...?"

Miss him? Was he kidding? I came back for him. Choked up with emotion, I couldn't even speak. I felt like I was about to burst.

The look of barely contained joy in my eyes must have been enough. With that gorgeously diffident smile, Gradd leaned down to kiss me again.

"*What are you doing?*" Scott's tone was anything but approving.

I jumped and my wide-eyed gaze trained on Scott and Lessandra right behind us.

They were probably walking in the garden, likewise wanting to make the most of the sudden good turn in the weather.

I started to pull away from Gradd but he held me fast. Lessandra only seemed mildly amused, a smile on her face. She was probably happy for us. But Scott looked mad. I wrinkled my nose in dread. That thing I was supposed to talk to him about? Yeah, I hadn't yet.

"What the hell do you think you're doing?" Scott demanded as he walked up to us, leaving Lessandra behind.

I winced. I'd never seen Scott so angry before. That couldn't be good.

Gradd just shrugged. "Just enjoying the night, like you are."

"What?" Scott's voice went up a few decibels in disbelief.

I winced again. Ignorance was such bliss. Managing to wrench myself from Gradd to stand to one side, I looked from one guy to the other, trying to rack my brain for how I could even begin this incredibly awkward conversation.

I was also internally kicking myself as it would have been way easier for me to have spoken to each of them individually before everything came to a head—to *this*.

Too late.

"What's going on, you guys?" Lessandra's puzzled voice was still trying to be cheerful.

"Scott," Gradd began. "I know you're like a brother to Sarah but don't you think you're taking the protectiveness a little too far?" Not doing himself any favors, his tone was a little condescending,

Scott scoffed to counter, "Gradd, *you* are like a brother to me but perhaps you are the one taking things too far by kissing the girl I've proposed to."

Gradd flinched like he'd just been sucker-punched. "Proposed?"

Lessandra's jaw dropped. "Proposed?"

Three pairs of eyes. Three angry glares. At me.

Swallowing hard, I froze in panic. *Oh my god, it's a nightmare. I'm now officially in a nightmare.*

Scott raised a self-confident eyebrow. "She didn't tell you?"

Gradd was shaking his head as if to clear it before he shot Scott a look. "It doesn't matter. She wouldn't have said yes."

"How do you know?" Scott sneered.

My eyes widened when Gradd's hand moved to his sword. The two of them looked to be squaring off for a fight. Like really.

"Oh come on, guys," I finally spoke up, attempting a jovial, good-natured tone to lighten the situation. "You're kidding again, right? Somebody tell me you're kidding, please?"

"Sarah loves me. And I love her," Gradd declared with conviction.

Scott's prompt was wry. "She does, does she? Are you absolutely sure about that?"

Gradd seemed to actually stop to consider this. Forehead creased, he shot me a look as though he was beginning to doubt that himself.

"Is this about winning again, Gradd?" Scott mocked. "You can't beat me at swords so you decided to take away the girl that I love?"

I gasped—but a louder, more outraged gasp overlapped mine.

Lessandra's hand was over her mouth in shock. Having heard enough, she whirled around and fled.

Wide-eyed in alarm, I bolted after her. "Lessandra!"

"Sarah!" Scott called.

I waved him away. "Princess breakdown! More important!" Dashing into the hallway, I looked left and right. "Lessandra!" But she was gone.

50

conspiracies

I turned the castle upside down looking for Lessandra so I could explain everything, but she apparently could hide better than Leila.

The entire castle had retired by the time I retreated to my room. Too caught up in my thoughts, I didn't notice that the usual guards at my door weren't there. When I walked in, Genesa was tidying up the bed.

"Oh hey, Genesa." I collapsed flat on the bed. "Have you seen Princess Lessandra, by any chance?"

Genesa's forehead was creased. "Actually, yes."

"Really?" I sat up eagerly. "Where? When?" Then I noticed her frown. "What's wrong?"

"M'lady has reassigned me to the kitchen." Genesa looked troubled. "She's also called off your guards."

"What?"

She bit her lip. "I'm not even supposed to be here. I just came to say goodbye."

I should have known this would happen. This was Lessandra's castle after all. I groaned in exasperation. "Ohh, I've totally messed everything up."

"I've seen the Princess like this before." Genesa's tone was a tiny bit reassuring. "Eventually, the King will rectify the situation but until he does..." She gave me a meaningful look. "I'd like to wish you luck. You'll be needing it."

Grateful, I gave her a small smile. "Thanks."

Genesa paused at the door and curtsied before she left.

"Ugh!" Rolling my eyes as I groaned, I flopped back on the bed.

Lessandra would probably have me kicked out of the castle altogether. *Ugh! Why did she have to be such a spoiled—* I stopped. *No, no. This was my fault. Everything was always my fault.*

Sitting up, I reached for my *Cubs* baseball cap on the corner of my bed. I'd been wearing it for the game the other day so it had crossed over with me. The rest of my clothes were still neatly stacked on the padded chair.

Chewing on my lips, I figured I should probably get dressed back into my own clothes, especially if I was about to be kicked out of the castle. I wasn't likely welcome to these dresses or this room any longer.

Sorting through my Earth clothes, I was looking for my shirt when there was a knock at door. "If anyone wants permission to come into the room, better ask Princess Lessandra who owns it, or anyone of similar ranking," I called out nonchalantly before I looked over.

Gradd stood by the doorway, nowhere nearer.

I met his sharp gaze. "Oh, it's you."

There was no amusement in his voice. "And clearly you were expecting someone else?"

"I had assumed it was either Scott coming to apologize or you— coming to argue," I relayed, a catch in my tone. "You were the less obvious choice."

"The less obvious choice," he echoed wryly. "Is that what I am?" Leaning against the doorframe, he crossed his arms over his chest.

Already aggravated, I rolled my eyes. *Oh, bite me.* "Look." I sat cross-legged on the bed, picking at the worn patches on my long-sleeved button-down baseball top before tossing it aside in disarray. "I have had a really, really long night. Are you going to get all testosteroney or are you at least going to give me a chance to expl—"

"He proposed to you?" Gradd burst out what seemingly could not be held back any longer.

"Yeah, didn't think so." *Let's get on with it.* Sighing, I steeled myself for the battle. "Yes, Gradd, that he did," I confirmed. Although, I was a little insulted by how he was making it as though the notion was ridiculous. Like someone like me didn't deserve to be proposed to by someone like Scott.

He ran his fingers through his hair in frustration. "That night in the woods, before we found the Phoenix, I should have known there was more to it when you mentioned his name."

"Look, I didn't expect him to follow through on it," I explained thickly. "Much less make some kind of claim. Honestly, I didn't expect you to make such a big deal out of it either."

"What? A proposal of marriage isn't a big deal to you?" Gradd's eyes were livid. "What the hell kind of world are you from anyway?"

"Hey!" I snapped in offense. "You leave my world out of this."

He threw his hands up. "Why didn't you just tell me?"

I shot him a look of annoyed disbelief. "I don't have to tell you everything."

His expression darkened. "Oh, that's great. So exactly what else are you hiding from me? What else are you lying about?"

"What?" I couldn't keep my voice down any longer. "That's not what I meant—"

"Well, what did you mean then?"

I was starting to lose my cool. "I can't believe you're turning this into something that it isn't!"

"Now I understand why it seemed so easy for you to switch feelings on and off." Gradd's tone dripped with resentment. "None of this really matters to you, does it? Scott was right about one thing. I don't really know how you feel. I guess I don't really know you at all."

My mouth hung open in wordless bewilderment.

Gradd's voice strained, his eyes were on the floor in dejection. "I suppose this is all just a lot of fun for you. And we're all so stupid to believe that you actually cared."

Anger bubbling up in my chest, I clenched my jaw. That was it. I'd had enough of this.

I began to nod. "You're right," I conceded eagerly, finding my voice as if I had just come to an awesome epiphany. "You are so right. I mean, what other conclusions could there be? I couldn't just be confused, concerned, or trying to be sensible about everything—of course not!" I snarled. "*Of course*, I was placed in this world to torment you all, because you're all so very, very special and so very easy to fool—yeah." I kept nodding so he couldn't cut in. "Because I'm the lying gremlin from Earth—or who knows where the hell I really came from, right?" I mocked flatly. "Yeah, Gradd. It's a big conspiracy."

Gradd glared at me without a word.

If I wasn't so infuriated myself, I would have shriveled to a pathetic heap from the look on his face. But instead, I raised my eyebrows at him expectantly, undauntedly.

Gradd's scowl deepened before he stalked away in a huff.

Once he was gone, I let out an exaggerated loud groan of frustration and I flopped back down in bed. Completely worn out, I let my head hang off one side, my long ponytail almost brushing my sneakers on the floor, the blood flowing to my head until I got a full-on headache.

Sighing heavily as I looked out the window, I twirled my baseball cap around my finger, the frown having not left my face all night.

Brainstorm. I had to fix this.

First, I had to find Lessandra and explain how I wasn't interested in Scott in any other way other than as a friend. With any luck, she might even listen to me instead of throwing me in the dungeon. Next, I had to tell Scott that I really wasn't interested in him in any other way other than as a friend. I was sure he'd understand. I figured if Scott cared about me, he would only ever want my happiness, right?

And as for Gradd...

Squeezing my eyes shut for a moment, I groaned again. How could he think I could just turn feelings on and off like that? Did he forget I was the one who didn't want to get involved in the first place specifically because I knew how difficult it would be if, after all this, we never saw each other again?

I scoffed in haughty self-assuredness. Really, this was all his fault.

A particularly cold breeze blew into the window. The curtains fluttered up and clanked against its metal frames.

I rubbed my hands up and down my arms, still in deep thought.

Surely, Gradd wasn't the only reason I was back here. I refused to believe that I didn't have any other greater purpose in coming back here aside from some *guy*. Seriously, how pathetic would that have made me?

I stopped as that creepy feeling churned in the pit of my stomach once again.

Still upside down on the bed, I darted my eyes around, narrowing them as I looked out the darkened windows. There was nothing there and the room was empty but somehow, I still had a really bad feeling.

My heart starting to pound, I was moving to sit back up when a shadow moved out of the corner of my eye.

Before I could even alert myself or anyone else, the shadow jumped into the room and scooped me right off the bed.

"Hey!" Yelping, I tried to push away but the next thing I knew, I was being whisked away out the window.

Glimpsing a pink pastel dress on the castle grounds as I was being carried off, my eyes lit up. *Lessandra!* I was already heaving so I swallowed first before I was able to shout her name.

Lessandra seemed to pause in suspicion, glancing around her, but before I could scream for her again, something muffled my mouth and nose and I was out like a light.

51

evil to meet you

Letting out a loud, anguished groan, I curled up on my side from the searing pain that struck every living nerve in my body.

What a way to wake up.

I tried to peel my eyes open but all my blurred vision could tell me was that it was dark where I was...

Where was I? My stomach turned over as I remembered being nabbed from the castle at Eleria by...I didn't even know. My head still spun from whatever it was they had used to knock me out.

Coughing, I hugged myself tight but the pain refused to go away. It was all I could think about.

Gritting my teeth, I groaned again. I had to find out where I was. I had to get out of here. Judging by how I was taken, there was no chance that these people were friends with Eleria. *I had to escape.*

A fresh jolt of pain went through me and somehow it occurred to me. *The Malkens.* Whatever I was doing here had something to do with the Malkens.

Managing to roll over to my other side, I clutched at my stomach, nausea threatening my every movement.

From this side, I could make out several shades of color that denoted I was probably inside a room. There was a bed across the way, a door to the right, and to the left, thick, heavy curtains that blocked any light from seeping in through windows. There was also something a few feet away from me on the floor. Something that seemed to glow a dim eerie blue light.

I hissed in pain from an intensified headache and when I clapped my hand up to my forehead, my fingers brushed something attached to my temples. Blinking, I reached up both hands to feel for what they could be. But something was stuck to my hands as well.

Holding my hands up near my face, I almost retched at the white circular plugs. Like those things scientists attached to lab monkeys for experiments. Even more frightened, I swallowed past the lump in my throat. I shut my eyes, wanting to cry.

The opening door creaked and I jumped. I squinted to see two figures walk. They came within about a few yards of me before there was enough light for me to recognize them and my heart jumped to my throat.

It was them.

Both men were tall as they hovered over me, a pathetic heap on the floor, and to me, they both looked like they were in cosplay for Darth Vader. One was the bald guy with the scar from before, the head of Malken, Tagbart, wearing the Malken scorpion emblem on his cloak. The other one was the strange guy whom Gradd didn't know. The nameless guy looked, to a degree, very normal. He didn't look much older than I, with his dark hair slicked back and those eyes... The ones I remembered seeming so void and deep and pure evil.

My chest started to heave in dread.

The nameless guy smiled at me with a sort of proud, haughty look. "You're finally awake." His deep, slightly amused voice sent chills up my spine—scary chills. "How do you like your room? We've had this room prepared especially for you, the legend of Centeria."

Despite the wrenching pain, I tried to glare up at him. I wanted to snap some sarcastic remark back, but really, I wasn't up to it.

He gave me a condescending look. "I apologize for the means with which you were brought to us. We merely felt it was the only way to avoid any more...unnecessary trouble."

"We've been keeping an eye on you since your first arrival," Tagbart started with a sneer. His voice was not as deep as the other guy's but it was just as oily. "I have to admit it's been quite a challenge to get an audience with your illustrious self. We tried to capture you in Centeria. But...you know how that turned out." He smiled as if he knew I didn't want to be reminded of the event. "We tried again a few other times. But even by sending several of our special relics, as you well know, you and your King friend still escaped us." Then he let out a small chuckle. "So, my friend here decided we should dispense with the pleasantries and just kidnap you, and well, here you are."

The nameless guy was just watching me, quiet for the moment.

I scowled at him.

"You almost got away from us too, going back to the other world," Tagbart continued he grinned. "But I guess that King of yours turned out to be of some use. After all, if it wasn't for him, you wouldn't have wanted to come back so much, it would have been impossible for us to retrieve you."

My stomach turned over. *If it wasn't for Gradd, it would have been impossible?* Oh, shit. I *did* do this to myself. I wanted to smack myself on the face just as a surge of pain went through my guts anyway, and groaning yet again, I curled back up into a ball.

"I'm sorry we can't make your unavoidable state any more comfortable," the nameless guy went on. "But don't worry, the pain will go away eventually." The grim smile on his face seemed to say the pain would go away—like, when I died.

Then they both started to turn away to leave.

They were nearly at the door when I managed to gasp out one word. "Why?"

Only Tagbart turned back. He shot me another sneering look. "It's too bad you yourself are unaware of your full potential. Do not worry. There will be plenty of time to find out."

The heavy door shut with a loud thud and I hugged my knees to my chest. A powerful wave of desperation and hopelessness surged through me and I burst into tears.

I couldn't sleep. The throbbing pain made it hard enough to even breathe for ten minutes straight, let alone rest. There were times when the pain got so intense, I would simply pass out. But when I came to again, the pain would still be there.

I had too much time to ponder what the two men had said. I had been right. They hadn't been trying to kill me. They had wanted me alive. But for what?

It's too bad you yourself are unaware of your full potential...

What? I wondered in bafflement. Aside from the dumb useless visions, it wasn't like I could do anything. Certainly nothing special. Did they think I could negotiate with Gradd, or anybody, to surrender their countries to the Malkens? Fat chance!

If it was possible, my headache got even worse as I racked my brain.

This was just great. I had gotten myself captured by the Malkens—and why? Because I was a stupid girl who thought stupidly that it would be super awesome if she stupidly saw some stupid guy again.

Obviously, there was no way I was going to voluntarily help the Malkens. They'd destroyed kingdoms, killed hundreds, if not thousands, of innocent people. The Malkens were evil. I was never going to cooperate. They would have to kill me first.

My heartbeat pounded harder in my chest. Was I really going to die to save an alien kingdom? An alien world?

Gradd's pained face as he told me of the things that the Malkens had done to his family and his kingdom, the only things he had, popped into my head.

The legend says, when the kingdom is faced with grave danger, a savior will come...a person who will save Centeria...

I clenched my jaw in resolution. *Save Centeria.* I had to save Centeria.

Another wave of pain washed over me. They seemed to come in intervals but weren't any less intense.

Gritting my teeth, I curled up again. The Malkens were responsible for this pain. I was going to loathe them for the rest of my life.

I was still lying on the floor, facing the bed, when another surge of pain hit.

I groaned and clutched at the floor but as it usually did, the intensity of the pain subsided in seconds.

My eyes were drawn to the blue glow of that 'something' across the floor.

I'd been in the room long enough to notice that every time I felt a wave of pain, that blue light glowed brighter. It also seemed to dim as soon as the pain ended too. It was as if there was a connection there.

Taking a deep breath, I crawled over to get a closer look, but it was nothing but a little koi pond entrenched into the floor of the room.

Disappointed, I narrowed my eyes at the water. Seeming to have depth but no bottom, calm as it was now, it was like a mirror over a faintly blue smooth surface.

Frowning at my reflection, I drew back abruptly. I looked horrible, my hair stuck to my face in a cold sweat, my eyes two dark hollows, my lips cracked, and face pale.

The intensity of the next surge of pain made me clutch the rim around the little pool and I realized why the pain felt somewhat familiar.

It was like... I was having a vision...

I peered into the pond, and as I'd suspected, the 'water' glowed brighter.

Violent ripples from out of nowhere disturbed the calm blue surface of the water, except upon closer inspection, it wasn't quite water. The fluid had a stodgy texture.

Furrowing my eyebrows, I watched as the continuous tremors in the water began to form distinct lines, and suddenly, I was looking at...

Genesa!

Wide-eyed, my jaw dropped. *What the hell is this?*

Genesa looked distressed. *"I don't know, your majesty,"* she was saying. *"I had just come in for a moment to tidy up the bed and then I left Lady Sarah alone. In the morning, she was just gone."*

The picture changed to Lessandra. *"Maybe she just went back to her own world where she belongs,"* she drawled. *"She didn't have the courtesy to say goodbye last time either."*

Then there was a puzzled Scott. *"It seems odd she would have left her clothes."*

With a gasp, I remembered that I'd left all my Earth clothes behind, my sneakers on the floor beside the bed.

The view in the blue pond seemed to pan back to show Lessandra in the garden with Scott, Genesa, and Gradd. The latter was standing with his back to the rest of them gathered by the fountain.

Lessandra dismissed Genesa. *"Of course, she went home. Where else would she have gone? What do you think? Some strange creature took her from her room in the middle of the night?"* she posed as though in ridicule.

My jaw dropped again. She had seen me! "Ohh..." I moaned, weakening and falling back to the floor.

The door to the room chugged open again.

The nameless guy noticed me by the pond and his eyebrow shot up. "I see you have learned a new trick. Congratulations."

Tagbart looked down at the water. "Amazing, isn't it?" he gloated. "This pool is filled with the raw form of the substance which enables our relics to camouflage. My friend here discovered and developed it himself." He gestured to the nameless guy. "I have to admit I had no idea about its capabilities, much less that it can harness your powers of vision which is quite useful. Well, except for the obvious side effects."

I glared at him even as my heartbeat was pounding from the implications of what he'd just relayed.

The nameless guy was watching the current scene in the pool. "I see your friends are already giving up looking for you. That's too bad."

"What the hell do you want from me?" I was able to spit out.

The nameless guy smiled and shook his head. "It really was unfortunate that you fell into the hands of the Centerians first. If you had come to us, you would have had the benefit of my guidance and your powers could have known no bounds. Imagine the things we could accomplish." His eyes gleamed. "The rebirth of Anthuria, the beginning of a new and better world which we would rule. Together."

"That's your plan?" I scoffed in ridicule. "To destroy everything and then rebuild Anthuria under your rule?"

"Basically, yeah. We all have to start somewhere." He shrugged offhand then turned to me. "Tell me that isn't a tempting offer. What do you say?"

I blinked but I didn't need to think about it. "I think you and your stupid kingdom can go straight to hell."

The nameless guy shot me a disapproving look. "Tsk, tsk." He clicked his tongue. "Sarah, are you really going to put yourself through all this for people you don't know? For an alien world? For people who claim to care for you, yet make no effort at all to find out what's happened to you?"

I frowned as I looked back down into the pool.

"It's been two days," Scott said in exasperation. *"We've searched the entire kingdom. Where could she be?"*

Gradd spoke up then. *"If she doesn't want to be found, you won't find her."*

My stomach churning, I swallowed hard but attempted a defiant look back up at the guy. "You can't psychobabble me. Gradd will—" I stopped short. "Scott will come to get me."

Tagbart roared in laughter. "Your blond King is the most naïve of all. He's too young to even realize how stupid he is. If he was any good a ruler, his kingdom would still be standing." He shot me a wicked look. "And that goes for your Centerian King as well."

Glaring at him, my blood started to boil.

"It's too bad his father didn't live long enough to see what a disappointment his son had become," Tagbart went on with an egotistic smile.

Snapping, I snarled, *"Bastard!"* making a lunge at him before I slammed my face into something hard that made me rebound back to the floor. "Ow!" It felt like I had hit a wall.

Tagbart had jumped in surprise but then he raised his eyebrows at me. "My, my, now I feel foolish. Did I forget to mention? There is an invisible barrier here." He gestured before him. "Naturally, we needed to have something like you well-contained. But how long your glass cage will serve as your home is up to you."

My bones aching, I slumped back on the floor.

The nameless guy was watching me again. He looked surprised at my stamina or determination. "You can choose to join us, be free of this prison and what I can only imagine is excruciating pain." He smirked before giving me a plain look. "Or we will continue to use what we can and your pain *will* end. One way or another." His smile was dark before he turned to leave. "We'll wait for you to change your mind. It shouldn't be long now."

I groaned and looked into the pool again. Gradd was still by the fountain, staring into space. Just then, another intense shockwave of pain came and I blacked out again.

5 2

❦

human determination

I was racked with pain. I could barely open my eyes, let alone move. It could have been for days but since the room never saw any light of day, I couldn't be sure.

The nameless guy came to observe me often and watch the pool. More often than not, all by himself, since I supposed Tagbart had some other business to tend to. Or that he was simply more sadistic.

When I opened my eyes, the nameless guy was bent down, peering at my face.

I attempted to give him a desperate tortured look, hoping maybe he'd feel a bit of guilt or pity.

But one corner of his mouth turned up. "You can stop the pain, Sarah," he coaxed. "We—well, *I* really—don't like to see you, the all-powerful legend of Centeria reduced to this." He gestured to offer his hand. "Join us."

Swallowing hard, I clenched my jaw and shot him a venomous look. *Not on your life!*

Chuckling, he sat back on his heels and clasped his hands in front of him. "I do understand how you feel. You believe those friends of yours will come to save you soon and you just have to stick it out. Be *tough*," he relayed with a feigned grunt on the last word. "What

283

you don't realize yet is, those friends of yours will give up. And do you know why?" He met my glare again with a shake of his head. "Because you're not like them. You're not even from this world. Now, what makes you think they'll waste all that effort just for you? An outsider?" He gazed off across the room. "Think about it. What have you ever done for them that they should owe you anything?"

I wanted to defend my friends but I had neither the strength nor willpower to. Also there was a sinking feeling in my stomach dreading that he was probably right. I averted my gaze, unwilling to listen any more of his sly words. I shouldn't let him talk me into anything.

"Look," he called my attention to something.

I didn't move.

Eyes narrowing, he barked his order again, "Look!" at the same time that he stretched out his hand toward me.

I gasped as my body stiffened and lifted a few feet off the ground. Stunned, my wide-eyed gaze darted up to meet his. He had powers too.

He gave me a half-grin, looking satisfied with my realization. With a wave of his hand, he led me to hover above the blue pool. "Look."

Hissing in pain, I tried to keep my gaze away but he forced my head to turn so I could see.

It was Eleria again. My friends were dining in the garden. All of them, except for Gradd. They were talking about the war and business and kingdom. Floating around like a butterfly, Lessandra brightened up everyone's day. Leila was playing with her food again. With a warm smile, Scott looked over to help her.

Everybody looked normal. Everybody looked happy.

Without warning, the nameless guy let me go and I groaned as I thumped on the floor.

"See?" he prompted, matter-of-factly. "They've forgotten all about you. They've abandoned you. You didn't belong there. You know you never did and you never will. They'll never treat you like they treat one of their kind. *Never.*"

Right then, I really wished my fury would let me literally explode. I didn't even mind dying as long as I took down this jerk with me.

But he went on. "Do you know why?" He leaned a bit closer. "Because you're different, Sarah," he noted, pausing for a moment, before adding something else. "We're different."

My gaze snapped up to his again.

What did he just say?

Straightening up, the nameless guy reached for my baseball cap that was on the bed. I supposed it had been on me when I was abducted.

He wrinkled his nose down at it as though in distaste. "And if you ask me, the Yankees are still, hands down, the greatest baseball team on Earth. I mean, Babe Ruth, the Great Bambino. He was a Yankee. That's all you need to know."

Stunned, I blinked again. *What in the seriously freaking hell?*

He was...he was a...

Pleased at my reaction to his dropping that little hint, he gave me another wry look. "Maybe now you understand. Together with our powers, there's no telling what we could accomplish in this world."

I struggled to understand exactly what he'd just said. How in the hell did he come to be here? Was it even possible?

He was like me. He was from Earth too.

Bile rose in my throat as I tried to make sense of things.

This guy—*he* was the real cause of all this destruction and suffering. Gradd had even said that the Malkens had only recently become a threat. It was all him! This guy was responsible for all the death and pain. *He* had started everything. How could he—*How could he?*

My scowl deepened in pure molten anger.

"I have to admit, when I found out about your arrival, I had just wanted to kill you. I wanted to be the only special one," he said with a haughty huff. "But then I decided you might be more useful. That is if we could incorporate your powers into my genius cloaked relics, they would be even more invincible. *I'd* be even more invincible." He shot me a look, his eyes gleaming. "We could be invincible together. What do you say?"

My glower at him darkened. He was truly sick. Why was he doing this? How could he possibly be from Earth? How could he have turned out so evil? And he expected me to ally myself with him to help him with his plan for even more death and destruction?

I shut my eyes for a moment to take a deep breath so I was able to sneer, "Don't hold your breath."

His pre-emptively triumphant mood instantly doused, his eyebrows snapped together as he lost his cool. "Then you are more stupid than I thought!"

But he recovered after a mere few seconds, donning a friendly expression once again. Turning back to me with a smile, he bid, "I'll leave now. Sweet dreams," before he left.

Once he was gone, I moaned again, curling back up into a ball.

I had to do something. I had to find a way to try to break free, escape, or anything to at least fight this. I rolled on the floor so I could peer into the pool again. If there was only a way that I could send a message to them. Still heaving desperately, I watched my friends have a normal, happy meal in Eleria.

Pushing out a shaky breath, my frown deepened as I wondered where Gradd was.

Crying out again as a particularly painful jolt shot through me, I collapsed, hanging over the pool like a limp noodle. I was about to close my eyes when the vision switched to show Gradd.

Standing by one of the castle windows, he had a faraway look on his face. But then he stopped short, his forehead creasing. It was almost as if he sensed something.

All I could do was clench my teeth. *Gradd... Gradd! I'm still here. Help me. Oh please, help me.* My eyelids getting heavy, I struggled to keep watching Gradd. After a moment, he turned and walked away.

"No." Groaned, I lay back again, my eyes refusing to stay open.

Help. Somebody help me. Anybody...

I writhed in pain inside my little glass cage. Keeping my eyes open was getting to be too painful, I could hardly watch what was going on in Eleria anymore. Besides, it wasn't like my friends were doing anything new. Or at least, nothing that I should be concerned about. They weren't trying to rescue me, that was for sure.

Moaning, I twisted about on the floor. My anguished cries seemed to pass through the walls. I bet they could hear it throughout the fortress.

I could only stop the visions somehow, maybe I could stop the pain.

I shook my head in ridicule. I had never been able to control the visions. It was like they had a mind of their own. I still wanted to be able to see what was happening outside and see familiar people in the little pool. At least, it made me feel a little less alone.

I was alone. My chest sank heavier as another wave of self-pity washed over me.

Nobody was coming to save me. If they were, I wouldn't still be here. I wouldn't still be in pain. If anybody really cared, I should have been out of here by now. But they didn't really care. They all wanted me gone. Lessandra, Gradd, everyone.

My face hot, I'd almost lost feeling in my extremities and I could barely breathe.

If only I wasn't breathing...

I kept staring at the ceiling. I was sure face was streaked with tears and blood from when I was coughing earlier. Blood already dried on my clothes. Maybe I would bleed to death. That would surely stop the pain.

Your pain will end...one way or another...

Stopping short, I blinked hard. *Oh great, now I want to die.* "You're useless, Sarah," I muttered in frustration. "You're useless!"

Yelling just about used up whatever energy I had left, I collapsed down beside the pool in a pathetic heap once more.

"Oh, Sarah, you're such a bitch." The familiar voice made me start. *"Yeah, I'm coming guys. I guess Sarah can find her own way home."*

"Ena..." I whispered in recognition and propped myself up to look into the pool again.

This time, it showed the baseball dugout back on Earth. With the rain having stopped, the players were emerging from under the bleachers. It looked as though everyone was just about ready to leave after the game.

"*Party! Party!*" Jamie howled as he ran around.

A small smile on my cracked lips made me wince but for a moment, my mood lifted. We had won the game. I bet everyone was going to celebrate.

Judy was scowling by one corner, surrounded by her girlfriends. "*Lucky*", she muttered as she squeezed rainwater out of her hair. She didn't look so prim and neat now.

Ena shot her a haughty look before starting to head out of the gate. "*Come on guys,*" she called. "*Let's go to the diner. I want to get there before the mud dries off.*"

Matt, Haley, and the others laughed.

"*Hey, shouldn't we wait for Sarah first?*" Jamie asked.

Ena looked around and shook her head. "*I didn't see her duck into the bleachers. But the rain's been over for a while. Wherever she went to hide, she should've been back by now.*"

"*Maybe she literally went straight home,*" Matt joked.

"*Hey, maybe Zack saw her,*" Jamie suggested and called out to Zack to ask.

But Zack shrugged. "*I don't know. It rained pretty hard and she knocked me down. I didn't see after she came to plate.*"

Ena pursed her lips. "*Well, I'm sure she's around here somewhere. She'll turn up later. She has to.*"

I have to...

Groaning in pain, I lay back flat on my back again.

This is stupid, Sarah. You can't kill yourself. You still have to go back home and gloat that win in Judy's face. You still have to go back to Eleria and pick some bones with Lessandra and Scott. You still have to prove to Gradd, to everyone, that you can take care of yourself. You can't give up.

Oh, Sarah, there's no hope for you if you give up...

Another urgent voice floated up from the vision pool. *"Something's wrong with Lord Gradd. He seems sick. He hasn't eaten in three days."*

My eyebrows furrowing in worry, I turned to look again.

Scott was being led down a hallway and into a dark room that must be Gradd's. A dark form was in bed but I could recognize that silhouette anywhere. Gradd seemed to be in a deep, unsettled sleep, tossing and turning.

"Call the doctor," Scott instructed the maid before trying to shake Gradd awake. "Gradd. Wake up, Gradd. What's wrong with you?"

Another streak of pain stabbed through me and I clutched my stomach with a gasp. "Aaahhh—"

Someone else groaned.

Swallowing in bewilderment, I glanced back into the pool.

Gradd was clutching his stomach, his brows furrowed even as his eyes were squeezed shut.

Groaning again, I balled up my fists.

Gradd moaned as well.

"Oh no." My eyes watered as I checked in on the vision pool once more.

Gradd hissed something out as he let out another groan at the same time I did.

"Sarah..."

"Oh, shit," I cursed with a grimace. *Damn you, Gradd.* Now I really had to get through this. Letting out an exasperated breath, I collapsed face down on the floor. I flinched when something blunt poked at my neck. It took an effort to reach up but I stopped short when I remembered what it was.

Scott's flute. It was still around my neck.

It might be of use to you someday.

You didn't hear that? Maybe there's something different about how I hear sounds because I'm not from this world.

You're different Sarah. We're different.

Big, flying rocks...a rock canyon...

The wheels started to turn in my head and I took a deep breath. Maybe if I played this...someone outside could get a message to Eleria.

Gradd knew the fortress was in a rocky canyon, just not which one. If the fortress walls let certain sounds pass through so well, perhaps the flute music might echo through the mountains and someone would hear it.

And since that nameless guy was human too, he wouldn't be able to hear it and suspect anything. With any luck, by the time anyone who could hear it warned him about it, someone else would already have heard me and sent a message through to Eleria.

I bit my lip, my pulse racing. It was an incredibly long shot but it was the only shot I had. I pushed myself up off the floor before slumping back down. "Oof—" *Now if I could only turn over.*

53

it's time

"Somebody get me the hell out of here!" I pounded on the invisible wall. "Hey! Come on, you jerks! What do you think you're doing to me? Do you know who I am? You don't know who you're dealing with!"

Having completely lost all notion of time, I was still in the Malkens' fortress and getting pretty hopeless. I'd been blowing on that stupid whistle for days on end and what?

Nothing. Nada. Zilch. Zip. Zero.

The only good news was that the other Earth guy hadn't seemed to get any wind of my call for help. Either that or no one had bothered him with it yet.

Of course, it was also a possibility that it could not have been working altogether and I had just been wasting my breath.

The Malkens had been watching me closely in the past few days and discussing my condition. Nameless Earth-guy had also been by several times himself with more lame attempts to brainwash me, flaring up in anger, and stalking off every time he failed.

Still in pain, I would keep crying out loud or bang my head against the walls. Then some days, I would recover a bit of strength and be able to stand up and pace for short bursts at a time. Like today.

"You've got no right to do this to me!" I paced inside my bubble like a caged panther. Maybe the Malkens intended to drive me insane. "Let me out of here!"

I didn't know what was going to happen to me. All I knew was that I was still here. There was no rescue. No rescue attempt. No plan for a rescue attempt. And I had a persistent splitting headache.

"Nobody's coming to save me." I scowled. "Nobody cares anymore." I threw up my hands in annoyance. "I have to do everything by myself and these stupid people don't even care that I haven't eaten a decent meal in like a week! Do you hear me? You don't treat people like...like this." I trailed off as my knees buckled and I began to weaken all over again.

I collapsed to a seated position on the floor, facing away from the door. I took a deep breath to try to recollect my wits.

Whatever connection Gradd had gleaned from me that had made him sick had subsided some days ago but he was still on bed rest. And, because of Lessandra, all efforts to search for me had been halted since everyone had assumed that I'd simply gone back to Earth like last time.

Meanwhile, the Malken war had kept on, and attack after attack, kingdoms fell one by one. As if I couldn't feel any worse, the vision pool was nice enough to make me watch those too.

Another tremor of pain rumbled through me and I crouched down. Grimacing, I looked at my hands—dirty, bloody, and weak. *Hopeless.* There was nothing more I could do now. I heaved a sigh in resignation, in defeat.

This was it. I was going to stay here, and rot, and die.

When the doors flew open, I jumped and whirled around.

There were two of them this time. I hadn't seen Tagbart in quite a while. I wanted to snap an 'It's nice of you to join us for a change' but thought the better of it and simply glared at them both.

Tagbart was studying my appearance with a curl of disgust on his lips but he didn't seem to have anything to say for the moment.

The still-nameless guy gave me a sympathetic look. "It's been weeks,

Ms. Peters. I would've thought we'd established some sort of rapport by now."

I flashed him a fake smile but gave him nothing, except the finger.

He just looked more amused. "Honestly, I don't understand why you're still counting on those so-called friends of yours to help you while we have been here for you all this time, through your pain."

I couldn't help but scoff. "Through my pain?" I echoed in disbelief as he had left out that he was the one causing me said pain. "I am never going to help you," I declared. "I don't see what you still need me for. These visions can't be that important and you obviously don't need my help to conquer anything."

"You just won't understand." The nameless guy's smile was mysterious. "As long as you're locked up in here, we can't fail. It's as simple as that."

My frown deepened. I was more and more convinced that he was the mastermind of all this and that Tagbart was just some puppet who, unfortunately, was too stupid not to follow some alien guy's plans for world domination. "Why are you doing this?" I asked again. "What do you even care about this world? Surely, you have family and friends looking for you by now. Why don't you and I just go back home to Earth, huh? Let's just forget about all this."

The nameless guy's eyes narrowed sharply. "You don't know anything about my life," he sneered. "Earth was not my home. It was a prison. Here in Anthuria, I have a chance to change things. I can have anything I want."

I shook my head in derision. "Dude, that's just pathetic."

"No, you're pathetic!" he blazed. He sure had a quick temper. "You'd better remember who you're talking to. As it happens, I am the one who holds your very life. You should see yourself now. No friends. No freedom. No hope."

"So kill me. I don't care." I shrugged offhand, as for some reason, I got a distinct sense that the nameless guy wouldn't go so far as to kill me. I didn't know how I knew that but I did. Perhaps, it was his twisted sense of camaraderie, or even sympathy since we were the only two humans on Anthuria. Or perhaps, something worse. I didn't want to think of the other possibilities for which he actually specifically needed me alive.

He scowled but before he could retort, the vision pool glowed again, drawing our attention.

"He said where?" Scott's voice was more urgent than I'd ever heard it.

There was some type of commotion. Scott and several soldiers were rushing down the hallway of Eleria. It looked like they were headed toward the gardens.

"In the rock canyons, your majesty," one soldier was speaking. *"Near the Bacathra peaks. There was a farming convoy passing through there and one of the group remembered hearing the distinct sound of a flute."*

My eyes widened.

"It only caught their attention as it was kind of strange and seemed to be playing the same succession of notes over and over," the soldier went on to relay.

"Scales," Scott affirmed as he burst into the greenhouse.

Gradd, Lessandra, and Leila were there. The servants were cleaning up after a meal service. Lessandra was with Leila by the fountains across the way so only Gradd looked up when Scott approached.

"There is news," Scott spoke to Gradd before directly explaining the situation.

Gradd's forehead was creased in puzzlement until Scott finished with, *"It's Sarah."* And his eyes lit up, his expression more than bewildered, more than alerted. *"What? She's still here?"*

Scott nodded. *"In a rock canyon, near Bacathra."*

Overhearing, Lessandra had glanced over.

"Rock canyon?" Gradd's posture stiffened with a start. *"The Malkens are—"*

"We think so." Scott's tone was grave.

Lessandra hastened over. *"The Malkens?"* she echoed, horrified. *"Oh my god, so she was taken after all?"*

Gradd's eyes blazed. *"What the hell do you mean?"*

Stammering, Lessandra looked close to tears. *"The-the night Sarah disappeared, I—I thought I saw...something but..."*

Scott's face was aghast. *"What? Why didn't you say anything sooner?"*

"I'm—I'm sorry," Lessandra implored.

I made a face. *Like hell you are.*

"How long ago did they say?" Gradd pressed Scott for more details.

"Possibly a couple of days ago."

"That means she may still be alive." Gradd stood up.

"Gradd, what exactly do you think you're going to do?" Scott called out as Gradd stalked away. *"You can't just show up there."*

"Watch me," Gradd snapped his reply.

I almost sighed in relief. Gradd was coming to save me. It was a miracle!

The nameless guy's scowl darkened as his eyes caught the flute hanging around my neck. With his powers, he raised his hand to whip the necklace away from me.

Jerking at the forceful tug on my neck, I yelped out.

My necklace shot through the glass barrier and then it was in his hand.

"How could you have missed this?" Unhappy, Tagbart almost growled at the nameless guy. He moved to leave the room, presumably to call upon his army.

The nameless guy gestured at him to stop. "It doesn't matter now anyway. It's time."

Swallowing hard, I edged away. *Time for what?*

With a diabolical glint in his eyes, the nameless guy turned back to me with a cold smile. Raising his hand toward me, he spoke in his creepy, low voice. "It's time for you, Sarah Peters, to die..."

My eyes widened but I couldn't resist as I stiffened and hovered off the ground again. The next thing I knew, it was as though someone reached into my body and torn me clean in half. "Aaahhh—aahhh!" I cried at the pain in my head, in my chest, in my stomach, everywhere.

I screamed and screamed. The searing, stabbing pain was worse than the last dozen visions combined. And it wouldn't stop. The pain went on and on. I could hardly breathe to scream anymore. I moaned before I took one last breath and everything went black.

54

reset

I woke up with a start to the loud rumble of thunder and rain falling outside. I opened my eyes but it was too dark to see anything.

Moaning, I shifted in bed. For some reason, I was weak, like I had just gone through a significant ordeal.

But I couldn't remember anything.

Once my eyes adjusted to the dim light, I noticed the shadow of someone seated beside my bed. "Wh-who's there?" I whispered.

A flash of lightning illuminated his face for a second and I squinted to try to recognize him.

He had dark hair and dark eyes. He was wearing black clothes with a black cowl. But when he spoke, his voice was calm and soothing.

"You're finally awake. I'm so glad you're okay." Sounding concerned, he patted my arm.

My throat was raw. Trying to speak made me all scratchy but I had too many questions. I tried to sit up. "Who—who are you?"

"Oh, dear. What horrible things they must've put you through."

"What? Who?"

"But don't you remember?" Sounding surprised, he moved to put his arm around my shoulder. "My poor sister."

I blinked, catching my breath. "You're...my brother?"

"Yes, it's me," he replied with a nod. "Don't worry. You're safe now."

Safe... I liked the sound of that. I was safe. I took a deep breath. "I don't remember anything."

"Shh, it's okay," he assured. "You just rest now and get your strength back. We'll talk about the evil people later."

A tremor of pain rushed up my spine. *Evil people? They did this to me.* I instantly hated them. "Who are they, brother?"

"The Centerians," he supplied. "But you mustn't think about them right now. Just rest."

The Centerians... I set my jaw in an already outraged resolution. *Centeria is the enemy.*

"Portia!" My brother called.

I turned back from looking out the balcony and strolled out of my room to find him. "Yes, brother?"

He was in the main chambers, speaking with Lord Tagbart, the head of our kingdom.

I avoided meeting Lord Tagbart's gaze as I walked up to my brother. Lord Tagbart always seemed to dislike me even though I had only re-met him two days ago.

"There you are." My brother's smile looked bright. "You're looking rested today."

Smiling back, I curtsied. "I like this new dress." I looked down at my long, black silk and taffeta dress.

"Look at this." My brother gestured out the window where our newly-improved cloaking relics were in training.

I glanced over, still smiling. I always liked watching the relics. It made me feel safe that our army was so strong.

"The enemy won't stand a chance against us," my brother declared.

I raised an eyebrow. "I don't understand why these pathetic rebel countries don't just surrender. They're obviously no match for us."

"You forget, sister, that they have the Phoenix."

I had been told of the Phoenix. It was a relic from that evil kingdom of Centeria that despite not being capable of cloaking, could supposedly still defeat our best cloaked relics. I hadn't seen it in action yet, not even in my vision pool, but I was confident that it couldn't possibly stand a chance against us.

"One pathetic relic couldn't possibly defeat an army of cloaked relics," I pointed out.

"Indeed," my brother remarked with a vague grin. "You know, when you're well enough and ready, I might let you train in one of the cloaked relics again."

My eyes lit up in eagerness. "Really? I'm ready now! I'm ready now!"

"Now Portia," my brother chided. "Don't make me remind you of the last time."

Frowning, I recalled what I had been told. That I had taken out one of the cloaked relics, even though I hadn't been fully trained on it. It was how I'd been captured by the enemy, who had probably tortured me so badly that I had lost my memory before I was able to be rescued and brought back here. I shivered at the thought then gritted my teeth. "It won't happen again. Never again."

My brother nodded in approval. "Go back to your room now. Lord Tagbart and I need to talk. You need to get some more rest."

I complied. "Yes, brother." Smiling to myself, I headed back to my room. I would be able to train again. I was excited at the chance to prove myself. I wouldn't fail this time. I would be the best fighter ever and destroy the Phoenix. I would make my brother proud.

I knelt in front of my vision pool on the floor of my room, which at the moment I had made look like a little pond with swimming fish. With it, I could focus my powers and see anything in the present and sometimes the future.

My brother had forbidden me from looking into the past. The one time I had sneaked a try, a vision of myself screaming in anguish flashed red hot in my mind and I had ended the vision abruptly. I had almost lost control.

My brother had said that the Centerians had been responsible for that. I hated them more and more every day. I was very glad we had destroyed their kingdom.

I waved my hand over the pool and directed it to show my brother. An image of the main chamber room appeared from the blue ripples of water. My brother and Lord Tagbart were still talking.

"...her powers, we will be unbeatable. So you see where her loyalty lies," my brother was saying. *"She is on our side."*

"Make sure you keep it that way," Lord Tagbart stated.

Sensing me, my brother paused. *"Portia, I told you. No eavesdropping."*

I chuckled. "Of course, brother!" I called out so he could hear me then waved the vision away and my little fish pond returned. I had always thought he might have simply been afraid I'd catch him taking a bath or something.

I walked back out to my balcony and breathed in the mountain air. My room had a great view of the granite mountains, the blue sky, the other flying rocks in our canyon, and our other relics training down below.

Leaning against the edge of the balcony, looking down until I was heady, it felt like I was on top of the world. I knew it wouldn't be long before we won the war. Because the good side always won. It was only a matter of time.

55

who are you?

Among other things, I had forgotten that I was an extremely light sleeper.

I'd also forgotten to close the balcony doors and the cold wind breezed in. But I was too sleepy to get up and shut it so instead, I pulled the blankets closer, burrowing deeper into my bed.

There were some faint swishing sounds and I opened my eyes in exasperation. It must have been my maid again as she bothered me a lot. But when I rolled over to face away from the door, I found myself staring straight into a shadowy face that was leaning down over me.

Gasping, I sat up and had begun to scream. But the stranger clamped his hand over my mouth, pinning my arms to my chest as he put his other arm around me to keep me from struggling.

"Shhh, it's okay, Sarah," he murmured. "It's me. It's me."

I tried to push away but he muffled my wails in his hand. My eyes widened as I caught a glimpse of a red symbol on his sleeve—*a phoenix*. It was the symbol of Centeria! I struggled harder then bit his hand.

"Aahh," he hissed and sprang back.

I stared at him, wide-eyed and heaving, as I edged back into bed. I pulled the covers closer to me. "Who are you? What do you want?"

"What?" He blinked in disbelief.

I squinted to study him up and down. The stranger was tall with dark hair and green eyes. He wore a heavy black cloak over a seemingly distinguished outfit. I'd never seen him before in my life.

"Take it easy, Sarah." He tried to calm me down. "It's me. Gradd. Now don't make too much of a commotion and let's go before they suspect anything."

"What are you talking about?" I mocked, making a face. "You better leave now before I call my brother."

"Brother? Sarah, what—"

"Who is this Sarah you're referring to?" I prompted in exasperation. "You must have the wrong room."

His forehead creased, he took a step closer. "Sarah—"

I held out my hand to stop him. "Don't come any closer," I warned. "I saw the mark on your clothing. I know you're from Centeria. If you don't want to get hurt, I suggest you leave now before the guards come."

He stared at me in bewilderment. "Who...are you?"

I narrowed my eyes. "My name is Portia. I am the sister of the Head General of Malken."

He froze as if in shock.

The doors to my chambers burst open and my brother and Lord Tagbart, along with several armed guards, barged in.

Tagbart smirked, his soulless eyes almost glowing. "Ah, the King of Centeria. Welcome back. We've been expecting you." He snapped his fingers. "Guards," he bid the men to march forward restrained the stranger.

He struggled, shooting me a look before darting Tagbart and my brother a dark look. "What have you done to her?"

My brother merely raised an eyebrow at the stranger as he was promptly dragged away.

Tagbart had already left the room before my brother looked over at me to give me a casual smile. "Sorry about that," he apologized. "Don't mind the prisoner. Go back to sleep."

A bit confused, I nodded. "Alright."

"Good night," my brother said as he turned to leave and closed the door behind him.

I settled back in bed before my eyes darted to the balcony door that was still wide open. Jumping up, I closed it shut before I dove back into bed to get back to sleep.

Even as my pulse still raced.

Who was that?

The next morning, I dashed into the main chambers and caught them about to leave to question the prisoner.

"Portia, go back to your room." Knowing exactly what I was up to, my brother waved me away. "Let us handle this."

"I want to be there. I *need* to be there," I amended in resolve.

My brother sighed. "Alright, fine."

Tagbart shot him a quick look of ire but my brother gave him a neutral look. "Let's try this."

Tagbart didn't look happy, which seemed as per usual, but he led the way to the dungeon.

My brother gave me a firm look. "We'll let you inside with us, but you do not talk to the prisoner. Is that clear?"

I pursed my lips and nodded. I just wanted to know what the evil was like.

I had heard from the maids that the stranger was the king of our enemy kingdom. It seemed highly irregular to me. As if this was part of some elaborate plan of attack against us, why would they send royalty—all by himself, for that matter—instead of an army of soldiers?

The stranger was inside a heavily guarded cell. His whole face seemed to light up when he saw me. But I glared back at him as

I remembered the pain his people had inflicted on me and his face darkened again.

"So, you've found us," Tagbart announced as the three of us stood in front of his cell.

The stranger was seated on the dirty floor, his knees drawn up. He glared at each of the two men in turn before his eyes settled back on me.

My pulse raced at his focus. It was like he was trying to measure me up.

"We'll make it easy on you, your majesty," Tagbart began, his smile sly. "Tell us where the Phoenix is and we'll leave you the use of your legs."

"I don't have it." The stranger's reply was flat, his gaze still fixed on me.

"Oh, come on, you couldn't have gotten here so fast without your relic," my brother reasoned. "Now tell us where it is and it will save us both the time. Our soldiers are already looking for it anyway and will find it eventually."

The stranger didn't answer.

What was his name...? I strained to remember from the previous night. *Grouch? Gary? Grape?* But he looked at me steadily and said nothing.

My eyebrows furrowed, I was trying to keep glaring at him. But his gaze was firm, imploring...almost pleading.

Gradd! I blinked in surprise as I remembered.

He wouldn't look away from me at all. It was as though he was looking for something in my eyes, in my face.

I swallowed and stepped back to stand partway behind my brother. The stranger's gaze was unnerving me. Like he knew something I didn't.

My brother noticed. "I'll thank you to stop staring at my sister."

Gradd turned the daggers in his eyes toward him. "What have you done to her?"

"What have I done?" my brother asked in ridicule. "I have only restored my sister's memory after her terrible ordeal with your people."

"What? Sarah's—"

"The girl you are referring to was a spy," my brother cut in, his tone patronizing. "She was sent to you to get information about the Phoenix. How do you think we knew of your arrival last night?"

Gradd scowled. "I don't believe it." He looked back at me and e moved to get up. "Sarah, whatever you think you know is a lie. He's lying to you, Sarah. Find a way to fight it—"

Tagbart prompted a guard and the stranger was whipped twice.

I winced as the stranger collapsed on the floor with a groan.

"The girl you knew is dead," my brother said. "It's too bad her last memories were of people whom she thought were her friends betraying her to the enemy and leaving her to suffer and die. If you don't tell us the whereabouts of the Phoenix, we have no need of you." He stepped back from the bars. "Come, Portia. I'm sure Lord Tagbart has plenty to catch up on with our prisoner."

I nodded and turned to go but not before I glanced back and met Gradd's gaze again.

Despite his obvious pain, it looked as though he was trying to give me a reassuring smile.

My frown deepened with a feeling I couldn't pinpoint. I hurried to follow my brother back up the stairs. "Brother," I began once we were back in the upstairs hall.

My brother was quick to respond. "You shouldn't be concerned about the prisoner. He plans to deceive us."

"Of course, brother," I agreed with a dismissive wave. "I was wondering about this girl he keeps looking for. Sarah? Who is she?"

"Was," my brother corrected. "She died. Another victim of the Centerians. The prisoner was just confused. You were likely both captured at the same time, except, unfortunately, she did not survive their mistreatment." He frowned and patted my shoulder. "Oh, my poor sister, how strong you must have been to have survived what they put you through. But don't think of it anymore. It's okay now, you're home."

Reassured by that, I nodded.

My brother met my gaze. "Listen, promise me you won't go anywhere near the dungeons," he instructed. "That is no place for a lady. And who knows what other lies the prisoner might concoct to fool you or make you pity him. Centerians are known for their deceit."

"Yes, of course, brother." I nodded again.

"There we go." He smiled before he started away.

I took a deep breath.

My brother was right. If anyone knew how evil the enemy was, it was my brother. He must also have been right that I was extremely lucky to have survived enemy capture and that I should be grateful.

Find a way to fight it...

Walking back to my room, I shook my head to clear it. That stranger... There was something about him. Something vaguely familiar...

Oh, Sarah, there's no hope for you if you give up...

Wincing at the jolt of slight pain, I threw myself face down on my bed. *Ugh. Forget about it.*

Mealtime was pretty quiet with the tension of the war and having such a distinguished prisoner within the castle. I tried to steer the conversation toward cheerier topics, relic cloaks and my upcoming training.

My brother looked to be half-listening but his mind was preoccupied with something else. Lord Tagbart didn't pretend to enjoy the meal at all. But I'd always found him to be rude. He stood up and left before the meal was even finished.

Frowning, I watched Lord Tagbart leave. "How come Lord Tagbart always seems to dislike me?" I asked my brother.

He waved it away. "Tagbart dislikes everybody. Don't take it personally."

"Oh, okay." I pushed my food around my plate. "Brother," I ventured dully. "The prisoner...have I...seen him somewhere before? He just seems familiar is all."

My brother's eyebrows snapped together in an instant blaze of anger. "I don't want to discuss the prisoner anymore. Is that clear, Portia?"

I flinched. "Uh, y-yes of course, brother."

He stood up and faced away from me. "You were their prisoner for quite a while. He is their leader. You must have seen him there. It is also highly possible that he could have killed our parents himself..." His voice subdued as he trailed off and stalked away.

My heart squeezed. I had been told that our parents had been captured while on a mission to rescue me. They didn't survive either. It made sense that my brother didn't want to talk about any of it.

My poor brother. I clenched my jaw. If it was possible, I hated the Centerians even more now than I already did before.

Especially the prisoner.

That night, I tried to sleep but every time I closed my eyes, I saw the face of that prisoner so clearly. As if I knew it so well. As if I could see his pained eyes from this morning as they seemed to tell me, reassure me, that he was okay... That he would be okay.

Turning to one side, I frowned. He looked familiar because he probably killed my parents. I shivered in disgust but also some frustration. *If only I could remember...* But everything before I woke up in bed several days ago was a blank.

Although for some reason I couldn't fathom, I could easily picture the stranger in the middle of a fight in the woods, could easily picture how he looked with his shirt off...putting bandages on his shoulder...

Totally awake, I groaned as I sat up in bed. I had to shake my head briskly in an attempt to clear it. *Forget about it. Forget about it.*

I glimpsed the blue glow of the pool to my side. It had been showing visions of the dungeon all day— without my instruction. It was like it had a mind of its own.

With a helpless frown, I leaned over my bed to watch.

Gradd was simply standing in the cell. Earlier, he had been pacing and punching the wall. The guards looked like they were slacking off as usual. It puzzled to me why he didn't even try to escape. As again, for some reason, it was something I was sure he could very easily do. But he seemed to be waiting for something. I let out a huge sigh.

Gradd stopped and blinked.

My jaw dropped. He sensed me. Only my brother could sense me.

Gradd narrowed his eyes before he whispered, *"Portia."*

Swallowing hard, I jumped out of bed, grabbed my coat, and headed to the dungeons.

The guards stood alert and then relaxed when they saw it was just me.

Gradd looked up.

Pulling my coat closed tighter in front of me, I glared at him as I neared the cell.

Without warning, Gradd smiled as if in relief and wistfulness.

I scowled deeper at him. "What are you smiling for? You're a prisoner here."

Gradd's smile faded and he shot me a look that seemed to say, *So are you.*

Taken a back, I winced. I was of half a mind to leave when he spoke.

"I'm glad you're all right," he said, again in that familiar tone as if he knew me.

"My brother says you're confused," I told him. "You're confusing me with someone already dead."

His face sobered. "He could be right. It's too bad. She was a strong person." A ghost of a smile laced his features. "She looked like you. She was really..." He trailed off with a shrug, gesturing to my clothes. "Black looks interesting on you."

My heart pounded and there was that feeling again that I couldn't describe. My lower lip almost trembled but I hardened my jaw.

Centerians are known for their deceit...

"You've killed our people," I tried to say with as much bitterness as I could muster. "You killed my parents. You've brought us pain. You people are evil. If you surrender now, I can help you to avoid more destruction and death."

"You really believe that?" He shook his head in incredulity before giving me a steady look. "I've got nothing left to lose."

Crestfallen, I frowned and started to turn away.

"Your name is Sarah Peters," Gradd called out. "You're from another world called Earth. You came to this world to save Centeria, not fight it. You have a sister named Annette. You play something called baseball with your best friend Ena. You don't know a thing about treating wounds or starting fires. I've saved your life like you've saved mine, time and time again, and I—I—" He broke off in hesitation.

My chest constricting, I didn't look back. Instead, I glanced up at the guard near the entrance to the dungeon. "I wasn't here tonight. Guard him well," I bid before starting back upstairs.

56

eliminate him.

The cracking of the whip from the dungeons echoed in my room because of the vision pool. I clamped my hands over my ears and gritted my teeth. "Stop it! Stop it!"

I tried to command the pool for what seemed like the millionth time. "Something else," I bid firmly but the view wouldn't change. Gradd's face contorted in pain as he groaned. I forced myself not to look, not to care, but every lashing he took was a spike in my chest.

I slumped down on my bed in frustration. "Why? Why?"

My door opened and my brother came in.

"Oh, brother." I whirled around in relief.

"What's wrong, Portia?" His eyes looked concerned.

"It's the pool," I pointed disdainfully to the blue hole in the floor. "I can't control it anymore. I think that the prisoner is able to manipulate it."

My brother glanced down at the pool and a shadow fell on his face but he looked back up at me with a small smile. "Now Portia. You are the only one with the powers to control the vision pool, you know that. Not even my powers can do so. What you're saying is simply impossible." He patted my back in encouragement. "Just concentrate harder."

"I just don't understand it." I sighed with a helpless frown. "I'm concentrating as much as I can but—"

"You just need to focus some more. Eliminate all the distractions from your mind."

Eliminate.

I started to nod eagerly. "Yes." It made sense. "Yes. Do that. Eliminate all distractions. That prisoner. He is a distraction."

My brother raised an eyebrow. "You want us to—eliminate him?" He looked surprised but, for some reason, also pleased.

I kept nodding. Anything to end this fixation. Surely, the prisoner wouldn't be able to bother me if he was dead.

I almost missed my brother's evil grin as he turned to leave. "As you wish, my dear sister."

I still kept nodding then tried to command the pool again, squeezing my eyes shut to concentrate as hard as I could. *Something else. Anything else.*

I was sleeping when someone touched my face. Opening my eyes, I was still groggy but the prisoner's dark face hovered above me again. Frozen still, I could only gasp. My tongue felt stuck to the roof of my mouth and I was unable to scream.

"Please don't." Gradd brushed my hair out of my eyes.

I blinked at him, dumbfounded. How did he even get in here?

"I'll be leaving shortly."

Why was he telling me? My pulse racing, I narrowed my eyes at him. "Are you here to kill me?" I croaked out.

His eyes widened in horror. "What? I could never—you of all people should know that I'm not a cold-blooded, unfeeling monster."

"Oh, yeah, sure," my reply was laced with sarcasm but I bit my lip right after the words had left my mouth. *How could I possibly know?*

His eyes which had lit up with a momentary flicker of hope fell again when I spoke next.

"The person you know died. I am not her. I am not in need of your rescue," I pointed out, matter-of-factly. "Why do you like to pretend that I am?"

Gradd pursed his lips. "I'm not going to force you to come with me. All I want you to do is consider the possibility that you are not who they say you are."

"My brother said you might try something like this."

"He's not your brother!" Gradd burst out. "You'd never even seen him before in your life, remember? You told me so. We'd been on the quest to find the Phoenix and the Malken relics attacked us. You almost drowned. Sarah, please try to remember."

I furrowed my eyebrows. "I am not...Sarah."

"Says who? Your brother?"

My frown deepened. "If you're going to leave, go. If I don't stop you soon, they might think I helped you. I'll count to five before I call the guards. One," I started.

He gave me a slightly haunted smile and despite the strain in his voice, his tone was self-assured. "You won't stop me. I came all this way to save you. I'd walk through hell for you, Sarah."

"I am not Sarah," I insisted under my breath.

"Please. Try to remember," he urged, his hand hovering over my cheek as if he wanted to touch me again. "You came to this world. I brought you to my kingdom. The Malkens destroyed it. We went to Thorb, to Eleria. You met a lot of people, Agarpa, the witch, Aella, Scott, Lessandra. Leila misses you very much. You have a yellow plant in Eleria. You went home and you came back again after four months, remember?"

Shaking my head, I refused to believe him. "Two."

His eyebrows furrowed in determination. "Sarah, we were in the forest, remember?" he relayed. "Some bandits almost killed me but *you* saved my life. You took care of me for several days. That was when I realized what I'd been trying to pretend wasn't true...that I had already fallen in love with you."

"Three." I didn't flinch.

Gradd looked into my eyes and sighed. He brushed his thumb

against my cheek again and despite myself, I shivered. His frown deepened at my response as I hadn't pulled away. His breathing turned heavy as his gaze dropped to my mouth. I could almost see the conflict in his eyes. He knew he shouldn't but...

"That night was also when I first..." He leaned down and covered my lips with his.

I tried to resist. But there was something in his kiss that I felt I could only find there, something I wanted, something I needed... My heart pounded harder in my chest and I clutched at the sheets as his kiss deepened.

His fingers slid into my hair and I shivered again. I didn't want him to stop. When he began to break off, I tipped my chin up for more. A helpless groan pulled from his throat and he obliged, leaning back down to kiss me again for the last time before finally pulling away.

Almost dizzy, my eyelids were heavy.

Breathless, Gradd's gaze smoldered. He touched my cheek again, his voice husky. "Remember?"

I swallowed hard. How could it be? How could I possibly have forgotten anything that felt like that? *But I couldn't remember.* My chest ached. *He was lying.* I blinked back warning tears before whispering, "Four."

His eyes glistened in the dark. He shook his head before he stepped back. "I'll come back for you," he promised, full of conviction.

Tears stung my eyes. "When you do, one of us will die."

Gradd took one last long look at me before he took off, jumping out my balcony exactly as my doors burst open again with half a dozen guards coming in along with Lord Tagbart and my brother.

I stayed frozen in bed, my pulse still racing. "He's gone."

Tagbart groaned aloud in disappointment before he stalked off, ranting and cursing.

My brother watched me. "Are you okay, Portia?" he asked after a moment, like any concerned brother would, if I do say so myself.

I forced myself to quit trembling. I set my jaw again. *My brother would never lie to me*, I thought with a new resolve. I met my brother's gaze. "I want to start training tomorrow."

What I had to do was clear. Eliminate the distraction.

"I want to join the next attack of Eleria," I told my brother during my break from training the next day.

"Portia, there's no way you can complete your training by then," my brother reasoned.

My vow was firm. "I will." I needed to destroy them all. The sooner the better.

I was certain that I would get the hang of it quickly if I worked hard enough.

After spending all day reacquainting myself with the cloaked relics, I was warming up for another test run when I overheard them again.

"This is insane," Tagbart was complaining to my brother. "You're letting that girl do whatever damn thing she wants!"

"Tagbart," my brother began. "What she wants is to destroy Eleria and the Phoenix. Give her a little credit."

"That girl can't operate a relic," Tagbart argued with a look of distaste. "Your kind is not strong enough."

"*She* can," my brother replied confidently. "I told you her heightened senses with the visions are incredibly compatible with relic operations. If she can master the new relic, I guarantee you, she'll be unbeatable."

"She's a human. She's not built for a heavy mech war," Tagbart pointed out.

"So am I and haven't I gotten you this far?" my brother rationalized. "Trust me. We cannot fail."

I was so determined, so incensed by Tagbart's insult that the 'human' reference completely went over my head.

I'll show that Tagbart, was all I could think. I'd be so damn good, he'll have to like me then.

For the next few days, I trained like hell, getting all bruised and beaten up. I only took breaks when I could no longer work the relic controls. I learned to maneuver and operate the special relic and soon, I could move within it with lightning speed as though the relic was my second skin.

My brother supported me all the way and I grew to hate the enemy more. They had the nerve to say that my brother wasn't my brother when he obviously cared a lot about me. He had rescued me from the enemy and taken care of me when our parents died. Despite all the trouble I had caused, he was the only one who was concerned about me. My brother couldn't possibly have just made all that up. He couldn't possibly be that good an actor or a liar. And I couldn't possibly be that stupid.

At night, when I fell into bed, exhausted, I was still orchestrating relic transformations, moves, and possibilities in my mind. I could just do it. Even though it shouldn't have surprised me that I was a natural at it, for some reason, it still did.

The vision pool came alive and I shifted over in bed to see.

We had been aware that in the past few days, the enemy had been preparing for a big rescue attempt based on the information that they'd gotten once Gradd had returned. It confused me even more that they should all suppose this Sarah person was still here and were still making such a big effort for a dead person.

Stupid, I thought haughtily. Regardless, they didn't stand a chance against us.

My gaze moved to Gradd in the vision pool and my expression neutralized. With a raised eyebrow, I watched his lips move as he spoke to this Scott person.

My face flushed when I remembered the intensity, the urgency, the desperate need in his kiss. I reached out as if to touch his face then stopped short in self-contempt.

Frowning again, I lay back down in bed.

He distracted me. I had to kill him.

I cried as I charged into a relic. "Aaahh!" I shouted as I whirled and clawed one behind me.

It was the last day of my training before we attacked the largest enemy kingdom of Eleria.

Tagbart was in charge of my training and I think he was really trying to kill me. He wasn't letting the training relics go easy on me at all.

But I guessed I surprised him. I could so easily fend off all his attacks since I was using the new relic designed for me. My relic reacted on impulse. It was so fast, I could practically control it with my thoughts.

"Bam! *Bam!*" I cried in triumph as I kicked the last obstacle relic before standing breathless in the middle of the big pile of fallen training relics.

My brother applauded.

I beamed at him then turned to check for Lord Tagbart's reaction.

Tagbart actually looked impressed. He turned to meet my brother's gaze with a conspiratorial smile. "I guess you were right, my partner."

I was ready.

57

❧

undertow

It was early morning on the brink of battle. Our relic armies were getting ready outside. Both my brother and Lord Tagbart were going all out with the day's wave of attack. We were bringing the floating fortress itself into the kingdom of Eleria. In fact, we were half-way there.

Admiring myself in the mirror, I smoothed back my hair into a high sleek ponytail. Turning to one side to adjust my armor suit, I raised an eyebrow at my reflection and smirked. *I do look good in black.*

The first rays of sunrise streaked through my balcony despite the sky being overcast again. I couldn't help a sardonic smile with my thought. *Perfect weather for death and destruction.*

Stepping around my bed, I sat down to watch the vision pool to pass the time.

Eleria was still quiet. I already knew their rescue attempt wasn't planned until tomorrow. Everyone was asleep except for Gradd and this other fellow Scott. They'd been talking all night about this Sarah girl.

I couldn't quite hear what they were saying but it still puzzled me. I didn't understand why they all seemed so concerned about her. She

317

couldn't have been that important. From what I figured, she was a spy who had failed at her mission and then died.

It seemed she wasn't even from this world and yet she still had all these people who seemed to care about her. I frowned as I studied Gradd's sober, urgent expression. And Gradd who seemed to love her. *Seemed to love me...*

Shaking my head to clear it, I wrinkled my nose in distaste. *Deceitful King of the deceitful enemy kingdom.*

I was moving to get up when a distinct hissing sound from the pool caught my attention and I glanced back down into it.

But the vision pool's surface was calm.

I narrowed my eyes at the pool again. *Where is that sound coming from?*

And then I could just feel it.

A presence... One that made the hairs on the back of my neck stand up on end.

"Who's there?" I whispered.

The vision pool began to distort into a dark shadow against its blue mirror and the figure hissed again. The sound made my blood run cold but somehow it was a familiar sort of creepy feeling.

"Sssarahh..."

I blew out a breath in exasperation. I was going to argue again that I wasn't this Sarah person but the shadow went on to speak in its particularly slimy voice.

"When the sun hits your eyes, the tables will turn. Alas, the spark has been lit and the fire must burn. To spare all the worlds the fates of hell, the legend must fall and all will be well..."

"What?" I blinked in great bewilderment at the creepy shadow's little riddle.

The door burst open just then and I jumped in a startle. But it was just my brother. "It's you." I took a breath to calm myself.

He walked over to me. "Something wrong?"

I glanced down at the pool. The shadow was gone. "No. Nothing."

His forehead creased with concern, my brother sat me down. "This is your first real battle. I wanted to make sure you had no doubts in proceeding."

In firm resolution, I shook my head. "No. None at all."

"This is a very important battle, Portia." His tone was as serious as I'd ever heard it. "We cannot afford to fail."

I nodded in solemn understanding.

"I just wanted to wish you luck." He patted my back. "As your brother, who's always been here to protect you, who has always been here for you—" He put a hand on my shoulder, his next words uttered in an almost frightening and grave voice. "Do not fail me."

I swallowed before vowing, "I won't fail you, brother. I'll make you proud."

"Good." As if the darkness lifted altogether, my brother cracked a bright smile and beckoned me over as he stood up. "It's time."

Beaming at him, I was more determined than ever. My brother wouldn't be so serious if he wasn't truly concerned, if he wasn't my only family. I watched him walk out of my room before following suit.

As soon I was loaded into my special relic unit, I focused my eyes straight ahead and followed the battalion take-off.

Getting into inner Eleria was super easy as the outpost fleets were nothing compared to our battalion of cloaked relics. I'd barely even worked up a sweat since the enemy's relics posed no challenge at all. They were a good warm-up but my goal was to destroy the Phoenix.

We pushed forward against barely any resistance at all and I was in good spirits. By mid-morning, we were only a few outposts away before reaching the heart of Eleria itself, the castle. Our recon group had come back reporting that the enemy relics had managed to form a barrier in front of the outpost with several dozens of relics. But I knew this was going to be a snap.

I had been hanging back for most of the outing so far, as per my brother's instructions, but I perked up when I heard that the Saber and the Phoenix were among the relics that had been sighted.

With our battalion hidden among the trees, still camouflaged, I moved a bit closer to see.

I spotted it immediately. Even if it wasn't standing right in the middle of the skirmish, beside the other special-looking relic, I would have recognized the Phoenix anywhere.

Curious, I tilted my head. I still didn't see why everyone was so scared of the Phoenix and their forces. I had been told that we had easily crushed the kingdom of Centeria. I didn't understand how it could be different this time. But I was eager to find out for myself.

Once the word was given, our battalion of cloaked relics advanced so sharply that the trees rustled, forcing the birds to fly away. Even as the commotion alerted the enemy, with our relics all invisible, they were still caught off-guard.

I was itching to jump in and join the fight but I wanted to see the Phoenix in action first. I wanted to see what the hell was so special about this stupid relic that scared everyone.

A bit smug, I stood back as I watched as our relics began their attack. I furrowed my eyebrows as I observed this illustrious Phoenix. I didn't see anything especially noteworthy in how the ancient-looking red relic fought. In fact, I had already noted that the Saber was significantly more adept in as far as fighting skills went.

"Watch the ground! Their relics are leaving tracks!"

I snapped to attention and looked over. The warning had come from the pilot of the Phoenix. Turning my attention to our relics, I noted they were indeed leaving a trail of mud on the ground. Gasping, I glanced backward. Our battalion had passed through a marshy trail in the forest on the way, with mud having been caught on the relics' feet, including mine.

I whirled back toward the fighting and narrowed my eyes at the Phoenix.

Cunning.

Several of our relics had been uncloaked after being tracked with the mud.

Cunning, but not good enough.

The order to take flight was given and I switched my helmet filter on to be able to see our cloaked relics in the sky.

Within a few minutes, our battalion had forced into the gate and was pushing the fight deeper into Eleria.

Self-satisfied, I remained standing back. Our relics didn't seem to need any help.

This is no challenge at all. I felt like yawning. Here I was thinking that something really important was going to happen today.

I was still entranced by the commendable swordsmanship of the silver Saber relic when a red spot in the sky distracted me.

The Phoenix had transformed into a flying red bird. It fought recklessly, aimlessly, battling the surrounding thin air as it looked to chance upon a cloaked relic.

I had to admit I was a bit impressed. *Well, it certainly has spirit.*

Something crashed near me and the ground shook with the debris and leaves flying up around. I looked up in time to see one of our relics uncloak just as another relic fell at my feet. I furrowed my eyebrows again. *What the—?*

The Phoenix seemed to somehow be fending off cloaked relic after cloaked relic.

How the hell—?

Another cloaked relic dropped from the sky—damn near right on top of me.

"Oh my god." I jumped to one side to avoid it but I hadn't even straightened up yet when something else crashed against me and I fell back with a heavy thud.

When I looked up, the sun glinted on the bright red metal of the Phoenix relic as it stood over me.

"I knew you were standing around there," the pilot of the Phoenix called. "Why don't you show yourself like a real soldier and fight me."

Gritting my teeth, I nimbly jumped up. "You'll have to uncloak me first," I mumbled in determination.

The Phoenix clawed at thin air, blindly trying to find me, and I used the pause to check on the battalion.

The gate behind us had already been trashed and we were nearing the last outpost. Everyone else was otherwise occupied. I glimpsed the skilled Saber relic across the way and decided that I would tangle with that one next. Once I had defeated the Phoenix.

This was it.

I turned to face the Phoenix who was still looking for me and I grinned. There was no way it was going to defeat me like that.

I began my attack, extending one of my relic claws to strike the Phoenix in the shoulder. Its response was a reflex, having somehow instantly calculated where my attack had come from and kicking in that direction.

My eyes widening, I wove away. It almost got me! I narrowed my eyes as I continued my attack, punching, clawing, and kicking. The Phoenix might have been really good but I was still certain it wouldn't stand a chance against an invisible enemy.

I cried out loud as I jabbed at the Phoenix and sprung away when it tried to return the favor. It missed me but I didn't see the combo double back hit and it grazed my arm. Groaning aloud, I attacked again on impulse.

There was a whoosh and the Saber relic arrived, landing quite close behind me. It was looking to assist the Phoenix. But I saw it and transformed to flight-mode, the Phoenix following fast at my heels.

I thought the Saber would follow us too but one of our other invisible relics arrived in time to keep the Saber occupied and grounded.

I glared back up at the Phoenix in triumph as I hovered around it. It was already badly beaten up from our fight. I was still trying to decide from which direction I would strike next when the Phoenix reared back. I thought it was going to claw around for me again when there was a sudden blow to my side.

"Oof!" Propeled sharply back, I gasped in disbelief.

"Keep hovering," the Phoenix pilot called. "I can hear your boosters."

Enraged, I growled as I clawed at it again but it was swift—and smart. I cried as I kicked it in its side and pummeled it backward.

"Gradd!" someone called and I glanced down.

It was the Saber having defeated our other relic and it was looking to help the Phoenix out again. But I was more gobsmacked by what he'd said.

Gradd? Stunned, I blinked up at the Phoenix. It was Gradd in there.

"I'm fine!" Gradd called back. "Help the others."

Furious, I narrowed my eyes at him. *He was fine, was he?* Crying out loud, I attacked him again. "Why don't you just die?" I shouted as I threw an extended claw at him. *We cannot fail*, I swore under my breath intently, fervently.

I managed to nick his headpiece armor but he found my invisible claw in the air and grabbed my relic hand. Whirling around, I thrust my relic fist into his stomach and he doubled over. Then grabbing both his relic arms, I squeezed until the metal started to give.

Groaning out loud, I put all my effort into it.

Unfortunately, in this position, Gradd knew exactly where I was and his next kick landed right across my middle. Groaning, I kicked him back, trying to twist away. "You'll have to do better than that!" I shouted as I lunged at him.

Gradd must have heard me and was so taken aback, he froze for a second, unable to disguise the stark disbelief in his voice. "Sarah?"

58

the best weapon

Hearing the name made me even more furious. "Stop calling me that!" I retorted, going for his arms again.

"Sarah, what the hell are you doing?" Gradd demanded. "Stop this right now!"

"No!" I yelled back, wanting to tear his arms out.

"Sarah, stop it!" Gradd pushed me back, harder this time that I hurtled to the ground.

When I crashed, my cloak disabled. "Shit!"

The ground shook as the Saber arrived and thundered toward my now-visible relic.

I scrambled to get up even as the gleaming Saber claw whooshed right toward me.

"Scott, no!" Gradd shouted.

The Saber stopped short.

"That's Sarah in there!"

"What?" Scott's tone was utter disbelief.

I had flinched when I saw him coming but he stopped so suddenly, I saw my chance. I kicked the Saber relic square in the chest and it flew back. Then I ran toward the other fighting relics again, ignoring them both.

"How can that be Sarah?" Scott was demanding. "It just kicked me."

"She's not herself. I think they've brainwashed her," Gradd replied.

More lies. Still fuming, I was able to down two more Elerian relics before Gradd caught up with me. He lunged at me from behind, restraining me, holding me back, but not hurting me.

"Sarah, stop this. Snap out of it!"

"Get off me. I'm not Sarah!" I grunted to break free.

The Phoenix pulled me to one side of a crumbling outpost and whirled around to pin me back against it. "Sarah, it's you. Listen to me. The Malkens have brainwashed you. You've got to believe me!"

Up at the mountain peak, the massive floating fortress finally arrived.

Brother! I shouted in my head.

As your brother, who's always been here to protect you, who has always been here for you. Do not fail me... So you see where her loyalty lies. She is on our side...

I moaned at the sudden, intense stinging in my head.

It's time for you, Sarah Peters, to die...

Your name is Sarah Peters, you're from another world called Earth. You came to this world to save Centeria...

You don't deserve to be the legend of Centeria...

I pressed my hands against my ears. "No!"

"Sarah, are you okay?" Gradd sounded worried.

Dizzy, a vision of the floating fortress, the vision pool, and my brother flashed in my mind all at once. When I turned to look up at the fortress, my eyes caught a strange glimmer of light which snapped something in me.

Do not fail me...

Blinking in resolution, I dropped my hands. *I have to destroy Eleria.* I pushed the Phoenix back with a strength I never knew I had and proceeded to attack more enemy relics and trash more structures.

"Sarah!" Gradd protested.

I didn't hear him. *I have to destroy Eleria.*

Nobody could stop me. I was the Malken's best weapon. Neither

Scott nor Gradd could touch me as I plowed through other relics, farms, and structures while the battle raged on around us.

I have to destroy Eleria.

"Gradd, do something!" Scott yelled.

"I don't know what happened." Gradd sounded desolate. "It's like she's under some form of mind control now. She stopped listening to me." Jetting over, he tried to block my way with his relic instead.

"Sarah, listen to me. You have to fight it. I know you can do it."

I charged straight at him.

Gradd groaned in helpless frustration. "I'm sorry!" he called out before rearing his arm back and taking a swing.

When he hit me, I fell but I couldn't feel anything.

I merely lay back on the ground, exhausted, debilitated.

Gradd knelt the Phoenix relic beside mine, reached down, and tore open the faceplate of my relic by force. "Are you okay?"

With my shielding damage, I squinted in the rays of high noon.

When the sun hits your eyes...

I blinked once, twice.

Gradd himself landed on my relic with a thud. Leaning over me, he carefully scooped me out of my pilot seat and propped me on his lap. Gazing down at my face, his forehead creased but he sounded relieved. "Sarah." He brushed back my hair which had worked loose from my ponytail. "Are you okay?"

I blinked again when I met his gaze and swallowed past the dry lump in my throat. "Gradd?"

Gradd's eager eyes lit up. "Sarah? Sarah!"

Moaning, I shifted in my position. "I am—not Sarah," I insisted. "Why do you keep calling me that?"

His face fell again. "Portia," he breathed in resignation before he scooped me up again and carried me into his relic.

That was when Scott arrived. "Aella and Agarpa are at the edge of the valley forest," he relayed, out of breath. "Agarpa says you have to bring Sarah to her. To break whatever spell they've put on her."

Gradd complied with a nod and both relics flew to the edge of the forest.

Lifting me out of his relic, Gradd set me down on the grass in front of a bunch of weird forest people I'd never seen before.

"We'll take care of her, Gradd." A tall, pretty girl wearing a large feathered headpiece assured him. "Go and take care of the Malkens."

Nodding, Gradd began to pull away. But I held him fast, my eyes wide. "You're leaving?"

"I'll go on ahead, Gradd," Scott bid with a gesture, "before the Malkens run Eleria over."

"Yeah." Gradd waved him away but he was only looking at me. Even with the intense fire burning in his eyes, he gave me a gentle smile. "Trust me. I'll be back. These people won't hurt you."

Still apprehensive, I managed a nod.

Gradd touched my cheek before he hopped back into his relic to fight the Malkens. My kingdom. My frown deepened in utter confusion.

"Hey Sarah, long time." The tall, pretty girl smiled at me.

I felt I hated her. "I'm not Sarah, for crying out loud!"

"Shut up, witch!" the one she called Agarpa hissed.

I recognized her as the shadow in my pool. "I'm a witch?" I made a face in incredulity. "Then what does that make you?"

Just then, two other forest women held me down. "Hey!" I struggled as Agarpa held her hands up over me. "What are you doing? Let go of me! Do you know who I am? I am the sister of the head general of Malken. You have no right to...to..." I trailed off before I fell under Agarpa's spell.

59

the prophecy

"Sarah! Sarah!" There were voices in my head.

"Annette, I've told you many times to watch your sister. Don't let her wander off into the neighbors again. She's your responsibility."

"Mom! Sarah's hogging the TV again! Dad, do something! I want to watch something besides Care bears!"

"And Pathetic Peters strikes again."

"Where the hell did you come from?"

"You don't mean me. You can't mean me. I don't know anything about fighting wars much less saving countries..."

"She comes from a place with no procedure..."

"I would think the legend of the Centerian kingdom would have been heavily guarded..."

"Scott Darabont. Pleasure."

"I wish my life was as dangerous as yours..."

"Centeria's pretty lucky to have you as the legend ..."

"Great. Will you marry me?"

"Gradd? are you okay? You better not die..."

"I wanted you to know how unbelievably lucky I feel that you've come into my life... Tell me you'll stay with me..."

"You're useless, Sarah!"

"It's too bad you yourself are unaware of your full potential..."

"As long as you're locked up in here, we can't fail..."

"Your name is Sarah Peters. You're from another world called Earth."

A sharp pain shot through my body and my eyes flew wide open as I woke up with a gasp. I started coughing as I rolled to one side.

Someone was rubbing my back. I blinked before I recognized her. "Aella?" I rasped.

"Oh, thank god." Aella looked relieved as she turned to Agarpa. "I think it worked."

I glanced over at the witchy shadow. I almost couldn't make out her form but somehow, I could tell she was exhausted.

Agarpa let out a breath before she whirled around and simply vanished as if she was never there.

Aella helped me sit up and I had to moan as my head swam. "Ugh, what happened?" I cast my gaze around in bewilderment. We were surrounded by the Kiffad people at the edge of some forest in Eleria. "What's going on? How did I get here?" I looked down at myself in distaste. "And what am I wearing?"

The last thing I remembered was that creepy nameless guy torturing me and saying it was time for me to die. A dreadful shiver ran up my spine.

"It's okay now." Aella put her hand on my arm in reassurance. "We got you back safe and sound. Thanks to Agarpa."

"Agarpa?" I wrinkled my nose. "She helped me?"

Aella had begun to chuckle when there was an explosion and a loud crash.

I snapped to attention. "What...was that?"

Aella's smile fading, she looked hesitant to tell me. "The Malkens...have attacked Eleria."

My heart sank in the heaviest dread ever. "No." I ran toward the edge of the cliff to see.

The Malken relics were fighting the Elerians at the last outpost, almost to the castle, meanwhile all that lay before them was a trail of destruction and devastation.

There was a constriction in my chest. *No. Not again. Not Eleria too.*

Fallen relics lay around—of every shape, size, and color. Even Malken ones.

I searched the battlefield for Scott and Gradd. Squinting, I thought I glimpsed Scott's Saber from far away as he fought with a badly damaged Malken relic. When I looked back toward the forest, another wave of Malken relics were flying in. It was as though they simply never ran out.

"Ohh no," I muttered in distress.

A fresh jolt of pain surged through me and I dropped to my knees on the grass at the an intense new vision.

Tagbart and that creepy nameless guy were arguing inside the flying fortress.

"*You've failed,*" Tagbart was ranting as he put on his armor. "*Starting now, we're doing this my way.*"

"*I didn't fail,*" the nameless guy retorted. "*Something must have gone wrong. Somehow they've used some kind of stronger magic to overcome my control. It's impossible! It's not my fault. Anyway, we don't need her. We have an army of cloaked relics and more where they came from. Have you forgotten you wouldn't even have them if it weren't for me?*"

"You are an ass. Why don't you just go home?" Tagbart snapped, whirled, and stalked out of the main chambers.

I groaned aloud as the vision ended, propping my hands on my knees to catch my breath.

I wasn't sure exactly what they were talking about but looking up at the mountain, I was surprised to see that the flying fortress itself was looming over the valley. The sun glanced off something large that shot out from beneath the fortress before disappearing into thin air and I guessed Tagbart was bringing out the big guns.

Continuing to search the field for Gradd in worry, I blinked alert when I finally spotted him.

Gradd was near the last outpost as well, halfway down the field from the forest. He'd just uncloaked a Malken relic. My jaw nearly dropped as I watched him fight. The Phoenix was incredible—agile, powerful. I'd never seen it in action before.

Grimacing at the heat, I raised my hand to shield my eyes from the early afternoon sun's rays. The last outpost to Eleria was on fire and there was a pit in my stomach as I feared we would not be able to hold out against the Malkens for much longer. I bit my lip and wished I could help.

The ground trembled with a crash and I looked over. The Phoenix had been thrown back against what remained of one of the outpost walls from the force of the Malken relic's claw. *Oh no, Gradd.* My pulse raced in concern.

Gradd was able to kick the relic off of him but it was persistent as hell. The Phoenix did an awesome spinning punch and a kick combo at the enemy and it finally fell.

Blowing out a breath in relief, I almost felt like clapping. *Gradd was okay.*

All of a sudden, Gradd's relic seemed to turn in my direction.

I was going to wave as he seemed to have seen me when I heard him shout, "Watch out!"

Furrowing my eyebrows, I glanced over my shoulder for any cause for alarm.

I found it.

An extending mechanical claw appeared out of nowhere from the trees behind me and whooshed right in my direction. I held my breath, frozen in place, and could only widen my eyes as the relic claw crashed into me and the ground around me.

I screamed as the impact tossed me aside like a pebble. The claw crashed into the cliff and the entire precipice gave way.

My whole body aching from the direct hit of the monster's heavy metal claw as if I'd broken every bone in my body, my head whirled and stung like hell as I plummeted straight down. I couldn't move anything. I squinted at the bright sky, warm blood oozing out of my mouth, my nose, my ears...

Everything muted out—the shouts, the explosions, the crashes, and all I could hear was my own heartbeat. It seemed loud in my ears, beating slower and slower.

The hard ground way below the cliff didn't feel like I thought it would. My back hit the ground squarely, the impact making me practically bounce, limp as a rag doll, as more pain exploded throughout my body.

The legend must fall...

When I hit the ground, I was able to groan weakly, shortly.

Then nothing.

60

the fall

Silence.

It was as if nature itself had stopped to watch as the girl from the mysterious other world plunged straight down the cliff from the cloaked relic's sneak attack. Even the very air seemed to hang still. She hit the ground. A breeze blew.

Frozen in sheer terror, Gradd had been watching from across the battlefield. His eyes were wide, and when the girl stayed limp on the ground, his breath that had caught in his throat released in a savage cry that seemed to echo throughout the valley.

"Sarah!" Aella emerged running out of the woods behind the cliff. She looked over the edge of the cliff in horror.

Scott had been fighting some distance away when he heard the shouts. He looked over in time to see Aella and half her tribe rush down the cliff to check on something that was at the bottom of the cliff. He narrowed his eyes and when he recognized what the unmoving form was, his blood ran cold.

"Sarah? Sarah, are you okay?" Aella's voice was insistent as she cradled the limp body of the girl. "Are you okay, Sarah? Wake up. Please be alive. Please!"

The girl remained motionless. Debris had torn her clothes and she was bleeding from everywhere.

"Sarah! Sarah!" Aella patted the girl's cheeks lightly at first then harder. "Sarah?" She bent her head to feel for breathing or a heartbeat. When she got nothing, she sat up and searched for a pulse on the girl's wrist then her neck.

Nothing.

"No, Sarah, no." Aella persisted, shaking the girl's shoulder again for another few seconds before she stopped. Blinking tears streaming down her face blurring her vision, Aella sat back on her heels with a sigh of defeat before she looked up in the direction of the red relic.

Gradd hadn't moved, his eyes were still wide. He saw Aella sit back in resignation.

Sarah was dead.

"No." He shook his head. "No," he repeated, his voice hollow.

A sinister laugh coasted the air. Everyone looked up as the Malken relic on the cliff uncloaked itself, leaped into the air, before landing in the middle of the valley. It was the Malkens' special relic, the Scorpion being piloted by Tagbart. His commentary was snide. "Some legend. Who's going to save you now?"

Gradd's eyes blazed in rage and pure fury. His muscles tensed and he let out a loud growl. The next thing anybody saw seemed like a split second flash of bright red light as the Phoenix charged headlong toward the Scorpion.

Scott had seen the Phoenix fight before but he stopped, taken aback, as he looked closer.

The Phoenix seemed to have erupted a crest of flames and its eyes were glowing bright red. It was fighting with a new, stronger force, driven from the depths of Gradd's soul.

Aella hardly noticed when Scott landed beside her to check on Sarah himself. She was entranced watching Gradd fight, her mouth hanging open in surprise and shock. "The Phoenix is alive," she murmured.

despair, Scott swallowed hard upon finding the same condition on the girl as Aella had. No breathing. No pulse. No heartbeat. He stumbled to stand up, only staggering again to collapse against Aella in anguish.

Patting his back, Aella pursed her lips. "We mustn't be disheartened, Scott. Sarah died for a reason and we can't abandon that cause. We can't give up. Not now." Sighing, she looked back out at the battle. "Poor Gradd."

Scott let out a deep sigh before shaking his head to clear it as he straightened up. He followed Aella's gaze in deep thought. "Even if Gradd wins this one, the other relics are practically at the castle already."

Aella shrugged. "If their leader falls, perhaps the others might surrender. But there are so many of them."

Scott turned his gaze to the flying fortress from where Malken relics seemed to be coming out in droves. He narrowed his eyes, setting jaw before hastening to his relic.

"Where are you going?" Aella looked up.

"I really have to blow something out of the sky right now," he replied with a glint in his eyes, hopping up into the Saber and taking off.

Aella tilted her head, not understanding, but she turned back to watch Gradd's fight. The attacks and counterattacks were lightning fast, they were almost imperceptible. Aella had never seen Gradd fight like this before. She looked down at the dead body before she bent down once more. "Bring some washcloths," she instructed the nearby Kiffads with a wave as she intended to at least clean up the body.

Another loud explosion made her look up, in time to see the big, flying rock base of the flying fortress shatter into several dozen chunks and the fortress began to fall from the sky.

Aella saw Scott's relic still flying among the debris. He wasn't done. He shot into the huge fortress and whatever he did made the structure implode so devastatingly, there was barely anything left to see afterward except a spray of rocks showering from the sky.

"NO! What have you done?" Tagbart glanced up in time to see his dark castle completely obliterated, falling to pieces.

Gradd took the opportunity while it was distracted to kick the Scorpion hard and it skidded backward but the Scorpion responded by reflex.

Aella, who was still watching, noticed the Scorpion's tail whip back to strike the unsuspecting Phoenix. "Look out!" she called out but quick as a flash, Gradd whirled to capture the scorpion tail in his hand and with a forceful heave, whipped the Scorpion right off its footing to crash down against the ground at the Phoenix's feet.

Tagbart was down.

Aella blew out a breath in relief just as the body she had been tending floated off the ground and emitted a strange red glow. "What the—?" Her eyes widening, she stood up.

The body was floating all by itself and its light grew brighter.

Aella stepped back. The rest of the Kiffads stepped back. They could all only watch as something emerged from the body of the dead girl—a bright ball of energy. This brightness rose, up into the sky, higher, until it was in the clouds. The body fell back on the ground, limp as before—but no one was watching that since the bright ball in the sky suddenly exploded into a spectacular red fire, momentarily taking the shape of a great big phoenix.

Still in his relic down on its back on the ground, Tagbart glared up at it in suspicion. "What's that?" His eyes filled with dread as the giant ball of energy glowed brighter again and then even brighter still until the glow was practically blinding.

Aella had to shield her eyes from its light which was intense as the sun.

"What-what the hell is that?" Tagbart tried to scamper back away but the energy ball reached out to the Scorpion, grabbed hold of its core, and dragged it into itself, sucking away at its being like a black hole. "What is this? Get me out of this!" Tagbart attempted to blast away from the reach of the energy ball to no avail.

Everyone watched as an intense force pressed around the Scorpion relic, making the metal creak and give before the Scorpion began to collapse into itself.

Tagbart screamed in terror as his relic crumpled into a ball, crumpling smaller and smaller until no one could hear Tagbart's cries any longer, and the metal ball that was once the Scorpion disintegrated into oblivion.

"Whoa," Aella mumbled in awe.

As if on cue, the entire Malken relic army withdrew. Their leader was gone. Their fortress destroyed. Most of them went running into retreat, likely in terror of what had happened to Tagbart and afraid the magic would get them next. The Elerian forces subdued the rest of the stragglers and chased them away.

Seeing this, the entire Kiffad tribe let out celebratory howls and joyous cheers, shouts, and applause could be heard from all over the valley and all across Eleria.

The war was over.

But Gradd was staring at the glowing energy ball that was still swirling before him. Uneasy, he blinked at this awesome power. *Was it going to take him too?* He pondered in dread when just then, a bright beam of energy shot out from the Phoenix relic itself—only to be sucked into the great ball of energy too but instead of crumpling up Gradd's relic, the Phoenix merely fell slack. Its crest of fire went out and its eyes dulled black once more as if all its power had been drained. The giant energy ball dimmed as it shrank.

With the Phoenix relic slumped on the ground, Gradd jumped out of it. He sprinted across the valley toward the bottom of the cliff. When he got close to the spot where Aella was, he dove down beside Sarah's lifeless form on the ground.

Gradd lifted her head, his face pained as he looked into hers. He turned back to glance over at Aella, nothing but urgency in his eyes. "She's going to be okay, right?" he prompted before he looked back down at Sarah who lay limp in his arms. "Sarah?" He brushed her hair aside. "Sarah, the war's over. We did it. We won." He patted her cheek in an attempt to wake her up. "Wake up. It's time to wake up.

Come on now. The joke's over. You can gloat about how you scared the living hell out of everybody all day if you just wake up. Please."

The body stayed slack.

Aella put a hand on his shoulder. "She lost too much blood, Gradd. It was too late..."

Gradd stared at the motionless figure for a moment before his eyebrows snapped together. "Sarah, this isn't funny. You wake up now!" he ordered, his tone almost vicious. "This isn't fair. You can't leave like this. I told you—I swore that I was supposed to—" He choked before groaning in frustration. Swallowing hard, he hung his head.

After a long moment, Gradd set the body back down on the ground. Straightening up abruptly, he cleared his throat, his face blank as if nothing happened.

Aella peered at him with a sympathetic frown. "Gradd, are you—?"

"Fine," he dismissed. "Let's get back to the castle. Where's Scott?"

"Uh...he uh...went to crash the fortress," Aella stammered, flustered as she watched him walk away. "I'll-I'll have Sarah brought back to the castle."

Gradd didn't respond.

"Gradd—" Aella caught his shoulder but he shrugged her off, looking irritable. She gave him a pointed warning look. "Don't you dare waste Sarah's death like this. She died for us. For you. If you want to be an ungrateful son of a bitch, that's your choice."

Gradd still didn't reply.

It was unfortunate that no one was watching the sky and what had become of the ball of energy to see that it had spread across the atmosphere in the form of a swirling cloud. It rumbled and crackled, as of a brewing storm, before a beam of light that streaked across the heavens like a bolt of lightning struck the lifeless body of the alien girl on the ground.

61

i'm okay

I was floating off the ground. When I managed to open my eyes, I saw that I was. "Whoa," I whispered hoarsely in surprise as I tried to sit up. But several guys wearing barely anything at all were carrying me off. One at my feet, two at my head. I blinked in a daze and swallowed. *Was this heaven?*

No such luck.

With said guys jumping startled at my sudden, seriously unexpected movement, I was unceremoniously dropped.

"Ow!" I squeaked. Rubbing my rear where I landed, I was still a little weak and everything was kind of fuzzy in my head.

"Chief!" one of the half-naked guys called out.

Aella who was walking ahead turned around.

I met her gaze and her eyes practically popped out of her head. Her jaw dropped in such astonishment that she was unable to speak.

"What?" I gave her an expectant look before I cast a glance around from where I sat on the ground.

Everything was quieter now. The sky was clearing up. I couldn't hear or see any more fighting. I thought I could even hear faint sounds of cheering coming from a distance. I craned my neck. All the Kiffad people had stepped back and were staring at me. Aella was here. Gradd was walking a few feet away.

I made a face. "Where's Scott? What the heck is wrong with everyone?"

"Y-y-you're—" Blinking hard, Aella was unable to finish her statement.

Gradd stopped short in mid-stride when he heard my voice. He turned around slowly as though still half in dread at what he might see.

I met Gradd's gaze and raised my eyebrows again in a puzzled prompt. But before I could ask again, Gradd lunged at me, enfolding me tight in his arms, and my eyes widened in surprise. "Whoa—!"

"Why are you always looking for Scott?" His demand sounded rough as he buried his face in my hair.

"Gradd?" I started to ask when he fell slack in my arms. "Hey." I shook his shoulder, trying to peer at his face. His eyes were closed. Looking up at Aella, I made another face. "Is he...dead?"

Aella let out a laugh. "No, I think he's uh...just tired and...awfully glad to see you."

"Oh." I shrugged and then frowned as I was being crushed under Gradd's body weight. "Ow—I think—ugh, my circulation!" I complained, trying to push out from under him.

Aella laughed again before she signaled her men to carry Gradd back to the castle.

Sitting on a chair beside his bed, in his room back at the castle in Eleria, I watched with a slight smile as Gradd slept.

Aella and I had laughed at the role reversal because usually it was me who was unconscious in bed and he was the one sitting up in worry.

The war had ended with a big bang, or so I had been told by Aella.

Apparently, I had died. Which was something I didn't usually hear every day. And that somehow, the phoenix had saved the world—*and* me. Which, if I thought about it, probably did make sense. I recalled what Gradd had said about the power of the phoenix when I had arrived in Anthuria and what the phoenix could make rise from the ashes. Not just kingdoms, it seemed. Although, I was definitely not keen on seeing if it would work a second time.

Regardless, I was also told that Gradd had defeated Tagbart. After which Tagbart's relic had got sucked into some type of black hole nothingness. Scott had destroyed the flying fortress. And even though everyone had tried looking for him in the wreckage, the nameless guy could not be found. Everyone assumed that he must have been crushed under all the debris when the fortress exploded. The Malkens hadn't reached the castle at Eleria. The kingdom was safe. Everyone was safe. The good guys had won.

Although nobody would tell me how I happened to be in the forest during the battle. My memories were still sort of fragmented from around about the time when the nameless guy had said that it was time for me to die. Then again, everyone was still exhausted and resting so no one was available for idle chitchat.

All I could do was sit, and wait, and wonder... Specifically, if the war was indeed over, what was I still doing here? Not that I couldn't wait to get back to fighting over the TV with Annette or stumbling through my life back on Earth. It was simply disconcerting not to know if I would disappear again to go back to Earth tomorrow, next week, perhaps this evening. Or even worse yet, perhaps this time around, never. *Yikes.*

I shrugged off my worry as I pondered with a smile what Ena might say in this situation. *Live in the moment.*

I couldn't help but reach over to brush Gradd's unruly hair off his forehead. I had been sitting here for what seemed like hours and I was getting hungry.

I leaned over to kiss him before straightening up to go and get something to eat.

But I hadn't moved a step away from the bed when Gradd caught my arm and pulled me back toward him. "Whoops—" I yelped out before I landed on top of Gradd.

He put his arms around me to pull me closer and I looked up at his face. He was awake. "Well." I gave him a pointed look. "For someone who's supposed to be exhausted, you've got quite a grip."

Gradd was gazing down at me in relief or perhaps disbelief. "I'm glad you're back," he began softly. "Don't you ever leave me like that again," he added, his voice almost a low growl.

When he noticed that I had changed back into my own clothes again (which Genesa had given me back earlier after crying her eyes out over them. 'Tears of joy' she had said.) I relayed, "Aella said that leather and armor didn't look good on me."

"Oh, it doesn't," Gradd said with firm conviction.

I looked at him in question. "Why was I wearing those weird black clothes anyway?"

His vague smile was slight. "Maybe I'll tell you some other time...someday." He shifted me up to kiss me and I kissed him back.

"What is going on here?" Scott's voice boomed as he came into the room.

Jumping in my startle, I looked over at him already with wide-eyed guilt as I stammered, "Oh crap, this is—I mean—I was going to tell you before I got—"

But a corner of Scott's mouth turned up into a grin as he met my gaze. He didn't say anything but I stopped short at the expression in his eyes and my smile widened in understanding and relief.

I glanced back up at Gradd who was also smiling.

Gradd called out to Scott even with his gaze still pinned on me, "Look away, man," before pulling me back down to kiss me again.

That's when Aella and Lessandra came to the door.

Aella cleared her throat.

Laughing, I tried to pull away from Gradd but he groaned in complaint. "Go away, guys."

"You guys," Aella remarked. "You'd think one of you had just almost died or something."

Chuckling again, I straightened up to sit on the bed beside Gradd so I could at least talk to them all properly.

"Anyway," Aella took on a serious tone as she began. "In case you were interested to know, we have received the official surrender from the Malkens. With Tagbart gone, there are quite a few good loyal soldiers who needed instruction. Some of whom have defected to join Eleria or Thorb and along with all the other kingdoms, they'll be helping to rebuild what the war has destroyed. It won't be everything. But it's a start." She shrugged and then looked over at Gradd. "This is your cue to lead negotiations. I'm sure they would be more than willing to help restore Centeria."

"Great," Gradd replied curtly. "*Now* can you guys go?"

Everyone laughed.

"Hey, what's happened to the Phoenix?" I wanted to know, looking at each of them. "Does it not work anymore?"

"Who knows?" Scott spoke up. "There are still mysteries surrounding it and its capabilities. But I think we can be assured that it will come to life again should the King of Centeria need it," he added with a slight bow to Gradd.

A little shiver shot up my spine at his words. *Gradd was King.* But then I realized, *Oh man, he sure has work to do.* Sighing, I looked around at everyone again. *Everyone* had a lot of work to do.

"Say, are you guys going to eat dinner soon? Because Louisa's in one of her fits again." Aella jerked her thumb in the direction of the door.

"Uh-oh." Scott made a face. "Can you smell mutton?"

"We'll save you guys some." Aella shot Gradd and me a knowing look as she turned to go, pulling Scott along behind her as he feigned his struggle with a "Help me! The monthter hath me!"

I was going to laugh again then I noticed Lessandra hanging back by the door. She hadn't said a word since she had arrived. She met my gaze, looking as meek as I'd ever seen her. I managed a small smile. I wasn't really in the mood to hold any grudges. Not today.

Lessandra pursed her lips and sighed. She still didn't say anything but I could read it in her eyes. I gave her a short nod and she smiled in relief and gratitude. She blew out a breath again, her smile widening before she returned the nod, acknowledged Gradd with another, and turned away to leave.

When we were alone again, I took a deep breath before meeting Gradd's gaze. "So what happens now?"

Gradd simply grinned before he pulled on my arm, sitting up a bit to meet me halfway and leaning his head toward me. "Now," he spoke with a catch in his husky tone. "We pretend as though you're leaving tomorrow. And tomorrow we'll do the same thing." He moved to kiss me again and murmured against my mouth, "and the next day, and the next day..."

***

62

him

I lounged at the hammock in our backyard waiting for Ena.

It had been over a day since I had come back to Earth again after having returned to Anthuria the second time.

Apparently, Ena had been looking for me all of yesterday and she couldn't understand why if I was indeed simply hiding under the bleachers from the rain after the game like I had told her, neither she nor anyone else had seen me.

I'd simply shrugged. I only remembered waking up under the bleachers last night. Sure, I had climbed into the Phoenix, a few days after the war had ended before it magically transported me back to Earth somehow, but it wasn't like that was something I could tell Ena about.

I'd had a perfect last few days in Anthuria. Everyone was bustling about getting rebuilds underway but everyone was in high spirits. I managed to reconcile properly with Scott and Lessandra. It even looked like they were getting their conflicts resolved since Lessandra looked to be branching out and setting her sights on Baron Ellingwood. Meanwhile, Scott and Aella seemed to have been developing something new between themselves.

And then the next morning, the Phoenix spoke to me in a dream—my last vision.

And I understood. I had to go home.

At least that time, I was able to say proper goodbyes to everyone.

Of course, Leila just insisted that she knew I'd be coming back.

"I'm counting on Leila being right," Gradd had said as he helped me into the Phoenix pilot seat through the translucent chest plate.

Neither of us understood exactly what was going to happen next, especially since the Phoenix was meant to have been drained of all its power. But we both knew well enough that we still barely knew all that the Phoenix was really capable of.

"What if she isn't?" I was almost overwhelmed with anxiety.

Gradd had just given me a meaningful look. "Then I'll come and find you. Even if I have to search all the known worlds, I'll find you —and bring you back," he had vowed, cradling my face in his hands before kissing me one last time.

I had wished he could come back to Earth with me but I knew Gradd would be more than busy enough. His mission now was to rebuild his kingdom. And mine was over.

I sighed as I swung around in the hammock. I was going to miss them all so much but I had to get back to my own life. I hadn't gone back to finish writing the story though. I was sure I would have plenty of time for that later. Besides, I wasn't planning on forgetting everything just yet.

Gradd... Wish you were here... Sighing again, I closed my eyes and swung on the hammock, my one leg on the grass.

Something sniffed at my leg.

When I looked up, I met the gray terrier's eyes with a look of disapproval. "Gray, what are you doing here again?" Sitting up, I glanced around for Derek with a shake of my head. He had better get that leash fixed soon as this dog was an accident waiting to happen. Scooping the dog up in my arms, I walked around to the front of our house and spotted Derek walking over.

"Hey," I called out, holding out his dog. "Lose something?"

He groaned his complaint, taking the dog from me. "I swear, this is the last time I do my sister any favors."

"Maybe you just bore him so much, he'd prefer to walk himself," I teased with a grin as I walked back to the front porch of my house.

Falling into step beside me, Derek chuckled. "Oh, hey." His face brightened. "I heard you won the game yesterday."

"Oh yeah, Judy must be having a manicure today to cope," I mused out loud with a nod.

"Saw you at bat. Close one, huh?"

"Uh, yeah." Nodding again, I gave him a puzzled look. "Wait a minute. Were you there?"

"Yeah, didn't I say I'd try to make it?" Derek reminded me. "I had to leave early though so I couldn't finish the game. I heard you got rained out."

"Rain or shine," I quipped, sitting back down on our porch steps. After a pause, I shot him a strange look. "Don't you have to be somewhere right now?"

He shrugged. "Not really."

I furrowed my eyebrows at him but he gave me a disarming smile. The way he was looking at me was making my pulse race for some reason. It felt strange.

Just then, Mr. Murphy's cat screeched and tumbled off some garbage cans across the street. The sound made Gray freak out and jump out of Derek's arms so suddenly that in trying to hold on to the dog, he lost his balance. I was the nearest thing he could reach.

"Whoops." I caught him against me.

Derek straightened up in front of me and looking up, I met his gaze again. I blinked in surprise as I noticed.

His eyes were green.

"Whoa, sorry about that." Derek was shaking his head as he pulled away.

I was still staring into his eyes. Then I narrowed mine. "H-have you always had green eyes?" I tried to rack my brain but I couldn't recall having ever been this close to him before.

He shot me a look like he wasn't expecting that question. "Um." He gave me a curt nod. "Yeah, green-blue, I guess." He paused for a moment, a curl of a smile coming to the corner of his mouth. "Why?" He gave me a curious prompt as he held my gaze.

"Hello!" Ena called out as she arrived.

Startled, I jumped and stepped back from Derek.

Ena had a suggestive grin on her face. "Am I interrupting anything?"

Derek gave her an easy smile. "Not at all."

Ena approached us and I shot her a disapproving look. "You're late."

Derek gestured backward. "I'll just get the dog."

I glanced over nonchalantly. "Right."

Ena squeezed my arm and mouthed 'Fate' again.

"Oh please. Not that again," I mumbled with a roll of my eyes, even though I had to shake my head to clear it.

So, he has green eyes. Big deal. I didn't like Derek anymore, right?

I watched Derek follow Gray around the corner toward the back of our house before following suit to help him out.

"Hey Derek," I called out in exasperation. "Do you need—" Stopping short, I whirled around. I thought I'd heard something—something that had immediately caused all the dogs on our block to bark like mad.

My eyes widening in alarm, I craned my neck, looking furtively up and down the street.

Scott's flute? I blinked in incredulity since I clearly remembered where I'd had it last and who might potentially have it right now.

Swallowing hard, I tried to calm my heartbeat which had gone into overdrive. *No...* I dismissed in skepticism. *It couldn't be. Of course not. There was no way.*

Just then, Derek poked his head around the corner, having retrieved the dog and come back to the front of the house from the other side. "Hey," he called and I snapped to attention. He gave me a mysterious grin. "If you're finished daydreaming now, how about joining us back in the real world?" he quipped before turning to leave.

Staring at his back in mocking, I started to smile as I followed him back out.

Ena was standing at the curb, waving me over, hands on hips. "And what are you waiting for, Ms. Thing? A royal assemblage?"

My smile widened and I ran over to them.

***

The End.

Sneak Peek: The Curse of the Arcadian Stone

She was solely created to guard a legendary relic. But when a rogue thief from Earth disrupts her dreary world, her job might not be the only thing she loses

***

"What are you doing here?" He was giving me an odd look. "Are you lost?"

I pursed my lips. I really would have come off as more credible if I were up in my tree.

"This place is dangerous." He waved me away. "You better get out of here."

I blinked. That was a switch. He was worried about *me*.

When I still didn't reply, he shrugged and turned to head in the direction of the Mystic Lake.

"Halt!" I stepped forward, raising my hand. "You mustn't go any further."

He stopped and turned back to look at me. "Halt...?"

I bit my tongue. I often forgot that languages evolved and that I had to adjust my manner of speaking. "I mean," I began again. "You must not go in that direction if you know what's good for you. If you are seeking the village, it is that way." I pointed in the other direction.

He looked up where I was pointing and then back at me. "I've just been to the village and trust me, babe, this direction is good for me."

I shot him a look of ridicule. *Babe?* I was over three thousand years old.

He continued to walk toward the Lake.

"Wait!" I went after him. "Please do not go any further. You must believe me. This is for your own safety." I tried to keep up with his long strides.

"Look babe, my safety is my business." His tone seemed firm, resolute.

"As the Guardian of this realm, it actually is my business," I declared. "And I am not a...*babe*." I made a face as I said it.

He paused and turned to me. "Oh, you're the guardian," he spoke as if in realization before his expression turned flat. "So?" he quipped and kept walking.

My serene smile faded when I saw that he was not about to co-operate. "Very well." I shrugged, finally spotting my tree and I drifted up to perch on one of the lower branches as I watched him walk past below. "If you keep going, you will die," I called down to him. "No living creature can withstand the magical barrier around the Mystic Lake."

He stopped walking.

"Are you here for the relic?" I queried with a casual tone, leaning against the tree trunk.

"If that relic is a broken piece of glass, then it looks like I am."

He'd started to walk but stopped again when I went on. "No one who has ever tried to obtain the relic has survived these woods," I announced. "Trust me. It will do you no good to try to get it."

That made him look up at me, way up above him, and I felt my words sink in. I always did feel better up in my tree. The Forest was my territory. I smiled regally down at him.

"What's your name?"

I blinked again, surprised. "The last person who asked me that died too," I replied instead of answering. "He tried to reason about how badly he needed the relic. I'm afraid it does no good to explain to me. I can't help you," I relayed. "I can only warn you. Please leave while you can."

He gave me a critical look, studying me from head to toe before his eyes met mine again. "What's your name?" he repeated, his tone gentler.

"Um..." I was about to explain that I didn't really have a name but then reconsidered. "I was called—Magenta."

Books by S. R. Breaker

Young Adult Epic Fantasy series
The Curse of the Arcadian Stone: Nameless Fay

The Dragons of Arcadia Fantasy Romance
Arranged to the Fae Warrior
Curse of the Dragon Heir
Reign of the Dragon Heir

Young Adult Portal Fantasy series
Selfless Series by S. Breaker

Sneak Peek: The Selfless Series

Feel like a fast-paced YA portal fantasy sci-fi adventure?

They're after you. But which you…? Mistaken identities. Parallel worlds. Government conspiracies. Out of time. Save the multiverse. Save yourself. Don't get erased. Ready?

***

"Did we lose them yet?" Laney rubbed her hands over her arms in the freezing cold.

Noah looked intently at the gadget on his arm, tapping a few keys seemingly in mid-air. "I wouldn't count on it."

The rain had abated but it was still dark. It seemed like they had run deeper into the city. She still didn't know where the hell they were.

The whole city was deserted. Old-fashioned cars were stopped in the middle of the streets, some having crashed onto other cars, or onto building facades with faded, cracked brickwork, fallen tarnished bicycles dotted the road, a vaguely iconic-looking red double-decker bus lay on its side at the far end of the street, almost out of view. There was no trace of any other people around, not even animals. Several doors to apartment buildings across the street had been left wide open. It was as though everyone had dropped everything to leave in a hurry.

"What…happened here?" she wanted to know, half-dreading the answer to her question.

"This is the dead city. Ground zero."

"Ground zero. For what?"

He sighed then as if it was no big deal, he relayed, "The global cascade bomb that nearly obliterated all organic life on our world sixty-seven years ago."

"Th-the *what*?" Laney gasped in shock, horrified.

He shot her a slightly annoyed look. "Look, can you keep up? We've already missed the rendezvous window and we're nowhere near where we need to be.

Laney braced her hands on her knees, still trying to catch her breath, and shot him an annoyed look right back. "Hey, we've been running all night. I don't know about the Laney from your world but *this* one is not a triathlon champion."

He didn't respond to her statement. "Come on." He motioned, leading them through a gap in the broken wire fence surrounding a construction site.

"You didn't answer my question earlier," Laney spoke up. "That guy, the one who tried to kill me the other night. He was looking for something. What is it anyway?"

Noah shot her a look, hesitating. "Do you know what spacetime is?"

"Of course," Laney replied dismissively.

He narrowed his eyes at her, dubious.

She blinked again. "I mean," she began. "I know it's like a *science* thing."

"Spacetime is the fabric of the multiverse within which all our worlds exist," he stated as if he was talking to a child. "Do you know what a wormhole is?"

She pursed her lips.

"What do you learn in school?" he asked in disbelief.

She made another face. "Once again," she said, gesturing to herself from top to bottom. "Normal person. *Not* genius nerd."

Noah rolled his eyes. "Look, the main thing is, there's a device. It makes it possible for a person to move back and forth between two distinct realities."

"Okay."

Noah blinked hard. "No. *Not okay*. What they're ignoring is the probability that this device is going to cause a break in the spacetime continuum, effectively erasing us all from existence. And life as we know it will be over. *Everywhere.*"

Laney mused, "I still don't understand what any of this has to do with me."

"Well, obviously, the government bureaucracies in my world really want this device back—badly. And unfortunately, they think *you* have it."

She stifled an incredulous laugh. "Why the heck would they think *that*?"

"Because...you created it, Laney."

***

Enjoyed the preview? Read **The Selfless** series now!

For Ben Sanders—traitor, thief, and temporal orphan—time is running out.

After three years as a fugitive, with the police task force led by Lysander O'Donohue and Jacob Ofori hot on his heels, Ben has to resort to desperate measures to evade capture and find the key to locating his missing father, lost in time for over two decades. With secrets and conspiracies at every turn, the net grows ever tighter around him.

Haunted by the people he betrayed, the loved ones he left behind, and the lives he ruined, it's too late to stop now. But no matter what Ben does, there's no escaping his past.

With this exciting conclusion to the *Out of Time* series, it is recommended to read the first four books for full enjoyment.